KITTENS, PUPPIES & LOVE

A SMALL TOWN SLOW BURN MYSTERY ROMANCE

HOPE & HEARTS FROM SWAN HARBOR
BOOK 2

SOPHIE BARTOW

CONTENTS

This book is dedicated to...

My street team;
The Wall-Giennie Wicks-Delaney,
Connector Inspector- Linda Hagerty
Reactor Inspector- Jami Fenton
Plot Catcher- Barbara Berry
Sign Crew- Kate Semenyuk

The Clean-up crew: Cindy, Laura, Kim, Maggie, Sylvia, and Diane whose feedback was valuable.
And my family, for not caring if the house was spic and span, while I wrote.

Inspiration began,
when a lost girl fell for a lost boy

Two Hearts Press
An Imprint of LLIPSS, INC
Copyright 2020 by Sophie Bartow

Regular Paperback ISBN: 978-1-965510-09-4
Large Print Paperback ISBN: 978-1-965510-02-5
Regular Print Hardback: 978-1-965510-05-6
Large Print Hardback ISBN: 978-1-965510-22-3

Edited and updated in September 2024

Cover Design by Kate Semenyuk

*Without hope, there would be
no happy endings.*

FROM DARKNESS INTO LOVE

KITTENS, PUPPIES & LOVE

BROTHERS, HOPE & HEARTS

KISSES, FAMILY & HOPE

A TREE, MISTLETOE & A SUNSET

HOPE, HEARTS & FOREVER

THE MEMORY OF LOVE

THE INNOCENCE OF LOVE

THE FORGIVENESS OF LOVE

THE POWER OF LOVE

THE CHRISTMAS LOVE SONG

THE KISS OF LOVE

THE LESSONS OF LOVE

THE HEART OF LOVE

THE JOURNEY TO LOVE

Hope & Hearts Historical Novellas

GUIDED BY LIGHT - 1952

GUIDED BY HEART - 1964

GUIDED BY LOVE - 1969

WELCOME TO SWAN HARBOR- 1979

FINDING HER LOST HEART- 1983/1990

GUIDED BY A KISS - 1995

SOME RESIDENTS OF SWAN HARBOR

Emma Foster: The Veterinarian and owner of Swan Harbor Veterinarian Hospital. Daughter of **Ava King** and Peter Foster.

Killian Reade: He is an Investigator for the Swan Harbor Sheriff's Department. Brother to **Liam Reade** and son of **Finley Reade** — both of whom live in New York.

Rusty Langley: He is an investigator for the Swan Harbor Sheriff's Department and the partner of **Killian Reade**. He is married to **Rene Langley.** His story is **The Power of Love**.

Rene Langley: She is the mayor of Swan Harbor, married to **Rusty,** and the mother of **Roland**.

Roland Langley: The young son of Rusty and Rene.

Dylan Prince: The Sheriff of Swan Harbor and married to **Molly Barnes Prince**. He is the brother of Jessie, twin to the late James, and son of the late Ruth and Robert. Their story is told in **The Innocence of Love.**

Molly Barnes Prince: She teaches first grade at Swan Harbor Elementary School and is married to **Dylan Prince**.

Grayson Hunter: Engineer at Hunter Construction and married to **Sadie Martin Hunter.** Their story is told in **The Memory of Love.**

Sadie Martin Hunter: The office manager of Swan Harbor Veterinarian Hospital and an accountant. Married to **Grayson Hunter**.

Hayden Patterson: He is a college student and works at Sally's Diner.

Tyler James: He is a professional singer and the owner of Siren's Song, a music club located on Swan Harbor's pier. He is also the father to six-year-old, **Bethany.** His story is told in **<u>The Christmas Love Song.</u>**

Mary Hunter: A Psychiatrist at Swan Harbor General Hospital. She is married to **Clint Hunter** and mother to sons Cameron and **Grayson**.

Clint Hunter: Owner of Hunter Construction (HCI). Married to Mary Hunter.

Liam Reade: Firefighter/Paramedic in New York City. Works at Queen's Court Medical Center, which King Industries owns. His story is told in **<u>Brothers, Hope & Hearts.</u>**

Finley Reade: Owns a real estate business in New York City. Father of **Liam** and **Killian**. His story is told in **<u>Kisses, Family & Love.</u>**

Ava King: Philanthropist and businesswoman for King Industries. Mother of **Emma Foster**.

Elsa Winters: She is a pediatric resident at Queen's Court Medical Center in New York City and is best friends with **Emma Foster**.

Captain Jack: He is a retired Naval officer and an eccentric resident of the small town. When he's not doling out sage advice, you can find him at his restaurant. Captain Jack's Fine Dining is built inside the seventeenth-century Spanish Galleon, moored at Swan Harbor's newly renovated pier. His story is told in **<u>The Journey to Love.</u>**

Welcome to Swan Harbor

A Haven of Hope for Lost Hearts.

The word cloak means to hide, cover, or disguise. Many have them to keep others from seeing their real selves. What does it take to push someone to remove their cloak, allowing others to see the person beneath?

ONE

Sheriff's Department
September 7
11:00 a.m.

KILLIAN READE CLOSED HIS EYES AND LEANED BACK IN HIS CHAIR. The sheriff's department was quieter than it had been for a few months, and he kind of enjoyed it. With the end of summer sending the tourists home, it gave him time to appreciate how much his life had changed in the past year.

Surprised you liked it, aren't you?

Before he could dive too far down the reflection hole, Dylan, his boss, dropped a pile of folders on his desk. "You're welcome.

"Bloody hell, Dylan! I've already finished my paperwork."

"Just think of them as a gift." Dylan gave him a cheeky smile. "When you're done, I'll take my usual from Sally's."

"But aren't these Rusty's cases?"

"He had to take Rene to the airport, so …"

"Welcome to Swan Harbor," Killian grumbled, more for show than annoyance at helping his partner.

"What can I say?" Dylan grinned. "We're a friendly bunch."

Killian sighed and opened the first file. "But next time you want to give me a gift, a pastry from Paula's will do."

"I'll remember that."

Killian laughed—an action that, even after being in Swan Harbor for seven months, still felt abnormal. In a way, it was comforting, especially after living in relative anonymity for much of the previous ten years. He didn't need to look over his shoulder or second-guess his actions. The sound of gunshots didn't wake him nightly, and the smell of blood didn't surround him.

Those thoughts were ones he rarely allowed, preferring more pleasant ones. Such as the bevy of beautiful women the picturesque town offered.

"All done, Killian?" Amy, the office clerk, asked.

"Thanks, love." He nodded toward the completed pile. "You can take those."

"Need anything else?"

The hopeful tone in her voice had him glancing back up. "Not right now," and because it was expected, he winked.

Her smile dimmed. "Well, okay, I'll just file these." She flipped her blonde hair over her shoulder and left the room with a little extra wiggle in her walk.

Women liked him, and with his tousled black hair, blue eyes, and square jaw, he was used to their attention. He treated them well and never made promises he didn't intend to keep.

However, people only saw the Killian Reade he allowed them to see. It was a behavior he liked—most of the time. Except lately, his once comfortable habits no longer felt so. They unsettled him, making him wonder what was around the corner. Yet, those were feelings he didn't understand, and ones he spared little energy on.

When he'd completed the folders, Killian left them on Amy's desk, slipped on his sunglasses, and stepped into the September sun. He was greeted, not by the peaceful sound of waves, but by the untuned engine of a bright yellow Volkswagen Beetle. The thought of ticketing them for disturbing the peace was just starting to form when he caught sight of the driver. *Bloody hell!*

Main Street
September 7
12:45 p.m.

EMMA GLANCED AT THE BUILDING AS SHE ROLLED PAST AND READ its sign, "Swan Harbor Sheriff Department," her second landmark. Unconsciously, she tightened her hand on the gearshift.

Just two more blocks.

Why was she nervous? This was what she'd been working toward.

Then, take a right.

She'd grown up in a world full of make-believe and had run far away.

125 Summer Ave, Suite 2A.

As an adult, Emma needed to be in control. Something she'd had very little of growing up. Which left her with a tendency to throw up walls, especially in situations where she might not be completely comfortable.

Attorney Ben Matthews, 1:00 p.m.

One way she retained control was by setting goals. Once they'd been achieved, she'd check them off. They allowed her to see where she'd been and make plans for where she wanted to go. Those were important to her well-being.

Emma pulled into a parking space in front of the early colonial home where Ben's office was located.

Her palms began to sweat.

She opened the door, and the *Rhopalocera* in her stomach swarmed. When she stepped from the car, her heart rate took off like a herd of *Equus caballus*.

It's okay, Emma.

Except the voice couldn't stop the feelings inside. Fear, anxiousness, excitement ... hope.

Goals equaled success, something she'd said to herself probably a million times. All she needed to do was sign a few papers, and one more item could be crossed off her list.

Graduate from High School. ✓

Graduate with her Bachelor's. ✔
Get into Veterinarian School. ✔
Graduate from Veterinarian School. ✔
Pass licensure exams. ✔
Get a job. She was doing better than just getting a job. Soon, she would be Doctor Emma Foster, Owner and Veterinarian.

Sally's Diner
September 7
1:00 p.m.

KILLIAN STEPPED INTO SALLY'S DINER, HIS THOUGHTS STILL ON the lovely lass driving the yellow car. She'd looked through him and not *at* him, a behavior that had him curious.

"Hey, Killian," Hayden, Sally's nephew, greeted him with a series of hand slaps. "Let me clean this table, and your order should be ready."

"My order?" Killian frowned at the younger lad. "I don't recall giving my order. Did I step through a time warp?"

Hayden rolled his eyes in typical late-teen fashion. "No, you're just one of my regulars, that's all."

"Regulars?" Killian glanced down at his black jeans and t-shirt. "I never thought of myself as a regular anything."

Hayden tucked his rag back into his apron and picked up the tray of dirty dishes. "Regular, as in you have lunch at Sally's three times a week, eat the same foods, look around for someone, and after paying, you leave."

"I'm that predictable?"

Hayden grinned. "Very much so."

"And when I look around, you're assuming I'm looking for someone, or do you *know?*"

"Killian," Hayden exclaimed with a slightly exasperated tone, "I'm not a kid. I know you're trolling for fresh meat. I'll check on your order."

"Maybe you should be the Investigator instead of me."

Hayden laughed. "Nah, I'm a computer guy, you know that. I'll be right back."

Killian watched the younger man bound across the room. His mannerisms and confidence reminded him of his younger days. However, life and experiences had gotten in the way and created the man he saw in the mirror. Predictable in his past life would have gotten him killed. Did he want that title? Or any of the titles Hayden had used?

"Dylan's order was ready too." Hayden handed him two bags. "See you at the gym tomorrow."

"I'm predictable about that, too?"

Hayden blushed, almost as if he was embarrassed to have divulged so much information. "Well ..."

Killian gave the younger man a break and changed the subject. "When do you head back to school?"

"Next week. Just three more years."

"Don't rush it. You'll get there soon enough. I'll see you at the gym."

He hadn't gotten far when the yellow car rushed past, loud music trailing in its wake. Where had she been? Where was she going, and who the bloody hell was she?

Veterinarian Clinic
September 14
4:00 p.m.

Emma's purchase, Swan Harbor Veterinarian Clinic, included two buildings on several acres not far from town. She would use the largest building, a barn, for treating horses and cattle. The smaller building was divided into her clinic on the bottom floor and a one-bedroom apartment above. It was perfect.

A week after taking ownership, she added to her list.

Make Business a Success.

Before she could contemplate the steps needed to complete the goal, the bell over the door rang. When she stepped into the front room, she was greeted by a petite brunette clinging tightly to a birdcage.

"Can I help you?"

"I was looking for the Doctor."

"I'm Doctor Foster," Emma replied. "Maybe I can help."

The woman studied her for a few seconds. "Okay, thanks. But what happened to Doc Thatcher?"

"He retired," Emma replied. "Now, how can I help, Miss ...?"

"Prince, Molly Prince," the woman murmured. "I found this bird tangled in some wires and thought maybe ..."

Emma took the cage and led her into one of the smaller rooms. While she examined the bird, she learned the woman was a first-grade teacher and married to the town sheriff.

"It looks like the bird has a broken wing," Emma murmured. "I'll try to set it ... and then we'll see."

Molly's smile fell. "Will it be alright?"

"I'll do the best I can, okay?"

It took several minutes of intense scrutiny before Molly finally nodded. "How much do I owe you?"

"This one's on me. You're my first customer."

"Thank you, and congratulations." Molly's green eyes sparkled. "You're new in town, aren't you?"

"Is it that obvious?"

"Small town." Molly shrugged. "Would you like to meet for lunch sometime? I could show you around."

While Emma wasn't sure how much free time she would have, she understood the benefit of knowing someone local. "That would be great, thanks."

"Will you let me know about the bird?"

"Even if it's not good news?" When Molly just nodded quickly, Emma promised to let her know.

"Thanks, we'll talk soon."

"Well, little bird," Emma crooned softly. "Let's see what we can do about your wing."

Sally's Diner
September 20
12:30 p.m.

MORE THAN A WEEK HAD PASSED SINCE HE'D SEEN THE WOMAN driving the yellow bug. He searched for the driver, but he didn't understand why. If he wanted a woman—there were plenty available. Since the incident with Violet, though, he'd changed. More often, he felt lost, something he didn't care for and was unwilling to share with others.

After a morning patrolling the beach, Killian was returning to the office when a flash of yellow caused him to slam on his brakes.

"Bloody hell!"

He pulled into the department's parking lot and ducked into the men's room. Once he swished with mouthwash and brushed his hair, he started across the street, a little extra bounce in his step.

When he walked in, the blonde sat alone at a table near the front. The curve of her cheek and the way the sun highlighted her hair took his breath, and only one word came to mind—gobsmacked. He wiped his sweaty palms on his jeans and sauntered toward his partner, sitting at the counter.

Be cool, Reade. You're just here for lunch.

"Who's the lovely lass?" Killian asked without greeting.

"Well, hello to you too," Rusty quipped.

Killian casually leaned against the counter. "Very funny. Hello. Now, who's the lovely lass?"

"That lovely lass?" Rusty thumbed over his shoulder.

"Bloody hell, Rusty!" Killian pushed his friend's hand down. "Are you in high school?"

"I could ask you the same thing," Rusty snickered. "After all, you *are* the town Lothario. Go introduce yourself."

Killian looked down, unwilling to admit the label embarrassed him. While it fit the man before he'd moved to Swan Harbor, he'd changed ... internally. In a way, Rusty was right. He'd never had difficulty talking to women before. Was this woman any different?

"Shoo." Rusty waved him away. "I'd like to eat in peace."

"You're grouchy," Killian retorted. "Problems at home?"

"Rene and Roland are still out of town. Rusty repeated the dismissive hand motion, "Now go meet the girl."

Killian stood a little taller and pulled his shoulders back. "I think I will."

He took several steps toward her table before his bravado disappeared. Then, as if being pulled by an invisible string, he detoured toward Dylan and his wife, Molly, sitting nearby.

"I think Emma needs to meet Killian," Dylan was saying. "Don't you agree?"

"I couldn't agree more," Killian jumped in, using the smile he pulled out when he needed to coerce members of the opposite sex to do his bidding.

"Killian," she cautioned, "Emma might not ..."

"Emma." He repeated several times, liking the way it felt on his tongue. "What could it hurt?" Then, when he noticed Molly weakening, he pushed a little more. "Even Dylan thinks it's a good idea."

Molly sighed. "Okay. Come with me. We were just leaving, anyway."

As he followed his friends toward the elusive Emma, Killian's heart beat a little faster. His steps grew a little slower.

What was it about her that made him hesitate? Since it wasn't a question he could answer, he did as always and pushed aside the feelings of self-doubt. To further hide his insecurities, he added a little extra swagger to his walk.

"Emma," Molly began. "I'd like you to meet Killian Reade. He's an investigator at the sheriff's department with Dylan. Killian, meet Emma Foster."

He smiled, using the one that never failed to get a smile in return. "I'd be happy to tune your engine any time."

"Killian!" Molly exclaimed.

Emma's expression had Killian taking a step back. It wasn't adoring, indulgent, or one that spoke of intrigue. Instead, she appeared aggravated, annoyed and bothered. Once again, she'd thrown him off his game, leaving him confused and unsure about his next step.

"Er, I'm sorry, Lass. You drove by me the other day, and your yellow car rattled, and I ..."

"Thought to impress me with your witty repartee?" she snapped, dismissing him.

He ducked his head and glanced up under his brow. "Oh, you're a tough lass, aren't you?"

"Some would say so."

Their eyes locked, Emma's a turbulent shade of green. She might look angelic, but the words coming from her mouth were anything but. Was she, too, trying to hide something?

"Just who are you?"

"Wouldn't you like to know?" Emma whispered, then turned her back to speak with Molly.

He thought she might ignore him and leave, but she glanced over her shoulder as if unable to resist. Her lips curled into the semblance of a smile that never reached her eyes. "It was nice to meet you."

"You too, Ms. Foster."

"It's Doctor Foster," she corrected. "I took over for Doc Thatcher." With a wave to Molly and Dylan, she was gone.

Killian stared at her retreating figure. He'd never met a woman who didn't behave as he expected. They usually fell all over him almost too quickly. Did he care enough to try to change what Emma thought of him? Or did he move on to the next challenge?

Veterinarian Clinic
October 14
10:00 a.m.

Over the next few weeks, Killian Reade and his lame pickup line floated through Emma's head at the oddest times. She couldn't decide if he thought he was charming or just socially awkward. That she was still thinking about him was annoying. Her next goal was not **Find a Man.** So far, though, her self-scoldings hadn't helped, and he'd pop back into her head at the worst possible times.

In the middle of inventory, when she exercised, and even when treating patients, it was a little disconcerting and a lot terrifying. Emma Foster made goals and checked them off one by one. She did not skip around.

Molly had been both a saint and a sinner regarding Emma's quest for control. She'd stopped by the clinic more than once, and somehow, Killian's name always entered the conversation. But when a kernel of anticipation flickered to life inside, she had no choice and slammed on the brakes. That's when she took down her goal list and revised her plan.

Make Business a Success
Buy Business Cards
Order stationery
Pass Out Flyers
Hire Help

The smaller goals made it easier to stay focused, even if it didn't eliminate the butterflies in her stomach. Every time she drove into town, they swarmed. When she pulled into a parking spot at Peter Pan Park, seeing the sheriff's department car caused her heart to race.

She'd been asked to help locate Fred, a black Labrador, who belonged to the hospital administrator. The dog had been seen roaming the woods surrounding the park.

"Fred, Emma," she reminded herself as soon as she stepped from the car. "You're only here to find the dog."

I know! I know!

"No detours," Emma repeated while skirting around the dog park.

A fresh paw print leading toward the woods distracted her long enough to refocus. She'd found the dog. Now, she needed to catch him.

Peter Pan Park
October 14
3:00 p.m.

Killian was standing behind a group of trees, watching Emma weave around the dog park. When she turned in his direction, he stepped deeper into the shadows, not wanting to be seen. He hated admitting it, but her brush-off at Sally's still stung. Some days, he was ready to move to the next name in one of his black books. While other days, he wanted a do-over.

He watched as Emma stepped into the shade the large trees provided. She stopped for several seconds, studied the ground, and then tilted her head. What she was listening for, he didn't know.

Seconds later, she turned in another direction, making him think she'd heard something. He couldn't say why he followed and didn't alert her to his presence. His only thoughts right then were staying out of sight.

They walked deeper into the woods, and still, no sign of the dog. Emma suddenly stopped and stared at the ground, leaving Killian to wonder about her abilities once again. Even more so when she pushed aside several branches and moved backward before taking off perpendicularly.

He thought she tracked Fred by following certain patterns on the beaten-down leaves. A behavior that should have surprised him. Instead, he added it to the list of what fascinated him. It was a new feeling, but one he didn't think he could ignore.

Not long afterward, he saw Fred's black nose behind a fallen log. Emma didn't move, but stood silently, waiting for the dog to come to her. He lost track of how long she stood still, communing with the animal. Goosebumps broke out on his skin when, slowly, the scared dog started toward the stranger.

Her ease with which she could get the frightened dog to trust her stole his breath. Yet, again, he was given a new item to add to his list.

Emma clipped the leash on the dog and led him back the way she'd come. When she walked within thirty yards of where he was standing, and didn't notice him, Killian let her go.

The unsettled feelings she left behind had him wondering how to regain the upper hand. Was a night out with the guys what he needed to get her out of his mind? Or was it female companionship?

TWO

Molly & Dylan's Apartment
October 28
6:30 p.m.

THE MINUTE MOLLY ANSWERED HER KNOCK, EMMA REALIZED SHE might be in trouble. Instead of the quiet evening she'd expected, the room was full of unknown faces.

"Emma, I'm so glad ..." Molly's smile faded. "Are you okay? You look a little pale."

"I'm ah..." Emma began breathlessly. *Come on! You know what to do.* "I just wasn't expecting this."

"Oh, I'm sorry. I thought this was the best way for you to get to know everyone."

"At once?"

"I could ..."

"No, no," Emma replied, not wanting to disappoint her new friend. "I'll be fine."

"Oh, good." Molly smiled. "Come meet everyone."

Emma took a deep breath and followed Molly from one group to another to be introduced. It reminded her of the many times she'd been paraded in front of people as a child. Those partygoers had exclaimed over her because of *who* her parents were. It allowed her to relax slightly, as the people she met weren't scary.

"Molly," she whispered. "I'm never going to remember everyone's name."

"No?"

"If they were holding a dog or cat, maybe, but without ..."

"You'll be fine."

With 'I'll be fine' echoing in her head, Emma followed Molly to the next group.

"Do you know Ben?"

"Ben helped with the sale of my clinic."

"And Emma helped me find Fred," Ben threw in.

"How is Fred?" Emma asked. "No more problems?"

"None," Ben sighed dramatically, "and I'm happy to say he's back home with Arthur."

"Be nice," Molly tsked. "Fred's a sweetheart."

"Just go on thinking that," Ben muttered. "The next time Arthur leaves town, you can dog sit."

"Oh, Wilby would ..." Molly began. Then suddenly, a panicked look crossed her face, and she muttered, "I forgot my crostini!" before rushing toward the kitchen.

"Her crostini?" Emma frowned. "Did I miss something?"

"Molly's feeling a bit frazzled lately," Ben explained. "Their house is being remodeled, and things are spread out between here and across the hall in Killian's apartment."

The man's name she'd been trying *not* to think about had Emma's curiosity peeking out.

"That must be tough."

Although, why was *this* something Molly hadn't shared, considering she rarely let any opportunity to mention Killian's name pass by?

"Whether it's tough or not," a tall man with sandy hair stepped into their circle, "Molly tells me it is every day. Gray Hunter," he introduced himself.

"Emma Foster."

"From the look on your face, I gather you've heard some of her complaints," Gray went on.

"Oh, I have," Emma laughed. "The last one had something to do with cabinet knobs."

He winced. "They did. I never knew she had such a colorful vocabulary."

"She did have quite a bit to say," Emma muttered tongue-in-cheek.

"I probably should talk to her," Gray sighed. "My brother, Cameron, is married to Dylan's sister, which makes Molly family, so ..." He shrugged, almost as if assuming she understood his meaning.

But family dynamics weren't something Emma was familiar with. Her family was different.

"So, you're the new vet Anita has been praising lately?" Gray returned her attention to the conversation.

It took Emma a second to connect the name with her treatment. "Four-year-old bay mare with a red-bag delivery, right?"

"That's Roisin, Anita's prized mare," Gray acknowledged. "I heard it was touch and go there for a while.

"I just did what any animal doctor would—helped a mother in trouble."

What she didn't say was that type of birth was very dangerous. Since the foal was born inside the placenta, it could have been life or death for the mother *or* the son.

"You're being modest." Gray tipped his beer bottle in her direction. "Anita said you were amazing."

"Thanks. Are you related to Anita?"

"I'm engaged to her daughter." Gray glanced across the room, and his face lit up with a goofy smile. The display of his emotions gave Emma a strange feeling. It didn't last long, but one she hadn't experienced.

"Get a room," Ben quipped.

Gray's response was succinct.

"Didn't I hear your mama tell you to watch your mouth around ladies?" a familiar voice drawled.

Emma's eyes flared when she realized who had joined their group.

"Well, if it isn't the local crooner." Ben nodded toward Emma. "Have you met ...?"

"Tyler James," she murmured. "I saw you in concert at the Illinois Fair two or maybe three years ago."

Their eyes clashed, and all she could see were shadows. Almost as if he was hiding his thoughts.

"More like four," Tyler responded in that husky voice that caused many females to swoon. "I stopped touring before Beth was born. She was three earlier this year."

"Oh!" *Which answered more than one question.* "Your wife and daughter must love having you home ..." Except, before she completed the statement, she realized she'd said something wrong.

"Kara, my wife, died right after having Beth," Tyler answered.

"I'm sorry."

Emma tightened the strings of her invisible cape, unsure how else to respond. After all, Emma Foster didn't have close relationships.

"We're doing okay."

But the shadows in his eyes made her wonder who he was trying to convince.

"I bet Beth's a handful."

While he talked about his daughter, the shadows faded. It made her wonder if anyone saw the same when they looked at her.

"I'm trying to find a new sitter," he continued. "Lois and Glynis, the women who currently watch her, are leaving for warmer weather soon."

"If it doesn't have to do with *Animalia*," Emma quipped. "I'm no help."

"I didn't want you to think I was suggesting ..." Tyler began.

"That *I* watch her just because I'm a woman?" Emma hummed. When deer-in-headlights expressions crossed the men's faces, she snickered. "You fellas are too easy."

"So, you're not mad?" Tyler asked hesitantly.

"Mad? No." Emma laughed. "I am, however, hungry. It's been nice talking to you."

She left them trading insults and made her way around the room. As the distance between her and the men grew, her need to pretend decreased. While it wasn't completely awful being in a crowd she didn't know, she still felt like she was on the outside looking in.

As she walked by, someone knocked on the door, and habit had her answering. "Oh, Killian."

"Emma." His lilting accent wrapped around the syllables, giving her the impression he was caressing her name ... and her. The feeling gave her pause and had her studying him a little closer.

"Come in. Dylan and Molly are here somewhere."

"Thanks, love."

Once he walked into the apartment, gone was the man who'd knocked, and the confident, cocky man had returned. He was the kind of man who sent her running. Except there was something about him, making it difficult to forget.

"Killian, there you are!" A redhead threw herself into his arms.

He grunted, making Emma snicker. However, it also allowed her to walk away without being noticed.

She forced her attention to the buffet table. When she glanced at the assortment of finger foods, she couldn't think about how different it was from when she'd been a child. Pigs in a blanket or a simple crostini would have been too common, not fitting for the upper-crust society she'd been born into. That didn't stop her from picking up a plate and starting around the table.

"Can you believe she just threw herself at him?" one of the women across the table whispered.

"She's so pushy," the other answered. "But that kiss! Just ugh!"

"Don't remind me," the first woman replied bitterly. "Although he does know how to kiss."

"Oh, yes, he does," the other purred.

Emma hurried away from them, uninterested in hearing all about Killian's women.

"You forgot one of these," a husky voice murmured close to her ear.

She looked up into the blue eyes of the man being discussed. It took several seconds before she could form a response. "What did you just say?"

"The shrimp." Killian lightly touched her bottom lip with the shellfish. "It's succulent." He leaned in slightly, and a gentle puff of air whispered across her lips when he popped his T.

Emma's jaw dropped, and her brain shouted Mayday. Finally, her common sense woke up, and she stepped back.

"What are you doing? For all you know, I could be allergic to that stuff." Then, without waiting for him to respond, she gathered her food and headed toward the other side of the room.

"Are you okay?"

Emma glanced over her shoulder to see a familiar-looking leggy brunette. "I'm fine. Why do you ask?"

The woman rolled her eyes in a way that said, '*Really, you're going there,*' causing Emma to laugh. "I'm fine. He's just …"

"Hot. Hunky. Gorgeous." The woman smiled. "Take your pick."

"Sadie." Gray slipped his arm around the woman's waist and kissed her quite thoroughly. "Are you trying to make me jealous?"

"How do you know I wasn't describing you?" Sadie kissed him again.

Gray side-eyed Emma, and a corner of his mouth curved. "Well, were you?"

"Of course, sweetheart," Sadie grinned, "right?"

Once Gray said the woman's name, Emma knew why her face was so familiar. Sadie was Anita's daughter. "Right," she muttered, tongue-in-cheek.

"See," Sadie gave Gray a toothy smile, "told you."

"You did," he grinned. "How will I make it up to you?"

Sadie leaned in and whispered something, causing him to blush. "Now shoo, we've got some girl talking to do."

"If I shoo, *you'll* have to make it up to me," Gray teased.

Emma watched them communicate, saying nothing, and a zip of envy rushed through her. She wanted that. *Wait*! *No detours, Emma, remember*?

"Sorry about that." Sadie's grin was wolfish. "He is just …" She glanced in the direction Gray had gone and sighed. "Anyway, where were we? Oh yeah, Killian."

He was easy to locate, as he was the only man holding court to a harem. In addition to the redhead who'd met him at the door and the two she'd overheard at the food table, he'd been joined by two others. "Does he always need to collect women?"

"Killian is …"

"Self-absorbed, cocky, shallow," Emma quipped. "Shall I continue?"

Sadie tipped her head as if she agreed. "But … I think there's more behind those blue eyes than he allows anyone to see."

"Really?" Emma frowned. "So, what's the story with those women? No pride?"

Sadie laughed. "The redhead, Morgan, seems to think if she buys him gifts, she'll have his undying love."

"Puhlease!" Emma drew out the single-syllable. "Guys like him aren't looking for just one someone."

"You sound like you're talking from experience." Sadie raised a brow.

"My father." Emma let go of a little laugh, wondering why she'd revealed that.

Thankfully, Sadie didn't ask any further questions. "The brunette is Chloe. She spreads rumors about people."

"That sounds immature."

"It is," Sadie agreed. "But it's been like that since elementary school. Boys, grades, clothes, you name it. Jealousy, I think."

"But why throw themselves at Killian?"

Sadie rolled her eyes. "Killian's new to town and fresh meat. They've already made the rounds with most other men here, including Gray, Cameron, Ben, and Dylan."

The news Killian had moved to Swan Harbor in February had come from Molly. As did the part about him not having any problems attracting company. A group always surrounded him. It had Emma wondering what it was about him that drew other people. While her encounters with him weren't entirely positive, he lingered in her mind.

"He's just a man."

"Who probably leaves the lid up just like my fiancé," Sadie quipped.

Emma snickered. "Truth. But I don't plan on being another notch on his bedpost."

"Good for you." Sadie hesitated a second before nodding across the room. "Ah oh, look."

Killian ushered Morgan and Chloe from the room and shut the door.

"Well, that was special," Sadie muttered. "I think I need a drink."

They made their way across the room to where Molly was manning the punch bowl.

"Is it spiked?"

"Maybe." Molly grinned, and a dimple peeked out on one cheek. "Want some?"

"Do I?"

"Taste."

Emma wasn't sure she should follow through but ended up taking a careful sip. "Vodka and rum?"

"Yeah," Molly grumbled. "Dylan and Killian made the punch."

"Speaking of them." Emma glanced around to make sure no one was listening. "Did you forget to tell me something?"

"What?"

"Okay, be that way," Emma laughed. "I just remembered I wanted to ask Sadie something."

As she walked away, the door opened, and Killian returned, arm in arm, with both women.

❧

KILLIAN CAUGHT SIGHT OF THE LOVELY DOCTOR FOSTER GLIDING across the room when he re-entered with Morgan and Chloe. As predicted, it had taken little more than a few kisses and a promise of dinner, and they were pacified. Why wasn't it as easy to get Emma's attention? She didn't seem to have difficulty giving it to others.

"Ladies." Killian kissed each on the cheek. "My mate, Dylan, needs my help. I'll see you two later."

"Promise, Killian?" Chloe ran a slim finger down his chest.

"Promise, love."

Morgan wound her arms around his neck and pressed her body against his. "Don't you forget now?" She tugged his head toward hers.

When he leaned down, his eyes met Emma's. Unconsciously, he jerked his head sideways.

"What was that?" Morgan snapped.

The image of Emma's arched brow and curled lip had him shaking his head to clear the picture. "Sorry, love. Dylan needs me." He walked away, not caring she'd stormed off in the opposite direction.

"Breaking hearts again, Killian?" Dylan questioned.

"As long as it's not mine."

Dylan started to say something, but after a few beats, he handed over a bottle of rum. "We've been instructed to create our punch again. Any idea how much of that stuff you added?"

"No idea." Killian glanced at the bottle in his hand. "Trial and error?" He upended the liquid into the bowl, where it mixed with the fruit punch, lemonade, and club soda.

"Works for me." Dylan did the same with his bottle of vodka. "Just don't tell Molly our secret."

Killian scooped a cup of punch for each. "Why didn't you tell Emma I'd be here?"

"Molly was supposed to," Dylan tossed the blame. "But you know how women are." Then, he quickly changed the subject. "I saw Ladies Monday through Saturday surrounding you earlier. Are you looking for Ms. Sunday?"

Killian refused to acknowledge he was in any way ashamed of his behavior. "And if I am?"

"I'd have to say, ha!" Dylan snickered.

"Ha?" Killian echoed. "What kind of response is ha?"

"Emma's not a groupie, Killian."

"A groupie?" Killian frowned. "What the bloody hell are you talking about?"

"You know, a groupie!" Dylan repeated. "One of many women who follows you, hoping for a tiny crumb of attention. Emma is worth more than all those floozies combined."

Killian dropped his eyes, unwilling to look at whether the statement was true. He enjoyed having a different woman on his arm every night. Didn't he?

His gaze drifted to Emma. The memory of how her green eyes became shuttered before she'd stormed off had him pasting on his cockiest smile. "If you'll excuse me, Ladies Monday and Tuesday are waiting."

When he walked away, he heard Dylan murmur, "You can only run so far, as the truth has a way of coming out."

The comment, combined with the memory of Emma's waspishness, had him planting himself in the center of his admirers. They soothed his ego. Yet, they didn't stop his thoughts. Somehow, he always knew where she was and with whom she was speaking.

"Are you listening to me?" Chloe pouted.

"I certainly am." He gave her his '*You're the only one I'm thinking of smile.*' "You were telling me about your dress."

"You *were* listening," she squealed.

Her high-pitched voice had him tightening his jaw to keep from saying something untoward. He felt like he was balancing on a wire tipping into the unknown, and his patience was wearing thin. When Chloe went off with Morgan, he couldn't help but sigh with relief.

"Are you okay?"

Killian glanced into Tia Patterson's brown eyes, his sometimes date, but always friend. "Just peachy."

Her look said, '*Don't-kid-a-kidder*,' which had him offering, "I'm alright. Why?"

"Because."

He followed her line of sight to where Tyler and Emma were engaged in what appeared to be an intimate conversation.

Bloody hell! It took every ounce of Killian's training not to storm across the room and demand an explanation. Thankfully, his common sense stood up before he did so. However, it didn't keep him from worrying he'd be asked questions he couldn't answer.

When Tia leaned her head against his arm, his chest relaxed. She wasn't worried about his heart, but her own.

"Have you met her?"

"Who?"

Tia's brown eyes sparked briefly. "Emma. The woman talking to Tyler."

"Aye," Killian admitted. "She seems to be a prickly sort."

"Really?"

While he wasn't privy to Tia's entire history with Tyler James, he knew her heart had been involved. It had him realize that even though she was no longer dating the singer, she didn't care to see him with another female.

"Really."

Tia kissed his cheek. "You're a nice guy, Killian Reade. Thank you."

"Of course, I'm a nice guy." He exaggerated his accent.

"I'm not fooled. Good luck."

"With what?"

"You know." She lightly squeezed his fingers and wandered off.

Killian's attention went back to where Emma was still in close conversation with Tyler. He decided he couldn't stand it any longer and put his expertise of hiding in plain sight into use. It took a while of weaving in and out of groups, but she turned toward the room at large just before he'd drawn next to her.

Bloody hell!

He slid behind several people and peered around, trying to decide if he should put himself out there.

She laughed before he could convince his feet to move, making him realize she was closer than he'd thought.

"Ready to go, Emma?"

What? Killian watched as Tyler helped her with her jacket.

You're such a dick! Tyler seemed to be a good bloke, but ….

Once Emma and Tyler were gone, Killian glanced around the room. Chloe and Morgan were in one corner, and Tia, Belle, and Amy in another. He had choices.

The decision was easy, and he quickly worked his way to the door.

"Going somewhere?"

Killian whirled around to Molly's laughing green eyes. "There's no need to sneak up on a man."

"Sorry about that," Molly murmured, not looking contrite at all. "I just wondered why you were tiptoeing out."

"I'm not sneaking anywhere," Killian tossed back. "I thought …" He searched his surroundings and spotted Wilby's leash. "I'd take the dog out to do his business. He's been stuck in my apartment for several hours."

"You'll need these." Molly reached for the leash, a little bag, and a shovel.

"Leash." Killian held up the flexible strap. "What's this other stuff for?"

"You said you were taking Wilby out to do his business, right?"

"Right."

"That's for his business."

"Oh."

"Is there something you need to tell me, Killian?" Molly's smile was all-knowing.

"His business," Killian muttered, "right. I'll be back." Before she could say more, he ran across the hall and grabbed Wilby.

After being cooped up, Wilby tugged on the leash, but Killian didn't want to look like he was in a hurry. "Slow down, boy. We can't appear desperate."

However, luck wasn't on his side. When he arrived downstairs, there was no sign of Emma or her yellow bug. That left him with options—a walk with the dog or returning to his bevy of beauties.

Once again, the decision was easy.

"Well, boy," Killian directed the dog away from the apartments, "shall we?"

THREE

Sheriff's Department
November 3
2:00 p.m.

The following Friday, Killian was alone at the office, and his conversation with Dylan kept replaying in his mind.

Emma's worth more than all those floozies combined.

Emma's not a groupie.

Are you looking for Ms. Sunday?

His week had been full. He'd spent Monday with Morgan, Tuesday with Chloe, and Wednesday with Tia. Thursday, he'd worked, and since it was Friday, he'd made plans with Belle. But he just ....

Which was the crux of the problem ... the *but*. Did he throw himself into his evening with Belle and forget about Emma?

He'd tried not to think about her. Tried not to imagine her and the singer together. But bloody hell, it wasn't easy. She was in his head, and he couldn't seem to get her out.

Her moss-green eyes haunted him whenever he bent to kiss the women he'd taken out on dates. Instead of thinking about the lips of the woman he was with, it was Emma's full-bottom, one he fantasized about. Just the idea of taking it between his own turned him on more than anything he'd done ... or thought about doing in years.

Why?

What was he going to do about it?

The phone rang, which was almost a relief. He dropped his feet to the floor and grabbed the receiver before it finished a second ring. "Yeah."

"Oh, Killian." Molly's anxious voice exclaimed. "Can I speak with Dylan?"

"I'm sorry, Molly. He's at a meeting with the mayor. Is there something I can help you with?"

"Well," she hesitated, "you know Rusty was supposed to come to my class, right?"

"Aye," Killian replied. "He was looking forward to it."

"It was today, and—"

"—Rusty is home because Roland is sick."

"Right," Molly sighed. "I was going to ask Dylan, but ... I'll just tell the kids we'll do it later. I hate disappointing them, though."

"I'll do it," Killian blurted before thinking the statement through.

"Really?" she squealed. "Thank you, thank you, thank you. Can you be here in an hour?"

On his way to the elementary school, Killian questioned his sanity several times. By the time he arrived, he still hadn't figured out what had caused him to volunteer. Boredom, he decided, as he waded into the fray.

"Killian, come in." Molly directed him to the front of the room. "Class, say hello to Investigator Reade."

As he walked toward Molly, the comments he overheard had him second-guessing his decision to volunteer. But once the pint-size humans began to throw out questions, he forgot he was supposed to feel awkward. They were open and honest and listened to *what* he said. It wasn't his glib tongue or its talent that mattered. What mattered was he'd taken the time to read to them.

"Today," Molly explained. "Our guest will read *Ten Big Toes and a Prince's Nose.* Come sit close."

The children gathered around Killian, and he began ....

"There once was a princess so lovely and fair ..."

It took him several pages to feel comfortable, but he hit his stride by the middle of the book. While he read, he didn't consider the possibility the words had a hidden message.

I am what I am, and that's alright with me.

But three-quarters of the way through, he began to wonder. Had he been wrong? Was there an underlying meaning, after all?

I don't have to be different; I just have to be.

He'd spent ten years pretending to be someone else. But moving to Swan Harbor and working for the sheriff's department allowed him to be himself. Didn't it?

I don't want to be somebody else. No sir-ree!

His life was moving in the direction he wished. During the day, he had work, and his evenings were filled with an assortment of beauties. He was happy, even without ....

I am what I am, and that's all right with me.

When he finished the story, a sliver of an unknown feeling ran through him. The feeling was so new and unsettling, he slipped back into his flirtatious persona. It allowed him to stay in control while he said goodbye to Molly and the children.

Hours later, he parked in front of Harbor Towers Apartments and still hadn't reconciled what was happening inside. He was out of sorts and had been since a certain blonde drove her yellow car across his path. What was his next step?

A part of him wanted to cancel his date. Before he could seriously consider it, his sixth sense warned him there might be trouble. His thoughts of a quiet evening flew from his head, and he backed against a wall. Once he was sure he was alone, Killian rushed toward his apartment.

They found you! raced by when he saw the opened door.

He drew his weapon and peered inside, expecting the worst. Except ... the furniture hadn't been overturned, nor was the floor littered with broken glass. Instead, the lights were turned down low, soft music was playing, and a bottle of champagne was chilling beside the sofa.

Bloody hell!

Killian holstered his gun and let the door shut behind him. "Hello."

"Oh, there you are!" Belle stepped into the dining room, holding a salad bowl. "Surprised?"

"I wasn't aware we were to meet here," he mumbled, working to keep his anger from bubbling to the surface.

"We weren't." She set the salad bowl on the table and started toward him. However, when I heard how you'd saved the day for Molly, I thought I'd surprise you with a home-cooked meal."

"Oh, I'm surprised, alright," he quipped. "How did you get in?"

"Oh, Dylan and I arrived at the same time. He let me in."

He'd have to talk to Dylan. Later, though, his decision to give Belle his attention had him pasting on a false smile. "Do I have time for a quick shower?"

Her gaze tracked up his body, and a sultry smile played along her mouth. "Do you need someone to scrub your back?"

"Uhm." Killian forcefully swallowed and backed toward his bedroom. "No, no. I'll be right back."

He stored his gun and locked himself in the bathroom. "What are you going to do now, Reade?"

When his reflection didn't respond, he shed his clothes and rushed through his shower. Ten minutes later, he was pulling out Belle's chair and sitting down to the meal she'd prepared. She smelled nice, and her skin was soft, but ....

The pasta dish, salad, and homemade garlic bread were perfectly paired with the wine. She was a good dinner companion, regaling him with stories from her day. When she spoke, her blue eyes sparkled, but ....

Killian listened to her talk but had to admit his attention drifted throughout the meal. It made little sense as her voice was soft and musical, perfect for a librarian, but ....

After dinner, they sat on the sofa, where he stretched his arm along the back and lightly fingered a few strands of Belle's hair. The candlelight flickered around the room, bringing out its auburn highlights, but ....

"Why don't I open the champagne?"

He took the bottle from the bucket and concentrated on peeling off the wrapping and working the cork free.

He thought he heard Belle say she would get glasses, but his mind was lost on the 'but' statements.

Her speech pattern was melodious, one perfect for a librarian, but ....

She didn't breathlessly say his name one minute and the next spit out comments challenging him.

When she spoke, her blue eyes sparkled, but ....

They weren't the moss-green ones haunting his dreams.

The candlelight flickered around the room, bringing out the highlights in her auburn hair, but ....

It wasn't thick and blonde, making him want to wrap his hand around it, tugging its owner closer.

She smelled nice, and her skin was soft, but ... she wasn't, "Emma."

A gasp had him swinging around. "Belle, I, I didn't ..."

"Goodbye, Killian." Belle grabbed her jacket and rushed out of the apartment.

Killian dropped the champagne bottle into the bucket, glad he hadn't gotten it open. A part of him felt awful for hurting her. The other part couldn't work up the desire to go after her.

What was going on with him?

The quiet of the night called to him, and with a flick of his wrist, he shut off the music. He poured a generous glass of rum into a glass and took it, along with the bottle, onto the patio.

He liked women, and women liked him.

Except Emma.

He liked Morgan, and she had fiery red hair.

She's not Emma.

He liked Chloe, and she was a brunette.

She's not Emma.

He liked Tia.

She's not Emma.

But she's blonde.

She's not Emma.

"Bloody hell, shut up!" Killian downed the rum, poured another three fingers, and immediately tossed half of it back. It burned on the way to his gut but didn't stop his thoughts.

Before he'd even parked his car, he'd known he was in a mood. Except with Belle waiting, there hadn't been time to get into the right frame of mind. He needed to thank his good buddy, Dylan.

"'Lo," Dylan barked after just one ring.

"You let her in." Killian groused. "How could you let her in?"

"Belle?"

"Of course, Belle. You know I don't bring dates to my apartment."

His apartment was his space. It was the one place where he didn't have to worry about what he said or how he looked. If he was out with a woman, they went to her place. Then, he could leave when he was ready.

"Sorry," Dylan sighed. "But she said you invited her. Why?"

"She left," Killian admitted. Then, he surprised himself by adding, "I called her Emma."

"What?!" Dylan chuckled. "How did Mr. Date of the Day make a mistake like that?"

"I don't know," Killian mumbled, wondering how he'd gotten himself into this ... whatever *this* was. "I've never done that before, and for some reason, I don't feel as bad as I think I should."

"And you called her Emma? Sounds like you need to go talk to Emma."

"Bloody hell," Killian sputtered, "she won't talk to me. Besides, who said I wanted to talk to her, anyway?"

"You never know until you try," Dylan pointed out. "Oh, thanks for helping Molly today. I gotta go."

The dead air had Killian frowning at the phone and shoving it into his pocket. He poured another two fingers of rum and wandered back onto the patio. But thoughts of Emma continued crowding him. What if they talked? Would he be able to move on? Or would it take more? Like a date? Was that what was needed for her to become *just* another woman?

There's no time like the present.

Before he could change his mind, Killian tossed back the rest of the alcohol and grabbed his keys. She was just a woman, and once he figured out what made her so elusive, he could purge her from his thoughts once and for all.

Veterinarian Clinic
November 3
9:00 p.m.

Emma rhythmically ran the small brush over the kitten's tiny head. Orphaned, barely three-weeks old, and Tyler's daughter was depending on her to save the *Felis catus.* Which she would, because that was what she did.

Who are you kidding, Emma?

She blew out a breath and amended her thoughts. Saving animals wasn't just *what* she did but *who* she was. Her entire life had been about collecting orphans and saving as many as possible. That included puppies, dogs, kittens, cats, birds, and whatever other animals had been dropped off. *They* had needed her ... and *she* had needed them.

However, tending to the kitten didn't stop her thoughts. Tyler was still charming and handsome, but she wasn't the one he'd been interested in. That had been her best friend, Elsa. It was too bad, really, as he would be easier to forget.

Emma Foster needed control. Which she usually got from her list. Except Killian ....

There will be no detours, Emma.

While she might have sensed more going on behind Killian's eyes, she couldn't take a chance. He reminded her of the people she'd run away from. Ones she had no desire to see again.

Swan Harbor had given her a business she could love. It was a slow process, but she was working to find her place in the town.

New opportunities and situations arose daily, and if she was prepared, then ....

"A moment, please." The quiet voice of the man she'd just vowed to keep at arm's length shattered her concentration.

Emma studied him for several seconds. There was something different about him, yet she refused to look too deeply. "I'm a little busy."

His eyes were trying to tell her something. Except she'd seen *that* too many times with her father. It would take more than a look to pierce her cloak. The one she'd grown to keep pain away that was always close.

"She needs me now." Emma indicated the kitten.

The chirp of an incoming text saved her from having to say anything else while she finished her task. "I need to ..." she began, schooling her features into a neutral mask.

"We'll talk later then," Killian finally answered. Then, just as silently as he'd entered, he left.

Once he was gone, Emma relaxed. "No detours, Emma." She cuddled the kitten again and placed her back in the warming bed.

When her phone buzzed again, Emma pushed any residual thoughts aside and answered. "Elsa, what's going on?"

They spent several minutes catching up before the real reason for the call was mentioned. "You're coming to New York for the holidays, right?"

Elsa's slightly pleading tone had Emma's curiosity pinging. Before making promises, she had to figure out the logistics of going away. However, a few days in New York would allow her to alert her friend about one of Swan Harbor's residents.

Sheriff's Department
November 6
1:00 p.m.

Killian opened his bottom drawer and pulled out his four black books. When he flipped through them, he realized he could put a face with only a few of the names. The others ... were just names.

When had choosing a date from his long list become not enough?

The answer floated by, but unwilling to acknowledge it, he shoved it aside. Except, he couldn't run from the truth. He didn't want any of those women, and the one he wanted wouldn't give him the time of day.

Killian tossed the books back in the drawer and slammed it shut. When he glanced up, the Sheriff was standing in the doorway.

"So, did you ask Emma out?"

"She was busy."

"You let that stop you?"

"But ... she's different."

And you have no clue what you're doing.

Dylan studied him for a few seconds, making it a fight to sit still. He sauntered into the room and hitched a hip on the corner of the desk.

"You mean that, don't you?"

"Aye." Killian ran his hand through his hair, not caring if it was standing on end. "I feel like a fraud."

"Talk to me. I've been a sounding board for Gray, Cameron, Ben ..."

"And Jessie?" Killian guessed, knowing Dylan had been her guardian after their parents' deaths.

Dylan tipped his head in acknowledgment. "Talk to me."

It took several seconds for Killian to formulate his thoughts, but then the ugly truth came out.

"When I was a teenager, I learned females liked what they saw when they looked at me." His smile was self-deprecating. "I shamelessly flaunted that, swearing I would never be foolish enough to allow a female to have control over me. I wrapped the love and leave persona around tight and held on until ..."

"What changed?" Dylan's quiet voice gave him the strength to go on.

"Violet."

"A woman?"

"A little girl."

"Yours?"

"No, not mine."

Killian took a deep breath and allowed the memory to wash over him for the first time in a long while. "The shortened version of the story is an undercover assignment that went horribly wrong. A blown identity and the life of a little girl was lost, caught in the crossfire."

He wiped his hand over his face, the smell of blood and smoke still clinging to his skin. "Her mom had been a kid and on drugs, and her grandmother was raising Violet."

"She got under your skin, didn't she?"

"Aye." Killian winced, thinking what an understatement. "Beatrice Morris made the best blueberry muffins I'd ever tasted." They had taken some of the loneliness away while he was undercover.

His thoughts traveled back to the apartment building, and he remembered how the little girl had always seemed to know when he passed by her door. "Violet used to ask, '*What did you do good today, Ian?*'"

Dylan smiled. "She sounds very wise. How old was she?"

"Ten going on thirty," Killian murmured. "That case is why I left the NYPD."

Swan Harbor and the people there had been a much needed change. After years of being undercover and always seeing the seedier side of life, it had been what he needed. However, some things were easier to shed than others.

"After her death, I needed to get away and start over. I moved here ..." Killian's voice faded as he thought back on the decision to leave everything he knew and how he'd assumed he was happy. Until a flash from a yellow car with music trailing in its wake ... had him questioning everything. Not only who he was but what he was doing.

"Did you ever think maybe Violet saw something in you no one else could?" Dylan's quiet words broke through his thoughts.

Killian started to deny it, but was his friend, right? Had he been a different person with Violet? He raised a brow, silently asking for more of an explanation.

Dylan opened the drawer and tossed the black books onto the desk.

"The man who collects those names is a shallow, cocky SOB who only cares about himself."

He flipped around a picture. It showed Killian sitting in a small chair in Molly's first-grade class, surrounded by tiny students.

"That man is introspective, caring, and will go out of his way to read to a bunch of six-year-olds."

Killian ducked his head, a little ashamed by the description. "Maybe you're right."

"I know I'm right," Dylan asserted smugly. "Maybe if you can find the man Violet knew you could be, *Emma* wouldn't be so busy. I've got a meeting. I'll see you later."

"Thanks." Killian watched him leave and, before he could second guess his decision, scooped up the books and tossed them into the trash. He was going to take his friend's advice. Maybe if Emma got to know the real him, he wouldn't have any need for the information in those books.

But who was he? Did he even know where to look? The words he'd read to the kids circled back.

I am what I am, and that's alright with me. I don't have to be different. I just have to be. I don't want to be somebody else. No sir-ree! I am what I am, and that's all right with me.

Before he could change his mind, he sent a quick text to his brother.

Killian: Changed my mind. I'll be there for Thanksgiving. I need your help finding someone.

Liam: Who?

Killian: Me

To uncover what lies beneath,
a journey must begin.

FOUR

New York City
Liam's Apartment
December 31
7:00 p.m.

Killian leaned on the bathroom vanity and stared in the mirror. His hair was black, and his square jaw held a hint of scruff. Blue eyes, black lashes, and slanted brows he'd been told had a life of their own. Externally, he looked the same. It was on the inside where he was different.

Dylan's question, '*Did you ever think maybe Violet saw something in you no one else could see?*' had sent him searching for answers.

His undercover persona, Ian Jones, was a low-life involved with drugs and guns. Killian's job had been to infiltrate the Callandra gang, hoping to bring them down. But once inside, something about the case tore at him, threatening his existence in ways he couldn't understand. Violet and Beatrice Morris had reminded him of who he was, often surprising him.

He'd first met Violet when, as Ian Jones, he'd stepped between the child and a group of punks. After that day, it had become a habit to keep an eye on her and her grandmother. The little girl made him laugh, and as she'd ordered him to call her, Mama B made 'melt-in-your-mouth' muffins. When he was with them, he didn't feel like the low-life he was pretending to be. Little by little, he'd allowed them to meet the Killian Reade that few knew.

Maybe if you can find the man Violet knew you could be, Emma wouldn't be so busy.

His quest led him to spend time with Mama B, something he should have done right after Violet's death. But his guilt had sent him running. He'd not grieved. Nor had he taken the time to be there for an older woman who'd lost more than her share. Finally, after a handful of visits, he felt closure. The time spent talking about the little girl had been cathartic, allowing him to remember things about himself he'd forgotten.

... I don't have to be different. I just have to be me ...

Since before Thanksgiving, Killian spent more time in New York with Liam than in Swan Harbor. He'd been fortunate his brother had been patient, but he knew the time was coming for them to talk.

"Let's just get through tonight," he murmured as he tied his black bowtie.

Liam had been instructed to appear at a New Year's party and was pulling Killian along. Except with no date on his arm, it would be a challenge not to fall back into old habits and hide. *Was he ready?* he wondered, leaving his room to see his brother pacing in front of the door.

"It's about time," Liam grumbled.

"Bugger off." Killian shot back. "I'm ready, aren't I?"

"Not quite." Liam held up a black scarf. "You forgot this."

Killian's eyebrow automatically arched as he eyed the silky scrap. "Bloody hell, no!"

"Sorry, little brother." Liam's lips lifted slightly. "It's a masquerade ball. Masks on until the countdown begins."

As Killian took the cloth and crammed it into his pocket, his lips twisted at the irony of the situation. He'd spent much of the past few weeks shedding layers, searching for the man beneath. Was it possible once the mask was removed at midnight, the new year would begin with the rebirth of the man Violet thought he could be?

New York City
Elsa's Apartment

December 31
7:30 p.m.

EMMA SURPRISED HERSELF BY JUMPING INTO THE SWAN HARBOR holiday festivities with both feet. There was caroling through town, ostentatious decorating, and more parties than she'd imagined. But she made it through often without her protective shields.

Except she'd gotten a little too comfortable with her newfound freedom. A cookie exchange and an overheard conversation about Killian had pushed her too far from her 'at-ease' zone, and she'd latched back onto her protective shell. If only she hadn't been so nosy ...

"Have you seen Killian lately?" Voice one asked.

"Not since before Thanksgiving," Voice two answered. "But after what happened with Belle, I can't say I'm surprised."

"What happened?" Voice one fired back.

"You didn't hear?" Voice two hesitated a beat. "Dylan let Belle into Killian's apartment, and she cooked him a nice dinner. Sometime during the evening, he called her Emma."

"What?!" shrieked Voice One. "I bet Belle was upset."

The sound of someone coming sent Emma scurrying for safety, but their words stayed with her. She couldn't put it out of her mind and searched for the man himself. When he was nowhere to be found, she reread her goals, tightened her protective armor, and took the train to see Elsa.

They spent an enjoyable week, and she'd once again felt centered. But then she learned where Elsa was taking her for New Year's Eve. With her friend working at a King Hospital, there was the risk of recognition. Should she come clean about her past or continue to pretend? Had living in Swan Harbor given her the strength to do what she must?

While Emma got ready, all the what-ifs rushed through her mind. By the time she zipped up her simple black dress and pulled her hair into a messy bun, she hadn't decided.

Even after fastening her gold chain, diamond earrings, and adding a slash of coral lipstick, her nerves were still pinging. "You can do this," she chanted several times while leaving the bedroom.

"Why is it we have to go to this masquerade affair?" Emma asked again.

Elsa grinned, "Because ..."

"Your boss strongly suggested you show up," Emma finished, repeating the answer she'd received every other time she'd asked.

"So, if you know the answer ..."

Emma thought about sticking her tongue out. But since it wouldn't do any good, she slipped a black wrap around her shoulders, ready to go.

"Besides," Elsa continued, her blue eyes twinkling, "I just might see ..."

"Oh, now," Emma smirked, "finally, the real reason comes out. Who might you see?"

"A man." Elsa pretended to study her nails for several seconds before an impish grin crossed her face. "He's just so darn good-looking."

Emma glanced at her friend, who usually wasn't so exuberant about meeting men, especially in the last few years. Was he 'that' remarkable to cause such a change.

"That's why you didn't ask questions when I told you Tyler lived in Swan Harbor." Elsa's eyes flared, but she was hesitant to push any farther. "You can tell me all about this new man in the car."

"There's not much to tell," Elsa confessed softly as they rode the elevator to the lobby. "I've just seen him in the hospital a few times. He's a paramedic."

Nothing else was said as they exited Elsa's apartment building and climbed into the limousine. While the driver dealt with traffic, taking them from the Upper West side to the Four Seasons Midtown, Emma prodded for more information. "Tell me, is he tall or short? Dark or light?"

Elsa grinned mischievously. "He's tall, has expressive blue eyes, and the most delicious accent."

Blue eyes that said more than you expected floated through Emma's mind. "Wait a minute. You said it's a masquerade party until the countdown starts, right?"

Elsa hummed in agreement, and just the tone said several things about her feelings for the man.

"Then how will your paramedic even recognize you?"

"I told him what color dress I was wearing."

"That's cheating."

Elsa shrugged one slim shoulder, "So ... sue me." Then she gave a very un-Elsa-like giggle and handed over a scrap of fabric.

Emma tied the slim scarf around her friend's head and then turned her back, waiting for reciprocation of the favor. "Someone's going to have a little more fun than I am," she muttered, stepping from the car.

Elsa grabbed her elbow in excitement as they entered the gorgeous hotel with its Christmas decorations still magnificently displayed. "Maybe not. He told me he has a brother."

"Great," Emma murmured for Elsa's ears only. "Just what I need."

"Oh, hush," Elsa scolded. "Love might be waiting for you tonight."

Emma glanced around the room with low lighting and soft music and considered making a snide comment. Except there was something about the words that touched her. Could she let go of control long enough to explore her options?

New York City
Four Seasons Hotel
December 31
8:00 p.m.

KILLIAN LEANED ON THE HIGH-TOP TABLE, WAITING AND watching for one of the colorful lasses to catch his attention. Several had asked him to dance, and although he'd accepted a few times, his mind and heart hadn't been engaged enough to stay for a second song. It had been too easy to fall back into the cocky SOB who was interested in padding his black books. Flirting without affecting an air of pretense was his hope. Was it possible?

"There she is," Liam murmured.

"Where?" He looked toward the door just as several women entered the ballroom simultaneously.

"There," Liam indicted, "the vision in peach."

Killian glanced across the room, and his gaze immediately locked on the woman standing next to Liam's date. "Emma," he murmured, wondering how he could know that.

Almost as if she'd heard someone say her name, Emma lifted her head, and while he knew it was impossible, it felt like she was staring straight at him. *What* was she seeing? *Who* was she seeing?

"No, Elsa." Liam corrected. "Come on."

Killian followed his brother through the crowd. With every step he took, his heart beat a little harder.

She never looked away, which was both a blessing and a curse. It made him worry about what to say and how to act.

His mouth felt like cotton. On the outside, he was the same man. On the inside, though, there had been changes. Would she see them? Would she stay and talk to him? Or would she run?

Her perfume reached out and wrapped around him, making him want to lean in and bury his nose against her neck. Yet, the fear of rejection had him standing back and waiting to see if she would meet him somewhere in the middle.

When Emma turned away to talk to her friend, it gave him a few seconds to catch his breath. *What would it feel like to have her smile at him? Was that a pipe dream? Could he even handle having her looking at him and not through him? Was he ready for that impact any more than he'd been prepared for the effect of a dressed-up Doctor Foster?*

"Good evening," he heard Liam say to Elsa. "You look lovely."

Her response was much the same, and Killian had to bite his lip to keep the smirk off his face. His brother was completely gobsmacked—something he'd not expected.

Liam cleared his throat, and a mischievous grin flitted across his face. "This is my brother," he hesitated a beat, "Zorro."

What could have been a soft snort came from Killian's left. It took digging inside for a shot of courage before he could allow his eyes to meet Emma's. He bowed in an old-world manner and inclined his head slightly. "It's a pleasure to meet you."

Emma's lips twitched, and he could have sworn her eyes twinkled behind her mask. "Well, Zorro," she teased, "should I ask where you're hiding your sword?"

Killian's mouth dropped open before he could catch it. "My sword?" He blinked several times behind the scarf and thought perhaps he was dreaming. Except, when he opened his eyes, and she hadn't disappeared, he couldn't stop his grin. Nor could he keep from playing along by lifting his jacket as if looking for a sheath. "I must have left it at home."

She stepped closer and pushed a little more, causing his heart rate to tick up a few extra beats. "And where is that?"

"Now that would be cheating, wouldn't it?" he quipped. "Dance?"

Emma studied him, and it was a fight to stand still. A battle to let her see he wasn't the same man who'd left Swan Harbor a few weeks ago. The question was, would she give him a chance? That wasn't something that could be easily answered.

Unable to stand still any longer, he finally took the initiative and held out his hand. "Please."

"Okay." Her husky voice caused a shiver to work its way up her spine. Then she placed her hand in his, and he was lost.

His palm tingled where they touched as he led her to the dance floor. When he pulled her close, he was amazed at how fragile she felt in his arms. She worked with much larger animals yet handled them with ease. Who was this woman who could take on a two-thousand-pound horse one minute and a kitten weighing less than a pound the next?

Again, an answer he wasn't privy to, but it didn't mean he wasn't going to ask ... eventually. There was a part of him that was scared to say anything. Scared he'd say or do the wrong thing, and everything would turn out to be a dream. Scared, he'd frighten her into running away. Scared they weren't on the same page.

EMMA FELT ALIVE—ALMOST AS IF SOMEONE HAD PLUGGED HER IN. Was it him? The scientist in her wanted to form a hypothesis, but the woman just wanted to enjoy. That was a new admission for her and something she wasn't sure how to handle. Give her a difficult man, and she knew what to do. But give her one who held her as if she were porcelain, and she was lost.

"Are you a true Zorro?" She tilted her head, and a corner of her mouth curled up. "Do you defend the poor and the victimized?"

Killian swung her around in time with the music, and his grin threatened to take her breath. "Not these days, Lass. I left my sword and bullwhip behind for a simpler way of life almost a year ago."

She wanted to ask more about what he meant but decided not to push. "A simpler way of life, you say," she hesitated a few seconds. "Would that be like Jimmy Buffett living in Margaritaville?"

"I can't say I live a Jimmy Buffett life," he murmured, "but I have been known to exercise at the beach a time or two."

"And listen to Margaritaville?"

He chuckled. "How about you, Lass? My brother whisked away your friend before you were introduced."

Emma glanced around but couldn't see Elsa or her paramedic. "They had eyes only for each other, didn't they?" she replied, still surprised by Elsa's behavior.

"Aye," Killian answered absently. "I'm happy for Liam."

"I'm hearing a but in there somewhere," Emma prodded for more.

"Oh, it's nothing." He jumped away from the subject, making her even more curious. "However, you still haven't told me what I should call you."

"Cinderella?" she tossed out, surprised a fake name hadn't easily rolled off her tongue. Which, if she thought about it, was odd. In a way, she was usually pretending to be someone else.

Not someone else ... just a different Emma.

Their eyes met, both hidden behind scarves, which was freeing in one way but frustrating in others. She wanted to read what they were saying.

But don't you know what they are saying? Didn't you say he was just like your father?

Questions she didn't want to think about. Just not ones that would magically disappear.

"So, tell me," Killian teased. "If you're Cinderella, does that mean your dress will become rags at midnight, and your friend will turn into a rat?"

Emma was shocked when she couldn't hold back a giggle. "No. Elsa's definitely not a rat."

"Good. I'd hate for my brother to get his heart broken." Killian smiled. "They actually look smitten with each other."

He swung her around a few times until she could see them. There was something about the scene that had tears immediately filling her eyes. The way Elsa and Liam seemed to be in their own little world belied the comment about just seeing the paramedic a few times. But she wasn't going to argue, as Elsa deserved happiness. If Killian's brother were the man who made her friend happy, then he would have had her blessing. In fact, it would be nothing less than Elsa would ho—

Emma's breath caught at where her thoughts had traveled. She glanced up and caught Killian watching her closely. Was he the predator to her prey?

That description certainly would have fit the man who offered to 'tune her engine' at Sally's in September. Just not the man in front of her. The man she'd been dancing with for a while hadn't said anything to make her push him into that category.

"Hope," she offered, thinking somehow, it fit.

"Hope?"

"Yes, Hope," Emma repeated. "It's part of my New Year's resolution."

"Hope," Killian echoed, his voice low and husky. "I like it."

His arms tightened around her, bringing her closer to his firm body. When the warning lights in her head were silent, Emma couldn't help but think it was because he made her feel safe. She leaned her head against his chest and, for the first time in forever, allowed herself to dream. For years, she'd believed her goals had to be accomplished one at a time and in chronological order. Whatever was going on between her and Killian had her wondering. Was it possible for her to focus on more than one goal at a time?

Hope.

That had become her resolution. What was she hoping for, though? Did happy endings begin with hope? Once more, her gaze drifted to Elsa and Liam. Would a man ever want her like that? If so, how would that make her feel?

"You're quiet." Killian's warm breath blew across her temple. "Are you alright?"

"I'm fine. Just enjoying the music."

And being in your arms.

The words to the song reminded her of Elsa's earlier comment, *love might be waiting for you tonight.* Was it possible?

KILLIAN LOST TRACK OF HOW LONG THEY DANCED. ONE SONG blended into another, but by the time the last song was cued, she had ruined him for others. She was the one he wanted, but was the reverse true?

The words to the song floated around them, wrapping them in a sensual cocoon. Were they building something? Or would she regret spending the time with him once the masks came off?

As the countdown started, Killian dropped his arms and reached behind his head to untie his scarf.

9

8

When Emma smiled, the butterflies in his stomach took flight, causing his heart to race.

5

4

Her scarf loosened on one side, but before the other side dropped, her attention was pulled away from him.

2

Emma's mouth dropped open, and her face lost all color. She raced toward the door as her white scarf fluttered to the ground at his feet, and the word "No!" hung in the air.

"Emma!"

FIVE

New York City
January 1
12:15 am.

EMMA WASN'T SURE HOW LONG SHE'D BEEN HIDING IN THE LADIES'
lounge, but every time the door opened, she panicked. Her pulse would race,
and it always took her several minutes to steady her breathing so she wouldn't
hyperventilate. Rationally, she knew she was being ridiculous, but
emotionally, she felt like a child all over again. Except if she went back into the
ballroom ....

"Emma?"

She peeked around a stall door. "Are you alone?"

"Are you okay?" Elsa asked without answering. "You look like you've seen
a ghost."

"Yeah," Emma murmured. "I ... I just need to get out of here. Can
we go?"

"Emma," Elsa pleaded, "tell me what happened. Did your dance partner
say ... or do something he shouldn't have?"

"No, but ..."

The look on her friend's face said the time for running was over. "Look,"

Emma grabbed Elsa's hands, "I know you have questions, and I'll answer them, but not here, okay?"

Elsa studied her for several seconds and finally nodded. "I'll get our wraps. Do you have your purse?"

"No, I gave it to Kil—I mean Zorro to hold for me. I think it's in his pocket."

"Okay. I'll get it and then come back here." Elsa took several steps before turning back. "Do you want me to say anything to Zorro for you? It seemed like you were having a good time."

Emma's thoughts returned to dancing with Killian. Elsa was right. She had been having a good time. It had been an evening of surprises. But what could she say that wouldn't make her sound like an idiot?

"Just," Emma shrugged, unsure what to say, "tell him thank you for the dances, and I'm sorry."

"What about your name?" Elsa suggested.

"My name?"

Let him in. Take a chance. Emma thought she read on Elsa's face.

While Emma was tempted, it wasn't the perfect way for Killian to find out who she was. "Tell him to have hope."

"Hope?"

"He'll understand."

With a little nod, Elsa disappeared, leaving Emma alone with her thoughts. *Time had run out.* In the past, she'd been content to shelve the questions until another day. That wasn't an option this time. She needed to decide what to say, and soon.

"Fine mess you've gotten yourself into," she grumbled, pacing back and forth within the small confines of the room. But as much as she was uncomfortable with the next step, she couldn't say she regretted the evening. Spending time with Killian while pretending to be a stranger had been good— in fact, amazing. If only she could move past her issues.

Once in the car, both women sat back, staring out their prospective windows, lost in their thoughts. It was after midnight in the new year, and the city never slept. The streets were still crowded, and the Christmas lights lit. But as the driver made his way back toward Elsa's apartment building, Emma's focus was on what was ahead.

"Get comfortable," Elsa advised as they walked through the door. "I'm going to change and make hot chocolate." She sent Emma a pointed look. "Then you can tell me why I'm here and not back in that ballroom kissing Liam."

"Brat." Emma's lips twitched at the way Elsa flounced from the room.

"You haven't seen anything yet," Elsa shot right back. "And you know how stubborn I can be."

Since that was true, Emma hurried to change into sweatpants and an oversized shirt. However, when she let down her hair, the *what* to say still hadn't completely coalesced in her head.

Start at the beginning.

Which sounded like a good idea, but ....

"Emma," Elsa called, "stop hiding and get your butt out here."

Emma grabbed a pillow from the bed, headed into the front room, and found Elsa seated, holding a mug of hot chocolate.

"Assume the position." She pointed to the other end of the sofa.

"Anyone ever mention how bossy you are?" Emma settled in one corner and placed the pillow on her lap.

"I only use my bossy voice with people who keep me from spending time with a man I've been trying to meet for months," Elsa sniped.

"Oh?" Emma's brow rose in question. "Tell me more."

"No, no, no," Elsa playfully wagged her finger. "Your turn. Now spill. What made you run away?"

"I saw my mother, okay?"

"You saw Ava?" Elsa frowned. "There has to be more to the story, Emma. We've known each other for a long time, and you've never behaved like this."

"You're going to make me tell you everything, aren't you?"

Elsa didn't even dignify the question with an answer. She just raised an elegant blonde brow and pushed, "Go on."

"Maybe I should start with the easier story of what's been happening." Emma gave Elsa a sheepish smile. "What have I told you about my life in Swan Harbor?"

"Well ... you told me about your clinic and the park and—"

"The people," Emma interrupted. "What have I told you about the people?"

"You've met some nice people, and the town has its own gigolo." She gave Emma a contemplative look. "Is that what you mean?"

"Yeah, that's what I said. Can you guess who that gigolo is?"

Elsa tilted her head, and a little frown appeared between her eyes. "How would I know who it is?"

"Because you danced with his brother all evening."

A myriad of emotions crossed Elsa's face. "Killian? Killian Reade is Swan Harbor's town gigolo?"

New York City
Liam's Apartment
January 1
1:30 a.m.

KILLIAN PRECEDED LIAM INTO THE APARTMENT AND DROPPED into the nearest chair. He buried his face in Emma's silky white scarf and inhaled her scent. It clung to the fabric and surrounded him, telling him that forever, the smell would remind him of home—vanilla, sugar, and something uniquely hers.

Liam shoved a glass in his direction. "Here."

"Thanks." Killian took the glass of rum and immediately downed half of it, relishing the rush of fire as it hit his gut. "Did Elsa say anything else?"

He'd replayed the evening over and over in his head. For the life of him, though, he couldn't figure out what had caused Emma to run. Plus, her message of not giving up hope? What did that even mean?

Liam sighed, his impatience apparent. "I've told you everything ... several times, in fact. Elsa said she would call or at least text me when she could."

Killian stormed to the window to stare over the city. "I'm bloody tired of feeling like I have no power over my life!"

He stalked across the room, poured another few fingers of the amber liquid, and once again dropped onto a chair. "If it hadn't been for that bloody yellow car blaring its bloody loud music, this would never have happened. I would be bloody happy with my four books filled with any number of beautiful women to help me ring in the new year."

"Dark hair and dark eyes. Great."

"Brown hair and blue eyes. Fabulous."

"Red hair and brown eyes. Yes."

"Blonde hair and blue eyes—too many to count."

The rest of the liquid in the glass slid down his throat, and when he set it down a little too hard, he gave Liam an apologetic look.

"'I can help you tune your engine,' I said to the most beautiful creature ever to grace this earth."

She'd looked at him like she would an insect she needed to squash. "'And you thought to impress me with your witty repartee?'"

"The next time I saw her, I tried a line I might have used with Morgan or Tia, Chloe, or Belle, and my arse was handed to me once again. What the bloody hell is she doing to me? She even had me calling another woman by her name. Do you know the last time I did *that*? Never!"

Killian forcefully undid his bowtie and several studs of his white shirt. When his agitation still hadn't settled, he ran his hand through his hair and stood to pace. It was the only way he could think of to get rid of some of his frustration.

"I even tried a third time because, you know," he scoffed, "third time's a charm. But no, no, no."

He remembered how she'd looked holding that tiny animal. "'I'm a little busy,'" Killian repeated, attempting to mimic her voice.

"'She needs me right now,'" he pitched his voice even higher. "Then she dismissed me before turning her attention to the kitten."

After making several more laps around the room, he stopped and pointed toward Liam. "But that's not the worst of it. No." Killian stretched out the word. "I even tossed my bloody books away for her."

"Killian," Liam's voice broke through his tirade, "who are you talking about?"

"Why, Emma, of course." Killian looked at his brother as if he were daft.

"Emma?" Liam questioned. "Elsa's friend Emma?" He fired question after question before Killian could answer. "The lass you were dancing with all evening?"

"Aye." Killian sent him a disgusted look. "Isn't it blatant?"

Liam chuckled. "You're telling me you knew Emma in Swan Harbor, and she didn't succumb to your charms? She wasn't another notch on your bedpost?"

"Bloody hell, no!" Killian snapped. "She barely even spoke to me."

"Yet, tonight, when both of you were masked, you danced with her for hours before she ran out?"

Killian rolled his eyes. "You know that's the case."

"Cor Blimey, Killian," Liam contended, "it's about time. My hat's off to Emma."

"Don't be cheeky, Liam."

"Come on, little brother," Liam asserted. "You cocked up. You've used that pretty face of yours to get females to do whatever you wanted since Mum left. It's about time someone called you on it."

Killian sent Liam a look that would have had many shaking in their shoes, but not his brother. He sat still with a little smirk on his face.

"After Mum left, you changed, but Violet's death pushed you even deeper into a downward spiral." Liam's tone was soft and persuasive.

"Violet?" Killian snapped, even though he sounded like a prat. Except where did Liam get that name? He knew he hadn't told his brother, and only a few of his friends on the force knew the complete story.

"I may just be a lowly paramedic, but I still have a few friends on the force," Liam confirmed, where he'd gotten his information.

Suddenly, Killian deflated. He sagged onto the sofa and buried his head in his hands.

"You sent me a request to help you find someone before you arrived," Liam prodded. "Do you remember who that was?"

"Aye," Killian answered. *The man Violet knew I could be.*

"Good. Because I know the first place to start."

Elsa's Apartment
January 1
1:45 a.m.

"Emma, you've told me about two encounters with Killian in Swan Harbor, where he behaved like a jerk," Elsa began. "You've also admitted you knew who he was the minute you saw him tonight. Yet you still danced with him—not just one dance, but all evening. What are you leaving out?"

Emma gnawed on her bottom lip while thoughts of being in Killian's arms echoed inside. She kept thinking about how their conversations didn't fit the man she'd thought him to be.

Several times throughout the evening, other females had asked him to dance. After he'd told the first woman his dance card was full, Emma thought it was only a fluke. But then it happened again ... and again. He hadn't flirted excessively with others, which would have been his prerogative—especially since she wasn't his date. *That* man confused her.

The man she'd spent the evening with was nothing like the man she'd first met at Sally's. That Killian's glib line had repelled even though his eyes captivated her. Tonight's man seemed to care, had a good sense of humor, and was so good-looking he took her breath away.

She wasn't sure if she trusted tonight to be real. One side of her heart said once back in Swan Harbor, the cocky man who wore his sexuality as a cloak would return. While the other side whispered, *Trust him.* Which side should she believe?

"What are you not saying?" Elsa repeated.

"Nothing," Emma quipped, but Elsa's evil eye had her relenting. "Even when he was at his most obnoxious, his eyes called to me. Something I've never experienced when a man looked at me."

"Why didn't you talk to him in Swan Harbor?"

Emma grimaced at her ping-pongy behavior. "I tried."

"But ..."

"At first, I thought I could forget how he made me feel and work on my goals."

"That sounds like the Emma I know so well."

Elsa's tongue-in-cheek response had Emma childishly sticking out her tongue. "Be nice."

"I brought you home, didn't I?"

"Sorry about cutting your time with Liam short."

"There will be other times." Elsa shrugged as if it didn't matter. "But don't change the subject. Why didn't you talk to him in Swan Harbor?"

"I," Emma rushed to deny the accusation, but even that wasn't the complete truth. "I—"

"—You wanted to ignore Killian, then tried to talk to him," Elsa prompted when she couldn't decide how to begin.

"I overheard something at a party."

"And?"

"It pushed me to look for Killian, but since he wasn't in Swan Harbor ..."

"You reread your goals and tried to put what you heard out of your mind."

"Hey!"

"What can I say?" Elsa laughed. "I know you too well. Now, what made you rethink talking to him?"

Emma told her about being at the cookie exchange and overhearing the conversation. "The need to know why he called another woman my name was so strong; I couldn't get it out of my head."

"Because you were on his mind," Elsa stated. "*You* were the woman he wanted. After tonight, can't you *feel* that?"

"But he didn't know it was me."

"Come on." Elsa's brow shot up in disbelief. "You knew it was him, didn't you?"

"Well, yeah, but women are better observers than men."

"Emma," Elsa snorted, "do you really think he didn't know it was you?"

Did she?

When she looked deep inside, the answer was there. She just ....

"Well?" Elsa pushed a bit more. "Killian was an undercover detective with the NYPD for ten years before moving to Swan Harbor. And he's still in law enforcement. I'm betting his powers of observation are better than yours."

"He worked undercover?" Emma frowned, wondering how he was able to blend, which would have been necessary. At the ball, even with all those people and each wearing masks, he stood out. "You asked Liam questions about Killian?"

"Are you telling me you didn't ask Killian about Liam?"

"Well, no, but ..." Emma smiled wryly. "Some things never change, do they?"

"We've been friends for a long time."

"You can run, but you can't hide," Emma muttered words she'd heard in the past when she hadn't wanted to share.

"We ..." Elsa began before her phone whistled an incoming text.

Liam's Apartment
January 1
2:15 a.m.

WHILE HIS BROTHER TEXTED BACK AND FORTH WITH ELSA, Killian paced, hoping for answers. But the more steps he took, the louder Liam's comment, *You've used that pretty face of yours to get females to do whatever you want since Mum left* rang inside his head.

Was there some truth in the statement? Had the way his father reacted after his mum left caused him to act a certain way? Or was he reaching for excuses?

But with Liam on the phone with Elsa, finding out why Emma had run was his priority.

Had he said something he shouldn't have?

Their conversation had been innocuous, basically getting acquainted without revealing who they were.

You knew who she was.

True, but she didn't know who you were, did she? Or was that why she ran?

When Liam hung up, Killian was ready with questions. "How's Emma? Did she say why she ran? Is she okay? Can I talk to her tomorrow ... I mean later today?"

However, he was wound so tightly it took Liam's shrill whistle to stop his tirade.

"Sorry," Killian grumbled. "But bloody hell, Liam. I'm dying."

"You really like this girl, don't you?"

"Aye." His quick response surprised him. Especially the fact he'd responded in the affirmative with no temptation to deny the truth. "There's just something about her that's mesmerized me from the moment I saw her. Big news to hear Killian Reade say that, isn't it?"

"A welcome one," Liam replied. "However, you can stop worrying because, according to Elsa, Emma is fine. You weren't the reason she ran. It seems she saw her mother."

"Her mother?" Killian frowned. "Why would that make her run?"

"I don't know." Liam shrugged. "But her mother is Ava King."

"As in King Industries?"

"The same."

"Oh." Killian let that hang in the air for a few seconds. "So she's rich. I can deal with that."

"You can handle it, eh?"

"Aye."

"Well," Liam pinched the bridge of his nose as if he had a headache. "We won't know the story tonight. Emma fell asleep, and I suggest we do the same. We're having a visitor in the morning, and I want you awake."

"Bugger that, Liam. I'll be fine." Killian didn't think he could relax and sleep without answers.

"Trust me," Liam urged him to listen. "Tomorrow, we'll find the solutions. I'm going to bed. Night."

Killian wanted to push, but decided against it and, after shutting off the lights, made his way to the guest room. Based on Liam's vocal tone, their visitor was someone he wouldn't expect. The question was, who?

SIX

New York City
Elsa's Apartment
January 1
7:45 a.m.

After a restless night, Emma woke early and was on her second cup of hot chocolate when Elsa stumbled out of her bedroom.

"I'm sorry I fell asleep."

"That's okay," Elsa grumbled on her way to the kitchen. "I didn't expect you to be up this early."

"Couldn't sleep."

"Busy mind?"

"How'd you know?"

Elsa disappeared for several minutes before returning with a donut and coffee, then settled on the sofa. "Please, Emma, don't do that."

"Sorry," Emma grimaced, realizing her reprieve was over. "But why don't you wake up a little more and tell me about Liam?"

"You're stalling," Elsa accused. "But I do have a message for you."

"For me?" Emma fought to keep the corners of her mouth straight. "From Killian?"

"See." Elsa beamed. "That wasn't so tough, was it?"

Emma considered denying everything, but knew it wouldn't do any good. "Okay, I'm interested. But just because he makes my heart go pitter-pat doesn't mean he's good relationship material. Even *if* I was in the market, for one."

"You don't think you owe it to yourself to find out?"

"Doesn't matter," Emma replied, "bad boys and loners have a tough time giving up their roving eye for just one person."

"That's not true," Elsa protested. "Bad boys and loners only stay that way until the right woman comes along. Don't you know that?

"Says who?"

"Come on," Elsa exclaimed. "Don't you ever watch romantic shows? Let's see." She held up one finger. "There's Johnny. You know Baby saved him in *Dirty Dancing*." A second finger flew up. "We can't forget Edward in *Pretty Woman*. Vivian saved him, and he saved her from a life on the streets." Up went the third finger. "And there's Danny Zuko. Who would he have been without Sandy?"

Emma shook her head. "Those are the movies, though, not real life."

"I've got more." Elsa went on, holding up a fourth finger. "How about Lee Stetson from *Scarecrow and Mrs. King*? He was a self-centered bachelor until Amanda came into his life. And, drum roll please," she held up her little finger, "Remington Steele, who was a con man and a thief until he fell for Laura Holt."

Emma laughed, but it felt hollow, telling her it was time to talk. "While that might be true in those shows you love, I know firsthand leopards never change their spots."

"What are you trying to tell me?"

Emma set her cup aside and wound her fingers together. "Did you ever wonder why my parents never came to see me in college? Why it was always just my mom."

Elsa shrugged. "Oh, maybe a few times. But you were always a private person, and I assumed your parents were divorced."

"No." Emma frowned, realizing she didn't know when ... or even if her parents were divorced. By the time she'd gone to college, her father had been out of her life for several years. "I was never high on my father's priority list."

"Oh, Emma," Elsa empathized. "I'm sure that's not true."

"It's true," Emma sighed, knowing it was time to talk about her childhood. "Need another cup of coffee? It's a long, convoluted story."

Elsa studied her for several seconds. "Okay, let me get reinforcements. Want more hot chocolate?"

After replenishing their drinks, Emma took a deep breath and began, "Unlike yours, I come from quite a dysfunctional family. I hope I don't scare you away."

Elsa shook her head. "Don't be silly. I'm your friend. Tell me only what you're comfortable with."

"Don't say I didn't warn you," Emma tried again, a part of her hoping to hear, 'Never mind. I don't really want to hear the story.'

But Elsa just raised a brow, and Emma found herself stepping back, almost as if she was detaching from reality.

"Once upon a time, a rich little girl was raised by her father in an ivory tower. You see, not long after the little girl was born, her mother died, and her father became very protective. The little girl tried hard to be good. Except, she had a wild streak inside, and her daddy often had to pay to make things disappear. Then, she graduated and went to college, which was very important to her father. Someday, he had plans for her to take over his business. You see, she was a King."

"King Industries," Elsa murmured, as if she'd only just realized it. "Your mother owns my hospital, which explains why she was at the ball last night."

Emma nodded. "Honestly, I'm surprised I didn't see more people I knew."

"But," Elsa frowned, "I know you aren't close to your mother, so why did you ...?"

"We haven't gotten to the convoluted part yet."

"By all means ..."

Emma recentered her thoughts and continued, "The little girl went to college, discovered she enjoyed learning, and four years later, graduated magna cum laude. As a gift, her father sent her on a month-long trip with promises of grooming her to take over King Industries once she returned."

"Where did she go?"

"Brest." Emma readied for the next part of her story. "It's located in Belarus, on the Poland border. But she had gone there with a purpose, as she knew her college crush was there working."

"Working?" Elsa broke in. "What did he do?"

"I'm getting there," Emma promised. "As luck would have it, she was sitting in a small cafe one morning, and he sat beside her.

Elsa practically swooned. "Oh, how romantic."

Emma hated admitting it, but her friend was right. Looking in from the outside, it was very romantic. "I guess so," she acknowledged, moving on with her story. "He was a consummate flirt, and when he wasn't working, he spent all his extra hours with her. She fell head over heels, forgetting her father's plans for her back in the States.

After a few weeks, she traveled with the object of her crush to Ternitz in lower Austria. He went to work daily, and she was content to play tourist. As you can imagine, her father was unhappy and wanted her to come home. But ... she was stubborn and in love.

Six weeks later, she defied her father and flew with her lover to Marseille in the Southeast of France. She was convinced he would propose, and they would live happily ever after. Except, when his work was done, with little more than a pat on the head, he flew on to his next job. The little rich girl was left heartbroken and pregnant.

Elsa's quick inhalation filled the silence.

"Yeah," Emma acknowledged, "it didn't end so well, did it?"

"That must have been a scary time for your mom."

"Maybe," Emma conceded. "She survived, and life moved on."

"Come on, Emma," Elsa scolded. "You aren't *that* jaded, are you?"

Was she? She used to think so, but as she grew older, she could study the situation with the eyes of an adult. The mistakes weren't one-sided.

"No? Yes?" Emma shrugged. "I don't think so. But now, for the convoluted part. My grandfather wasn't happy, and with the swipe of his pen, he ruined my father's career. My parents were pushed into marriage, and any negative press was squashed."

"They were unable to rekindle their feelings for each other?"

"I don't know," Emma confessed. "I never asked. Looking back, though, I think they tolerated each other. Several times yearly, my grandfather commanded the appearance of a happy family. On those occasions, my dad could be bought—a new watch here, ten thousand dollars there. What mattered was it looked as if he had the perfect family: a beautiful daughter, her adoring and famous husband, and their little princess."

"What about you, Emma?" Elsa asked gently. "What did you need?"

"Nothing," Emma quickly denied. "Johanna and the other staff members doted on me. They're the reason I became a veterinarian."

"Oh?"

"Yes, but that's for another day."

"Well, okay," Elsa grumbled. "But before I grab a refill, tell me. Who's your father?"

"Peter Foster."

"What!?" Elsa screeched. "The actor?"

Liam's Apartment
New Year's Day
8:45 a.m.

Since waking, Liam's comments had been at the forefront of Killian's mind.

After Mum left, you changed, but Violet's death pushed you even deeper into a downward spiral.

That comment was nothing new. What he didn't know was what precipitated his desire to change. Had it been Emma, or was there more?

You've used that pretty face of yours to get females to do whatever you wanted since Mum left.

But that statement didn't feel right either. While his behavior might have changed when his mum left, he didn't believe the cause was just her behavior. What stuck in his head was seeing his larger-than-life father crying like a baby and hugging a bottle of scotch.

Afterward, he'd gone through school, college, and the academy, treating women like trophies.

You behaved like a git.

He had. At least, he was man enough to admit he'd collected females for years, but never allowed them close enough to touch his heart.

Until Emma.

She had already gotten under his skin, and he didn't want to let her go.

He tugged on a clean shirt and studied his image in the mirror. What did people see when they looked at him? Was it his black hair that looked like he'd just run his fingers through it? Or his blue eyes, which, in the morning light, showed tiny wrinkles from squinting in the sun? Could it be his mouth, chin, or the nose he'd always thought a touch too large?

Had he ever paid attention to *how* he looked? Or was it just the behavior his looks elicited?

He couldn't say for sure about the past. But for his future with Emma, he didn't want his looks to matter. His heart, his protective nature, and his being a good listener. Those were the things he wanted to show her.

Would she give him a chance, though?

Bloody hell, he hoped so.

"It's about time you showed your ugly mug," Liam groused.

"Bugger off, Liam," Killian shot right back. "I'm here, aren't I?

"You are." Liam's eyes twinkled. "But if I were you, I'd grab a cup of coffee as our guest," he hesitated a beat just as the doorbell rang, "is here."

There was only one person Killian knew who was that punctual.

"Dad."

"Hello, Killian." Finn Reade entered the room, a broad smile on his face. "It's good to see you again."

"And you," Killian replied. "Liam didn't tell me you were coming by this morning."

Liam gloated. "I'm going to run out and pick up some bagels while you two catch up."

Talk to him, Liam's eyes pleaded. "I won't be long."

It took several awkward moments before Killian was able to recover his wits. "Coffee with a splash of milk?"

Finn smiled. "You remembered."

"It's just coffee." Killian poured cups for both before joining his father at that table. "You look good, Dad. How have you been?"

His father wore a dark, obviously tailored suit, a light blue shirt, multicolored tie, and shiny black shoes. Several steps up from the jeans, plaid shirt, and dirty tennis shoes he'd worn the last time they'd been together.

"Thank you." Killian felt Finn's dark eyes studying his appearance. "I was just going to say the same about you. How long has it been, son?"

"A couple of years." Killian's cheeks heated, and he had to look away from his father's intense gaze.

"That's right." Finn leaned back and crossed one foot over the other knee. "Just before you were going undercover, right?"

Killian nodded, ashamed he'd only gone to see his father because he was worried he might not make it out alive.

"I heard you moved away from New York after it was over," Finn's soft voice continued. "What happened?"

Somehow, just like when he'd been a kid, Killian spilled the entire story. He explained Violet's zest for life. Explained how much he regretted not being able to save her. How, in a way, she'd saved him.

"I shoved the pain and the guilt so far away I thought it would never touch me."

"But it found you, didn't it?"

"Aye," Killian admitted, giving his father a self-deprecating grin. "I've been staying with Liam for several weeks, laying a few ghosts to rest."

Finn nodded in understanding. "Has it worked?"

"It's worked, but ..." Killian left the sentence hanging, wondering how best to bring up the next subject.

"Just say it," Finn spit out. "Whatever it is. I'll help if I can."

"Liam commented the other day about using my pretty face, which made me question ..."

"Tired of the love 'em and leave 'em lifestyle, Killian?"

His initial impulse was to quip, but with a crooked smile, he confessed, "I met someone."

"And?"

"I, I want to be a man who is worthy of her heart."

"I get the feeling you're after something specific," Finn prodded a little more.

"Liam believes my behavior is linked to mother's leaving," Killian confided in a rush. "I just don't ..."

"You don't want to lose yourself to someone like I did," Finn concluded. "And you want to know how come I was bloody arseholed all the time after your mother left?"

Killian opened and closed his mouth several times. "What happened?"

"You're doing a brave thing facing your ghosts," Finn confessed. "I should have done that much quicker than I did. Have a seat, and let me tell you my story."

"I met Claire when I was 21, and she was just 17. With her long black hair and big blue eyes, I thought she was the most beautiful girl in the world. It wasn't long before we were inseparable."

Finn told him that as soon as Claire turned 18, they had run off and married. Nine months later, Liam was born, and less than two years after that, Killian. With two children under three, her behavior became unpredictable, even more so when they moved to the United States.

"Except she wouldn't allow herself to be happy." Finn ran his hand across his mouth as if what he was about to say next was distasteful. "And you know the rest, Killian. She left, and I fell apart."

"Why?" Killian pushed, still not understanding. "Why allow her to have such control?"

"I was young and foolish. But Killian, loving someone doesn't mean losing who you are. When you love someone, you want to be your better self. Your mother and I ... we weren't right. However, she gave me you and Liam, and I am thankful for that."

For years after his mother left, Killian knew his father was unhappy. He'd spent much of that time bladdered, and his real estate business had suffered.

"You've changed too," Killian replied, noting the man from those days was gone.

Finn chuckled, "Finally! Wasn't it about time?"

He stopped talking when the door opened with Liam's return. "Sorry, it took so long. Fresh bagels are on."

Once Liam had gone into the kitchen, Finn leaned closer. "Killian, when you're talking about love, you have to be patient. Do you have any other questions?"

"Not right now."

Finn's dark eyes clashed with his. "If you think of something, you can call. You *do* still have my phone number, right?"

"Aye." Then, he changed the subject because he wanted to distance himself from his less-than-admirable behavior. "Liam told me you're selling high-end real estate these days."

The little smirk that crossed Finn's mouth said he knew what was happening, but Killian relaxed when he started talking about his new business. Even more so when his father called Liam into the room, and the conversation flowed smoothly.

"I'm sorry to say, but I need to leave." Finn gave a long-suffering sigh, however the sparkle in his eye belied his unhappiness. "The life of a real estate agent is often at the beck and call of others."

Liam frowned. "Who's looking at a place on New Year's Day?"

"A beautiful woman who doesn't enjoy American football."

"Well, well," Liam began.

"Stop being cheeky, Liam." Finn quipped. Then, surprising Killian, Finn hugged them and waved goodbye.

"How did it go?" Liam asked as soon as the door shut.

Killian studied his brother, but his thoughts were on his conversation with his father. "It went well ... and as much as it pains me to admit this, thank you."

"Wasn't so hard, was it?" Liam laughed. "Did you get your questions answered?"

"He gave me a lot of fodder for thought," Killian conceded. The question was, would Emma think he was different? Would she spend time with the man she danced with last night? "Liam, do you think Emma might talk to me today?"

Elsa's Apartment
January 1
11:30 a.m.

It had taken Elsa a while to calm down, and for the last few hours, she'd been peppering Emma with questions about her father. Which was why she told no one she was related to Peter Foster. It made her feel too vulnerable to admit how little she knew about him.

"Sorry," Elsa apologized. "I know I'm acting weird. But my mom had the biggest crush on him. She'll pester me for news when I tell her he's your dad."

"You'll have to tell her you have none," Emma confessed. "I, I haven't seen him in years."

"Years?"

"My grandfather passed when I was in high school, and my father took off. I haven't seen or heard anything about him since. And," Emma continued with the sad truth, "the last time I saw my mom was three, maybe four years ago."

"At graduation?"

Emma hummed. "She was supposed to come to my vet school graduation, but King business took her away."

"Do you talk to her?"

"An email here and there." Emma shrugged. "Phone calls a few times a year."

"And that doesn't bother you?"

Emma pondered the question for several seconds. "It is what it is. Would I have changed my family dynamics? Sure, who wouldn't? But aren't we products of our experiences, so change one thing—"

"—And we become an entirely different person," Elsa murmured.

"Exactly. But, as much as I've enjoyed this confessional, I need to finish packing and head to the train station. Sadie is expecting me in the morning."

"I hate that you must go," Elsa moaned, "even though I understand. But Emma, what are you going to do about Killian?"

The feeling of being in Killian's arms warred with the memory of him surrounded by groupies.

The sweet things he had uttered to her last night fought with the memory of his glib tongue those times in Swan Harbor.

Who was the real Killian Reade?

"I need time."

"I'm here ..."

"I know."

When Elsa's phone rang, and it was the hospital, Emma sighed with relief and finished packing. Anything else could wait.

SEVEN

New York City
Liam's Apartment
New Year's Day
12:30 p.m.

KILLIAN'S HEART FLIPPED SEVERAL TIMES WHEN LIAM TOLD HIM to grab his jacket because they were going to Elsa's. The question was ... what would Emma think when they showed up? Would she be okay? He wasn't sure, but as they'd opted to walk, he had a few minutes to gather his thoughts.

When they crossed Fifth Avenue into Central Park, the memory of long-ago dates flashed through his mind. He'd taken women for romantic carriage rides around the park, but had little recollection of their faces. They were just names left behind in the books he'd tossed out.

"Do you think Father is still in love with Mum?"

"What?" Liam quickly glanced in Killian's direction.

"I was just thinking about my conversation with Dad. He never said he no longer loved Mum. Do you think if she returned, he'd take her back?"

"I don't know." Liam shrugged, his voice a tad frostier than before. "You didn't ask?"

Asked? No, his father somehow had anticipated what he'd wanted to know, except there had been holes in his confession. "He admitted he'd *finally* laid his ghosts to rest. And, I admit, he does look good."

"I say it's about time," Liam snapped. "Claire Reade didn't care to be a mum, and I say good riddance."

His brother's anger and resentment threatened to spoil their easy camaraderie, pushing him to change the subject. "So, how did you meet Elsa? You never said."

While Liam was talking about Elsa, Killian half listened. The other half was focused on Emma.

Emma said to tell you to have hope.

Were there limits to how much he could hope for?

He could hope she would spend time with him, but could he hope it was because they were on a date?

He could hope they would be friends, but could he hope they would be lovers?

He could hope she would like him, but could he hope she would love him?

He could hope for an hour, a day, or a week of her time, but could he hope for always?

"Here we are," Liam interrupted his thoughts as they entered the lobby of a modern building.

"Nice."

"I looked at an apartment in this building when I went to work for Queen's Court Medical," Liam grumbled. "Wish I would have taken it now."

Elsa lived on the tenth floor, and the higher the elevator climbed, the faster Killian's heart raced and the clammier his hands. *Bloody hell, I'm not some sixteen-year-old.*

When the elevator stopped, Liam pointed to the door. "Come on, little brother, you'll be fine."

Liam reached to knock on the door, and the closer his hand got, the faster Killian breathed. "Wait!" he hissed around the black spots in front of his eyes. "I need a moment."

Liam studied him for several seconds and then forcibly tugged him down the hallway. "Killian, you're white as a ghost. What's gotten into you, man?

"What do I say to her?"

"You didn't have any difficulty speaking with her last night, did you?"

"No," Killian muttered, "but I was wearing a mask. Now I'm not. What if she doesn't like this man?"

"Little Brother, I don't mean to burst your bubble, but you've been hiding behind more than a mask since mum left. Last night, for the first time in years, only your eyes were covered. Trust me."

With his breathing returning to normal, Killian gave Liam a little nod and followed him down the hallway.

"Ready?"

"Aye." But his heart jumped into his throat while he waited for the door to swing open.

The Train to Swan Harbor
January 1
1:00 p.m.

THE VIEW OUT THE WINDOW CAPTURED EMMA'S ATTENTION. SHE couldn't help but think how different the view was depending on where she looked. She could see a mass of buildings in one direction and wide-open spaces in another.

She picked up her phone and opened the newest message. In addition to Killian's phone number, Elsa sent a picture from the dance. The impact had one word echoing inside ... wow!

Since moving to Swan Harbor, she'd done a lot of self-reflection, but none more so than in the past twenty hours. That she'd shared her childhood with someone surprised her. It had always been her closely guarded secret. However, the biggest revelation wasn't *that* she'd shared. It was how she felt with it behind her—free. She felt free.

But just because she felt good about sharing her past, she still had concerns about Killian. The man she'd met in Swan Harbor was too much like her father, and even though she was drawn to that man, she wasn't willing to risk her heart. As a child, Peter Foster had shattered hers too many times.

Except she couldn't help thinking about how she'd felt when Killian held her. Couldn't forget the sound of his voice when he said her name. Or the way one corner of his mouth hitched when he smiled. If that were the real man, she'd gladly hand him her heart, knowing he would guard it with his life.

Which man was he, though? The cocky jerk or the gentleman? They were such opposing personalities. One she would have no difficulty running toward. The other, she would run from as fast as possible.

Her attention returned to the picture of the two people at the ball. What she saw had her heart doing a dance she was unsure how to handle. If you looked closely, there was more going on than just a man in a black tuxedo holding a woman in a black dress.

If you looked closely, you couldn't miss the way her body melted against his. Or the way her smile said she trusted him.

If you looked closely, you couldn't miss how their eyes were locked on each other. Or the way their clasped hands rested over his heart.

"Until you saw Ava."

Emma leaned her head against the cool glass. If she focused, she could still feel Killian's touch. Every dance, every song, every word played over and over.

Elsa's Apartment
January 1
1:00 p.m.

"LIAM," ELSA GREETED HIS BROTHER BREATHLESSLY.

"We're not too early, are we?"

"You're fine." She stepped back and opened the door wider. "Come in."

Killian followed Liam into the apartment and immediately knew, "We missed her, didn't we?"

"I'm sorry. Emma had to catch a train," Elsa apologized. "I started to text, but ..."

She wanted to spend time with Liam.

"That's alright," Liam assured her. "We needed to get out of the house, anyway."

"Can I get you anything?" Elsa drew them further into the apartment.

Both men declined, and while Liam and Elsa were talking, the photos on the wall captured Killian's attention.

"Emma."

"We were young and silly," Elsa alleged.

"You went to college together?"

Killian couldn't look away from the pictures and studied each one. A part of him felt like he was privy to a piece of Emma's life she didn't let many see. In fact, he doubted few people in Swan Harbor knew the woman featured in the photos.

"Yes." Elsa waved at one picture of twenty girls standing in a group. "This was taken our freshman year of college right after all the parents left. Emma and I were roommates."

She pointed out several other pictures, each depicting moments in the girls' lives. He couldn't help but think the more he learned about Emma Foster, the more she fascinated him. Most images needed no explanation as they showed typical college activities: studying, sporting events, dances, cooking, eating, etc. Others, though, piqued his curiosity.

"Do I even want to ask?"

He'd been looking at photos showing Emma and others in comical situations. In one, she was pulling on numerous articles of clothing. Another had her holding a spoon with an egg on it. Her face was buried in what looked like a pie in a third. Then, in the last one, egg yolk spilled from her hands.

"It was a bonding exercise for the girls on our floor." Elsa's laugh was lighthearted. "Our RA had a quirky sense of humor."

"Looks like it worked." Killian studied the other girls in the pictures. "Everyone looks like they're having fun."

"It did," Elsa agreed. "But for months afterward, I couldn't make myself eat pie."

Elsa's collage of various events of Emma's life gave him insights into some of her behavior. The girl in the photos was kind, caring, and empathetic, but she had walls. She was smiling and laughing in most pictures but only completely carefree in a few. There was something in each image where he thought she was holding back. Her smile didn't quite reach her eyes in one. Her body language was off in another. But in some of them ... it was almost like she was another person.

"There are two Emmas." He exclaimed, then immediately felt his face heat.

"Show me."

Killian glanced at Elsa and saw only acceptance. "See these," he indicated a few pictures. She looks happy, but her smile is just a touch off. In these," another couple were shown. Her smile is open, relaxed, and reached her eyes."

He hesitated a second and thought, it's as if her heart was in her eyes before he moved on. "This one," the picture showed Emma sitting in a grassy field surrounded by puppies and kittens, "is the real Emma." *And she's beautiful.* "How can I get through to that, Emma?"

Elsa studied him, probably trying to determine if he was worthy. "Emma matters to you, doesn't she?"

The need to wrap himself in his protective cloak and flirt his way through the uncomfortable situation was intense. It took more than one deep breath before he could again meet Elsa's eyes.

"Aye. Possibly more than she should at this point in our acquaintance."

"That's good." Elsa hesitated a few beats. "But it won't be easy. Emma's not easy," she reiterated. "However, once you've gotten inside her walls, there's no better friend."

He'd figured out that much on his own. But where had her walls come from? Why were they so high? Those were the questions he needed to answer.

"Somehow, I knew that," he admitted. "I could see it the other night when you two were talking. You're close, aren't you?"

"We are." Elsa smiled and linked her arm with his, leading them to the sofa. "Let's sit and chat a while."

"Said the spider to the fly," he quipped, immediately pressing his lips together.

Elsa's giggle had him releasing his breath and meeting her smile with one of his own.

"Tell me how you met Emma."

Killian wasn't sure what had gotten into him, but he shared just as he had with his father. While there were pieces of his story, he held back. He found himself telling Elsa the reason behind his love 'em and leave 'em behavior.

Her lack of judgment allowed him to share everything that had transpired in Swan Harbor. That included his lame attempts to treat Emma like every other female he'd been interested in.

"I'm sure that went over well," Elsa grinned.

"Ripped me a new one."

"Did you immediately know it was Emma at the dance?"

Killian thought back to that night and how all it had taken was a glance. "Aye," he confessed. "Liam pointed you out, and I immediately knew who she was."

"She knew it was you, too. Even though I didn't know until later, it helped me understand some of her behavior that night."

He couldn't stop the smile that bloomed on his face. "And she still danced with me."

The pictures on the wall once again captured his attention. "She still flirted and told me to have hope." *But then why* .... "You gave her my number, right?" Elsa nodded. "Then why haven't I heard from her?"

"Perhaps she needs time to think through a few things."

"Will you give me her number?" Killian asked, even though he knew it wasn't Elsa's to give. "Never mind. But help me. I'm not sure where to go in this situation."

"Give her time," Elsa suggested. "I've known Emma for ten years and learned some new things about her this morning. Just be her friend and be patient."

Could he be patient when patience wasn't his strong suit?

For Emma. Anything for Emma.

The Train to Swan Harbor
January 1
1:30 p.m.

EMMA HAD BEEN ON THE TRAIN FOR OVER HALF AN HOUR AND still couldn't get her thoughts to settle. The same things spun around and around.

If she had stayed in NYC another day, would she have wanted to talk to Killian?

Maybe.

But ....

Which was what it all came down to ... the but.

A family sitting across the aisle from her captured her attention. The mother was reading with her young daughter. At the same time, the father and a young boy were laughing at a video they were watching on an iPad. What would it be like to be a part of a family like that? Had Ava ever read to her? If so, the memory of it was missing.

Ava hadn't known how to deal with a small child, preferring to leave her with Johanna, her nanny, until she'd become a teen. It was then that Ava tried to befriend her. Except Emma hadn't wanted to shop or spend time at the spa. Instead, she preferred volunteering at the local animal shelters. The animals touched an empty space inside.

And her father ....

The conversation with Elsa had her wondering what had happened to him, a thought she hadn't allowed in years. Before she could change her mind, Emma typed his name into her search engine. The headline **Peter Foster to Wed His High School Sweetheart** caught her eye.

Peter Foster and Amber Waters will be wed in a quiet ceremony on Saturday.

She read the article's first line and skimmed the rest, surprised to discover he'd returned to Ferndale, Washington. What was he doing in a place with very little limelight?

Curiosity led her to save the picture of her father and Amber and search for a similar one of her parents. The differences were striking.

In the picture of her parents, both were angled toward the camera, almost as if they were alone. Whereas, in the photo of Peter and Amber, they were turned into each other. His arm was around her, holding her close, and her hand lay over his heart, displaying her engagement ring.

He looks happy.

"Leopards don't change their spots," she reminded herself.

Are you sure about that?

Unconsciously, her finger slid across the screen, bringing back the picture of her and Killian. *They look happy. Dare I trust myself and the way I'm feeling?*

Her phone vibrated with an incoming message.

Elsa: Killian and Liam were here

Emma: Was that your doing?

Elsa: Yes, so sue me. But Killian was like a whipped puppy when I told him you'd left.

What would he have said if I were still there?

Emma: I'm sure. He's not getting his way.

At least, that was how she would have expected the man from Swan Harbor to behave. The man from the dance confused her.

Elsa: He's a good guy, Emma. We talked for a long time.

Emma: About?

I bet he grilled her for information about me.

Elsa: Him.

Emma: Him? Really?

That wasn't the answer she'd expected.

Elsa: Really? He told me about his stupid comments.

Emma: Wow.

Why would he voluntarily tell someone about his ridiculous attempts to impress her?

Elsa: Give him a chance, Emma. He asked if I gave you his number. He wanted yours.

Emma: Did you?

Elsa: No. I told him to be patient.

Something told her patience wasn't one of Killian's strong suits.

Emma: Thanks, Elsa. I'll think about everything.

And if I don't, she won't let me forget.

Elsa: Good.

Emma: TTYL

Emma slid her phone into her pocket and closed her eyes. She had some thinking to do before her train arrived in Portland.

New York City
Liam's Apartment
January 1
9:00 p.m.

KILLIAN'S PHONE BUZZED, AND WITHOUT LOOKING, HE KNEW IT was the alarm he'd set hours ago. The one allowing him to track Emma's train, telling him she was pulling into the Portland station. Then, once she'd gathered her belongings, she'd climb into her yellow car and begin the drive back to Swan Harbor ... without him.

Should he cut his trip short and go home?

A part of him was ready to return to Swan Harbor. But as he rode the elevator to Liam's apartment, Elsa's words kept banging away in his head.

My suggestion is to be her friend.

He could do that, right?

Do you even know how to be friends with a female?

I have plenty of female friends.

Right! Who?

Molly.

She's married.

So?

He could see his subconscious arching its brow, not buying his excuse.

Sadie.

She's engaged and off-limits.

Dozens of females popped into his mind, but just as quickly, he disregarded them for one reason or the other.

Bea Morris.

She's old enough to be your mother. Try again.

Alright, he admitted, slamming the lid on the voice. But what could he do?

Killian pushed open Liam's door and hung the key on a hook.

"Where've you been?"

"Walking. Thinking about what Elsa said."

"About?"

"She suggested I be Emma's friend."

"And?"

"Come on, Liam." Killian felt his frustration level rise. "Help me out here. How do I make friends with a female?"

Liam's chuckle quickly turned into a full-blown belly laugh. "You want me to tell you how to be friends with a female?" His laughter grew louder until he was bent over, holding onto his stomach.

"I don't find this particularly funny." Killian clenched his teeth so hard his jaw hurt.

"Sorry." Liam wiped his eyes. "I just didn't expect that question. Now," his lips twitched, "friends, right?"

"Aye." Killian snapped. "Friends."

Liam's shrug made Killian feel daft for even asking the question.

"The same way you make friends with men. Common interests. What does Emma like?"

"How the bloody hell do I know what Emma likes?" Killian barked. "If I knew, I wouldn't have made such an arse of myself."

"Think about it, little brother. What makes Emma happy?"

What made Emma happy?

Unwittingly, the multitude of pictures on Elsa's wall came to mind, one sticking out more than others. The one of her surrounded by small animals had caused a genuine smile, which hadn't been so in the others.

And her ease with Fred when she'd found him in the woods around Peter Pan Park.

"Animals make her happy."

"There you have it," Liam noted, turning on the television. "Talk to her about animals."

"Animals?!" Killian faltered slightly. "Bloody hell, Liam. We never had animals growing up."

Liam gave him a disgruntled look. "Google can help. Now, hush. Liverpool's playing."

"Animals." Killian picked up his iPad. "How hard can it be to learn about animals?"

His finger hovered over the search box while he tried to decide where to start. But the only animals he knew anything about were the ones he saw on a vacation trip to Disney World ... a mouse, a dog, and a duck.

"It's a start," he murmured, typing Ani ....

EIGHT

Swan Harbor
Veterinarian Clinic
January 5
4:00 p.m.

When Emma returned to Swan Harbor, several emergencies happened simultaneously, and she realized help was needed. Surviving on little sleep and too much caffeine, her sense of losing control rose a little more every day.

But it keeps you from having to decide about Killian.

It did that, but after the freedom she'd felt sharing her past with Elsa, being out of control made her uncomfortable. Especially when she couldn't find notes she'd taken when speaking to a former professor. Emma Foster didn't lose things.

"But you did this time, didn't you?" Emma whispered, flipping through several piles of folders on her desk. When the last group hadn't revealed her treasure, she dropped onto her chair and slammed the drawer. "Damn!"

"What's wrong?"

Emma glanced up to see Sadie enter the office with a pile of folders in her arms. "I'm looking for something."

"Really?" A teasing smile crossed Sadie's face. "Did you say you're looking for something?"

"Yes," Emma asserted, refusing to be pulled wherever her office manager was trying to lead. "I'm looking for some notes."

"Are you the same Doctor Foster who makes lists and subdivides them?"

"Come on, Sadie, I'm not that bad."

"Oh, I didn't say it was bad," Sadie assured her. "But ... you have been frazzled lately."

Emma had been more distracted since returning to Swan Harbor, but wasn't willing to acknowledge that. "Come on," she sputtered, "it's been crazy since I returned. Mitzi Fisher's prized poodle almost died giving birth—"

"Her precious Ribbons and Bows," Sadie added.

"And Bo Peep," Emma continued as if she hadn't been interrupted, "was hit by a car."

"But you saved her."

Emma grinned. "No thanks to my assistant, who passed out at the first sight of blood."

"Yeah, sorry about that." Sadie gave her a sheepish smile. "I didn't think it would bother me that much."

"Seems I need to hire someone to help. Preferably someone who can watch over the animals in recovery and help in surgery."

"Makes sense." Sadie handed her a piece of paper. "Call Leroy. He's a nice guy, although a bit of a busybody. But he's great with animals and did similar work for Doc Thatcher."

"Okay, thanks." Emma left the paper in the center of her desk with her phone on top.

"But there's something else."

The way Sadie was staring gave Emma the same feeling as when Elsa was trying to pull information from her.

"I've been ... busy," Emma tossed out, hoping to throw Sadie off track. "And *Felis catus* have taken over my office."

Sadie picked up an orange ball of fur. "I'll agree six kittens can be distracting, but this is different."

"Different? How?"

"Oh," Sadie hummed. "You're distracted. It's almost as if it involves a man."

Emma's face heated, and she quickly turned away to point at her board. "Puhlease. You know that's not next on my list."

"Oh, I know. But this is Swan Harbor, Emma," Sadie flashed the diamond on her left ring finger, "where the heart wants what the heart wants."

"Well," Emma yawned, "my heart wants sleep. And my notes. Have you seen them?"

"Would these be the notes written on a bag from Sally's takeout or on the box your pink gloves come in?"

Emma winced at the fact her uncharacteristic behavior was out on display. Instead, she tried remembering what she was doing when taking said notes. "Sally's bag, I think. They had to do with the treatment of the Mayor's horse."

"You're in luck then." Sadie tossed the file on the desk. "It was tough, but I managed to read your chicken scratch and made you a copy."

"Thanks. What about the *Canis lupus familiaris*?"

"Bo Peep, Ribbons, and her puppies are home with their owners, and follow-up appointments have been scheduled."

"Okay. Thanks again, Sadie." Emma covered her mouth when another yawn snuck out. "I'm heading to bed. I'll see you Monday."

With Sadie gone, Emma trudged up the stairs to her apartment. She had a date with a pile of mail and her bed.

Sheriff's Department
January 12
8:00 a.m.

KILLIAN RAN UP THE STEPS TO THE SHERIFF'S DEPARTMENT, HAPPY to be home. He'd been gone for more than six weeks, and he'd missed it—the town, the people ... Emma. Now that he'd allowed her to see the real man, he only hoped she would call.

"Welcome back," Dylan greeted him as soon as he stepped inside. "How was New York?"

"Good," Killian smiled. "It was nice to be with my brother over the holidays."

"Glad I could help."

When a fax arrived, it pulled Dylan from their conversation, giving Killian a moment to say something to Amy. Except the way she was looking at him made him uncomfortable.

It's because you've changed.

Just a few weeks ago, those words from the quiet voice inside his head would have terrified him.

"How were your holidays?" he asked after a few minutes of silence.

"Good." Amy continued to watch him.

Killian cleared his throat and tried again. "Did I miss anything important?"

"Not really. I left the incident reports on your desk. Read them, and you'll be caught up."

"Thank you." Killian took a step away from her desk, his feeling of discomfort increasing even more.

"You're very welcome," she preened, her smile becoming more predatory than he'd ever seen her aim at him. "Let me know if there's anything else you need."

"Will do."

As Amy had promised, the report was in the middle of his desk and smelled of her perfume. But, just as she had said, it wasn't very long, and after living in New York, he had to marvel at a few of the incidents.

"Underwear on Christmas decorations?" Killian read, sure it was a mistake.

"It was a sight." Dylan laughed, coming into the office and hitching a hip onto Killian's desk. "You should have seen Sally's undies on a snowman."

"Granny panties?"

"Oh no," Dylan's blue eyes twinkled. "Let's just say our Sally has good taste."

"Or Danny does," Killian added, wondering about the older couple and their closeness.

"That's a possibility. He and my dad grew up together. I heard some ... interesting stories when I was young."

Killian had a hard time understanding the longevity of those types of relationships. But now that he lived in a small town ....

"We haven't found the culprit either," Dylan moved the conversation back to the underwear caper.

"A kid?"

"Maybe," Dylan hummed. "It's happened before. Amy's looking into it for me."

"A serial Underwear Bandit," Killian chuckled. "That's a new one."

"You get all kinds in a small town. Just wait. Now ..." Dylan hesitated, as if waiting for something.

"Now?" Killian played dumb, unsure what to share about his trip to New York. However, his friend's expression had him asking, "What is it you want to know?"

"Did you find what you were looking for?"

More than Killian couldn't help but think. "I'm working on it," he admitted. "The time away was educational. But I've laid quite a few ghosts to rest."

"And Emma?" Dylan prodded a little more. "What about her?"

"I have hope this year will be a good one."

"It's about time you got your ugly mug back to work," Rusty replied when he entered their office. "You've been taking it easy way too long."

"Wanker," Killian taunted.

"Prat," Rusty shot back.

"Boys," Dylan shook his head. "Must you resort to name-calling so early in the morning?"

"Sorry, Boss," Rusty snickered. "We'll wait until after lunch. Won't we, Muppet?

"Muppet?" Dylan grinned. "Reminds me of that children's show Molly loves."

"I wouldn't use that word as an endearment, mate," Killian cautioned.

Dylan glanced from one to the other. "More British slang?"

"Aye."

When Killian joined the department and met Rusty Langley, they'd immediately bonded. It had been more than their law enforcement background, British heritage, or love of soccer. There had been an inherent connection that said someone had his back. That they could rile their unflappable boss was a bonus.

"Together, you're like children." Dylan softened the insult with an indulgent grin. "You'll make me gray before my time."

"You used to say that about Jessie," Rusty chuckled. "Now that she's married and out of town, Killian and I are just picking up the slack."

"I appreciate it … not," Dylan began.

"Rusty, Killian, you two are up," Amy interrupted. "We've got an … incident."

The laughter in her voice had all three men exchanging looks and following her to the front.

"What's up?" Dylan stopped next to her desk, immediately taking over the situation.

Amy flipped a piece of paper toward them.

Woman awakened when she heard her neighbor screaming, 'I'm tied up, and the person with me has been knocked out.'

Dylan laughed. "Have fun."

"Welcome home," Rusty smirked on their way to the car.

"I thought I'd seen it all."

"See," Rusty pointed out, "it's true what they say, 'you do learn something new every day.'"

"I'm not worried about what I learned today," Killian grumbled. "It's what we might see."

Their call took them to the Camelot Arms Apartments, an older complex on the other side of town from where Killian lived. He was familiar with the sprawling old building in the sense he'd picked up a date there a time or two over the past year. However, since his name debacle in November, he'd made a point to use his evasion skills whenever a past acquaintance was in sight. It wasn't fear causing his unease, but the fact that every time he saw one, the saying about a woman scorned popped into his head. As Rusty parked, he had to wonder if his *Dodge and Dash* days were over.

"Do we have a name for who called?"

Rusty pulled the report from his pocket. "Chloe Lane. Isn't she one of yours?"

"I've been out with her a few times," Killian admitted. "Maybe you should do the talking."

"I'd be happy to." Rusty began. "But …"

Chloe was waiting for them at the top of the steps, and immediately latched onto Killian's arm. "It's about time. Poor Audrey is beside herself."

"We—"

"You're here now," she interrupted, pressing closer to his side.

Killian met Rusty's smiling eyes, and the thought *She's not Emma* floated through his head. "Do you have a key?" He disengaged his arm and stepped away.

"No," Chloe denied, "and the manager is out of town."

Rusty kicked at the door. "It's metal, so we can't break it down."

"I've got this." Killian pulled a black leather case from his pocket, removed a silver lock pick, and opened the door.

"Audrey," Killian called, picturing the nondescript, tall, thin woman. "It's the police."

"Hurry," Audrey yelled. "Leroy needs your help."

"Leroy?" Rusty whispered. "And Audrey?"

"Interesting," Killian mused, picturing the short, brash man who often drank and became rowdy on the weekends. "Wouldn't have expected that pairing."

The sight that greeted them when they reached the bedroom door had Killian backing up a step and telling Chloe to call 911.

"I'll check Leroy." Rusty moved quickly toward the man on the floor, whose head and bare feet were the only parts of his body not covered by a large, red cape.

Killian glanced toward the center of the room and quickly took in the scene. Naked, Audrey lay spread eagle on top of the sheets with each hand and foot bound to a bedpost. He tossed a blanket over her, then worked on the knots. "What happened?"

"Oh, Leroy," Audrey sputtered, her face red with embarrassment, "woke up wanting to play Superman. Except when he tried to fly, he missed, and ..." She sat up and wrapped the sheet around her body. "Is he okay?"

"He's breathing." Rusty left Leroy's side when the paramedics rushed in with a stretcher. "Why don't you get ready and ride with him?"

"Thank you." Audrey went to dress, and after ensuring the paramedics had everything under control, Killian followed Rusty outside.

"Get cases like that often?"

"Oh, you don't know the half of it."

Killian grunted and climbed into the car. When he glanced back toward the building and caught sight of Chloe's face, he couldn't help but think, *Hell hath no fury ...*

"Whoa," Rusty whistled, "looks like you're in trouble."

"No promises were made."

Rusty lifted a brow, pushing Killian to add, "Didn't sleep with her either.

"Want to talk about it?"

Did he? And say what? That he'd spent time with Emma, and she'd had his number for over a week and not used it. Or should he share the fact he was trying not to lose hope? He wasn't ready.

"Nothing to talk about," Killian sighed. "Just pent-up energy, I guess."

"Sounds like you need to hit Giennie's."

"Perhaps you're right."

Killian searched for a change of topic and finally asked about Rusty's family. Thankfully, his partner picked up on the unspoken message and began talking about his wife, Rene, and son, Roland. But even the redirection didn't save him, as by the time they arrived back at the department, Emma's name was mentioned more times than he could count.

Rene's horse had come up lame, and he had to hear about how wonderful Emma, the vet, had been with the animal. Then Dylan mentioned Molly was meeting Emma, the friend, after school at Sally's. The entire time he suspected they were across the street, he'd fought not to run to her. But after Gray and Sadie stopped by, and Killian overheard them talking about Emma, the employer, and how she was distracted, he'd given up the fight and headed to the gym. He needed to calm his insides.

On the way to Giennie's, it was Elsa's words to be patient that kept him from taking a detour. Otherwise, he would have been heading to Emma's vet clinic to find out why Emma had been distracted. But it wasn't only Emma, the vet, who interested him. He wanted to get to know Emma, the woman.

Killian parked and hurried inside, hoping he wouldn't be required to socialize. In a town like Swan Harbor, that was no small feat, but after running into Chloe, he wasn't sure he was strong enough not to fall back into old habits. His cape was fraying, and if he saw ...

"Hey, Killian." Tyler James was standing in front of an open locker, a wet towel around his neck. "Haven't seen you around lately.

Bloody hell.

The image of Tyler and Emma leaving the party together popped into his head.

You forgot about Tyler.

Shut up! "Spent the holidays in New York."

And dancing with Emma.

"That's nice," Tyler went on. "Bethany and I spent time down south with family. Christmas is tough for Kara's parents."

Killian wanted to be abrupt and not like the singer, but it was hard to see Tyler as competition whenever he talked about his daughter. "I bet they appreciated that."

"They did." Tyler dropped his towel in a duffle bag and pulled a sweatshirt over his head. "We had a good time, but Beth was happy to be home with her kitten.

Kitten? He seemed destined to be reminded of the lovely Doctor Foster, no matter what he was doing.

"Anyway," Tyler went on, "gotta run. See you later."

"Later."

You behaved like a git.

Sue me, he wanted to say, heading toward the boxing area, but as soon as he'd taken several steps, his senses heightened. The hairs on the back of his neck stood on end, and his heart raced.

They found you.

"Bloody hell!" Killian cursed, stepping back into the shadows.

Emma!

She wore black spandex shorts, a bright red sports bra, tennis shoes, and nothing else. Her concentration told him she was working on those demons that were distracting her.

Be patient.

Have hope.

A jab with her right hand, a cross with her left. Every move showcased her lean body, making him long to touch. She mesmerized him. If he stayed, though, he wouldn't be able to keep away from her. Instead, he opted for jammers and the indoor pool.

As soon as he dove into the water, he immediately moved into the butterfly. Back and forth, he swam, trying not to compare the feel of the silky water to a lover's caress. His goal—to purge the vision of Emma in her tight clothing from his mind.

After losing count of how many laps he swam, he flipped over for the backstroke. Except Emma's image was still there. When that didn't help,

Killian tried the breaststroke. He just couldn't get the picture of her in a red sports bra out of his head.

Once he'd pushed himself as far as possible, he wearily pulled his body from the pool. His chest heaved, and his arms felt like jelly. Yet the images of her were bright in his mind.

"Bloody hell!" There were issues with his current lot in life. They had him practically running to the locker room, changing from wet to dry clothes and leaving Giennie's behind.

At home, Killian tossed his wet clothes in the washer's direction and went to the bathroom. He shed his clothing and, with a flick of his wrist, turned the shower on full blast. When the water was hot, he stepped in and leaned his arms against the tile, allowing it to pulse down on his weary shoulders.

Her fists rapidly pummeled the bag, and with each movement of her body, the slight muscles rippled in her arms.

"Stop being an arse, Reade!"

Killian adjusted the spray and turned his face up, allowing the mist to rain down upon him.

When her leg swung around to level a perfect roundhouse kick, the spandex stretched even tighter, showing the perfect curve of her taut behind.

Another part of his anatomy stood up, paying attention to his wayward thoughts.

"Friends!" he snapped. "Just friends."

A cross was thrown with her right hand and a kick with her left leg, showing off the lower part of her back and her flat stomach.

The Killian Reade who watched the yellow bug fly by last summer would say, *To hell with it*, grab hold with both hands, and pleasure himself. But this man ... this man would be her friend. "I'm here, Doc," he murmured, flipping the water to cold.

NINE

Veterinarian Clinic
January 19
6:30 p.m.

IT HAD BEEN TWO WEEKS SINCE EMMA UNCOVERED A TATTERED envelope in her pile of mail. She'd left it on the table with her copy of the Merck Veterinary Manual on top of it. Yet, just because she couldn't see the letter didn't mean she could forget it was there. Every time she walked through the kitchen, the hidden object whispered her name.

She tried working long hours and exercising until she fell asleep at night. But the whispers remained. They haunted her, telling her she needed to face what was inside the envelope. Once she did, she could move forward into the future—except saying it was easier than doing.

But that didn't keep her thoughts from veering into the danger area. She'd forced images of their New Year's Eve away more than she cared to admit. Yet fear held her back. It kept her from reaching out and taking a chance.

Lunch with Molly revealed Killian had been on a journey to find himself, making her wonder if he'd found what he was looking for in New York. That information and Elsa's comment about him being a good guy kept showing up. It had her asking herself. Should she listen to what her friends were saying?

Before she could change her mind, Emma moved the Merck, picked up the envelope, and slid the letter from its housing ....

My Dearest Emma,

If you are reading this, it's probably more than I deserve. I wouldn't be surprised if your first inclination was to hide the letter thinking, out of sight, out of mind. You see, that's what I tried when it came to you. But that you've read this far means you inherited my determined nature, which has led us to this point in time.

Let me start at the beginning. I was born on the proverbial wrong side of the tracks to a mother who was underage and a father who liked beer better than he liked his wife or his son. When I was ten, my parents were killed, and I went to live with my grandmother. She made me go to school, but anything beyond that, she didn't know how to give. The day I graduated from high school, I left Ferndale behind and moved to Hollywood.

I was fortunate to be in the right place at the right time and landed in a movie, and then another and another. Before long, I believed my press, and the only genuine thing I cared about was making it big. I'm not proud of the man I was, but it was that man who met your mother.

She was beautiful and carefree, and she adored me. I took advantage of her adoration, and we conceived you. When Leo King found me and torpedoed my career, I hated him. Not because he forced me to marry your mother or because of you, but because of what he did to me.

Fast forward to your birth, and the second I looked into your eyes, and you wrapped your tiny fist around my finger, something inside sparked to life. But that feeling? That feeling terrified me, and I did the only thing I could think of and turned away from you. If you weren't where I had to see you every day, I could pretend you didn't exist, and the hate I felt was safe.

Did it work? Not completely. Every time Leo King felt it would benefit King Industries, I was summoned for a command performance. I would be expected to appear with Ava and you as if we were a happy family. My hate was at war with my heart. Whenever I saw you, you owned a bigger piece of me. Yet, when we arrived back at the house, the hate won, and I ran instead of staying with you as my heart wanted.

When your grandfather died, the story you know is I was given money and disappeared from your life. Except the actual story is much more complicated. You see ... you weren't the first person who caused me to feel. That was Amber Waters, a kind girl who befriended a poor boy when they were teens.

She was shy and sweet and cared. When I left Ferndale, Amber went on with her life and became a psychologist who runs a successful practice. After Leo's death, I learned he'd created a fake dossier about Amber and me. However, if the information had leaked to the public, it would have destroyed her.

My choices were ....

Take the money and leave Boston and you behind, and the dossier would be mine.

Or

Stay in a marriage neither Ava nor I wanted, and the dossier would be made public.

I felt I had no choice but to take my freedom.

For months, I tried to find an agent, director—anyone to give me a chance, but it had been too many years. I was over forty, and just like my father, I tried to numb the pain. My drink of choice was vodka.

I lived in a drunken fog for a year. Then, one morning, I stopped for coffee and was flipping through a New York Times. My eyes locked onto your image in the paper, and my heart stopped. But *when I looked at that picture, my heart started beating again.*

I left LA behind, moved to Ferndale, and found myself. Amber was there for me, helping me become a better man. I went to college and currently teach high school drama. I thought my life was complete until Amber helped me see I needed you to feel completely alive.

According to my agreement with Leo's lawyer, I couldn't contact you. But that didn't mean I couldn't watch you grow.

When I saw you, I took pictures and wrote down my thoughts. I've since transferred everything into a blog. I was never prouder of you than when you graduated from veterinarian school and became Doctor Emma Foster.

I know I don't deserve it, but I'm hoping we can start over and get to know each other as adults. Amber and I are getting married in January, and I would like you to meet her. That would make me complete.

I love you,
Dad

When Emma finished reading the letter, she didn't know which emotion coursing through her system was the loudest: hate, anger, frustration, sadness, hurt ... love ..., or hope.

He had included the URL to his blog, and curiosity had her settling on the sofa with her laptop.

Blackbeard's Bar & Grill
January 19
8:00 p.m.

It was a Friday night, and just like he'd done before, Killian was out with friends. Dylan and Molly, Gray and Sadie, and Rusty and his wife Rene, the mayor of Swan Harbor. He'd been out with them many times. But this time was different. This time … he felt alone.

It had been another week without hearing from Emma, and he was close to feeling defeated. But whether it was inadvertent or on purpose, Molly had helped when she asked him to read to her class.

He'd read the book *Llama Llama Red Pajama* to the first graders. While he certainly didn't have motherly feelings about Emma, the book had a good lesson about patience. One he took to heart. This was why he couldn't seem to work up the need to be too offended when his friends began ribbing him about his reading style.

"So, you're telling me," Dylan laughed. "Killian used different voices when he read to your class?"

"Oh, yes." Molly sent Killian an impish grin. "In a high-pitched voice, he'd read, 'What is Mama Llama doing? Baby Llama starts boo-hooing,' and then he'd pitch it lower for the mama."

"The kids loved it," Killian defended his reading style.

"They did!" Molly agreed. "And after a few pages, Killian sat on the floor with the kids spread around him."

"Seems children bring out a new you." Dylan pinned Killian with a knowing gaze. "If you get bored at the sheriff's department," he continued, "perhaps Swan Harbor Elementary would hire you."

"The kids love it when he reads to them," Molly jumped into protective mode. "Especially the little girls."

"Oh!" Rusty chuckled. "I bet they did. We met one of Killian's 'girls' this week.

"Would that be Ms. Tuesday or Ms. Sunday?" Dylan prodded.

Killian understood that was Dylan's way of being nosy, but Blackbeard's Bar & Grill was not the place to spill his problems. Instead, he gave a subtle head shake and asked Sadie about wedding plans, effectively changing the subject.

"Don't ask her about them," Gray grimaced. "If you ever get married, elope. Getting everyone on the same page is a disaster."

"Oh, it can't be that bad, can it?" Killian laughed at Gray's disgruntled expression.

"Don't listen to him," Sadie smoothed her hand along her fiancé's thigh. "Most of the decisions are fine."

"It's our siblings who are the problem," Dylan complained.

Killian knew Cameron and Jessie were off volunteering with an organization that took them worldwide. Finding a weekend when everyone could be back in Swan Harbor at the same time was difficult.

"It's not just them," Gray groaned. "It's my parents too. My mom is presenting at a few psychiatry conferences that need to be scheduled around."

Killian had met Gray's parents, Mary and Clint, several times the previous summer. He'd even worked a case with Gray's mother when he'd happened upon a runaway. They had the kind of relationship he was beginning to realize he wanted.

The conversation went on around him, and while he didn't feel completely comfortable, neither did he feel as if he didn't belong.

Llama llama red pajama feels alone without his mama.

Emma was friends with Molly and Sadie, and he could easily imagine her sitting beside him. She'd fit in as if she'd been a part of the group forever. Was that what he was hoping for?

Llama llama red pajama in the dark without his mama. Eyes wide open, covers drawn .... What if Mama Llama's gone?

Killian's attention drifted for several minutes until he heard Emma's name in conjunction with Rene's horse's treatment. He dialed back into the conversation, hoping Sadie would offer some news. A part of him wanted to ask about her, but it didn't feel right. *Emma,* he sent out a silent plea to those around him.

Llama llama red pajama hollers loudly for his mama.

Baby Llama stomps and pouts. Baby Llama jumps and shouts.

As the evening progressed, candlelight replaced the overhead lights, and the music became more romantic. Killian's loneliness grew, and he decided to leave, thinking being home alone was better than at a date night event without a date.

Llama llama red pajama weeping, wailing for his mama. Will his mama ever come? Mama Llama, run, run, run!

"Sadie," the tone of Molly's voice kept his arse on his chair, "Grace told me about her dog, Bo Peep. Is she okay?"

Sadie shivered. "She's fine now, but it was touch and go for a few days."

Dylan frowned. "What happened?"

"Bo Peep was hit by a car," Sadie murmured. "It happened right after Emma returned from her trip. She was wonderful."

Emma's been busy.

"She is a good vet," Rene added.

Sadie agreed. "She's a natural,"

"I heard from Grace," Molly explained, "that poor Bo Peep had to have surgery."

"Let's not talk about that," Sadie laughed. "Good news is Emma hired Leroy to help with surgeries and at night."

Leroy? Killian's gaze met Rusty's. *He's been busy this week.*

"Sadie doesn't do so well with blood." Gray kissed her cheek. "She was white as a ghost when I picked her up that day."

"Thank goodness for Leroy," Sadie leaned into Gray. "Between the phones, the surgeries, and all the kittens roaming the clinic, the place is quite hectic.

Baby Llama, what a tizzy! Sometimes Mama's very busy.

Please stop all this llama drama and be patient for your mama.

Veterinarian Clinic
January 19
11:45 p.m.

BLOGS. EMMA CLOSED HER COMPUTER AND SET IT ASIDE. HE'D BEEN there from her senior year in high school until she graduated from veterinarian school. How had she not seen him? How had she not known he cared?

"He's changed," Emma murmured, thinking about her discussion with Elsa about bad boys and loners.

Didn't you know bad boys and loners only stay that way until the right woman comes along?

Was that what Amber was for her dad?

Emma flipped through the photos on her phone and found the one of her father and his fiancé. Peter Foster looked happy and at peace, something she couldn't remember him ever being.

Elsa had listed television and movie couples where love had tamed the bad boy. But what about Killian? Her first two encounters with him directly contradicted what she'd felt when they were dancing.

Killian had been on a journey to find himself.

Could she be the right woman for him?

He's a good guy. Give him a chance.

"Okay, Elsa, I'm going to trust you." Emma punched in Killian's cell number, attached the picture Elsa had taken at the dance, and wrote a short note.

It was time for her to take a chance.

✿

Killian's Apartment
January 19
11:50 p.m.

KILLIAN WAS IN BED, HALFWAY BETWEEN SLEEP AND wakefulness, an area that often helped him solve problems. However, it also reminded him that he was alone.

The gentle buzz of an incoming text had him turning away from where the phone lay and punching his pillow into submission. If he kept his eyes closed, he could pretend he was asleep. Besides, he was sure it was a text from Liam talking about his date with Elsa.

The languid feeling, dragging him into sleep, washed over him.

What if it's not from Liam?

Who else could it be?

Emma?

His eyes flew open, immediately going to the clock.

Would Emma really be texting this late?

She's been busy. Check.

The more Emma's name floated through his head, the faster his heart raced and the more awake he became. "Bloody hell! If it's Liam, I'll ..."

Little Llama, don't you know, Mama Llama loves you so?

Mama Llama's always near, even if she's not right here.

When he lightly touched the screen and saw the message, his heart rate skyrocketed, and with a shaking hand, he brought the phone close.

"Emma."

> Emma: It seems we weren't very good at hiding our identities from each other, were we? We should talk soon. Emma.

The picture of the two of them proved what he already knew. They belonged together.

His thumbs hovered over the keyboard, trying to decide how to respond. He wanted to scream, *I love you. Marry me!* But he wasn't that big of a prat and typed a simple message.

Opening the picture, he lay down and let himself get lost in the memories of the night it was taken.

Llama llama red pajama gets two kisses from his mama, snuggles pillow soft and deep….

Baby Llama goes to sleep.

"Goodnight, Emma," he whispered as the lethargy pulled him under.

Veterinarian Clinic
January 20
9:00 a.m.

WHEN EMMA WOKE UP ON SATURDAY, SHE WONDERED IF SHE'D dreamed everything from the evening before. There had been a letter and an online journal from her father. And she'd sent Killian a text and was taking a chance leopards could change their spots. Neither of those were things that happened to her every day. But the letter on the sofa beside her laptop convinced her it was true. She had always been loved. In fact, she was loved.

Her phone had fallen between the sofa cushions, but once she found it, a text had her heart beating a rapid pitter-pat inside her chest.

> Killian: Good morning, Doc. The picture is one I will treasure. Are you okay?

Why would he ask me if I was okay?

Emma: Am I okay?

Killian: Aye. I worried my ugly mug sent you running from the Ball.

Emma: Not you, Killian. Just someone from my past.

Killian: Ghosts can show up when you least expect them.

He didn't know the half of it, Emma thought, looking at the journal blog she had reopened.

Emma: True. Sometimes, things happen you would never expect.

Don't push me, she silently pleaded.

Killian: I heard what you did for Bo Peep. Nice job, Doc.

His compliment created a warm feeling inside she hadn't expected.

Emma: Thank you. It was tricky repairing that poor dog's degloving.

Killian: Degloving? I wasn't aware dogs even had hands.

Emma laughed at his statement but then quickly sobered. *He's not serious, is he?*

Emma: You know dogs don't have hands, right?

Killian: Of course. I'm not completely daft.

No, but there certainly seemed to be more going on with him than she'd thought.

> Emma: Degloving is where the top layer of skin is removed from the underlying tissue.

> Killian: And you had to put it back together?
> Delicate work.

Emma typed a response, but lack of time had her rushing through their communications. She had a few routine appointments, and then she planned to get more acquainted with Killian. Now that she'd decided to take a chance, some facts needed to be gathered. More importantly, though, she needed to make sure she wasn't making a big mistake.

Hours later, Emma waved goodbye to the last patient and, as soon as the door was locked, pulled out her phone. "Well, poop!" She'd never hit send on her last message and would need to revise.

> Emma: Sorry, I had to vaccinate a Felis catus and do a checkup on a Canis lupus familiaris.

> Killian: What color was the Tabby Cat?

His response had her giggling and wishing she could have seen his face when he first read her text.

> Emma: Google help with the answer, Killian?

> Killian: Don't get cheeky, Doctor Foster.

His quick answer made her laugh.

"You win this one, Elsa," she whispered, making a note to reach out to her friend soon.

TEN

Sally's Diner
January 23
11:45 a.m.

Emma tossed the last bite of her grilled cheese onto the plate. Her favorite comfort foods hadn't provided the much-needed solace she'd hoped.

"Everything okay?" Peyton asked, setting a fresh cup of hot chocolate on the table.

"It's fine." Emma smiled. "Just been one of those days, you know?"

"Oh, I get that," Peyton grimaced. "I have a biology test *and* an English lit paper tomorrow, and I'm here ... working. Isn't that just awful?"

"Awful," Emma agreed, tongue-in-cheek. "Have you started?"

"Have I started?" Peyton's eyes almost bugged out. "You mean my paper?"

"Well, yeah."

"No," Peyton stretched out the vowel.

Maybe you should have ... Emma wanted to say but finally settled on. "Good luck."

"Thanks. Anything else?"

Emma glanced at the hot chocolate and considered asking for it to go, but then decided against it. "No, I'm good."

"Okay, let me know if you change your mind."

"Thanks." Emma watched as the girl bounced across the room. Would she want to be eighteen or nineteen again? She didn't think so, but she might exchange her morning with Peyton ... at least temporarily.

She'd been pulled from bed for an early morning emergency that hadn't ended well. From there, she'd gone on a home visit, which was also disappointing. Even her favorite meal at Sally's hadn't helped her mood. Before she left, though, she needed to recenter herself.

Emma leaned back in the booth and closed her eyes. A deep breath in, a deep breath out. The surrounding conversation faded. Another deep breath in ....

"Killian was there."

Hearing his name caused Emma's heart to race, breaking her focus. She knew that voice ... but from where?

"Rusty was with him," the same voice continued.

The cookie exchange. That's where she'd heard the voice.

"I called them to rescue Audrey."

When the woman's voice grew softer, Emma pressed her head against the booth, focusing only on the two voices.

"Audrey had been yelling for help for several hours," the first voice continued.

"She lives next door to you, right?" the other voice questioned.

"Yes," the first voice replied. "Apparently, Audrey and Leroy were playing sex games, and Leroy was hurt."

Emma's breath caught. *Leroy? Her Leroy?* How was she going to be able to look at him and keep her brain from going down a path she didn't want it to go?

"I hadn't seen Killian since before the holidays," the first Voice said. "But he barely even looked at me. He even removed my hand from his arm and stepped away."

The second voice gasped. "Has Killian been dating anyone since that situation with Belle?"

"I don't know," the first voice answered. "I was going to ask you the same thing."

It was silent for several seconds, allowing Emma to relax and finish her hot chocolate.

"Oh, he just walked in," the first voice whispered. "How do I look?"

A zip of electricity shot up Emma's spine. Killian just walked in? What should she do? What should she say?

A part of her had to fight to keep from turning around, but the other part panicked, thinking, I must look awful!

Self-consciously, Emma slid a little lower in the seat. Her feelings about seeing him weren't the same as before New York. They'd exchanged numerous texts over the weekend, giving her new insights about him. She found him funny, and the way he tried to impress her was sweet. But she wasn't wearing makeup, her clothes were wrinkled, and her ponytail was droopy.

Vain, Emma? That's not you.

Her phone buzzed, and before she glanced at it, she knew it was him.

> Killian: Are the Felis catus still creating chaos in your clinic?

> Emma: Did Google help with that, or did you remember on your own?

Killian didn't want to sound cheeky, but she sent another message before he decided what to say.

> Emma: I'm sorry. That was rude.

Her response unsettled him, but not because of what he felt. She made him nervous, something he hadn't experienced in well ... forever.

> Killian: Rough Day?

When she didn't immediately respond, Killian weighed his options. Chloe and Morgan were sitting in the booth behind Emma and watching him. He knew what they were expecting ... but he had no intention of being that man again. Except, how was he to behave when he saw women he'd dated?

Before he'd come up with an answer, Emma laid money on the table, which had him hurriedly typing another message. That he typed it, deleted and typed it again was a sign of just how much was at stake.

Killian: Want some company?

Waiting for her response was almost worse than staring down the barrel of a gun. Both situations had the power to hurt him.

The three little dots appeared ...

She's responding.

His palms started to sweat.

She's responding.

His heart raced.

She's responding.

His hands shook.

Emma: Sure. I have a little time.

Killian sagged against the counter and worked to control his breathing.

You can do it.

He repeated those words more than once as he walked across the diner.

"Was it good?" He nodded at the remains of her lunch.

You've wanted to talk to her for ages, and that's the best you could come up with?

Emma smiled, but it didn't quite reach her eyes. "Sally's has the best grilled cheese and chicken soup."

"What brings you to town this early in the day?"

"I had a home visit and decided to have lunch before returning to the clinic."

"But there's more, isn't there?

Her behavior said she was involved in an internal debate. He wanted to slide into the booth beside her. They would be closer and less likely to be overheard. But a quick movement over Emma's shoulder reminded him of Chloe and Morgan.

"You done here?" He tapped her plate.

Their eyes met again, and her shoulders visibly relaxed. "Yes."

"Walk with me?"

"Don't you need to wait for your lunch?" Her lips twitched as if she already knew the answer.

"I didn't come in for lunch."

"No?"

"Should I apologize?"

Emma giggled. "No. I'm ready."

Killian lightly guided her through the diner with his hand on her elbow. Once outside, he forced himself to put some space between them. He flipped up his collar and tucked his hands into his pockets. "It feels like snow."

"Think so?" Emma glanced up at the sky. "I hope not."

They walked along in companionable silence for several minutes. He wanted to ask her for a date, but Elsa's words about being patient held him back. Instead, he was content to just walk with her and let her set the pace.

"You were right," Emma blurted.

Her unexpected response had him running to catch up. "Right about what?"

"About my having a rough day," she sighed. "Today has just been one of those days, you know?"

"I've had those," he murmured. "I've been told sharing your burdens helps."

Emma smiled, making her eyes crinkle at the corners. "You're not one who usually asks for help, are you?"

"Not normally," he admitted. "But in the last few months, I've asked for it a few times."

"Did it help?"

"Sharing my burdens?"

"Yes."

Killian blew out a laugh. "As much as I hate to say this, it helped."

"I'm glad."

She was quiet for a few more minutes before she suddenly stopped. "I was up early trying to save another dog hit by a car, which ended badly. Then I had to check on Rene's horse."

"And those didn't end well?" He prompted, thinking about what Rusty had told him about his wife's horse.

Emma shook her head, a pensive look on her beautiful face. "I couldn't save the dog, and," her lower lip trembled slightly, "the news on Rene's horse could have been better."

"Rene knows you're doing your best."

"I know." She frowned as if something had just come to her.

"What is it?"

"That's the fourth hit-and-run victim I've treated since I returned to Swan Harbor."

For some reason, the comment set off Killian's investigative radar. "Wait, what did you just say?"

Emma gnawed on her bottom lip. "In the past three weeks, I've seen four dogs hit by a vehicle, and the driver left the scene. The first was Bo Peep. There were two stray dogs, and the one this morning belonged to Shawn."

"Shawn?"

"My mechanic," Emma explained.

Killian bit back a response about Shawn tuning Emma's car to ask, "And no idea who's responsible?"

A teasing grin crossed her face. "I don't know, but," Emma placed a hand on her chest, "I just try to save them. Aren't you," she pointed at him, "the one who investigates?"

"Touché." Killian met her grin with one of his own. "I'll look into it."

"Good. I've got to run." Emma took a couple of steps before turning back. "Oh, and thanks."

"For?"

"Taking on some of my," she made quotation marks with her fingers, "burdens."

"Anytime, Doc." Killian's grin grew bigger. "Anytime."

Veterinarian Clinic
January 25
3:00 p.m.

EMMA STOOD AT THE WINDOW OF HER CLINIC, WATCHING THE white flakes rapidly cover the ground. "Sadie," she glanced back at her friend, "you should go home. It's getting pretty bad out there."

Sadie barely looked up from the computer screen she was studying. "Oh, poo, that's nothing. Besides, Gray's picking me up in his work truck. And you know how big that is."

Emma snickered. "Men and the size of their ..."

"Now, now, Emma. In this case, it's–"

"La la la," Emma sang, "TMI, my friend."

"Someday," Sadie teased.

An image of Killian smiling down at her floated through Emma's mind. But she wasn't ready to go there yet. Instead, she turned her attention back to the snow.

When her phone buzzed, she hurriedly pulled it from her pocket.

Killian: You're home safe, right? We've already had several accidents because of this weather.

Having someone, especially someone of the male species, concerned about her was a new experience. But ... in a way, she had to admit, it was kind of nice.

Emma: I hope no one was hurt too badly. And yes, I'm home.

Killian: Nothing major ... yet. Any more dog incidents?

Emma: No more dogs. Have you solved the mystery yet?

Killian: Not yet. Stay warm.

She shoved the phone back into her pocket, fighting the smile threatening to break free.

"So?"

Emma could feel Sadie's curious gaze without even turning her head. "What?"

"Come on, Emma," Sadie coaxed, "spill the details about you and Killian."

"There is no me and Killian," Emma responded hurriedly.

Sadie linked her arm through Emma's and directed them into the all-purpose room, "Me thinks you protest too much. Come on, have a seat, and tell Aunty Sadie."

Emma studied Sadie for several seconds, shocked to realize she wanted to discuss what had transpired. "If I tell you, it has to remain between us."

Sadie made a small X over her heart and then raised her hand as if making a pledge. "I promise. Now give me the details."

"Well," Emma began, "when I was in New York, I attended a masquerade ball on New Year's Eve with my friend Elsa, and guess who was there?"

"Killian?" Sadie squealed, practically bouncing up and down in the chair.

"Yes," Emma confirmed. "It was bizarre, but my friend Elsa and Killian's brother, Liam, are interested in each other."

"If it was a masquerade ball, how did you know it was Killian?"

Emma thought back on that night. "I think it had something to do with the way he walked."

"The way he walked?" Sadie tilted her head in thought, "I could see that. But wasn't his face covered?"

"It was." Emma's heart raced with the memory of watching him stroll across the room toward her. "He wore a black tux, a white shirt, a black bow tie, and a cummerbund. Around his head, he'd tied a black scarf. He reminded me of the Lone Ranger."

"Is that what you called him?"

"No," Emma giggled. "Liam introduced him as Zorro."

"Zorro?" Sadie nodded. "I can see that. But how romantic."

"It *was* nice," Emma murmured. "Since I've been back, well ..."

Sheriff's Department
January 31
2:00 p.m.

IT HAD BEEN OVER A WEEK SINCE HE'D LEARNED ABOUT THE mystery surrounding the dogs. But after a three-day whiteout and another two days of digging out, there hadn't been time to investigate the situation. However, after an uninterrupted night's rest and barring no further disasters, he was moving it to the top of his daily agenda. He was even more determined after Emma's latest message.

Emma: Sadie's mother's dog is the latest in the hit-and-run mystery. That makes five.

The text left him unsettled. Just as he'd done with the first four incidences, he grabbed a piece of paper and added the new information. He then pulled the file he'd started the week before and spread the papers on his desk. With five of them, maybe he'd see a pattern.

"What's captured your attention?"

Killian glanced up as Dylan strolled into his office. "Something Emma mentioned to me—"

"Emma?" Dylan interrupted. "You're finally talking to Emma?"

"That's such a girl thing to say," Killian grumbled. "I saw her at Sally's last week."

"And?"

"And nothing." Killian pasted on his best neutral expression. "Anyway," he steered the conversation back to the problem, "it seems there's been a rash of hit-and-run incidences involving dogs."

"Dogs?" Dylan frowned. "Well, I guess I could understand someone not wanting to let on that it was them, but multiple. How many are we talking about?"

"Five this month. Anything like this happened before?"

"Never," Dylan replied. "What have you found out?"

Killian flipped around the pages he'd created for Dylan to see and grabbed a map of Swan Harbor. "So far, this is what I have." He opened the map and marked several points showing where Bo Peep and the dogs belonging to Shawn and Anita were hit. "Two of the dogs were strays I'll need to ask Emma about."

"So basically, no one area has been targeted, right?"

"Right." Killian frowned, annoyed the pattern he'd wanted wasn't there. "So, either it's just a coincidence, or it's several people, or they've been drinking too much, or ..."

"We have someone deliberately targeting dogs in our little town."

"Bloody hell," Killian snapped. "How evil do you have to be to target helpless dogs?"

"Pretty evil," Dylan sighed. "Damn, a serial dog killer. Told you we had some crazy cases in Swan Harbor."

"You were right about that."

"Okay," Dylan grunted. "Get the word out, and maybe it will make our killer think twice. Keep me posted."

"Will do."

Killian wrote some notes and was getting ready to call Emma with a few questions when his cell phone buzzed with an incoming text. The message had him quickly dialing Emma.

"Killian?"

"You busy, Doc?"

"Not currently," she replied hesitantly. "Why?"

"Because I need you."

"What?"

"I'm sorry, Doc." Killian chuckled. "I didn't mean to make you uncomfortable, but ..."

"Oh, you didn't," she denied. "You just surprised me. Did you find out who's hitting the dogs and driving off?"

"No, not yet. I need your help with something else."

"Do I want to hear this?"

"I'm sorry," he apologized again. "I'm mucking this up, aren't I?"

"Killian," she broke in breathlessly, "just ask."

"It's a rescue mission. Are you game?"

"Uh, Uh, a rescue mission?"

With the slight stutter of Emma's words, a zip of excitement ran up Killian's spine. *Could* she have thought he was going to ask her *out*?

"It's not another dog that was hit-and-run, is it?" she asked in a voice that was, dare he say, disappointed.

"No hurt dog, Doc," he assured her, "that I know of, anyway."

"Well, okay. If you're sure. Where should I meet you?"

"I'll pick you up in one of the station's trucks," he offered. "The roads are better, but the bigger tires might be necessary where we're going. I'm on the way."

"I'll be waiting."

Calm down.

Stop acting like a schoolboy.

However, the entire time he shut down his computer and stored the file, he had to keep repeating the words. Finally, after months of hope ... he would be spending time with Emma.

"Leaving already?" Rusty asked, entering just as Killian exited.

"It's just a rescue mission," Killian offered, hoping his partner wouldn't turn into a busybody.

"Need some help?" Rusty asked hopefully. "It would get me out of writing this report."

"I'm ah ... I'm taking Emma with me," Killian finally got out. "This type of rescue is right up her alley."

"I see." A knowing look crossed Rusty's face. "Is Lothario turning into Galahad?"

"Something like that," Killian tugged on his ear, back to feeling much like the schoolboy.

"Well, if you're sure," Rusty stretched out his torture.

"Positive. See you tomorrow."

He'd gotten halfway down the steps when Rusty called, "Oh, and Killian."

"Aye?"

"Good luck."

For a second, Killian wasn't sure what Rusty was trying to say. Then he got a good look at his partner's face, and he couldn't curtail his smile. "Thanks. Thanks a lot."

ELEVEN

Veterinarian Clinic
January 31
4:00 p.m.

"I'M DONE FOR THE DAY, RIGHT?"

"Yes, all done," Sadie confirmed. "Why? Who was that, and what are you getting ready for?"

"That was Killian," Emma offered nonchalantly. "He needs me for a rescue mission."

A suggestive smile crossed Sadie's face. "Rescue what ... or should I ask whom? Him perhaps?"

"I'm guessing an animal of some sort. I'd better get my supplies."

She didn't wait for further questions but double-checked her home visits' backpack. Once it was stocked and ready, she laid out a few cages of assorted sizes.

You busy, Doc?

She didn't want to admit that hearing his voice caused her heart to race.

I need you.

Nor did she want to admit she'd been disappointed when he hadn't asked her on a *date*.

However, she would admit that hearing his voice made her happy. That was evident when she looked in the mirror, and her sparkling green eyes were looking back.

"Not bad." However, a glance at her scrubs, covered in who knew what fluids, sent her rushing for clean clothes.

"Well, well." Sadie slowly made a 360-degree inspection of her clothing. "Dressed up to," she made air quotes, "rescue animals, didn't you?"

"I, I just ..." Emma cleared her throat and tried again. "These old things? My scrubs were dirty, and it's ... uhh ... it's cold outside."

Sadie hummed, but the twinkle in her eyes said, 'I don't believe a word you're saying.'

"Really," Emma insisted. "Besides, why would I care how I looked?"

A car door slammed outside and captured her attention. *Yum* was the first word that popped into her mind when she saw Killian step from the large, black truck. His swagger as he walked toward her building was just so ... sexy. It projected both gracefulness and confidence and took her breath.

"See, Emma," Sadie whispered, "hot, hunky, gorgeous works just fine."

"Shh."

The door opened, bringing with it a blast of cold air. Killian stepped in, and with his black hair blown around his head, Emma had to squeeze her hands into fists to keep from reaching up to fix it. "Hi."

"Emma." He tugged at his right ear, causing her heart to flip. "Ready to go?"

"What are we rescuing, anyway?"

"Kittens. Gray found them, and they won't let him near them."

"Kittens?" Emma's brows rose. "Why didn't he call here?"

"I'm law enforcement and supposed to protect the community?"

"From kittens?"

Her eyes cut to the leggy brunette, who had made several suggestive comments since learning about the New Year's Eve dance.

"What?" Sadie glanced up from her computer, pretending she hadn't been listening.

"Did you know about the kittens that needed rescuing?"

"No," Sadie quickly denied. "But if stray kittens need your help, shouldn't you go?"

Emma glanced between Killian and Sadie, trying to figure out what she'd missed. But unable to read his expression, she mentally stepped back.

Control, Emma.

"Shall we go?" She grabbed her backpack and pointed to the cages, leaving Killian to follow.

He tossed the cages in the back and helped her onto the cold seat.

"Thanks."

"My pleasure."

His smooth baritone, combined with his British lilt, sent a thrill rushing along her skin.

Control Emma, she reminded herself when they bypassed the road leading to Peter Pan Park.

"Where are we going again?"

"An abandoned farmhouse on the outskirts of town," Killian shared. "Gray's business is thinking about buying the property."

"Any idea who the house belonged to?"

"Not really. I've only lived in Swan Harbor since last February, but maybe Dylan knows."

"What brought you to Swan Harbor?"

His jaw tightened, making her feel like she'd stepped over an invisible line.

"I'm sorry," she apologized. "That sounded nosy."

"It's alright."

He gave her a quick smile, but it wasn't as relaxed as before.

For the next few miles, both seemed lost in their thoughts. It wasn't until he pulled into a long drive that he turned toward her. "Ready?"

Their eyes clashed in the truck's low light, and several thoughts flew through her mind. "I'm ready."

He jumped from the truck and was halfway around the cab before Emma could release her seatbelt.

"Need some help?"

"Did you know this belt sticks?" Emma glanced into Killian's upturned face.

"Who, me?" He stepped on the runner, braced his left hand on the outside of the seat, and reached around her with his right. "It just requires a little ... finesse!" he purred, his face mere inches from hers.

The air blew across her mouth, causing her to slide the tip of her tongue across her bottom lip.

His breath hitched, his eyes dropped to her lips, and a rosy hue dotted his cheekbones.

Emma tightened her muscles to keep from leaning forward. "It's stuck, isn't it?"

"Aye," he uttered, a mere second before there was a click, and the seatbelt loosened. "Sorry about that, Doc."

"Thank you."

"My pleasure."

She climbed from the truck and, once again, had to remind herself *control*. But he wasn't making that easy.

Old Farmhouse
January 31
4:30 p.m.

KILLIAN SLUNG EMMA'S BACKPACK OVER HIS SHOULDER AND followed her from the truck. He was having difficulty forgetting how her breath had hitched when he was undoing her seatbelt. How she licked her full bottom lip and bloody hell—he'd wanted a taste.

Friends. Just friends.

Words he had to remind himself of several times because he wanted them to be different.

Her question about his move to Swan Harbor was also something he needed to decide about. Was he prepared to share the reason he'd moved with her?

"Did Gray bring others with him?" Emma asked as they neared the house. "It looks like there's more than one set of footprints."

"He just said the kittens were inside, and the house was empty."

"Hmm. I'd like to know how a stray cat ended up giving birth way out here."

So did he, but since he was with Emma, he wasn't complaining too loudly.

"There they are."

"Why are you whispering?"

"Because I don't want to scare them."

"Oh. I see."

Emma grinned. "They're wild and aren't used to people. If we're lucky enough to catch them, it will take some work."

Killian had to bite his tongue to avoid issuing a challenge. He'd wait until they were inside and then show her he wasn't completely useless.

"I see at least four." Emma moved from one window to another. "I'm not sure where the mama is, though. Do we know how Gray got inside?"

"No, he didn't say."

"Okay. I'll take my backpack, and you can get the bigger cage from the truck."

"Will you be alright while I'm gone?"

"I'll be fine," Emma assured him. "Don't worry."

He wanted to say many things, but in the end, he gave a slight nod and left to get the cage. However, telling him not to worry about her was as impossible as telling him not to breathe.

As soon as Killian hopped off the porch, Emma worked on getting into the house. It felt lonely, as if once upon a time, a family had lived there, but something tore them apart. "And all that's left is a family of *Felis catus*."

She tried several doors before locating a window opened as if someone else had done so recently.

Gray?

Emma dropped her bag inside and climbed through, shutting the window behind her. The lonely feeling from the outside gave way to a feeling inside she couldn't name. It was unsettling, and for the first time since he'd disappeared, she wished Killian were back. She shoved the uneasiness away and focused on why they were there ... the kittens.

The room she was standing in was once vibrant and colorful, but it was now old and faded. Although several pieces of furniture were left behind, the cushions were covered with dust, and the wood floors were full of scratches and debris.

An unpleasant odor made of dust and decay permeated the air. However, it wasn't as cold inside the house as she'd expected, which explained how the kittens had survived. But where was the mama?

Several doors led to various other rooms, one into a kitchen. Bags of cat food were stacked in the corner, one open and spilling onto the floor. Had Gray left them?

She reversed her position and found another door leading to a large bathroom, where water dripped from the bathtub and sink. Why wasn't the water turned on and not frozen? Was that Gray's work, too?

A quick perusal of the other doors revealed a small sitting room, and another led to a blocked-off hallway. Since the kittens were confined to three rooms, she crossed her fingers that catching them wouldn't take long.

When she returned to the front room, Killian had just climbed inside.

"Bloody hell. What's that smell?"

"You're a cop," she teased, "and you're complaining about a little kitten poop. I'm sure you've been around worse."

A look crossed his face that was gone before she could decipher it. "Did you find them?" he asked, ignoring her comment.

A behavior she found interesting but filed the subject change away for later.

"I brought some gloves for you."

"Why would I need gloves to catch a couple of tiny kittens?"

"Because they have claws," Emma reminded him. "Think needles, really sharp needles."

"I don't need them."

She raised a brow, but his smirk had her shrugging. "I guess it's your skin."

"I'll be fine."

Emma considered making a wager but decided against it and pointed toward the small setting room. "You can look in that room, and I'll look in here."

"You'll be alright alone?"

"I'll be fine," Emma parroted his words. "Yell if you need me."

Killian side-eyed her, but went off to do her bidding, leaving her alone to search. She found two huddled under a chair, pressed as tightly to the wall as possible.

"Ah, poor babies," she crooned. "I won't hurt you."

She stretched out her arm and released a piece of string. Then, slowly, she pulled it toward her. It took only a handful of seconds until temptation was too great, and one kitten moved closer.

When she tugged on the string, the kitten followed, and inch by inch, it moved closer. As soon as it was close enough, Emma transferred the string to her left hand, intending to grab it with her right. Just as she reached for the tiny body ....

Killian yelled, "Bloody hell! Get back here, you little bugger."

The sound sent the scared animal back under the chair, making Emma want to bang her head against the floor.

"Do you need some help, Killian?"

His prolific use of colorful language had her fighting a giggle, but that probably wouldn't help the situation.

"I've got everything under control."

"Sure you do." Emma checked on the kittens, only to discover they'd darted from their hiding place to a new one. "Damn!"

It took rethinking her strategy before she was able to find and capture the two little buggers, as Killian had called them. The third one proved to be a bit more challenging, and by the time she caught him and hadn't heard from Killian, her curiosity got the best of her.

She followed the sound of his voice and peeked around the door. Killian was on his knees with his butt in the air, looking underneath a sofa and talking to a kitten.

He would never get that baby to come to him, but instead of taking over, she watched.

"Come on out, love," Killian crooned. "There's a pretty lass."

Emma bit her lip to keep quiet. She couldn't decide whether to laugh or cry watching him sweet talk the tiny, helpless kitten.

"That's a good lass," he continued. "I'm not going to hurt you."

The words became inconsequential as he spoke to the scared animal, but the longer he spoke, the faster Emma's heart raced.

"I'm right here, pretty baby. Come to Killian."

Emma decided she would give him a few more seconds when she heard, "I've got you," and he stood, cradling a tiny grey kitten in the palm of his hand.

The look on his face as he gazed at the animal caused Emma's heart to flip several times.

Stop that. He's just a man!

"Look at the little lass, Doc. Isn't she pretty?"

"You sound sure it's a girl," she teased, hoping playful banter would lessen the size of the lump in her throat.

A chagrined look crossed his face. "I just assumed. Will you check?"

Emma grinned. "You trust me to hold your little love?"

He held the furry baby out to her. "Of course."

On the way to the other room, Emma peeked under the animal's tail. "It's a girl," she confirmed, placing the kitten with the others.

KILLIAN PREENED AT HER RESPONSE BUT SOBERED WHEN HE SAW the blood on his hand. "Have a bandage in that bag?"

"Hold on," Emma murmured. "Let me get these in the cage to keep the kittens warm."

He unwrapped the bloody cloth from around his hand to see a jagged cut across the fleshy skin at the base of his thumb.

"What happened?" Emma asked when she materialized at his side with a first aid bag.

"Just a misunderstanding between myself and the wee lass."

She took his hand, and her touch sent a live current zipping along his skin. "Killian, that's not little. Follow me."

Anytime.

She pushed his hand over a sink and poured a cool liquid on the cut. "Bloody hell, Doc."

"Quit being a baby." Emma grinned. "It's just hydrogen peroxide."

"You were right," he murmured, "her claws were like needles."

"Told you so."

Her smell tantalized him, making him fight not to bury his face against her neck. Being so close to her caused his senses to heighten, and every time she brushed against him, his body hardened a little more. *Down boy*, he warned. *Friends, remember.*

"There. Good as new." She taped the end of the gauze, then put the trash in a Ziplock bag.

A loud crash had Killian tucking her behind him and drawing his gun at the same time.

"What's through that door?" he growled.

"Kitchen."

"Stay here!" he demanded, taking several steps toward the other room. When he realized Emma's hands were tangled in the back of his jacket, he stopped abruptly, causing her to bump into him. "That's not staying here!"

"The one who stays behind is always the one killed."

Killian sighed, but continued toward the kitchen and peered around the door frame. When there was no apparent problem, he stepped into the room, only to be greeted by a cat meowing vociferously. "Well, who do we have here?"

"I would guess this is mama cat. But why is she just now showing up?"

"I don't know." He gazed down at the cat, who was winding around his feet. "What's the problem, Little Mama?"

The cat looked up and blinked her green eyes. A shiver raced up his spine when she turned and walked toward one of the cabinets. She stopped, looked over her shoulder, and meowed again.

"I think she wants us to follow her."

Mama Cat stopped in front of a lower cabinet and pawed at it several times. When Killian gave a forceful tug and pulled it open, the mother ran inside. It wasn't long before she returned carrying a kitten and dropped it at his feet.

Killian sent Emma a panicked look. "Is it ...?"

Emma picked up the baby. "No, it's alive, but barely. We need to get it back to the clinic. Here, can you put it with the others?"

Killian took the small ball of fur from Emma. Its weight so slight he could have been holding a piece of paper.

"We need to hurry, Killian." Emma rushed toward him, holding the Mama. "She's sick, too."

"Let's go."

After Emma picked up her bag, Killian grabbed the cage and led the way to the truck. There was no way the mama was going to lose one of her babies on his watch.

✿

Veterinarian Clinic

January 31

9:00 p.m.

Hours later, Emma was settled in a corner of the sofa, contemplating her day with Killian. Their time together had been ... comfortable, yet uncomfortable. Conversation between them flowed, but an awareness simmered just under the surface—one she wasn't sure how to handle. When combined with how she felt watching his behavior with the kittens, she was left confused and floundering.

She took a sip of her hot drink and pulled out her phone, discovering an unread text.

> Killian: Call me as soon as you can.

It was late, and she wanted to talk to Elsa, but she couldn't resist calling Killian first.

"Emma?" The background noise blared in her ear. "I'm sorry," he apologized as it suddenly quietened. "That's better."

"Having a wild party, Killian?"

His low laugh sent a tiny shiver up her spine. "Nothing like that. Just sharing a few drinks with friends."

Friends?

What felt suspiciously like jealousy coursed through her system. "I was just calling you back," she responded self-consciously, "but if it's unimportant, then ..."

Killian chuckled as if he knew exactly what she was thinking.

Damn him!

She swallowed the words on the tip of her tongue, determined to maintain control.

"What you have to say *is* important to me. The boys can wait," he assured her. "How's the family?"

Hearing that he was with the boys had her relaxing. "The family?"

"Aye, Doctor Foster. The little buggers we rescued today."

"The mother and baby are resting peacefully, but it was touch and go there for a while."

"I'm glad you could save them, Doc. Does she have a name yet?"

"That will happen after they're adopted."

"Oh, I see."

He sounded upset by the prospect, but did he think she kept every animal she rescued?

"So," she began hesitantly, "did you need something specific?"

"I just," he cleared his throat, "I just wanted to check on the family. Also to let you know, the bags of food from the farmhouse are in your front room."

"Thanks. Was Gray the one who left them?"

"No," Killian admitted. "Where those bags of food came from is a big mystery."

"Weird."

He hummed in agreement. "Will you keep me informed about the family?"

"I promise. And," she leaped, "I'm glad you asked for my help."

"Just sharing my burden," he murmured in a husky voice—one that affected her more than she cared to admit.

"Thanks for calling, Killian. Goodnight."

"Night, Doc. Sweet dreams."

Emma clutched the phone to her chest, her heart racing. She was in big trouble. "The list. The list," she repeated. "Don't forget the list."

Emma: Help!

When the phone rang, Emma pounced. "Elsa, help!"

TWELVE

Veterinarian Clinic
February 2
6:00 p.m.

On her way home from the store, Emma tried to wrap her head around what had happened in the last few hours. She'd grabbed the newest issue of the PetVet Magazine and settled in with a cup of hot chocolate when Molly called ....

"Oh, Emma," Molly exclaimed. "I'm so glad I caught you. I have a problem, and I don't know what to do."

"What's up?"

"You know Sadie's bridal shower was supposed to be at my apartment, right?"

"Right."

"Well," Molly sighed. "Our refrigerator broke, and there's no way we're going to ..."

As Molly rambled on, an article in the magazine caught Emma's attention, so she'd offered. "We can have it here," to get off the phone.

"Then what did you do, Foster?"

She'd finished reading the article, looked up a recipe for punch, and gone shopping. But now that she had the supplies, she kept wondering what she'd done. While it was easier to be around people she didn't know, the memory of how she'd felt at Molly's party was still fresh in her mind.

"Molly's your friend," she reminded herself. "You can do this."

The kittens would need to be locked in her clinic, and, if necessary, she'd pull on a cape and pretend. It wouldn't be the first time.

With a plan in place, Emma felt a little more in control. That only lasted until she pulled into her driveway, and her headlights bounced off the rear bumper of a sheriff's car.

"Emma," Dylan cried. "Please help Wilby."

He rushed off, leaving Emma to grab the groceries and run to catch up.

"Dylan, what's going on?"

"Wilby was hit by a car." Dylan lifted the English Shepard from the backseat.

The dog's whimpers broke her heart. If he needed surgery, though, Leroy wasn't expected for a few hours.

"I can't do it alone."

"I'll help," Dylan immediately offered.

"You're not squeamish, are you?"

"I'm good," he promised.

Once inside, Emma left the bags on a table and led Dylan to the operating room. "Are you sure?"

He gave her a quick nod and placed Wilby where she wanted him. Then she began tossing him instructions.

The type of surgery needed to save the dog's life was a complex one. But Dylan proved to be competent at taking directions and didn't ask many questions. He gave her tools, provided an extra set of hands, and, most importantly, remained calm throughout the procedure.

Once she'd done all she could do, Emma tossed her gloves in the trash. "Dylan, can you tell me what happened?"

"We were playing fetch," Dylan's eyes telegraphed his pain, "and the phone rang. I turned my back ..."

The break in his voice had Emma blinking rapidly and swallowing to push down the lump in her throat.

"Sorry." He wiped his eyes with the back of his hand.

"It's okay." She gently squeezed his arm. "Just take your time."

"Wilby yelped," Dylan went on, "and I remember feeling impatient." He hesitated a beat before continuing, "The whine of an engine caught my attention, but when I turned around, he was on the ground … not moving."

Somehow, Emma knew Wilby was the sixth victim of the dog killer. "You didn't see the car?"

"Not really," Dylan sighed. "When I turned around, all I saw were the red taillights and Wilby. After that, he was my focus. I wrapped him in a blanket and drove straight here."

"Wilby was lucky, Dylan. It's going to take some time, but he should be back chasing things really soon."

"Thanks, Emma." Dylan smiled for the first time since he'd arrived. "Swan Harbor is lucky to have you."

No, I'm the lucky one.

"I just want whoever is doing this to stop."

"Don't worry," Dylan replied. "Killian's solve rate in New York City was high. He'll find the person responsible for harming these defenseless animals."

"I just hope it's soon."

"Me too." Dylan agreed, running his hand over Wilby's head.

Watching Dylan caress his pet, Emma found herself comparing the behavior to Killian's treatment of the kittens. The dichotomy between their professional and personal personas was interesting.

For most of her life, she'd pretended to be someone else. However, while working to show others the real Emma, she wondered—did the concept fit her? Was there more than one *Emma*, but they were all still her?

"Help me move him."

They transferred the canine into one of the recovery cages, where Leroy would monitor him throughout the night. With that done and their protective gowns tossed, they found Molly and Leroy in the waiting room.

After a few words, Leroy led the Princes to the back while Emma worked on Wilby's chart.

Molly returned a few minutes later with a request. "Emma, please convince my husband Wilby will be fine without him. He won't listen to me."

Emma grinned. "Somehow, that doesn't surprise me. Let's see what I can do."

Killian's Apartment
February 2
9:30 p.m.

"Bloody hell!" Killian hung up from speaking with Dylan and quickly made a few notes for the dog killer's case charts. Then he called Emma.

"Hello," she answered after several rings.

"Emma?" Killian hesitated. "Is everything okay?"

"It's fine. I'm just dealing with ... stuff."

"Dylan told me about Wilby," he offered, hoping she would share.

"Yeah, it was a rough few hours, but he's going to be fine."

There was still an underlying *something* in her voice he couldn't place.

"I'm glad." His voice gentled. "There's more going on, though, isn't there?"

Her dry chuckle surprised him. "You could say that."

"Any burden you want to share?"

"Killian," she began after several heartbeats, "you know how a picture is worth a thousand words?"

"Aye."

"Okay, I'm going to send one." As soon as the line went dead, a picture and a text appeared.

The image had him slipping on his boots, grabbing his coat and keys, and driving toward the vet clinic. She'd shared her burdens, and he wanted to help.

When he walked into the clinic, his senses were immediately assaulted with the typical smells he'd expected—cleaning fluids, antiseptic, and animal. It was the underlying sweet scent of strawberries that had him following his nose.

"Whose idea was it to create this mess?" he heard when he reached the door to see Emma sitting on the floor, running a rag over a ball of fur.

The kittens were spread around the room, some batting at strawberries that were spilled on the floor. Others were pawing at puddles of ice cream melting on the floor. While the remaining were chasing each other up and down a carpeted contraption.

"Bloody hell," he murmured, amazed everything looked like the photo.

Emma's eyes met his. "I didn't hear you come in."

"So, *this* is the *stuff* you were dealing with?"

"Blame these guys." She indicated the kittens. "They were quite busy while I worked on Wilby."

"Need some help?" Killian lifted a brow. "I can handle a mop as easily as a gun."

Emma wiped her hands on the rag. "Thank you. I'd like that."

As would he ....

❧

Veterinarian Clinic
February 2
9:45 p.m.

HAD SHE KNOWN HE WOULD COME RUNNING AFTER SEEING THE picture? Maybe so. But having another set of hands to help clean the sticky mess was nice.

"What happened?"

"Well," Emma laughed. "Dylan was here when I got back from picking up a few things for Sadie's shower."

"And in your haste to treat the dog, you left the bags on the floor?"

"No, on the table."

"But," he frowned, "how did the bags you left on the table end up all over the floor?"

"You've never been around kittens, have you?"

"It's that obvious?"

"No cats? Dogs? Hamsters?"

"No pets at all."

"Oh, okay." She filed the information away for later. "The kittens made the mess."

Killian glanced around the room full of felines. "You're telling me those little buggers created this mess?"

"That they did." She shook her head, thinking about the first time she'd seen the mess. "They're nosy, and when you have fifteen in one place, well ... nothing is sacred."

At his blank look, Emma continued, "Imagine the bags standing on the table and several kittens wanting to look inside."

"They pushed the bags over?"

"Yes. Then, on the way down, the bottles hit the edge of the metal cage and bounced on the cement floor."

"And split?" Killian hummed. "Did Millicent help them, or did she turn her back and ignore them?"

"Millicent?"

"Aye, Doc." He pointed at the mother cat, who was grooming herself away from the mess. "I've dubbed her Millicent. It means one who has great strength. After all, leading us to her kitten showed just that."

"True, she did, but," Emma murmured, worried he was becoming attached, "what happened to not naming them?"

He ducked his head and looked up at her through his lashes. "Everyone needs an identity, Doc. Don't you agree?"

She did, but she'd learned if she didn't see her strays as individuals, it was easier to be objective. Allowing personal feelings to develop made the tough medical decisions even more difficult.

Are we only talking about animals, Emma?

"And did you come up with names for the others?"

"Nina, Trudi, Bree, Tiger, and Maximus." He proudly named the five kittens they'd rescued.

Once again, his behavior unsettled her. How was she to figure out who the real Killian Reade was if, every time they were together, she saw a different persona?

Killian scooped up the tiny feline who'd fallen for his charms at the farmhouse. "Meet Trudi." He made a face and held up wet, red fingers. "She needs a bath."

"That's what I was afraid of," Emma groaned. "You only suggested it because you've never given a kitten a bath."

"How bad can it be? She's just a tiny thing. We can handle it."

"Let's just say be happy they're kittens and not cats," Emma cautioned.

"Come on, Doc," he grinned, "where's your sense of adventure?"

"Cleaning this mess is pretty adventurous," she laughed. "Especially when you promised to help."

"Hey now, Doc."

"Quit complaining," she teased. "Get busy."

EMMA'S COMPANY MADE KILLIAN HAPPY. SHE CALLED HIM ON HIS bull and seemed more open when he wasn't flirting, but just being her friend. He liked she was getting to know *him*.

"What do you think the odds are of my best friend being interested in your brother?" she tossed out. "And that we would meet in New York City?"

"It was serendipitous, Doc," he quipped, and something in her eyes had him following that with, "After all, I deserved another opportunity to show you what a nice guy I could be."

Emma laughed as he'd hoped. "You don't think our early," she made quotations with her fingers, "encounters were memorable?"

"Oh, I'm sure they were memorable," he grumbled. "It just wasn't the first impression I'd intended."

"And what would that have been?"

There were so many things he wanted to say, but he wasn't convinced it was the right time.

"Emma," his voice dropped an octave, "whatever we become is up to you as much as it's up to me. Elsa suggested I be your friend. If that's all you want, then so be it. I won't like it, but it's your decision. No pressure. Alright?"

They stood still in silent communication for a handful of seconds before her lips curved into a tender smile. His heart flipped, and his hands tingled with the need to touch.

"Alright," she murmured. "Now, are you ready to bathe some kitties?"

Her low chuckle briefly gave him pause. Yet, it didn't stop him from putting away the cleaning supplies and starting the water.

When she returned from collecting supplies and laid them on the table, he asked, "Bandages and antiseptic?"

Her eyes twinkled. "Just wait."

The words *Run! Run!* echoed inside, something he wasn't willing to do.

Emma handed him a bottle and cautioned, "Here's the shampoo, but just use a little."

Killian nodded once and, since Trudi hadn't ventured far, decided she would be first. "Come here, Little Love. Let's clean your fur."

The tiny grey kitten's gaze met his, and when she blinked her amber eyes, his heart melted a little. *Was that it? Did animals creep in and take hold of your heart just like people?* His epiphany nearly had him confessing, but one glance at Emma's look of anticipation changed his mind.

Does she think I'm going to fail?

Does she want me to fail?

"Here we go, Trudi," Killian alerted the feline as he prepared to plunge her into the water.

"Killian, watch ..." Emma cautioned just as Trudi squealed. The kitten's four legs went in different directions, and she sank her claws into his hand.

"Bloody hell!" he grumbled, fighting his natural inclination to drop her.

Trudi's trembling body and frightened eyes squeezed his heart a little tighter.

"It's okay, Little Lass," he promised, bringing her tiny body close. "I'm right here. Just trust me."

It was several seconds before the kitten stopped shaking, allowing him to try again. This time, he gently lowered her until she hovered just above the water. With the other hand, he wet her fur and, using a small amount of the shampoo, removed all signs of the sticky mess.

If he crooned, no matter what was said, she was calmer, but even then, it was more difficult than he'd anticipated. "Here's the pretty girl, Doc. One down ..."

"And fourteen to go." Emma wrapped the kitten in a towel.

"Piece of cake," he winked.

Emma had to admit he was tenacious in his determination to outwit the felines. He coaxed, and they fought, but after the seventh, she took pity on him. "Let's take a break, shall we?"

"We only have eight more to go." Killian gave her a hangdog expression. "I can do it."

She placed a clean towel over the scratches on his hand, covering the outside of his thumb and wrist. "You're bleeding, and your clothes are soaking wet."

"But I was doing it." His grin turned boyish. "Wasn't I?"

The just-cleaned floor was covered with water and dissolving bubbles. His hands were covered with scratches, most of them deep enough to bleed. His wet shirt, which clung to his chest and lean stomach, sported dozens of tiny holes she bet hid wounds from the tips of claws. But the expression on his face was so exuberant she pretended not to notice and returned his smile.

"Yes," she switched from one hand to his other, "you were definitely doing it."

The air around them had been charged since he'd arrived. But when his eyes dropped to her lips, they tingled ....

Unconsciously, she licked her bottom lip in an attempt to tame the sizzling effect he had on her.

Whatever we become is up to you as much as it's up to me.

I want a taste. A thought she shouldn't be having.

What would Elsa say?

Elsa would say, Well, duh. Go for it!

Should she?

Her eyes moved from his to the base of his throat, where his pulse fluttered just as quickly as hers. One step closer ....

"Emma!" Leroy barged into the room, causing her to drop Killian's hand and jump back. "What happened in here? Smells like someone farted in a strawberry field."

Her lips twitched, and she pressed them together to keep from laughing. "Just a little accident, Leroy."

Killian's snicker was almost her undoing, but she maintained her facade long enough to ask her assistant what he needed.

"Hmm," Leroy grunted, as if he wasn't quite sure she was telling the whole truth. "I just need you to show me something."

"PROBABLY HIS WAY OF PAYING ME BACK BECAUSE I SAW HIS HAIRY ass," Killian grumbled after Emma followed Leroy from the room.

Millicent wound around his legs several times. When he bent over, she fell on her side, exposing her clean-shaven stomach. "You like that, don't you?"

She rolled farther onto her back, her green eyes staring into his, completely trusting him. Emma accepted something was growing between them, except she was scared—of what, though?

Him?

Or something inside?

"Will she ever trust me?"

Millicent trilled and burrowed her head into his hand. "I'll take that as a yes."

"I'm sorry about that," Emma said when she returned. "I needed to show Leroy where I put Wilby's pain medication."

"That's okay, Doc. I had this beauty to keep me company."

"She's a love," Emma grinned. "You ready?"

Before he could regain his equilibrium, Emma had drained, refilled the sink, and washed a kitten.

"Here you go." She handed him the wet animal.

"You're quick."

"Practice." She gave him another.

"I guess I need to practice."

"Guess you do. But you'll never be as fast as I am," Emma teased.

"Is that a challenge?"

"Maybe." The flirty smile she gave him had his body heat skyrocketing, giving him ideas wholly inappropriate at this point in their relationship.

"Watch it, Emma." His smile felt predatory. "I *always* rise to the occasion.

You didn't just say that, did you?

Instead of the waspish retort he'd half-expected, a little smile played along her mouth, warming his insides.

You didn't blow it.

His attention was pulled from Emma to the pain in his lower limb. "You little buggers!" he cried as three of the kittens were attempting to scale his pant leg. With every step they took, their claws pierced the material, digging into his skin. "Uhh, Emma, a little help, please."

"What is it?" She thrust another wet kitten toward him, then dropped to the floor.

He caught the kitten, but the quick motion scared the animal so badly, its claws dug into his chest. "Bloody hell."

Emma plucked the kittens off his pant leg one at a time. "There," she glanced up from where she was kneeling, "you're free."

Killian looked down, and his body reacted immediately.

Down, boy!

"Killian?"

"Thank you, Lo ... Doc," he quickly amended, focusing on the pain in his chest. *He needed to leave.* "Are we done?"

"Bathed your share of kittens?"

"I just, I just," Killian pulled his wet shirt away from his chest, "I just need to get out of this wet shirt."

Her expression transformed from teasing to concern. "Oh, I'm sorry."

"I'll be fine. Let me help you clean."

"I can ..."

"No. I promised to help." He tossed the used towels in the appropriate bins. "I want you to know I'm a man of my word."

"But ..."

"But nothing, Doc." Killian grabbed an old string mop to wipe the floor, only to be waylaid when Trudi jumped at the strings.

"Demanding little thing, isn't she?"

He trailed the mop along the floor, and every time the kitten pounced on it, she took another step into his heart.

Just like Emma. What are you going to do about it?

Not treat her like the others!

The sound of food lured Trudi away, giving him the opportunity to grab his jacket and prepare to leave.

Emma tugged on the sleeve of his leather coat. "Killian, you can't put your jacket on over that wet shirt."

He took a deep breath, pulled the shirt off, and dropped it on the floor. Emma's quick intake and the way her eyes were glued to his chest had him clamping his molars together, willing his body not to react.

"Those have to hurt."

She reached to touch the red marks, but the tenuous hold he had on his emotions had him catching her wrist. "I'll put something on them at home."

"Are you sure? I *am* a doctor."

"I'm sure." He slipped on his coat and zipped it halfway. "I'll be fine."

"Thank you for the help," she swept her hand around the room, "for everything."

Her smile was so tender he had to tighten his legs to keep from closing the distance between them. "Next time, I'd advise against leaving the punch supplies within the kitten's reach."

Her eyes sparkled. "I'll keep that in mind."

Only the strict regime of his career had him reaching for the door, not her. When he did, the lighted sign in front reminded him of her question. *What brought you to Swan Harbor?*

"Last week, you asked what brought me to Swan Harbor."

"I did."

He stared over her shoulder as an image of Violet's bullet-ridden body materialized. "When I worked for the NYPD, a life was inadvertently lost because of me. That's why I had to get away."

"I'm sorry, Killian," Emma whispered. "Perhaps someday you'll share more of that burden."

"Perhaps." In lieu of what he wanted to do, he traced a gentle finger over her cheekbone. "Goodnight, Emma."

THIRTEEN

Emma's Apartment
February 3
10:15 p.m.

Twenty-four hours later, Emma had replenished the punch ingredients and was standing next to Molly, watching Sadie's shower guests move around the room.

"Sadie knows all these people?"

"Yes." Molly lowered her voice. "But that doesn't mean she likes all of them."

"She wanted them at her party, but doesn't like them?" Emma frowned. "Then why?"

"To keep the peace."

"That makes no sense."

"I didn't think so either when I first moved to Swan Harbor." Molly pointed to a cluster of women standing off to the side of the room. "See the one with dark hair? That's Chloe Lane. Her brother is married to one of Sadie's best friends."

"Ahh. A tangled web."

"More than you know." Molly helped herself to some strawberry punch. "Hey, this is good."

"Thanks. I'm just glad I had time to pick up more punch supplies this afternoon. The strawberry smell seems to be lingering downstairs."

"Strawberry smell?" Molly's brows rose in question. "What happened?"

"Yesterday, when I ran to take care of Wilby, I left the bags with the punch ingredients on a table. It was my fault they didn't make it to the refrigerator." Emma chuckled at her blunder. "Let's just say, who knew how much fun melted sherbet, fruit punch, 7-up, and strawberries could be for fifteen rambunctious kittens?"

"Oh, no!" Molly giggled. "What a mess!"

"Now, it's funny." Emma rolled her eyes. "But when I first walked into the room and saw it, oh my ..." she continued, not considering the repercussions of her words, "Killian was a big help. Poor guy had claw marks all over him from bathing the kittens."

"Killian?" Molly's voice rose a few tones. "Killian was here?"

Emma sucked back what she'd been about to say, especially when she saw Molly's grin.

"He just stopped by to help," she sputtered.

"Oh, ho ho!"

"It's not an oh ho ho," Emma muttered. "He's just a friend."

Molly continued to grin but, surprisingly, remained silent.

"You're making this way bigger than it is." Emma gave Molly a pointed look. "You also sound just like my friend Elsa."

Molly's smile turned mischievous. "I need to talk to your friend and tell her all about our Killian Reade."

"Oh, Elsa probably knows more about him than you do," Emma murmured. "She's dating his brother."

"What!" Molly grabbed hold of Emma's arm. "This, *I* didn't know. Tell me more."

Emma shrugged, determined not to say too much until she figured out what was going on. It was interesting that Molly didn't know, as it meant Killian hadn't shared what had happened with Dylan. Begging the question—why?

"Come on," Molly whined, "give me some details."

Emma side-eyed her friend and pressed her lips together. She wanted to be annoyed but couldn't deny how giddy the situation made her.

"Come on, Emma. You were in New York. Killian was in New York. You see where I'm going?"

"You really don't know?"

"Was it so good you're afraid to say something that might reveal too much?"

"I saw him at a dance on New Year's Eve," Emma blurted.

"You spent New Year's Eve ..." Molly's attention suddenly shifted over Emma's shoulder. "Belle, have you met Emma?"

At hearing the woman's name, Emma remembered what she'd heard at the cookie exchange. Was this the Belle called by the wrong name?

"No, I haven't." Emma's eyes clashed with Belle's.

"Emma Foster." She held out her hand. "It's nice to meet you."

"You too." Belle shook Emma's hand, but her smile didn't quite reach her eyes.

There was a moment of awkward silence before Molly jumped in to ask about a book for her first-grade class. When Belle turned her attention to the conversation, Emma put a bit of distance between them.

While the other two were talking, she found herself unobtrusively studying the newcomer. Belle seemed nervous, which was understandable. What went through her head when the mishap occurred? What were her thoughts on meeting that person face-to-face?

Whatever we become is up to you as much as it's up to me.

Emma hadn't been able to get Killian's words out of her mind since he'd left the evening before. Especially in light of his abrupt departure.

He was uncomfortable when you saw his chest.

And what a chest it was!

The thought of his flat stomach, defined pectoral muscles shielded by a light covering of black hair, still had the power to make her hot.

"Thanks, Belle. I'll be there by Monday to get that book.

"Emma."

Molly's voice effectively shattered her daydream. "Yes?"

"What were you thinking about just now?" Molly snickered. "Your face is quite red."

"Nuh-nothing," Emma forced out and quickly changed the subject. "That conversation with Belle was a little strange. Who's she talking to now?"

"Oh, that's Catherine," Molly whispered. "She dated Dylan before he and I met."

"You man-stealer!"

Molly shrugged. "The heart wants what the heart wants. Just like Killian's."

"Stop that. We're friends."

"Sure, you are," Molly giggled. "However, I'll give you a bit of peace if you take me to Wilby. I brought his blanket."

With a glance around to make sure they wouldn't be missed, Emma led the way downstairs.

Molly tucked the old blanket around the dog and cooed at him for several minutes before her impish smile returned. "Now that we're away from Killian's castoffs, spill."

"I did feel a little like the proverbial doggie in the window up there." Emma chuckled.

Molly laughed. "I could see that, especially having Belle, Chloe, Tia, *and* Morgan all in one room. Sorry about that. They're just jealous."

"But ..."

"Did you know Killian threw his black books away?" Molly surprised her by saying.

"Books?" Emma's brows shot up. "As in more than one?"

"Yep. He had four."

"He threw them away? Why?"

"Don't you know, Emma?" Molly replied softly. "It's you. You're the woman who's taming the bad boy."

That was the second person to offer the same sentiment. One that made her heart race?

Emma showed Molly the photo on her phone. "Yes, I spent much of New Year's Eve with Killian, and we danced."

"Oh, Emma!" Molly exclaimed. "He's enamored with you."

Emma blew out a breath and decided to share her thoughts with Molly. If she couldn't help her sort through her confusing thoughts, there was always Elsa.

Sheriff's Department
February 8
2:00 p.m.

THE FOLLOWING MONDAY, KILLIAN AND DYLAN WERE STUDYING A map of Swan Harbor, hoping to discover a pattern in the dog killer's behavior. Except, no matter how long they looked at the map, nothing jumped out.

"It appears random," Killian snapped. "What are we missing?"

"Think it could be a drunk driver when on a bender?" Dylan pointed to the map in the order the animals were hit.

"Wilby and Anita's dogs aren't an easy drive to any bar," Killian noted.

"True," Dylan sighed. "Has anyone seen anything?"

"You saw taillights," Killian replied.

"Well, keep looking. Surely, something will break for us soon." Dylan stalked off to answer a call.

It unsettled Killian to think about someone purposely targeting dogs, as narrowing the search was more difficult. He kept taking second looks at every person he saw. In his line of work, quite often, the guilty party was the person you least expected.

"You're up, Reade." Dylan slapped a note down in front of him. "Take your girlfriend."

"My girlfriend?" Killian arched a brow. "Who said she was my girlfriend?"

Dylan smirked. "Emma and Killian sitting in a tree, K-I-S-S-I-N-G."

However, an hour later, when they drove away from the clinic, Killian side-eyed Emma. She was quiet, almost too quiet. There were no teasing glances or barbs thrown his way. He hated it, and before they arrived at their destination, he was determined to figure out what had changed since Friday evening.

While he'd been with the boys on Saturday, the women were at Sadie's party. Had something happened there that created the divide between them?

"Emma? Is everything alright?"

"It's fine. Why?"

Because you're suddenly acting shy around me.

"How was Sadie's party?"

"Fine," she hummed. "It was fine."

What the hell does fine mean?

Before he asked another question, pieces of his conversation with Gray, Dylan, Rusty, and a few others floated through his mind.

"Who have you been fighting with?" Gray tapped the side of Killian's hand where the remnants of kitten scratches remained.

Killian brushed off his concern. "They're just souvenirs from helping Emma bathe her naughty kittens last evening."

"Oh, lucky you." John Brown saluted him with his beer bottle. "I'd love to get a piece of that action."

Killian was halfway out of his seat before he realized Dylan had jumped on the chance to say something first.

"Thanks." Killian glanced across the room to where John was leaning against the bar. "I would have punched him."

"Our families go way back," Dylan told him. "Now, about this 'bathing naughty kittens' story?"

"Anyone tell you you're all like a bunch of old ladies?" Killian took a swig from his bottle before offering, "No, I didn't spend the night. We're friends, alright?"

Three pairs of eyebrows rose simultaneously. "The great Killian Reade is actually just friends with a woman?" Rusty quipped. "Will wonders never cease?"

"Cut it out," Killian tossed back. "Emma's not like that."

"Our boy's growing up," Gray mock whispered to Rusty and Dylan.

"I'm right here," Killian grunted.

"Sorry, Killian." Gray grinned. "Just never thought I'd see the day when a woman would make you change your ways."

Killian gave a self-deprecating laugh. "I guess it's true what they say, 'It just takes meeting the right woman to make you see the error of your ways.' After all," he let his eyes land on each of them, "you can't tell me you were perfect before your women came along."

It helped move the conversation off of him until later in the evening when Dylan cautioned, *"I hope Chloe, Belle, or whoever else was listed in those books doesn't decide to give Emma the low down on your Don Juan ways.*

Bloody hell! While his behavior in Swan Harbor hadn't been as loose as most assumed, several women he had dated had been at the party. Had they said something to upset Emma?

Killian tapped his thumbs on his steering wheel while he decided the best course of action.

Talk to her.

I'm trying, but she won't talk to me.

Are you trying hard enough?

The turn to Peter Pan Park was on his right, and without any warning, he swung into the closest lot. Emma gave him a quizzical look and then quickly turned back to the window to watch a dog and its owner running on the track.

Killian slid his arm along the back of the seats. "Emma, look at me."

She turned toward him, and her gaze settled in the center of his chest. "Is this where we're going?" Their eyes met briefly before hers skittered away to look out the window.

"Emma." He tucked a finger under her chin and tilted her face, forcing her to *look* at him.

Gradually, her eyes traveled up to meet his, and what he read in them was not what he'd expected. Not anger. Not disgust, but humor.

"Bloody hell, Doc," he cried in exasperation. "I thought you were pissed because of something you were told."

"Oh?" she teased. "Who could have said something that might make me pissed?"

"Someone from my past," he sighed. "I know there were several women I've dated at Sadie's party."

Emma's brows rose. "Just women you've *dated*?"

Killian's heart raced at her words, hoping her interest meant she cared. Except his thoughts and feelings were new and uncomfortable. In the past, if any woman asked questions, such as Emma, he would have told her where to get off. This time, that wasn't an option. Even though she'd only been a part of his life for a few months, she was firmly entrenched in his heart.

"Emma, I …"

"Never mind," she interrupted. "It's none of my business."

He couldn't help but think she was protecting herself. Who from, though? Was it because of what she assumed the truth to be? Or was she worried he would ask her questions about her past?

Killian caught her left hand, the fingers of his right one gently running back and forth on her wrist. He could feel her racing pulse and wondered if she was affected by his nearness.

"Emma," he tried again, "you understood what I meant the other night when I said, 'whatever we become is up to you as much as it is up to me,' right?"

"Yes."

"You also understood I want more with you, right?"

Her gaze dropped to the middle of his chest before once again meeting his. "I get that, but I ..."

She slid her tongue across her full bottom lip, distracting him momentarily.

Killian tightened his jaw, more determined to lay all his proverbial cards on the table. "There's no pressure, but I want to make a few things very clear, alright?"

"Okay."

"Parts of my past aren't pretty. Parts of my past I don't really remember. Today, though, I want to clarify any questions you might have concerning my time in Swan Harbor."

"You don't have to."

"Yes, yes, I do. I don't want you hearing stories and wondering if they're true or not."

Again, her gaze moved away from his, this time settling on the person and dog still running around the track.

"I'm listening." She straightened as if readying herself for upsetting news.

"I haven't slept with *any* of the ladies I've dated while living in Swan Harbor," he admitted huskily.

Emma arched a blonde brow. "In this case, is," she made air quotes, "'slept with' a euphemism meaning you didn't have sex with them? Or are you telling me you didn't spend the entire night *after* you had sex?"

"Would it matter?" he purred, feeling a little thrill when her eyes flared.

"I want to lie and say no, it wouldn't matter," she whispered. The defiance in her eyes when their eyes clashed gave him hope.

Killian saved her from an admission and placed a finger over her mouth. "Both. I never stayed over, and I certainly never had sex with *any* of them."

"Why?"

A bark of laughter escaped before he could stop it. "What? I thought that was a good thing."

"Well, it is. But why?"

"Why didn't I make them notches on my bedpost?" He smirked when a look of annoyance flitted across her face, and she nodded. "It was too easy."

"Is that why you're interested in me?" She confronted him with a question he'd asked himself more than once. "Is it just the chase?"

How did he tell her all the reasons he was interested in her without scaring her off? He cupped her jaw, and his thumb rested lightly on the slight indention below her bottom lip. "You," his voice dropped an octave, "make me *feel*."

"Is that a good thing?"

Was it a good thing?

He could honestly say it was just about the best bloody thing that had ever happened to him, but that was saying too much. Killian inclined his head, giving her a gentle smile. "It is ... but it scares the bloody hell out of me."

Their eyes engaged in a heated confrontation, one that had Killian's pulse racing and his breaths coming faster. In hers, he saw everything he could ever want and questions neither were ready to have exposed. A part of him needed to look away, afraid she would see too much and worry she would find him lacking. While the rest wanted to meld his mouth to hers and show her exactly what he felt.

The muscles in her throat moved up and then down as she swallowed, and her eyes dropped to his lips.

"It scares me too," she confessed breathlessly. "In fact ..."

"What is it, Emma?" he probed, unwilling to allow her to shut him out just yet.

She frowned, and the twinkle in her eyes belied her anger. "Did you really call one of those women Emma?"

Killian leaned his head back against the seat. "Not one of my finer moments," he groaned, going on to explain what had happened. "That was before Thanksgiving."

"Smooth move, Reade."

"Somehow," he sent her a pointed look, "I knew my life was going to change when your yellow bug crossed my path."

"Really?"

"Aye," he quipped. "After all, who else would have taught me the art of bathing kittens?" Then, needing to lessen the intensity of the conversation, he winked.

She studied him for a heartbeat before laughing. "And you were such a good student, too."

"I even have war wounds." He showed her one hand.

"That little thing?" She traced the scratch on the side of his thumb, making his skin tingle. "Poor baby."

Once again, the air sparked as their eyes clashed. The tingling on his hand spread up his arm, and against his will, his eyes dropped to her mouth. Her pupils dilated, her lips glistened, beckoning him forward. "Emma."

"Buster! Get back here!" a voice outside shouted, causing Emma's breath to catch, and she jumped back.

"Bloody hell!" Killian ran his fingers through his hair in frustration.

"Seems Buster isn't listening so well," Emma retorted as they watched the dog run back and forth in the snow, barking at something.

Killian studied the scene, wondering if he should have a look around. "What do you think he's barking at?"

"Probably some wild animal." Emma leaned forward to take a closer look. "It could be a skunk, a hare, or maybe even a deer."

"Okay. I guess we'd better go."

"Guess so."

It was quiet as they left the park behind and turned away from town.

"Where are we going again?" Emma asked. "This area is unfamiliar to me."

He mentally scolded himself for not telling her where they were going. "Have you met Allen Little?"

"I don't think so."

Killian gave her a '*You-won't-believe-this-look*.' "He's taking his neighbor's cats again."

"What?"

"Oh, he doesn't hurt them," Killian hastened to assure her. "Apparently, he's done it for the past three years. He takes them and returns them with no problem when asked."

"And no one knows why?" Emma frowned. "No charges are filed against him?"

"Not that I'm aware of. But once you meet him, you might understand. I think the neighbors protect him."

"Protect an animal thief?"

Killian just shrugged. "You'll see."

FOURTEEN

Cat Thief's Home
February 8
4:00 p.m.

EMMA GLANCED AROUND THE WELL-KEPT NEIGHBORHOOD WITH carefully shoveled walks and driveways. "Why am I here again?" she asked when Killian parked the car in front of a charming cape-style home.

"Because you're the cat whisperer," he teased. "Besides, Dylan claims the 'law' has had no success in getting Allen to change his ways, and we're hoping…"

"I would have more luck."

"Exactly."

"And he's not dangerous?"

"No, Doc."

Emma couldn't help it, but his husky voice had her glancing up at him.

"But if he was," Killian continued. "I'd protect you with my life."

His words had simultaneous thoughts running through her head.

Who's going to protect me from you?

and

He's thinking about the person he couldn't save in New York.

The intensity with which his eyes were locked on hers rendered her incapable of speech. They didn't move for another heartbeat, and then he rested his hand at the base of her spine and guided her up the last step.

"Ready?"

The combination of his nearness and touch made her knees feel like jelly. After several minutes, and no one had responded, Killian knocked again. This time, with a little more force than she thought was needed.

The door opened, and the largest man she'd ever seen was standing just inside the house. "You didn't tell me he was a giant," she whispered.

"Oh, hello," Allen greeted them in a friendly voice. "I wondered who would visit me this year."

Killian sent her a look that said, *'Is-this-guy-for-real?'* "You were expecting us?"

"Oh, sure. Come on in."

When Emma stepped inside, she didn't expect the neat and orderly room that smelled like cinnamon and chocolate.

"Allen, have you met Emma Foster, the town's new veterinarian?" Killian introduced her, shutting the door with a little too much force. Did he realize his attempt to intimidate wasn't working?

Allen beamed. "Welcome to Swan Harbor, Doctor Foster."

His tone was soft and friendly, but when their eyes met, she could see there was more going on.

Much like someone else she knew. Emma glanced in Killian's direction before turning her back to the big man. "It's nice to meet you, Allen."

"You need to give your neighbors their pets, Allen," Killian snapped, unwilling to make idle conversation. "They aren't yours."

Allen's face quickly morphed from happiness to sorrow. "I know."

Emma sent Killian a look of reproach for his impatience and encouraged Allen to join her on the sofa.

"Killian tells me this isn't the first time the neighbor's cats have 'visited.' Is that true?"

"Yeah," Allen muttered. "It's been a few years."

"But why?"

When he glanced up, the combination of pain and something she couldn't decipher looked back. It reminded her of times she'd used a 'cloak' to mask what she really felt.

"I was lonely."

Allen's answer reminded her how much easier it was to work with animals. They couldn't hide what she needed to know.

"But why collect other people's pets?"

"For years, I took care of my father and his cat, Mr. Bubbles," the gentle giant replied. "When Dad passed, and Mr. Bubbles followed immediately afterward, I was lost. Except for the winter, I had my work."

"What do you do?"

She learned he was a gardener who was busy most of the year. In the dead of winter, when his business was at its slowest, he grew lonely and wanted company.

"But why the neighbor's cats?"

"Because I can give them back when it's time to work," Allen stated, as if it was apparent. "Mr. Bubbles hated to be alone."

While there seemed to be a sliver of truth in his comment, Emma still felt like something was missing.

"Allen, have you thought about getting two pets? Then, when you're working, they can keep each other company."

"They could do that?" His voice was childlike, unlike the look in his eyes.

"It just so happens," Emma went on. "I have several kittens at my clinic ready for new homes. You could even have the first choice if ..." she hesitated, "you promise you won't do this again."

"I can do that."

Emma studied him, still convinced he was 'cloaking' his real thoughts.

When the front door opened, and Killian entered with several people she didn't know, Allen's face shuttered. The real Allen Little had cloaked himself behind a persona of simpleness.

"Allen, it's time to return your visitors," Killian said impatiently.

The way Allen greeted his neighbors and led them out of the room confused Emma. He was hiding something, but she had no idea what.

EVEN AFTER HEARING THE NEIGHBORS THANKING ALLEN FOR caring for the pets, Killian was still confused. Why were they taken, treated as if they were on vacation, and then returned? If the neighbors were happy with the way their pets were treated, why did they call the sheriff's department every year?

"Were you serious, Doctor Emma?" Allen asked. "You'll let me choose my very own kittens?"

Killian's head danced with visions of Trudi, Millicent, Nina, or Bree living with a stranger. *Did he want that?*

Trudi blinked her amber eyes at him, stealing a piece of his heart.

Millicent rolled over to expose her stomach, stealing another piece.

Emma hesitated, making Killian wonder if he'd get a reprieve, but then she said, "I will, but why the cloak?"

"Why do you say that?" Allen responded defensively.

"I grew up around people who pretended," Emma murmured, pushing Killian closer to hear what they were discussing.

"I can tell you're holding something back," she went on. "What is it? Why let everyone believe you're something you're not?"

Allen held Emma's stare for so long that Killian almost stepped between them. Somehow, she'd known and, with a gentle touch, stopped his interference.

She dealt with beings daily who couldn't talk to her. So, staring down one man was easy. It just showed him that dealing with Emma Foster would require his full attention.

Then, just as he'd anticipated, it wasn't long before Allen wilted, and he sank onto the couch.

"How did you know?" Allen asked, his voice more confident and slightly lower in pitch.

Emma gave Allen a crooked smile. "Never kid a kidder, right?"

How did she do that?

"You know how it is—people see what they want to see," Allen explained.

"There has to be more," Emma pushed. "What are you leaving out?"

Allen sighed. "Look at you—pretty, blonde, smart, and thin." He nodded toward Killian. "And he can have any girl he wants, but look at me ..."

Killian winced, uncomfortable with his past behavior and how he might have ignored someone like Allen.

"But," Emma began.

"When people look at me," Allen went on. "They see someone who is overweight and must only care about one thing … eating. No one sees a guy who's shy and has no idea how to make friends and talk to others."

"When you pretend to be a dumb jock or a simple gardener who borrows cats for company, you're treated differently?"

"Yeah," Allen admitted. "Then, I can pretend I have friends."

Killian exchanged looks with Emma before walking away. Cloaking came in all forms.

How, then, do you know if the person you meet is someone real or just pretending?

"Think about what I said." Emma gave Allen her business card. "Call me when you're ready to choose the two kittens you want."

"Okay. I will. And Emma … thanks."

As they said goodbye and climbed into the car, several thoughts and feelings coursed through Killian. The emotions, though, were foreign, and he didn't know what to do with them.

"Do you think that was a good idea?" he asked as soon as he was backing away.

"What?" Emma hesitated. "Offer him kittens?"

"Aye."

"Studies show animals give a person a reason to live, and cats are pretty independent. As long as he feeds them, they'll be fine. He'll have two friends who will love him unconditionally, and those two friends will have homes."

"True."

Except, if Killian were honest, he didn't like the idea she was giving his cats to …

"In addition, there's the possibility that communicating with the cats will help Allen in other ways," she added almost as an afterthought.

"Meaning?"

"Maybe he can drop the pretense." She gave him a look that had him metaphorically squirming in his seat. "Seems we all know something about that, don't we?"

"Touché," he murmured, realizing he needed to explain some of his behavior from their first meetings. The question was when and how much to share.

"Killian," her voice broke into his thoughts, "what's going on?"

"I don't like the idea of Trudi going to live with someone else," he exclaimed, deciding the kittens were the most pressing matter.

He fought to keep his eyes on the road but knew Emma was staring at him. It felt like she was trying to decipher what he hadn't said before getting to what was said.

"Oh!" she giggled, allowing him to deal with one thing at a time. "She stole your heart, didn't she?"

"Aye, she did."

"So, what does that mean?"

The words, "I'm going to adopt her," were uttered before he realized the thought had formed completely.

"And?" Emma prodded, already reading him better than anyone besides Liam.

"One of her siblings," Killian acknowledged out loud, but internally he was screaming. *Bloody hell, what are you doing?*

"That wasn't so hard to say, was it?"

"I've never had a pet before," Killian admitted breathlessly. "I've no idea where to begin."

"I'll help you," Emma promised. "You won't be going into it blindly."

"Promise?"

"Promise. Now, which of Trudi's siblings will you take? Let me guess."

"Think you know me that well, Doc?" Killian paused. "I'm not so sure ..."

"It shouldn't be too hard," Emma teased. "Why a sibling, though, when it's obvious you love Millicent?"

"Because you're going to keep Millicent." He grinned at her quick intake of air. "You're an open book ... about some things anyway."

"Huh," she snorted softly. "I guess I am."

The tone of her voice had him glancing in her direction. "Is that surprise because I read you or because you just realized you were going to keep her?"

"A little of both ... maybe," Emma murmured. "I never had a pet growing up either."

"No cats, no dogs, no fish?" Killian tossed back.

"Not a one." Her laugh was self-deprecating, "Poor little rich girl who collected strays, helped them heal, and then gave them all away. Grandfather was allergic. Cook didn't want them around. Always an excuse."

"What about college? Didn't you and Elsa adopt any strays?"

"I volunteered at a shelter where I was able to love them, but never kept one for myself. Strange, isn't it?"

"Maybe you were waiting until you were home."

"Perhaps."

She smiled, causing his heart to flip several times.

To Emma's Home
February 8
4:00 p.m.

While Killian focused on driving, Emma thought back on their earlier talk. He had a gentleness she hadn't expected. Nor had she anticipated how unsettled that side left her.

You make me feel.

His touch had sent her pulse skyrocketing but soothed her at the same time. How was that possible?

Even Trudi realized he would never harm her.

It's okay, Little Lass. I'm right here. Just trust me.

Plus, Trudi had trusted him from the beginning.

"I've got you." He stood, cradling the tiny grey kitten in the palm of his hand.

The more time she spent with him, the more she wanted to rearrange her priority list. But that behavior was foreign to her, as Emma Foster lived and died by her list. Didn't she?

She glanced in his direction, and when a lock of black hair fell across his forehead, she wanted to push it back. He was deep in thought, but about what?

When the sign for Peter Pan Park came into view, her thoughts once again returned to their conversation.

Oh no!

It took only a second for her brain to register what she was seeing. "Stop!"

Emma's panicked yell caused Killian to slam on the brakes. They locked just as the car hit a patch of black ice, sending it into a spin.

Emma's seatbelt tightened, almost painfully, as Killian fought for control of the car.

Time raced and slowed simultaneously while she waited for the car to stop. Finally, he regained control, and the car came to a rest sideways in the street. Before the rocking motion ceased, Emma unlatched her seatbelt, threw open the door, and ran.

"Emma!"

"Buster. It's Buster," she chanted, running to where the large brown dog lay on the road. Her thoughts from earlier caused tears to run down her face. She'd been annoyed his barking broke the moment—one that could be recaptured. But Buster ....

Emma dropped onto the cold ground and gently touched the matted fur.

"Emma?"

Killian's soft voice, accompanied by his gentle touch, was almost her undoing.

She'd known the dog was gone before she ever touched him. It was evident in the unnatural way he was lying.

In the bits of brown fur stuck to the asphalt.

In the streaks of red in the white snow.

It was several seconds before she was able to pull her emotions back under control. Once that happened, she wrapped her professional cape tightly around her feelings. In doing so, she answered her own question about personas.

Was there more than one Emma, but they were all still her?

"It's Buster." Emma moved closer to Killian's warmth.

"Is he?"

"Yeah." She closed her eyes and tightened her cloak a little more. "It's for the best, as, based on the scene, it was painful. Poor Buster."

"That's seven," Killian spit out, anger flowing off him in almost palpable waves.

"Yeah." Emma forced down the bile rising in her throat. "I met Buster a few weeks ago when he came in for vaccines. He was a sweet dog."

"I'm going to get this guy, Emma," Killian promised.

"I know you will," she sighed. "I just hope it's soon."

"I need to make a few calls." He looked around the crime scene before once again meeting her eyes. "Do you want to wait in the car?"

"Actually, if it's okay, I'm going to go break the news to Sydney, Buster's owner." Emma pointed to a mailbox not far from where they were standing. "He lives at the end of that drive."

"Do you want me to go with you?"

Her thoughts spun with what needed to be done, but even she knew Killian Reade, the Investigator, was working against time. She could point out what she *thought* happened, but he was the one collecting evidence. And with the light not lasting forever ....

"I can handle it, but first, I need something from my bag."

He walked her back to the car, and the way his hand rested at the base of her spine felt natural. A connection she was growing more comfortable with each day.

"What do you need?" he asked when she grabbed the small pack behind the passenger seat.

"Gloves." She took a pair of disposable ones and a clear bag from a zippered pocket. "I want to remove Buster's collar and give it to Sydney."

"Do you—?"

"No," Emma assured him. "I've got this. You take care of solving that," she waved toward the scene, "and I'll go talk to Sydney."

"Okay, Doc. Yell, if you need me."

"Thanks."

She gave him a crooked smile, and by the time she walked away, he was on the phone with Dylan.

Chin up, Emma. You've got this.

With Buster's collar removed and placed in a bag, she needed to do something about his remains. But it was a crime scene, and for that, she had respect.

The dog killer had struck again, and this time during daylight hours. From watching police shows, she knew the body and road held clues. With a lot of luck, casts of the tire tread would be made, and the dog killer found.

After a quick wave in Killian's direction, Emma started toward Sydney's mailbox. At the bottom of the drive, footprints surrounded its base, going in both directions.

"So, after running in the park, Sydney picked up the mail on his way back inside," Emma murmured. "But why did he leave Buster behind?"

The driveway continued for about fifty feet before making a sharp right.

Emma tried to follow the same path as Sydney, but since he hadn't been very diligent in shoveling his driveway, it was trial and error. She slipped several times until finally giving up and moving into softer snow.

Emma had just rounded the curve when the scene in front of her sent a rush of fear up her spine. "Killian! Come quick!"

FIFTEEN

To Emma's Home
February 8
5:30 p.m.

Emma's anxious voice had Killian dropping the tarp and cones he'd been using to preserve evidence, draw his gun, and take off running.

What had she discovered?

Was she in danger?

When she didn't yell again, he considered calling her name. But the possibility he could somehow jeopardize her safety had him continuing in silence.

Once he reached Sydney's driveway, Killian navigated the ruts, trying to follow the fresher footprints. As he neared the bend, he slowed, listening, hoping to hear something ... anything to assure him his girl was safe.

"Killian! Hurry!"

Emma's cry caused him to forgo quiet for speed as he continued to race up the main path.

"Killian, it's Sydney," Emma yelled again. "He needs help."

He shoved his gun back into his holster and didn't stop until he reached where Emma was kneeling next to Sydney's prone body.

"Is he ...?"

"No. But he needs a doctor."

Killian called for an ambulance and then scanned the area. Sydney was lying on his back, his feet facing the road. He was still wearing the running suit from earlier, and pieces of mail were scattered around him.

"Has he moved since you arrived?"

"No. But I did a cursory exam and saw no obvious wounds."

She toed the snow, looking so defeated Killian couldn't keep from pulling her into his arms. "Are you okay?"

"I'm fine. It's just ..."

An ambulance's siren had her stepping back and giving him a lop-sided grin.

"I know." Killian dropped his arms and immediately felt the loss. "I'd better go."

"Go." Emma gave him a shy smile. "I'll wait with Sydney."

He wanted to say more. Instead, he donned his professional cloak and went to meet the others.

EMMA DIDN'T HAVE TO WAIT LONG BEFORE SLAMMING DOORS shattered the silence, and two men with a stretcher rounded the corner.

"How long has he been unresponsive?" one of them asked.

"A half hour or so."

Except if the accident occurred just before they arrived, would Buster have felt as cold as he did?

"Is there anything else you can tell me?"

"Not really. I'm sorry."

"We'll take it from here. Detective Reade said he would meet you on the road. He was talking to the sheriff."

"Thank you."

Emma retraced her steps to the main road, where she found snow beginning to cover Buster. With Killian huddled with Dylan and Rusty, she took one of the tarps and covered the dog's body.

"Emma?" Killian's husky voice soothed something inside. "Everything okay?"

"Yeah," she sighed. "I know you still need him, but ..."

His eyes said he understood what she was feeling better than she did. "It's okay, Emma. Are you ready to go home?"

"Go home? Aren't you still needed here?"

"Aye, but Dylan and Rusty can handle it while I drive you home."

"Okay, thank you."

Killian opened the car door and whispered, "My pleasure," when she climbed in.

It had Emma's heart flipping several times, but she tucked the feeling away to examine later. There were more important things to focus on right then.

"Have you learned anything yet?"

He was quiet while he turned the car in the opposite direction and started toward her clinic. "We got a nice cast of the tire tread."

"A tire cast? But, since it's winter, don't most cars in Swan Harbor have the same seasonal tires?"

"I didn't say it was going to be easy." Killian winked. "Nothing worthwhile ever is."

Sexy. Whenever he winked, it disrupted her concentration.

"So now what?"

While Killian gave her a few details about the investigative process, he kept the details light and quickly changed the subject.

"How's Leroy working out?" He gave her a crooked grin as the little man's timing still annoyed him.

"Oh, he's fine. I just don't ask too many questions, and we get along."

Killian chuckled as the image of Leroy lying on Audrey's floor was still a bit too fresh in his mind. "A little free with information, is he?"

"You could say that. But at least he doesn't pass out and can help with surgery."

"Like Sadie?" Emma's look of surprise had him adding, "Gray shared."

"Ah, okay. Sadie was pretty embarrassed. It's good she didn't hurt herself when she fell."

"No more strawberry disasters?"

Emma laughed. "No, thank goodness."

Once on her property, Killian followed her directions around the main building to the opposite side of her clinic. "I didn't realize there were separate entrances."

"This one leads directly to my apartment."

"Good to know." His flippant reply was out before he could stop it.

Emma gave him an '*Is that the best you can do?*' look. It reminded him their *best* encounters were when he wasn't pretending. Why, then, were there moments when his mouth still got away from him?

Change is hard.

"You can just let me out right there." Emma waved to a spot in front of her door.

Since there was no bloody way he was just going to *let her out,* he parked next to her yellow bug.

"Don't you need to rush back?"

Killian removed the key and shoved it, along with his hands, into his pockets. "Emma, earlier today, when ..."

Something in her eyes told him to tread lightly. "It takes a special person to do what you do," he murmured, relaxing when the veil he'd seen lifted.

"In my line of work, I've seen some terrible things." Killian forced the image of Violet's body away. "But I'm not sure I could have done what you did with Buster."

"You do what you're called to do, right?"

"Aye."

"Good luck with your clue gathering."

"Killian Reade always gets what he's after," he quipped.

The look she gave him as he exited the car had him thinking through his words again. "I, I didn't mean that as it sounded. I just meant I'm a good investigator."

"Oh, I know."

She stepped in front of him to unlock her door and an image of bringing her home from an actu*al* date blossomed. His imagination had him tugging her into his arms and tasting her lips.

"Emma, I ..."

She turned quickly, and the pack on her shoulder unbalanced her, causing her to fall hard against his chest. His arms tightened, and his body jumped in reaction to having her close.

Their eyes collided, making him want to promise her the world. They were so close that every time she exhaled, her warm breath sent tiny shivers up his spine.

Cor blimey, he wanted to kiss her. Just a taste. Just a little taste. But would that be enough?

No, never.

Earlier at the park, he'd thought she was ready. Then, when he'd considered bringing up their talk, an almost panicked flicker had come and gone in her eyes.

Be her friend.

Be patient.

Once again, he relied on some untapped force deep inside, deciding the move *had* to be Emma's. He dug into that resource and gently kissed her forehead.

"Killian?"

The look in Emma's eyes when they flew open gave him hope.

"Lock up behind you, Doc. Thank you for your help with Allen."

"You're uh," she stammered, "welcome."

"Let me know when I can pick up my kittens." Killian tore himself away and, with a jaunty wave, jogged to the car.

When he drove away, the view of her still standing in front of her door assured him he'd made the right move.

Veterinarian Clinic
February 14
2:00 p.m.

THE FOLLOWING WEEK, AFTER SAYING GOODBYE TO MOLLY AND Wilby, Emma got lost in the memory of an earlier phone call from Killian.

"Hello," she answered, somewhat breathlessly.

"Doc," Killian's husky voice whispered across the line. "How are my girls?"

Emma swallowed hard, picturing Killian's blue eyes as he bent toward her. "Your girls?"

"Aye." His chuckle was low and sexy, confident in how he was affecting her. "Trudi and ...."

"Nina!" The fog cleared in time for her to realize it wasn't she he was referring to, but his new kittens.

"Huh!" Killian huffed. "How did you know Nina was the other kitten I would choose?"

Emma giggled. "I'm not the only one who's an open book. But your girls are fine and ready for their new home."

"That's ah fine," he stammered, just as she had when he'd kissed her forehead.

His hesitant reply had her heart turning to mush. "Just fine?" she teased.

"Okay, more than fine," Killian blurted. "But bloody hell, Emma. What if I cock up and harm comes to those little buggers?"

Emma's knees joined her mushy heart, turning to jelly over his concern for a pair of barely one-pound kittens. "You'll be fine. Trust me."

"I do, Emma," he sighed.

"What is it, Killian?"

"It's Sydney."

"He's not ..."

"No," Killian hurried to assure her. "He's fine ... at least physically."

"I sense a but is coming."

"Aye, Doc," Killian acknowledged. "Seems Sydney's suffering from some form of amnesia."

"He can't remember anything?"

"Let me clarify," Killian specified. "The last thing he remembers is running in the park with Buster. After that ... nothing until he woke up in the hospital."

"Which means he could have seen something, but we don't know, right?"

The conversation had worked its way back to his kittens, and after she promised to send him a list of the necessities, they hung up.

Were they going to catch this person before more blood was shed?

Millicent hopped on her desk and spread out across the computer keyboard. "I needed that," Emma scolded, but it didn't stop her from scratching underneath the cat's chin.

"This was your goal all along, wasn't it?" Emma crooned to her purring pet.

With what could have been an excited trill, the cat moved closer to rub her head against Emma's hand. "Already spoiled, aren't you?"

Then again, that's what they're for, right."

"Emma," Sadie called from the front. "Come quick."

"Please don't let it be another hit and run." Emma gave Millicent one more pat on her way to the front.

"Sadie, it's not …" Emma reached the doorway, but the sight before her had her grabbing the doorframe. "Do I even want to know?"

"Oh, these aren't all from Gray. These roses," Sadie tapped the huge bouquet next to her, "are from my fiancé. But those," she indicated the heart-shaped mylar balloons bobbing around the room, "are for you … kind of."

"But why?" Emma glanced at the balloons, unwilling to admit how hard she was fighting a smile.

"Emma," Sadie scolded, "duh, it's Valentine's Day."

"But but I don't have a Valentine."

Yet. You could, though.

Sadie handed her a red envelope. "They are for you, kind of. Except two of them, and this," a pink envelope was handed over, "explains everything."

"Oh."

The writing on the outside of the envelopes had Emma's heart flipping. Instead of opening them, though, she turned the attention back to Sadie's gift. "Should I ask how you rated four-dozen roses?"

"Five dozen," Sadie giggled, laying a magazine next to the roses. "I bought a few items from that magazine, and he's thanking me."

"Rebecca's Fantasies," Emma hummed. "Fulfilled his fantasies, did you?"

Sadie's chuckle was low and naughty. "You have that all wrong, my friend. It was he that filled …"

"La la la," Emma interrupted laughingly. "Between you and Leroy, I feel like a voyeur."

"You never know, Emma," Sadie winked. "Might give you some ideas for when you and Killian …"

Emma had gotten used to Sadie's innuendos and let her prattle on for several minutes. Only the arrival of a well-dressed older gentleman and his mixed-breed *Canis lupus familiaris* quieted her.

"Captain Jack!" Sadie rushed to hug the newcomer. "And Bandit! Have you met the new doctor, Emma Foster?"

Emma held out her hand to greet the newcomer. "It's a pleasure to meet you."

"You," when their eyes met, his voice faltered, and a surprised look crossed his face.

She sent Sadie a look that said, '*What's up?*' and slowly let her hand fall to her side.

"I'm sorry," Captain Jack stood a little taller. "Your beauty overwhelmed me. It's nice to meet you. We'll just wait for you in the treatment room."

"Any idea what that was about?" Emma asked once they'd disappeared into the exam room.

Sadie shrugged. "Who knows? He's a bit eccentric. Even been known to talk to the swan that shows up every summer."

Since eccentricity seemed to fit Swan Harbor, Emma let it go and checked on her patient.

"Aren't you going to read the cards?" Sadie whispered.

"Later." Emma crammed them into her pocket.

"Chicken."

Emma childishly stuck her tongue out. *Yep, I'm chicken and scared of not being in control.*

Sheriff's Department
February 14
5:00 p.m.

KILLIAN SPENT THE BETTER PART OF HIS AFTERNOON SETTING UP A large evidence board in the conference room. Each time he added a new clue, he hoped for a clearer picture. Yet, a part of the puzzle was still missing, and he was at a loss as to where to find it.

"Tell me you have some good news," Dylan instructed.

"It's a dog's breakfast."

"What the hell," Dylan laughed, "does a dog's breakfast mean?" His face sobered, more than likely thinking of Wilby. "And I'm sure it's anything but *a dog's breakfast* for the dead dog's owners."

"Sorry, mate," Killian apologized. "It means this," he waved at the board, "is a mess. Maybe I cocked up, and the case has gone pear-shaped."

The door banged against the wall, breaking the quiet. "That means he thinks he's screwed up." Rusty waved a piece of paper around.

"What did you find?" Killian barked.

Rusty gave him a cheeky grin. "Play nice, or I won't share."

"Sorry." Killian pressed his molars together to stay quiet.

"Temper, temper." Rusty handed him the page.

"Bloody hell, Rusty. Is this all you have?"

"What did you expect, Reade?" Rusty snapped. "A name and an address?"

"*That* would have been nice."

"Calm down, children," Dylan retorted. "Break it down for us, Killian."

He pinned the newest information to the board and started at the beginning. "There have been seven hit-and-run accidents spread throughout our town. As of today, only two canines have survived. Five dogs belonged to residents of Swan Harbor, with the other two considered strays."

"Where were the strays found?" Dylan asked.

Killian pointed to the two places he'd learned from Emma.

"So, most of the incidents are occurring around the perimeter of Swan Harbor," Dylan murmured.

Killian indicated the two outlying blue pins. "All except for Wilby and Bo Peep."

"Why would that be?" Rusty wondered aloud.

"I'm not sure," Killian grumbled. "However, it brings me to witnesses. So far, Dylan is the only one who's seen anything. I was hoping Sydney had, but ..."

"Nothing new with him?" Dylan inquired.

Killian shook his head. "Not so far, but I have an appointment tomorrow, so maybe."

Dylan glanced back and forth between the two men. "What about canvassing?"

"That's my agenda for tomorrow," Rusty reported.

"Okay, and this," Dylan pointed to the paper Killian had just pinned next to the picture of Buster's body.

"It's nothing specific," Killian grumbled. "The cast was from a 15"

Dunlop Winter Maxx WM01, which is on approximately 40% of the vehicles in Swan Harbor."

"Nothing stands out?" Dylan frowned.

"Bloody hell, no!" Dylan's concerned look had Killian taking a deep breath. "Sorry, I just feel ..."

"So bloody frustrated!" Dylan and Rusty exclaimed simultaneously.

"What the bloody hell?"

Dylan laughed. "You've mentioned how you feel a time or ..."

"Two thousand," Rusty asserted. "We get it."

"Listen," Dylan added. "There's nothing else we can do now, so let's call it a night. Besides, I have plans with my Valentine."

"As do I," Rusty replied. "See you two later."

With them gone, Killian dropped into his desk chair and studied the picture Emma sent. Their new collars were the smallest possible, but they still hung off the kittens. "Guess we'll be growing into them, won't we girls?" He thumbed to the next picture, which was the *list* Emma had promised.

"Are you talking to me?" Amy asked, holding a pile of folders.

Killian jumped, embarrassed to be caught talking to himself. "Sorry, no. I was just thinking out loud. But why are you still here?"

"Just finishing up." Amy indicated the folders. "What has you so interested? Do you have a hot date?"

"You could say that." Killian showed her a photo and pointed to the gray kitten. "Meet my girls, Trudi," he indicated the marble-colored one, "and her sister Nina. I'm picking them up later."

"Kittens!" Amy reached for his phone. "They're adorable."

"They are pretty cute, aren't they?"

"They are," she agreed. "See you tomorrow."

Once alone, Killian went back to Emma's message. He'd wanted to spend Valentine's evening with her, but he didn't think she was ready for that just yet. However, based on her behavior when they'd seen each other last, she wasn't completely immune to him. Something that gave him hope but questioned his ability to be patient.

"No choice, Reade," he murmured, scanning the never-ending list of kitten supplies. "Bloody hell."

Killian: Doc, what's a litter scooper?

Emma: It's used to scoop waste out of litter.

Since the only litter he could think of was the waste that lined the side of the road, Killian invited Google to fill him in:

Litter - *absorbent material, typically in granular form, used to line a shallow receptacle in which a cat can urinate and defecate when indoors.*

Unbidden, the smell from the farmhouse came back to him. "What have I gotten myself into?"

Killian: Where does one find a litter scoop?

Emma: Stop by Patti's Pampered Pets. You should be able to find everything you need.

It seemed like he had much to learn.

❧

Veterinarian Clinic
February 14
7:00 p.m.

WITH THE CLINIC 'CLOSED,' EMMA PULLED THE RED ENVELOPE from her pocket. It was bent from having taken it in and out of her pocket multiple times, only to cram it back in. She was scared, though, especially after the way the card to his 'girls' made her feel.

For My Girls,

He'd written in a unique and distinctive style.

Trudi and Nina, Welcome to the Reade family.

Two of the mylar balloons had collars attached, one red and the other pink.

Short, simple, and sweet. Words often thought when it came to him and animals.

"Come on, Emma. It's just a card and doesn't bite."

Her name, written in his loopy letters, made her heart race.

> *Emma,*
> *The journey isn't only where you've been but where you're going. Thank you for being a part of mine.*
> *Killian*
> *P.S. Somehow, I knew you would open this one last. Follow the numbers on the balloons and walk with me.*

Eight mylars, each with a red ribbon tied around a gift, waited for her. She unwrapped a miniature yellow car, a DVD of the movie *Grease*, a copy of a book titled *Ten Big Toes and a Prince's Nose*, and a silky white scarf like the one she'd worn at the ball. There was also a collie resembling Wilby, a tiny grey kitten, a bunch of plastic strawberries, and a picture of the Peter Pan Park parking lot. With the exception of the book, they were all symbols that meant something to her.

But then she read the story. Killian had given her a glimpse of what his journey had been about.

Uncovering Killian.

Untying the strings and letting go of the cape.

Just like you.

Was she a catalyst in his wanting to change, just as he was one in her fight to stay focused on her list?

A knock on the door startled her, but since she was expecting Killian, Emma opened it without checking to see who it was. "Oh!" She swallowed and tried again. "Mother, what are you doing here?"

"Hello, Emma," Ava King replied. "May I come in?"

SIXTEEN

Veterinarian Clinic
February 14
7:30 p.m.

AVA'S WORDS TRIGGERED A SWITCH INSIDE EMMA, AND SHE couldn't keep her childhood cape away. As she wrapped it around her, she became the Emma Foster she thought her family expected.

She stood a bit taller.

Don't slouch, Emma. Chin up. Chest out.

Her smile didn't quite reach her eyes.

It's important to keep your thoughts to yourself.

Her voice grew clipped, losing much of its intonation.

Overexcitement will never do.

Hands that cared for animals one minute and were used to express the next were glued to her side and bunched into fists.

Don't wave your hands around when you talk, Emma. It's quite distracting.

"Mother," Emma exclaimed. "Won't you come in?"

When Ava stepped inside, Emma expected the space to shrink. After all, she'd always seen her mother as larger than life. But it didn't happen. This time, when Ava stepped into *her* clinic, she was just another occupant.

"Emma," Ava gave her a cheery smile, "this place is very ..."

Here it comes. What derogatory comment will she use? Pedestrian, perhaps?

"Professional." Her mother finished, giving Emma pause.

"How did you find me? Walter?" She named the private detective her family used.

"You sent me a birthday card, remember?" Ava murmured. "Your return address was included."

Emma vaguely recalled grabbing a card and addressing the envelope but couldn't recollect mailing it. "I've been busy."

Ava inclined her head in the same regal manner, making others feel they had her undivided attention. "I'm sure. It's not easy running a small business all on your own."

"I have help," Emma bristled at what felt a little like an insult. "Sadie and Leroy ..."

But with her mother perusing the room and not listening, Emma studied her. She looked different. This Ava was dressed in jeans and a beat-up old leather jacket, not the designer dresses and heels she'd always worn.

Her feet were covered in old, very scuffed boots—not designer ones with heels so high you had to worry about falling, though. Ava King was wearing cowboy boots.

She even smelled different. Her usual fragrance had been exchanged for a clean, musky one, making Emma feel as if she'd been thrown into an alternate reality. Why all the changes?

"Were you in the area?"

"No," Ava answered, absently studying the pictures on the wall.

"Business?"

"No." Ava moved to look at the fish tank in the corner.

"But—"

"I'm sorry to just show up like this," Ava shrugged. "I just ..."

Something about her mother's behavior made Emma think she was nervous. Except ... Ava King didn't get nervous. Did she?

"I just wanted ..." A knock on the door had Ava lifting a brow in question.

Knowing it was Killian to pick up his kittens sent a sense of panic zipping through Emma's system. She didn't know if she was ready for her past and present lives to crash into one another.

"I need to get this. Would you like to wait upstairs in my apartment?"

"That's okay," Ava smiled, "go right ahead."

Emma took a deep breath and pulled open the door.

"Evening, Doc."

His smile almost melted her resolve, but with her mother listening, it felt like she was frozen in time. Once again, she was the twelve-year-old looking for acceptance.

"Killian."

"Are my girls ready?"

He stepped inside so close she could feel his body heat. Her breath caught, and with her insides screaming, she searched for control.

"Where's your cage?" Emma retorted. "That was number one on the list."

"Oh, come on, Doc," Killian asserted. "They're just tiny things. They'll be fine without a cage."

Her sense of smell betrayed her, allowing his essence to seep around the edges of her cape. *Damn*, she thought, straightening her spine even more. "Never mind. I have something you can use. Follow me."

"Emma," Ava glanced from her to Killian, "aren't you going to introduce me to your friend?"

"Mother," Emma took a breath, "this is Killian. He's here to pick up his new pets. Killian, my mother, Ava King."

Killian turned his charm in her mother's direction. "Ms. King, I see where Emma gets her beauty."

"It's Ava, please," her mother dimpled, "and thank you. It's always nice to meet Emma's friends."

What the heck is she talking about? Since when had she ever wanted to meet my friends? Elsa was the only one she knew.

"Mom, if you'll excuse us. This way, Killian."

"Do you need any help?" Ava asked before they'd escaped.

"No, no help. I'll be right back."

Emma rushed into the other room before saying more. "Now, let me get you something to transport your kittens."

"Emma?"

The tenderness in his voice had her tightening her cape strings while she went to get a temporary cage.

"Run into some of those ghosts?"

Her sense of hearing failed her, allowing his voice to reach inside and touch her heart. It wasn't just the smooth cadence of his British accent or the fact he used words similar to those in an earlier message. There was so much more.

"You could say that." She glanced up, and what she saw melted her cloak. "How did you know?"

"I encountered my share in New York."

"And what happened?"

She knew the answer before he said anything. His ghosts were what he'd laid to rest.

"Conquered them," he admitted before amending. "Most of them anyway."

Could she do that?

"Perhaps we have more in common than I thought."

He smiled, and his eyes crinkled at the corners. "I'd bet on it." Killian's voice dropped an octave. "If I can be so bold and give a bit of advice. When it comes to ghosts and parents, try to remember behaviors viewed through the lens of childhood, often look much different when viewed as an adult."

Her father's letter and blog entries were prime examples of all not being what they seemed.

"I get that." His nearness made her head swim. "Thank you again."

"Anytime, Doc." He winked. "Anytime."

While she set up the travel carrier, captured the kittens, and gave Killian instructions, Emma didn't worry about her cape reappearing. She didn't need to pretend with him. Could she do the same with her mother?

"Understand?"

"Aye, Doc," Killian assured her. "I'm not a complete prat."

"I know that, but ... if you need me ..."

"I'll call." His voice grew huskier. "And if you need me to slay a few ghosts for you, let me know."

"You'd do that?" Her cloak had been no match for Killian's persistence.

"Aye."

She wanted.

"I'll walk you out," Emma settled on, knowing her mother was still waiting.

When they returned to the front room, the pictures Ava was studying caught Emma's eye. "Anything new with Sydney?"

"No, sorry."

"And Buster," she thumbed over her shoulder. "I thought maybe I'd hold him ..."

Killian's gaze scooted away before meeting hers once again. "He's at the morgue."

"At the morgue?" Emma frowned. "But why?"

"It's still an active investigation."

Something told Emma there was more, especially when he followed up with, "I *am* going to get this guy." With that said, she could only trust him.

"Emma, Killian?" Ava took several steps toward them. "Buster? A morgue? An investigation?"

Emma almost asked her mother why she even cared. Except too many years of what was proper had her biting her tongue.

"Just a sick individual running over dogs."

❧

Killian stepped between the two women, hoping to lessen the tension. "It was a pleasure meeting you, Ava." He pasted on his most charming smile. "Will you be visiting our fair city for long?"

Her arched brow and sparkling blue eyes told him she saw right through him, but allowed him to have his way. "Just a short time. I hope to see you again."

It was then Trudi and Nina made their presence known from inside their makeshift cage. "I'd better go."

"Remember, Killian," Emma reminded him. "Keep the girls in the box until you get home."

"I know what I'm doing, Doc. Trust me."

He bounded to his car and placed the box on the passenger seat. Even before he'd driven off Emma's property, the kittens began making noise.

"Poor little loves," he crooned. "Shall I let you out?"

Their mews were his answer, and stopping, he opened the box and tilted it on its side. "There you go. Now be good, girls. We'll be home in a flash."

The night was cold and cloudy. As he drove, he found his thoughts divided. A large part of him was back at the clinic, curious about the relationship between Emma and Ava. In contrast, the other part was thinking about the case.

Until he glanced to his right in time to see Trudi and then Nina peering out just before disappearing.

"Bloody hell!"

Killian slammed his hand on the steering wheel and began searching for them. He flipped on the light and glanced over the seat. When he swung back around, a white flash darted in front of his car, forcing him to slam on the brakes.

The carrier slid forward, barreling into the dash, and his seatbelt pulled taut across his chest. *Was that a dog or a wolf?* had barely begun to form when he was nearly blinded by the high beams of a car heading directly for him. Killian braced for impact, but at the last moment, the car veered around his and disappeared.

"Bloody hell!" He reached for the door latch, hoping to get the car's license plate number. Before he could lift it completely, he realized if he opened it, the kittens might escape. Then he'd never find them.

"I'm such a git!"

Disgust climbed because, as sure as he knew his name, he knew the car had belonged to his dog killer.

If he'd listened to Emma, he might have been able to get their license plate numbers without worrying about his pets.

"Face it, Reade! You're a dick! An arrogant, self-important, stupid dickhead."

His anger temporarily abated, Killian put the car in gear and started for home. He'd wait and use the well-lit parking lot of his apartment complex to locate his new friends and return them to their carrier.

Before he'd gone far, tiny pricks in the lower part of his pant leg hinted he had a visitor. "Well, hello there, Little Love," he crooned, capturing Trudi and feeling her body vibrate as she purred. "Did that scare you?"

As soon as he'd set her inside the box, Killian searched for her sister.

"Nina," he called in a low voice. He'd just driven into the apartment parking lot when a gentle rustling allowed him to grab the wayward kitten and slip her into the box.

Killian climbed from the car, holding the carrier close. He'd just shut the door when the sound of a car engine brought his attention to the darkness beyond his complex.

Had the dog killer followed him?

Even though he couldn't see anyone, his sixth sense had been alerted. He knew they were out there and made a promise. "I will get you."

Veterinarian Clinic
February 14
10:00 p.m.

Several hours later, Emma was still trying to connect the images of the mother she remembered with the woman in her apartment. Ava had cooked and, while they ate, asked pointed questions about life in Swan Harbor. Details that, as a child, she'd wanted to share, but as an adult, she couldn't stop thinking about an ulterior motive. What had precipitated the behavior change?

"Mom, are you sick?"

When Ava didn't immediately deny the question, and her eyes skittered away, a coldness appeared inside. She might not have the relationship with her mother she desired, but she didn't want her to die.

"No," Ava frowned, "why would you think that?"

"Well, let's see." Emma held up a finger. "No designer clothes. Jeans and boots. New perfume. Grilled cheese and idle chitchat. And," she hesitated and lifted a fifth finger, "you've never just *shown up* without wanting something. So, what is it?"

If she hadn't been staring, she wouldn't have noticed it happening, but her mother transformed before her eyes. Suddenly, it was as if a light had gone off, and Killian's words about seeing things through the eyes of a child made sense. Her mother had a cloak, too. How could she have missed it?

"I'm sorry." Ava stood quickly. "I'll get out of your way."

Emma blinked, but it wasn't until her mother disappeared she moved and caught Ava at the bottom of the stairs.

"Mom, wait. I'm, I'm sorry." Then, she repeated words she'd said to Killian, "Seems we have more in common than I thought."

"What are you talking about?" Ava's clipped voice was the same from childhood.

"We're both good at pretending, aren't we?" Emma addressed the elephant in the room.

Ava's crystal-clear blue eyes bore into hers, making her feel like a *cheyletiella* under a microscope's lens. The longer she stood there under her mother's scrutiny, the harder she had to fight the urge not to grab her cape and hide. Where had that come from? Swan Harbor had changed her in ways she'd never anticipated. So much so she didn't want to look backward but instead move forward. Would her mother meet her halfway?

The music, the clock's ticking, the rustle of the kittens, and her heartbeat their only company.

Must be where I got my stubborn gene.

Millicent chased one of the kittens out and back through a door just beyond Ava, pulling Emma's attention away from the showdown. It would be so easy to walk away and allow the felines to distract. But a soft sniffle and tears running down Ava's cheeks had her sinking to the top step. For the first time in her life, she was seeing her mother cry.

"I guess we are," Ava sniffed, letting go of her pretense. "Are you sure you want to hear what I have to say?"

"I've been told sharing your burdens helps." Emma gave her mother a crooked smile. "I'm here ... you're here ..."

A resigned look crossed Ava's face, but with a little nod, she followed Emma back upstairs.

"Have a seat, mom. I'm going to grab us something to drink. What would you like? Wine?"

"Actually," Ava surprised her by answering. "Do you have hot chocolate, by any chance?"

Who could have known she shared those likes with her mother?

A short time later, Emma handed Ava her drink and sunk onto the sofa. The situation was similar to her talk with Elsa. Would what her mother had to say be freeing ... for both of them?

"Did you ever know," Ava began, "the cause of your Grandfather Leo's death?"

The question startled Emma, and a sinking feeling appeared in the center of her chest. "Heart attack, I think." Except she couldn't remember it being discussed.

"Massive heart attack, brought on by hypertension." Ava's lips twisted in disdain. "Stubborn old coot. Doctors tried to warn him, but he didn't pay attention."

Ava told the story of a father who sheltered his young daughter by keeping her locked in an ivory tower. Of how she'd always felt there was something she needed to find. Of how she escaped many times, only to be returned empty-handed.

"I thought Peter Foster was going to be my Flynn Ryder," Ava admitted with a sad smile. "Instead, he turned out to be the Gothel in my story, and the tower I was locked away in was much taller, much stronger than I'd ever expected."

"But why?" Emma frowned. "You could have done anything you wanted. Why stay in an unhappy situation?"

Ava paced around the room as she continued to talk. Her story was one of being born at a particular time and being groomed for a high-profile position, but as a female, being told she couldn't have it all. Her sexuality, her family, and her needs were shoved aside for the greater good of King Industries.

"Then, by the time my father passed, it was my *normal*." Ava shrugged. "I'm not trying to make excuses. I'm just trying to explain."

There were parts of Ava's story Emma knew, parts she was unfamiliar with, and parts she could relate to. Her profession alone had undergone a massive shift from being 98% male to 80% female in fifty years. But even with that, she felt she needed to work harder—to be better. She couldn't imagine what it was like for a woman in her twenties to take on a huge, primarily male, corporation. It must have been a daunting task, even for someone who was groomed from birth for the job.

Her mother stopped in front of an ornate mirror hanging on the wall and studied her reflection for several minutes.

"Have you ever looked at yourself and not recognized the person looking back?"

"Sure," Emma murmured. "I think everyone does that at one time or other. Our family especially, hence my pretending comment."

"I'm talking literally, not recognizing yourself," Ava clarified.

"Prosopagnosia?" Emma asked, remembering a diagnosis in a textbook from long ago. Ava nodded, forcing Emma to dig into her memory. "It usually follows a brain injury or ... a stroke."

"Just a mini one, thank goodness," Ava confessed. "But scary enough to force me to take a hard look at my life and realize that fifty was too young to die."

When she returned to the sofa and calmly resumed drinking her hot chocolate, Emma had a million thoughts.

Her mother had a stroke.

"When did this happen, and why am I just hearing about it?" she snapped, annoyed such a life-altering situation occurred without her knowledge.

"Not long after the new year," Ava replied. "As to why you didn't know, well ... I'm telling you now."

Emma could think of a dozen things to say, each having the power to create a greater division between them. Besides, what right did she have to demand answers when she was just as guilty of holding things inside?

"What happened?"

It began with the story of the high-powered corporate lifestyle that involved too many late meetings, stressful negotiations, and constant travel.

"Those led to too little sleep and too little time to be in tune with my body," Ava sighed. "Then, one morning, I woke up and just felt off. Instead of listening to my body, though, I went into the office."

The emotion in her mother's voice affected Emma almost more than the words. The emotion showed how much the situation scared Ava King. Emotion that if she hadn't heard it, she wasn't sure if she would have believed it to be true.

"I was in the middle of an international teleconference," Ava continued. "Multiple conversations were going on at once, and suddenly I felt dizzy. I stepped into the ladies' room, splashed cold water on my face, and looked in the mirror."

A cold kernel of dread plopped into the pit of Emma's stomach.

"When I looked in the mirror, I didn't recognize the woman looking back at me."

"But, you're okay now?" Emma asked hesitantly, the kernel opening slightly.

The cold spread as Emma learned how her mother had been found unconscious and rushed to the emergency room. It seeped into the tips of her fingers with the realization that Ava King, President of King Industries, had been felled by a stroke. Then spread to the tips of her toes with the knowledge that modern medicine had saved her when she was given an injection to reverse any damage.

That she had such a strong response surprised her, making her wonder if that was where she'd been heading since arriving in Swan Harbor.

"Several hours later," Ava went on, "I looked in a mirror again, and this time, you know what I saw?"

Emma shook her head, the lump in her throat keeping her quiet. Somehow, though, she guessed it wasn't the black hair, bright blue eyes, and creamy complexion everyone else saw.

"I saw an empty life." Ava's laugh was harsh. "Imagine that. I had wealth, power, and, thanks to modern medicine, my health." She stopped talking and took hold of Emma's hand. "But I didn't have my daughter standing next to me or her respect. I didn't have someone to grow old with. My stroke was both a blessing and a curse. Now, I have a chance at a do-over. How many get that opportunity?"

"Not many." Emma looked down at their joined hands. "So now what? Somehow, I don't see you sitting around eating bonbons and twiddling your thumbs."

"I want to mentor women who are interested in starting their own businesses."

"A worthwhile endeavor," Emma replied. "What about King Industries?"

"The family keeps the majority stock. However, someone else will run its daily operations. I want to get to know my daughter and," a twinkle appeared in her eye, "find my own Flynn Ryder."

"Did you add that to your day planner?" Emma teased, knowing part of her list-generating had come from watching Ava write things down.

"And what if I did?" Ava's smile turned impish. "A girl can never be too prepared." She hesitated a beat before continuing playfully, "Is Killian your Flynn Ryder, by any chance?"

Emma side-eyed her mother. "Whuh-what makes you say that?"

Ava chuckled. "The sparks were flying back and forth between you two."

"Well, we're ..."

"Emma," Ava's tone turned serious once again. "If you find you have a good thing, grab hold with both hands. You never know what the next day holds."

The unshed tears glistening in her mother's eyes propelled Emma forward into Ava's arms. It was a new beginning.

"You know, Mom," Emma grinned. "I've been told the journey isn't only where you've been, it's where you're going. I think maybe we're finally on our way ... together.

"Me too, honey," Ava hugged her tighter. "Me too."

SEVENTEEN

Sheriff's Department
February 19
9:00 a.m.

THE FOLLOWING WEEK, WITH SOME HELP FROM HIGHER-UPS, images from the traffic cameras began to arrive. Killian was halfway through the first one when a jaw-popping yawn had him press pause and take another drink of coffee.

"You look like you've been ridden hard and put away wet." Rusty dropped a box from Paula's Pastries on the desk.

Killian reached for a fresh, sweet roll. "Just what I needed."

"Paula sends her love."

"Did she send extra frosting for me?"

Rusty fished a small container out of his pocket. "You're such a child."

"You're just jealous." Killian peeled off the lid and licked the frosting off. "Thanks, Mate."

As the sugar and caffeine worked their way through his system, his energy returned. "Anything new?"

"I have a call to make, and then, maybe."

"Well, what are you waiting for?"

Rusty flipped him off on his way out of the office to make the call.

While he was gone, Killian continued through the footage. "Bloody hell."

"Nothing new?" Rusty slid into his desk chair.

"No."

"Wrong camera angles?" Rusty asked. "Or poor quality?"

Killian twisted his chair around to face his partner. "It's location. Almost as if our killer knows where the cameras are and which way they face."

Rusty nodded in understanding, "That makes sense, but ..." He flipped to a page in his notebook.

"What?"

"Hold your horses," Rusty grumbled. "I'm looking. Here, this is from Shawn Jackson. His neighbor, Krystal Salas, has a security camera attached to the front of her house."

"Krystal Salas?"

"Swan's Spirits," Rusty reminded him. "Wears spandex, has high blonde hair, and really high heels. She knows just as much about the happenings in this town as Sally."

"Which is saying something," Killian nodded. "I've seen her around town."

"Don't tell me she was another one of yours," Rusty snorted.

"Wanker."

"Nutter."

"Tosser." Knowing they could insult each other all day had Killian circling back. "Did you get the tape?"

"She's going to email it to me sometime after noon today."

"After noon?" Killian grunted. "Why the bloody hell do we have to wait? Can't she just go to her computer and punch, beep, bip, boop, and hit send?"

"Beep, bip, boop?" Rusty laughed. "What kind of gibberish is that?"

"Or whiskey, scotch, rum," Killian countered. "We need those images."

"She'll come through."

"Bloody hell, I hope she can be trusted. I hate that the dick who's doing this has gotten away with it so far."

"And it's making you bloody frustrated."

"Don't be cheeky," Killian scolded. Then his phone buzzed, and he switched directions. "Hello."

"Killian, it's Claudia Joyce. I finished my examination of the dog's remains. Do you want a report, or can I just tell you?"

"You found something?"

Her answer had Killian's pulse speeding up. "I'll be right there."

❧

Veterinarian Clinic
February 19
4:00 p.m.

AVA STAYED FOR FOUR DAYS, AND WHILE THEIR RELATIONSHIP wasn't perfect, it was better. They spent most of the time cooking simple meals and talking. It was a cathartic visit for both, and she'd even shown her mother the letter from her father. Ava's response gave her more to think about than the answers she craved.

"Emma, while some of your Grandfather Leo's behaviors made me angry, I never doubted he loved me. But love to him had a different definition than what I wanted or needed. Would I be a different person had he been different? Possibly. But my health scare showed me I can't change what's happened or go forward unless I dig inside and let go of the negativity. Does that make sense?"

"So basically, what you're saying is I'm in charge of my destiny?

"Yes." Her mother's blue eyes held her attention. "Your father's letter has given you an opening. The question is, will you walk through?"

Yet a week after her mother's departure, Emma still hadn't decided what to do about her father. Between the clinic, worrying about the dog killer, and trying to make sense of her emotions, she'd almost decided she could only handle one wayward parent. The fact her mother showed up, forcing her to confront those ghosts, was something she was thankful for, but the rest ....

Her phone rang, saving her from making any heavy decisions right then. However, the way her treacherous heart pounded when she saw who it was said she'd relaxed too quickly.

"Hello."

"Good afternoon, Doc." Killian's melodious voice sent a little thrill through her. "Busy?"

"Not right now. Why? What's going on?"

She hadn't seen much of him since he'd picked up Trudi and Nina, especially with her mother in town, but they'd texted daily. While his messages kept her apprised of the investigation, she was sure his goal was a little sneakier. *And darn if it didn't work*, as he'd popped into her thoughts over the last week more times than she wanted to admit.

Killian's low, sexy laugh added to the shivers working their way up and down her spine.

"Why, Doctor Foster? Can't a man just call to say hello?"

"That's not something you would do."

"I wouldn't call you just to say hello?"

"No," Emma chuckled. "You'd send me a kitten picture or try to stump me with an animal fact first."

"Oh."

His brief response was so unlike Killian that Emma hurried to reassure him she enjoyed his unique style of communication.

"I like your pictures, and you've not stumped me yet."

"I'm glad, Doc, but ..." He paused a beat before continuing in a huskier voice. "Seems I've been remiss with how *friends* treat *friends*."

"Killian, it wasn't a critique."

"Maybe not, Doc, but I can be such a git sometimes. As your friend, I plan to do better. Alright?"

"I would like that," Emma surprised herself by admitting.

His quick intake of air had her heart doing a mini-flip.

"Yeah?"

"Yeah," she replied breathlessly.

"Good. I wondered," he cleared his throat, "if you were available to meet me?"

"You need me?" Her stomach swirled. "Are you going to tell me why?"

"You sound suspicious, Doc. It's important, trust me."

"Another rescue mission, Killian?"

"You could say that," he murmured. "I'll text directions, alright?"

"Okay. What do I need to bring?"

"Your bag and a cage ... or two. I'll be waiting."

"Damn that man and his sexy voice." Emma slid into her boots, grabbed a coat, and headed to the clinic to gather supplies.

Once on the road, she worried about how to continue to ignore their connection. Especially since each new trait she uncovered made him even more irresistible?

Tiny kittens turned him into a big marshmallow, and his Valentine's Day gift had been thoughtful. He'd shown her several sides of Killian Reade, causing her to forget her cloak more than once. Even her mantra of '*No detours, Emma,*' and '*Remember the list*' no longer worked. He pushed her to rethink her life, making her wonder if a small-town veterinarian could someday have it all.

Her visceral reaction to the cocky Killian she'd first met still surprised her. It had been strong and unexpected, sending her into a panic. Had the response been *because* some part of her knew he was a danger to her plans?

When she arrived at their meeting place, he was leaning against his car. Her heart skipped a beat, and her breath lodged in her throat.

Killian sauntered toward her. With his swagger on full display, it made her mouth water. She looked away to keep from moaning with pleasure.

"Everything okay, Doc?"

"Everything's fine." Emma took her time getting out of the car, allowing her racing heart to slow down.

"Need some help?" He helped her down from the clinic van. "This is much larger than that other vehicle you use to zip from one end of town to the other."

"Hey." Emma eased her hand from his and immediately noticed the loss of the current between them. "Don't make fun of Elli. She's been a good friend for a lot of years."

"Elli is," his eyes twinkled, "short for *Coccinellidae*?"

"Very good, Detective Reade. It was one of the first texts you sent me."

"Guess I should have expected your car would be named after a ladybug."

"Perhaps. Are you ready to tell me what we're rescuing?"

"A family." Killian took her hand and led her away from their cars.

"A FAMILY?" EMMA TUGGED HIS HAND A LITTLE. "COME ON, Reade. You can do better than that."

With their hands clasped, Killian allowed himself to breathe again. He couldn't get over just how right holding her hand felt. Something had changed since the last time they'd been together, and while he wondered what, he didn't care.

"A family of *Canis lupus familiaris*," he capitulated.

"Hmm," Emma grinned, "so it's a family of dogs?"

"Right."

"But they aren't in danger?"

"Detecting, Doctor Foster? You don't trust me?"

"Oh, I trust you. I'm just nosy."

He laughed at her confession, completely charmed by her flirting.

"So …"

"Remember the night I picked up Trudi and Nina?"

"Yes."

"I was on my way home and had to slam on the brakes when a white dog ran in front of the car."

He left out the part about why he hadn't searched for the dog. Some things, after all, were better left ….

"Could you tell if the dog was running from anything?"

"It all happened so fast," he sighed. "As soon as the dog disappeared, I was blinded by the headlights of an oncoming car."

Her quick inhalation told him their thoughts had gone in the same direction. "You don't think …"

Killian gently squeezed her fingers, acknowledging the unspoken conclusion, before moving on. "After that night, several of us began actively looking for her and …"

"You got lucky?"

"Aye," he agreed. She didn't need to know he'd traded shifts to get where he was today. "I'm glad you were available, Doc. I tried to get closer, and the little dam wasn't happy with me."

"I bet. Mother dogs are quite protective."

It was another few minutes before Killian spotted the clump of bushes and broken branches. "They're in there."

Emma slowly started toward the animal's hiding place. When she was about two feet away, a black nose appeared, followed by the same low growling he'd been privy to earlier. Killian took a quick breath, ready to say something, but a frown from his dog whisperer had him biting his tongue.

She took another step, and this time, the growl was lower and more menacing, causing him to rethink inviting Emma. He'd once wondered if it was a dog or a wolf. What if it wasn't a dog? Wolves lived in Maine, didn't they?

The growling grew louder and so sinister that fear rippled along his skin. The image of an animal flying from the bushes, aiming straight for Emma's throat, became so realistic he couldn't keep quiet.

"Emma, be careful."

His voice, albeit soft, shattered the silence, causing the animal to disappear back under the brush.

Emma stepped away from the family. "Killian, you have to let me do this."

"But ..."

She stepped into his space, close enough he could smell her unique fragrance. Close enough that he could reach out and touch her.

"I'm okay." She smoothed one hand down the lapel of his leather jacket. Her touch settled his fears and raised an awareness of another kind.

Killian's heart raced, and unconsciously, he pulled her against him, resting his hands on her hips. "Emma, what if it's a wolf?"

The corners of her eyes crinkled. "Is that what you're worried about?"

"Well, I didn't get a good look when it ran in front of my car the other night."

"Oh, Killian," Emma grinned. "It's not a wolf.

"How can you be so sure?"

Her eyes flared, her voice softened. "I just know."

"And just how exactly," he swallowed, "do you know?"

With every word, Killian leaned a little closer until his lips hovered over hers. Their breaths mingled, and while he'd been this close before, he'd never had the pleasure of a taste.

He wanted to kiss her—had wanted to kiss her for weeks. Their first missed kiss was because of Leroy. The second time was after their talk at the park when Buster had gotten in the way.

Bloody hell, Reade. You're not why she's here.

"I'm sorry, Doc." He took a step back. "This wasn't why I brought you here."

The look of frustration on Emma's face surely mirrored his own. It's all about timing. *Soon, very soon.*

"You didn't answer my question, Doc. How do you know it's not a wolf?

Don't tell me you can discern the growl of a *Canis lupus familiaris* from a *Canis lupus*?"

Emma laughed. "No, nothing like that."

"Then what?" Killian stepped toward the animal's hiding place, its growl beginning again. "That's not the sound of a friendly sort."

She placed her hand on his arm—whether it was meant to stop him from moving closer or to calm him—he wasn't sure.

"I saw her face, okay? She's a scared dog—a terrier mix, maybe 25 pounds. Can you bring the large cage, the blue blanket, and a leash from the van?"

"Be careful, Doc." Killian took her keys and left to do her bidding.

ONCE SHE WAS ALONE, EMMA GRADUALLY EASED CLOSER TO THE mother dog. She hoped by the time Killian returned, the dam would be accepting of help. That the momma was scared was a given, but her behavior was atypical of a stray. Was there a family close by looking for her?

"Here, Doc."

Emma took the leash and, murmuring nonsense words, gently clipped it around the mother's neck. "Now, let's see those babies."

The dog's black eyes bore into hers and then, as if deeming the human trustworthy, moved aside. When she did, Emma removed six puppies and laid them on the ground.

"Here," Emma handed one puppy to Killian. "Let's see if the mom will come out of her hiding place."

"It's so small," he whispered, holding the puppy as gently as he'd held the kittens.

"They're not very old."

After several minutes of crooning and gently tugging on the leash, the larger dog began to move. Once she did, the dam didn't stop until she'd determined her puppies were safe.

"They should be fine now," Emma explained once the family was transferred to a cage.

"You sure? Maybe I should follow you back to the clinic and help you get them settled."

Emma's heart flipped. "I'd like that. Ready?"

On the drive back, she lectured herself about what would happen once inside. He'd made her giddy on the phone and breathless when he'd offered to help. Neither of those times could even touch her feelings when he'd pulled her close.

"Focus! He's just a man."

Except if watching him walk toward her caused the butterflies to swarm, she had to wonder if she'd made a mistake.

Once inside, she no longer needed to wonder. Killian was quiet and followed her directions. He weighed the puppies. She bathed the mother and surreptitiously studied him. Something was on his mind, but so far, he hadn't shared.

"All done, Doc. Where should I put them?"

"Put them in that bottom cage." Emma nodded toward the one she meant. "Then come and hold the mom for me. I want to scan her for a chip."

It was a struggle to keep from staring at him as he transferred the six puppies. He was careful with them, just as he'd been with each kitten. A few soft words, a gentle rub against his jaw, and he'd place them in the cage. It was no wonder she struggled to stay aloof. Detective Killian Reade drew her.

Once the puppies were taken care of, Emma had Killian hold the mother and took out her microchip scanner. While she wasn't expecting anything, something about the way the dog behaved made her wonder ....

"There now," Killian murmured. "Don't you feel a lot better?

The mother nudged his face, and Emma's heart flipped.

"Your puppies are doing well," he continued. "You have three lads and three lasses. Did you know that?"

His soft words made her knees feel weak.

"Let's see." Emma aimed the scanner over the dog and moved it around until .... "Well, look at that."

"What is it?" Killian's eyes brightened when he saw the scanner. "Her name is Summer?"

"Yes. I wonder where her family is."

"I wonder why Summer was running free?" Killian added. "Where's your home, Summer?"

The dog whined, a mournful sound making the hairs on Emma's arms stand up. "What's she trying to tell us?"

"I don't know, Doc." He wrapped an arm around her and drew her tighter against his side. "I promise you, though, I'm going to find out."

"I know you will. At least you saved Summer."

"Emma, I ..."

She placed a finger over his lips. "I don't care why you didn't go after her the night she ran in front of your car."

His gaze skittered away, confirming her suspicions. There *was* more to the story.

"But, I ..."

"What matters is the family is safe from the sick person out there."

Since arriving at the clinic, she'd known Killian was worrying about something. Right then, though, Emma needed them to celebrate the victory.

"I know, but I," he ran his hand through his hair, "I'm not quite the hero you're making me out to be."

"Maybe not," her eyes twinkled, "but I do think it earns you a mark in the hero column."

Killian smiled, one of those smiles that caused her heart to somersault and her knees to weaken.

"It's all about timing," he murmured so softly she didn't think the conversation was still about the dogs.

How's my timing?

Since when had he cared about bloody timing? In the past, if he wanted, he took—until Violet. Then, outwardly, he'd behaved the same—until Emma.

"My timing?" His voice dropped. "It's an area I've been working to develop some patience."

"That's ah ..."

Their eyes locked, and Killian fought the urge to step forward .... Then, one of the puppies squeaked as it pushed its way closer to its mother's warmth, interrupting the moment.

Emma grabbed hold of his arm. "Killian, tell me about Buster and the morgue."

Wait! his thoughts bounced from the invisible wall she'd just thrown up.

"What did you say?" Then he backpedaled, realizing how he sounded.

"Forgive me, Doc. That was rude. What I should have said was what brought on that question?"

"See that puppy?" Emma indicated the one she meant. "Its coloring reminded me of Buster."

He glanced at the little family and then back to her with a resigned sigh. "What do you want to know?"

"Why take him to the morgue?" she asked what he'd anticipated.

Killian knew she deserved answers, and he knew she was trustworthy.

"Evidence," he settled on. "Something was stuck to Buster's fur, and so ..."

"Really?"

"Aye," Killian barked. "Our killer got out of the car and stood over that dog! Bloody hell, I want to know why!"

Once he wound down, he was embarrassed ... frustrated he'd let his emotions get the better of him. *Stupid move, Reade!*

"I'm sorry, Emma. I should go." He slipped on his leather jacket before he worked up the nerve to look at her.

"Feel better?"

"Maybe."

"You'll find the answers, Killian."

"I hope so. My patience is wearing thin." *In more areas than one.*

Emma studied him as if she wanted to say more, but then she turned to check on the dog family before heading out of the room. "Hungry?"

"Why?" *Are you wondering if that would tame the beast?*

"No, I just wondered ..." Emma's gaze dropped from his to study a spot on the floor.

"What is it, Doc?" Killian tilted up her chin. "What did you wonder?"

"Well," she took a deep breath, "I was going to make something easy to eat and watch the movie Grease. Interested?"

"One friend spending time with another?"

"Yeah ... if you don't have any plans."

"I think Trudi and Nina will be alright for a few more hours, so ... I'd like that." He sounded like a breathless git, but right then, he didn't care.

"Good," Emma started up the stairs, "follow me."

Killian climbed behind her, watching her hips sway. "Anywhere, Doc. Anywhere."

EIGHTEEN

KILLIAN PLACED THE LATEST PIECE OF THE PUZZLE WITH THE others and leaned back to stare at the board.

"Now, speak to me."

"Talking to yourself again, Reade?" Dylan joked.

"She's not saying much," Killian muttered.

Dylan snorted. "Your evidence board is a female? I don't believe I've heard that one before."

"Stop being a dick," Killian sighed. "When you look at what she's offering, what do you see?"

Dylan took his time reviewing each document. "Summer and Buster?"

"Aye. Rusty's ..."

"Here," his partner burst into the room, holding a folder aloft like a prize.

"Was I right?" Killian forced himself to remain calm while he waited for the answer.

"You are one lucky SOB," Rusty grunted. "You know that, right?"

"Absobloodylutely." Killian spread the papers out on the table. "Once I found out Buster sired Summer's pups, I started trying to knit together a few holes. Sydney just helped tighten the loop."

"How?" Dylan prompted.

"I've always felt Summer running in front of my car, and the headlights from the car that almost hit me were connected," Killian began.

"Sydney put Buster and Summer together?" Dylan guessed.

"Not quite," Killian replied. "I finally spoke to Summer's owners, and they added a few parts I didn't know."

"Then I interviewed Sydney," Rusty added. "While he still has memory issues, his calendar was quite informative."

Killian pointed to the pages and explained the Andersons, Summer's family, had left town a few days before Sydney's accident. "It means we need to account for the two weeks between the accident and when Summer ran in front of my car."

Dylan glanced up with an understanding look. "You're trying to find the person caring for Summer, aren't you?"

"We are," Rusty nodded. "Killian believes it was the perp."

"Which is why Rusty was with Sydney again," Killian continued.

"Any conclusions?" Dylan asked.

Rusty chuckled. "Ever questioned an amnesiac? Sydney wasn't sure, but thinks someone was in his house while he was in the hospital."

"Our killer?" surmised Dylan.

"That's my guess. For some reason, the perp stood over Buster's body and then left the scene," Killian snapped. "They knew about Summer and took care of her until she ran away."

A satisfied smile crossed Dylan's face. "So, our perp knows Sydney?"

"Aye," Killian agreed. "And if we can retrace Sydney's steps, then …"

"We find our perp," Dylan concluded.

"That's our hope," Rusty concurred.

"So, what's next?" Dylan followed up.

Killian tapped the calendar. "Sydney liked his routines. Sally's, the library, and the sheriff's department on Monday. Sally's, and the police department on Tuesday. Same thing every week."

"It's still quite a few people," Dylan replied. "Any luck with the video from Ms. Salas?"

"Unfortunately, no," Rusty sighed. "The camera showed a small portion of the front driver's side panel, but not enough to determine the make or model."

"We only know the car is black," Killian added.

"Wait," Dylan frowned, "you didn't tell me what was found on Buster's body?"

A dangerous smile crossed Killian's face. "Hair." He pointed to a picture of a ziplocked bag. "Our perp left us a light-colored hair."

"Any chance of DNA?" Dylan questioned.

"Claudia believes the hair broke off, which means we don't have the root," Killian said.

"Damn!" cried Dylan.

"Agreed," Killian sighed. "But we know more today than we knew yesterday. We can rule out brunettes."

Randy's Arcade
March 16
8:00 p.m.

EMMA PARKED IN THE LOT NEXT TO RANDY'S ARCADE, HOPING she wasn't the first to arrive. While it was getting easier to be in groups of people she didn't know, walking in some place blind wasn't her favorite thing to do.

"Emma." Someone called out to her. "Emma Foster."

Emma glanced around the parking lot, landing on a blonde standing next to a dark car.

Great! The first person I see is one of Killian's floozies.

The woman grinned, almost as if she knew what Emma was thinking.

"Tia Patterson."

"We met at Sadie's bridal shower," Emma remembered. "You'll have to forgive me. I'm horrible with names unless I've treated your pet."

Tia laughed. "No pets, at least not right now. But when I was a child ..."

Emma let her ramble as they entered Randy's and located the group of women they were to meet. Once seated, even though she knew almost everyone at the table, it was hard not to feel like the little girl who was always the outsider. While she hadn't been born in Swan Harbor, something about the town called to her.

"Hi, Emma." A second blonde offered her a refill.

"No, I'm good," Emma grinned.

"You don't remember me, do you?" The woman smiled. "I'm Amy. I work with Killian."

Why would I know that?

Tia laughed. "Emma only remembers names if you have a pet."

"Sorry." Emma gave Amy a sheepish smile. "Names are not my forte, except for people and their pets. Then watch out."

"I bet." Amy's easy-going nature had her relaxing. "Killian talks about Trudi and Nina *all* the time!"

The image of Killian bending over while coaxing Trudi out from under the sofa still had the power to make Emma's heart flip. As did the picture of him crooning nonsense to the little grey kitten when he was bathing her.

"Really?"

"Oh, yes!" Amy exclaimed. "They can do no wrong in his eyes."

Emma shook her head, thinking of the strawberry disaster. "Something tells me they'll find a way to test him soon."

"I wouldn't be surprised," Tia agreed, but then threw Emma a curve and asked, "You two are dating, right?"

Emma's pat answer, "We're just friends," was out before she'd really processed the question.

When several of her table mates immediately disappeared, she frowned. "What did I say?"

"You just gave a few females the opening to go after Killian," Tia replied.

"Killian's here?" Emma glanced around, but since their table was in a side alcove, she couldn't see much.

If he's here, why hasn't he said anything?

"The guys are in that far corner." Tia's dark eyes sparkled. "I saw them come in. In fact, Gray was talking to someone I'm dying to meet."

"Have fun."

Killian never told me he'd be here.

But did you tell him you would be?

Oh, shut up, Emma scolded, thinking this was why she didn't like emotional entanglements. There were too many rules.

Her gaze clashed with Sadie's. "Would you like to come to the ladies' room with us?"

The breath Emma had been holding escaped when Molly stood as well. "It was nice talking with you, Amy."

"You looked like you needed saving." Sadie looped her arm through Emma's. "Some of those girls can be a bit much, and besides," she pointed toward another part of the arcade, "I spy with my little eye encroachment."

The sight of Killian sitting on a high stool with Belle, Morgan, and Chloe draped over him set Emma's teeth on edge. "We're just friends."

"Ha!" Molly chuckled. "Then explain why your aura just turned green."

"Oh please," Emma scoffed. "You have no clue how to read auras."

Molly grinned. "True, but admit it. Seeing those women touching your man made you want to claw their eyes out—at least a little."

Emma's lips twitched. "Okay, okay. But ..."

They entered the ladies' room, and she moved directly to the mirror.

What should she do?

"Remember what I told you a few weeks ago?" Molly's face appeared next to hers. "The heart wants what the heart wants."

"But—"

"No, buts," Molly interrupted. "When your heart speaks, it's best to listen."

Whatever we become is up to you as much as it's up to me.

"You want Killian, don't you?" Sadie's twinkling eyes appeared in the mirror on the other side of her.

It only took a heartbeat for her to decide to leap. "I do."

"Then come on," Molly grinned evilly. "Let's take those bitches down."

With a lighter heart and a plan in place, Emma followed her friends, slowing only when her phone buzzed. The message made her chuckle.

"Looks like I'm just in time. It's from Killian."

Killian: I need you, Doc. Please rescue me!

KILLIAN MOVED TO TAKE HIS TURN AT THE DARTBOARD, HAPPY for the reprieve from the three women. The smell of Morgan's perfume,

Chloe's clinging vine arms, and Belle's constant chatter were getting to him. Things he'd not noticed before.

You've changed.

He aimed at the dartboard, stopping when bright red fingernails trailed along his hand. "Morgan, why did you do that?"

She giggled, and the sound reminded him of grinding gears. "I wanted to wish you luck. So, good luck."

"Thank you." Killian gritted his teeth. "Now, could you please move?"

Once she was out of the way, he aimed again. This time, Chloe's arms snaked around his waist.

"Now what?"

Chloe squeezed a little closer. "I wanted to give you a good luck hug."

"I need some space," Killian grumbled, not caring he sounded like a twonk.

"If you're going to be like that, I'm going to get another drink."

"You do that."

He caught sight of Gray as he inclined his head toward the third female. "And you," Killian practically spit at Belle, "wouldn't have any words of wisdom to impart, would you?"

"Not if you're going to be mean."

"Good." Once again, Killian aimed at the board, thinking if he hit a bullseye, he'd win the game and could find Emma.

THE WAY KILLIAN'S SHIRT STRETCHED ACROSS HIS BACK AND then tapered to his lean hips brought Emma up short.

"Go," Sadie hissed. "Surprise him."

Emma regained her focus, stepping close enough behind Killian to whisper, "You needed me?" just as he let go of the dart.

"Bloody hell!" Killian whipped around so quickly that she had to step backward.

"Oops." Emma waved toward the dart, now on the floor. "You missed."

Gray snickered. "Let me show you how it's done." With a flick of his wrist, the dart hit the board. "I won."

Sadie draped an arm around Gray's shoulder. "You deserve a reward. Dance?"

"Belle," Gray sent Killian a look that said, '*You're going to owe me.* "Have you met my friend, Nic?"

"No, but," she glanced from Gray to Killian, "I thought ..."

Sadie looped her arm through Belle's. "Come meet Nic. He'll be in town for a few weeks."

"Nic ...?" Emma arched a brow. "Another one of your castoffs was looking to meet him earlier."

"Really? Bully for him."

"That's all you have to say?"

Killian stepped closer, invading her space and forcing her to tilt her chin slightly. "You caused me to *lose*," he emphasized. "I don't care to lose."

Emma's heart raced, and every time she took a breath, his cologne surrounded her.

"Wasn't my fault. You're the one who couldn't hit that little board. Surely, it can't be that hard."

"Oh? It's like that, is it?" Killian's voice dropped an octave. "Perhaps we should play and set up a small wager."

Emma glanced at the black and white board rimmed with numbers. "You want to play a game and wager?"

"Aye."

"And if I win? Will we still be friends?"

"You wound me, Doc." He picked up the darts. "Now, black or red?"

"Hmm, red."

Emma took one dart and weighed it in her hand. It was about seven inches long and much like holding a pencil. She ran her fingers up and down it and glanced at Killian under her brows. His gaze was locked on the movement of her fingers. He looked up, and the heat in his eyes made her forget to breathe.

"Ladies first."

His husky voice rippled across her skin.

"Are you sure?"

"Aye." He stepped back, allowing her to breathe again.

"Just to make sure I'm clear." Emma held up the dart. "I hold the base—"

"The shaft," Killian corrected.

"Shaft," Emma repeated, watching his eyes widen. She wrapped her fingers around the center. "I hold the shaft, and then …"

"Barrel," Killian corrected.

"Huh?" Emma grunted. "You just said it was the shaft."

Killian tapped the slender portion. "This is the shaft, and this," he pointed to the broader part, "is the barrel."

"I don't know why it matters, but okay," Emma mumbled. "I hold on to the base of the shaft," she popped her T, "and aim the tip for the … board, right?"

"Just throw the bloody dart, Doc," Killian sputtered.

"We never did set a wager." Emma's gaze was drawn to his full bottom lip. Except something stopped her from suggesting what she thought they both wanted. "The winner chooses dinner."

"Fine, now throw. Unless … you're chicken."

She huffed, lined up the dart, and let it fly. It hit the rim of the board, bounced off, and fell onto the floor.

Her competitive side kicked in for the second dart. It hit and stuck … to the wall and not the board. "Oops."

Killian stepped behind her, and it felt like her heart stopped.

"Let me help."

"Help me how?" she squeaked out, as being so close to him stole her thoughts.

"Like this, Doc." Killian placed his left hand at her waist and slid his right one next to hers, grasping her hand. "Now, lift slowly."

His hot breath ruffled her hair, causing goosebumps to dance across her skin. How was she supposed to concentrate?

"Aim for the center," he purred close to her ear. "Cock your hand, just so."

Emma slammed the brakes on her wayward thoughts.

"When I let your arm go, let the dart fly."

Emma tightened her resolve and held her breath. As soon as he let go, she let the dart fly. The time it took the missile to travel the short distance felt like hours and not minutes. When it hit, she froze, waiting to see if it would stick. Once it did, she immediately threw her arms around Killian's neck and squealed, "I did it!"

His arms closed around her, and he lifted her off the ground. "Congratulations, Doc. Not bad for a beginner."

The feel of being pressed tightly against every hard inch of his body rendered Emma speechless. Her arms relaxed so she could gaze into his face, where she quickly got lost in the heat of his eyes.

"Ahh, your turn."

"Do you really want to keep playing?"

No.

Before she could respond, their friends swarmed, tugging them in separate directions.

❧

HE'D BEEN BIDING HIS TIME PLAYING POOL, HOPING FOR AN opportunity to find Emma, when suddenly, she was there.

"Can anyone play?" She glanced over her shoulder to where Gray and Dylan were finishing a game.

Killian tightened his hold on the pool cue to keep from reaching for her. "Are you sure you can handle it?"

Her chuckle was low and sexy, and the sound rippled along his skin. "Are you sure you can?"

Not just no, but bloody hell no. Especially if it was played in the same manner as their game of darts. There was only so much frottage one man could handle.

"Do you need to be shown how to hold the pool cue?" He wiggled his brows mischievously.

"I don't *need* you to." Emma sauntered closer and placed one hand on his knee. "But ... what if I *want* you to show me? Would you be up ... for that?"

"I'm *up,*" Killian growled, "for whatever you have to offer."

The flair of her eyes and the pink tint covering her cheeks had him second-guessing his suggestive comments. Was this *his* Emma, or had someone plied her with too much alcohol?

When Dylan sank the eight ball to win the game, Killian stood and casually stretched his legs. A particular part of his anatomy, skinny jeans, and close proximity to the lovely Doctor Foster were not a good mix. He'd spent most of the night feeling like his nuts were in a vice, and if he wasn't careful, he'd be singing soprano.

"It's about time someone beat Gray," he congratulated Dylan. "Are you ready for another opponent?"

"Haven't I already beaten you once tonight?" Dylan quipped.

"Only because I allowed you to win," Killian scoffed. "Beating my boss might get me in trouble."

"Uh huh," Dylan laughed. "So, if not you, then who?"

"Me." Emma stepped in front of Killian and took his pool cue.

"Ready to play the intrepid Doctor Foster?" Killian teased Dylan. "Think you can handle her?"

Dylan glanced at Emma. "Rack 'em up."

Emma bent over the table and slid the pool cue along her left index finger. The sight of her pants stretching tightly across her taut behind had sweat popping out on Killian's forehead.

Bloody hell! He adjusted on the stool.

She pulled the cue back and stretched as she shot. When the muscles of her ass flexed, Killian had to adjust his stance yet again. As the game wore on, he wasn't sure how the night would end, but one thing he knew was she might be the death of him. His masculinity, anyway.

Emma sunk the eight ball. "I win."

"Well played, Emma." Dylan grinned. "Can I get you two another drink?"

Killian waved him off, but his gaze never left Emma. Once again, he'd been privy to another side of her. In addition to being beautiful, smart, and a bloody amazing veterinarian, she was sexy, seductive, and a siren. Was he reading her signs correctly? That it was *their* time?

"Ready to take me on?" Killian picked up Dylan's pool cue. "Are you Emma?"

She studied him for several seconds, but before she finished, her phone buzzed, and she tossed him an apologetic smile. "It's Leroy. I'll be right back. Okay?"

"Bloody hell," he mumbled, going after her.

EMMA STEPPED OUT OF THE LADIES' ROOM AND, WITHOUT PAYING attention to her surroundings, sent a few more instructions to Leroy.

"There you are." She was suddenly pulled back against a hard-male body that reeked of whiskey and sweat. "I've been waiting for you."

Her reflexes kicked in when she heard Killian growl, "Get your hands off her, John," and suddenly, she was free.

"Are you okay?" Sadie and Molly flanked her in full protective mode.

"Gray," Killian spit out, still holding his forearm across John's chest, "can you and Sadie see Emma gets home safely?"

Emma could feel her anger rising. She'd spent four years in veterinarian school trying to prove she was capable of handling anything. "I don't need someone to see me home," she hissed, stepping closer to where Killian was holding John.

"But, Emma," Killian began.

Emma placed her hand in the center of Killian's chest and pushed him away. "I know how to handle animals," she sneered, bringing her face close to John's. "And you know what happens to male animals who get too wild, don't you?" She made cutting motions with her fingers. "I'll be fine, Killian." Emma tossed a frosty look in John's direction. "You won't bother me again, will you?"

"No, no, ma'am," he uttered before scurrying away.

Emma leaned up and kissed Killian's cheek. "Thanks for the dart lesson ... and for being my knight. I have to leave. There's an emergency."

"It's not—?"

"No, not another hit-and-run," she assured him. "It's complications from a surgery. I'll see you later."

Before starting her car, Emma turned on her Bluetooth and dialed Elsa. "Hello."

"Busy?"

"Ah, oh. What happened?"

"I'm just annoyed," Emma sighed. "Some jerk just got a little handsy."

"Threaten to castrate him?"

"Used that one, have I?"

"Oh yes," Elsa snickered. "Remember the time we were ...."

NINETEEN

Sheriff's Department
Monday 19
8:00 a.m.

"Bloody hell, Killian," Liam snapped. "Do you know what time it is?"

"Who cares? I need help."

Liam sighed. "What is it now? Hmm, let me see. Which kitten food or perhaps which color toy balls to buy?

"Those were important questions," Killian mumbled. "But no, this is about Emma."

"Is she okay?"

"She's fine," Killian replied. "I just need to know how to ask her out."

Liam's laughter was so loud, Killian held the phone away from his ear.

"Bloody hell, Liam, this is important. Possibly the most important thing I've ever done."

"You figured out how to be her friend," Liam reminded him. "I'm sure you'll know what to say to ask her out."

"But ..."

"Let me know." Liam hung up.

A lot of bloody good talking to his brother did. Even Nina and Trudi hadn't helped. His feelings for Emma were different from anything he'd ever known. Taking it to the next level needed to be different.

H practiced in front of the mirror.

"Hey, Emma. Want to go out with me?"

"So, Emma. How about a date?"

"Dinner tonight?"

Except he sounded like a git.

He even read up on animal mating rituals. The idea of using body fluids like porcupines, giraffes, and hippos had him cringing and cramming his phone back into his pocket.

By the time he arrived at work, he was in a peevish mood.

Killian made his way back to his office and tossed the messages he'd picked up on his desk.

"Another hit and run?" Rusty asked.

"No."

"Then what has you behaving like a total cockwomble?"

Killian dropped into his chair and leaned back. "What?"

"Why are you behaving like such a git?" Rusty grumbled.

"Emma."

Rusty lifted a brow. "Emma? Why? What did she do?"

"Nothing," Killian sighed. "She didn't do anything."

"So that's the problem?" Rusty gave him a cheeky smile. "She hasn't *done* anything."

"No. Yes ..." Killian blew out an exasperated breath and jumped up to pace from one side of the small office to the other. "I want to ask her out."

"Then ask her out."

"Didn't you hear what I said?" Killian muttered. "I don't know what to say. There, are you happy?"

When Rusty didn't immediately say anything, Killian stopped to face him. "What?"

"You're not used to this, are you?"

"Definitely not."

Rusty let go of a light laugh. "Knowing you have some insecurities is actually quite charming."

"Only when it comes to Emma," Killian muttered.

"Listen, mate," Rusty began, "we all get tongue-tied when we want to make a good impression. Just ask her."

"Ask who what?" Dylan asked, stopping in the doorway.

"Emma," Rusty answered. "Killian doesn't know how to ask her out."

Dylan's stare had Killian fighting not to make sure he hadn't grown an extra head.

"Get your haircut, put on a different shirt, and go ask her," Dylan smirked. "Then get your ass back to work. I'm sure you have some calendar pages to follow."

Killian's surly mood vanished as he left to follow the instructions. After the haircut, he stopped by his apartment for a clean shirt. When he reached for a blue one, it reminded him of a peacock, preening to find a partner.

"We danced around each other like swans," Killian murmured. "And now I'm dressing like a peacock."

You're talking to kittens.

So, I am.

He grabbed his leather jacket on the way out the door. However, no matter how many ways he practiced the words, by the time he parked, they continued to sound stilted.

"It's time to man up, Reade."

"Sadie," Killian greeted Emma's assistant once inside the clinic. "Is Emma busy?"

Sadie lifted a brow. "Do you have an appointment?"

"You know bloody well I don't have an appointment," Killian snapped. "I just need to, ahh ..." he tugged on his ear self-consciously, "ask her something."

"About Trudi and Nina?" She lifted a brow. "Or is this personal?"

"Sadie," he growled before relenting, "please."

She chuckled, and he knew once he walked away, the gossip line would be busy. "Emma's in exam room one, finishing some paperwork."

"Thanks, Sadie." Killian grinned. "I won't be long."

"See that you don't." She pointed at the clock. "Her next appointment is in twenty minutes.

He gave her a cheeky grin. "Yes, ma'am."

Killian quietly entered the examination room and, needing to say his piece before he lost his nerve, blurted, "Doc, will you ...?" His voice faded when he got a good look at what she was doing.

Emma was staring at a set of X-rays, her expression telling him what she saw wasn't good.

"What is it?"

"More puppies and kittens, Killian?"

"Forget about me for a minute." Killian took her hand, forcing her to face him. "What has you troubled? Do these pictures paint a bleak story?"

Emma glanced at the wall of film again, her smile sad. "It's Rene's horse. None of my treatments are working."

"Oh."

In the past, when Rusty talked about Rene and how upset she'd been over Romeo, he hadn't understood. And then Trudi and Nina came into his life. In just a short time, the kittens had wormed their way into his heart. If anything happened to them, he wasn't sure what he'd do. Nor could he imagine having to deliver such bad news.

"I'm sorry."

"Yeah, it sucks." Emma stepped away to remove the films and slip them into an envelope. "What brings you by this early on a Monday? Not another incident?"

"No."

Just ask her.

"And no one needs rescuing?"

Just me.

He tucked her hair behind her ear and lightly caressed her neck.

Emma giggled. "That tickles."

Stealing mating rituals from swans, peacocks, millipedes, and now painted turtles? Just ask!

"Will you go out with me?" he blurted.

Her mouth dropped open, making Killian wish the floor would open and swallow him whole.

You big git. Now you've ruined things.

And then ... the most beautiful sight he'd ever seen appeared. Her eyes twinkled, and her smile took his breath.

"It's about time," Emma exclaimed. "I was giving you until Friday."

"Until Friday, Doc? And then what?"

"I was going to ask you. So, yes, Killian. I will go out with you."

"Really? Good." However, with that task completed, he needed to clarify one more thing. "Emma," his voice lowered, "just so we're clear. This is a date. I pick you up. We'll go someplace nice, and I pay. Then, when I bring you home, there will be a kiss goodnight. Alright?"

Her eyes flared, and it took all his willpower not to tug her close and kiss her. It was even more difficult when her smile turned sexier.

"I'll see you Friday."

He took several steps toward the door when Emma called him back.

"Aye."

"I was just thinking." She started toward him with slow, deliberate steps. Her expression was a touch anxious and a touch shy. While he had no idea what was on her mind, but it caused his heart to race and heat to spark deep inside. "It would be a shame to spend the entire week wondering..."

"Wondering what, Doc?"

Emma tangled her hands in the lapels of his leather jacket, tugged him forward, and kissed him. The impact was electric, sending millions of tiny currents rushing along his skin. His body hardened, his heart raced, and once his brain began functioning, he closed his arms around her.

She tasted just like he'd imagined. Sweet as honey, with an underlying flavor he couldn't identify but knew he'd never forget.

Their ragged breathing reverberated around the quiet room. Their moans spoke of desperation and a need that had been simmering too long. It took every ounce of his willpower to release her lips.

Unconsciously, Killian leaned his forehead against hers and willed his body to cool.

"That was ..." Words failed him at how to describe what had just happened.

"I know," Emma whispered.

"I'd better go." He kissed her once more, and only the knowledge Sadie could interrupt had him stepping back. "I'll call you later."

"I'd like that."

"Good." Killian squeezed her fingers and then turned to leave. He'd only taken a few steps before he stopped and looked over his shoulder. Emma was standing in the same position, her right hand resting on her bottom lip. Somehow, he knew that image would stay with him for the rest of the day.

Veterinarian Clinic
March 23
6:00 p.m.

THE WEEK CRAWLED, BUT WHEN SHE CLIMBED THE STAIRS TO GET ready for her date, Emma struggled to walk slowly. Since kissing Killian on Monday, her emotions had been all over the place. Something that gave Sadie and Molly plenty of opportunities to tease, but somehow, she didn't care. She hadn't tossed out her goal list for good, but was exploring the possibilities of having it all. Was her heart really telling her something?

Did that mean Molly was right in saying, 'Your heart wants what your heart wants'?

That wasn't something she could answer, but being close to Killian had her female parts doing a Hallelujah dance! When she closed her eyes, she could feel his arms around her. Her lips still tingled from his kisses. What else could she do but jump in with both feet?

After changing her mind several times, she dressed and moved to the living room to wait for Killian. She was nervous, excited, anxious, and scared. Then the phone rang, and when she saw who it was, her heart dropped.

"Hello," Emma answered hesitantly. "You're not calling to cancel, are you?"

The noises coming through the phone line indicated he was out on a case.

"No, Doc, but ..."

"You're running late," she guessed, "and you want me to meet you at the restaurant, right?"

"Bloody hell, Doc," Killian sighed. "I'm sorry."

"It's okay, but these things happen in both of our professions. I'll see you at Captain Jack's."

He grunted, which made her smile.

"Alright, but ..." he paused. "I will be seeing you home."

"Oh?" Her heart raced. "I'll look forward to it."

"As will I."

"Should I call and change our reservations?"

"Bloody hell, no!" Killian exclaimed. "Tonight is our night. Alright?"

"If you're sure, but ..."

"No buts, Doc. I need to go, and I *will* see you later."

"Okay, bye." Emma slid her finger across the screen to read a text.

"Damn."

Since it wasn't the kind of news to impart over the phone, she knew what she had to do—even though it wasn't her favorite type of house call to make.

Emma first met Rene Langley and her horse, Romeo, when she'd stopped for a routine visit. After she completed the assessment and was drawing blood, an offhand remark about the horse's gait caused alarm bells. The horse was old, twenty-eight at the time. If, as she expected, he'd injured his coffin bone, a full recovery would be a challenge.

She parked Elli in front of Rene's house and knocked. When the door wasn't immediately answered, she second-guessed her decision to stop by. If she'd called, though ....

"Emma." Rene gave Emma a half smile. "I thought you had a date tonight."

"I do, but Killian's running late, so ..." Emma held up the file. "I thought ..."

Rene opened the door wider. "Come on in.

"I should have called—"

"No," Rene sighed. "I get it."

As the mayor of a small town, somehow Emma thought maybe Rene did get it. Possibly more than others would.

"Let's go to my study." Rene led the way down a long hallway. "Roland's watching *SpongeBob*, and I don't want him to overhear."

"I know why you're here," Rene began in her forthright manner as they crossed the threshold.

Emma couldn't think of anything to say that wouldn't come across as an empty platitude.

Rene settled behind her desk, effectively creating boundaries between them.

"There's nothing else we can do?"

Emma sighed, as this part of her job never got easier. "We've tried it all. Stabilization, cortisone, antibiotics, but now," she pulled her professional cloak a bit closer, "the infection from the soft tissue has spread. I'm so sorry, Rene. I know he's been a part of your family for a long time."

Rene's bottom lip trembled, but she buried her feelings behind a resolve

Emma had seen in very few women. Was that something she'd learned growing up, or had she developed it as a civil servant?

"My daddy bought him for me for my fifth birthday." Rene took a deep breath and blinked several times, almost daring her tears to fall. "Do I need to make the decision right now?"

"Of course not," Emma assured her. "Take your time, say goodbye, and then send me a text." She tightened her cape even more and forced down the lump in her throat. "I'll come when you're ready."

"Okay," Rene sniffed. "I'll let you know."

Emma squeezed Rene's arm in support as she exited the big house and wished not for the first time her news had been better. She didn't want anything else to get in the way of the evening.

Captain Jack's was a twenty-minute drive, which gave her plenty of time to shed her professional cloak. At least, she hoped.

Captain Jack's Fine Dining
March 23
7:15 p.m.

KILLIAN PULLED INTO A PARKING SPOT OUTSIDE CAPTAIN JACK'S Fine Dining. The restaurant, located inside a seventeenth-century Spanish galleon, was moored at one end of Swan Harbor's busy pier. While he'd lived in his new town for over a year, he'd never brought a date to the old ship. That had been important to him. But with Dylan giving praise to the romantic atmosphere and Rusty the food, he'd been sold. He just hoped Emma liked it.

When he looked around and didn't see any sign of his date, uncertainty zipped through him. It had been four days since he'd seen her, and he could still taste her sweetness. He could still feel the impression of her kiss—could the same be said for her?

She was the one who initiated the kiss.

Alright, so perhaps he was behaving like a schoolboy going out on his first date, but ... this was *Emma.*

And?

He wanted to impress her.

Then just be yourself. No cape. No cloak. No pretense.

That would be easy to do, wouldn't it?

An older model Cadillac pulled in next to his car, and the restaurant owner stepped out, immediately followed by his dog.

"Evening, Killian."

"Captain Jack," Killian greeted him. "You're bringing Bandit to work with you now?"

"Oh, yes." Captain Jack glanced around furtively. "You know, with the dog killer around, I can't be too careful," his voice dropped to a whisper.

"But doesn't Bandit stay inside when you're at the restaurant?"

"Yes," Captain Jack replied. "But I saw Sydney at Sally's yesterday, and he said the killer was in his house."

"Oh, he did, did he?"

Killian ground his molars together to keep from spewing a few colorful words. He should have known that a potential clue wouldn't remain hidden, especially since Sydney was the editor of *The Swan Harbor News.*

"It's okay. Sydney mentioned that, isn't it?" A slight frown appeared between his brows. "I'd hate for him to get in trouble."

It was bloody stupid of him, Killian wanted to say, but the distressed look on the other man's face had him changing his mind.

"I don't think you need to worry about anyone getting to Bandit when you're at work. You lock your doors, right?"

"My doors?" Captain Jack hummed. "Well, sure. Most of the time, anyway."

"That's good. Bandit will be fine."

"I'm holding you to that, son," Captain Jack smiled. "Now, what brings you by my establishment on a Friday night? Do you have a hot date?"

"Aye. She should be here any minute."

"What?" Captain Jack's expression sobered. "Your young woman is meeting you here?"

"Well ..."

"In my day, no man worth his weight would allow his date to drive herself," Captain Jack went on. "What is it with men these days? I understand women are capable, but what happened to courting rituals?"

Killian didn't think the Captain would appreciate the mating rituals he'd considered recently. "There was a wreck, and I was running late. Believe me, I hated asking Emma to meet me, but—"

"Emma?" Captain Jack repeated. "Emma Foster?"

"Aye," Killian replied, relieved to see Emma's yellow car pulling into the parking lot. "In fact, here she is now. Have you met her?"

"Emma?" Captain Jack nodded. "Yes. Lovely girl."

"Would you like to say hello?"

"Not ... not tonight. I'd better go. Come along, Bandit." He hurried across the parking lot with his dog trailing behind him.

Killian wondered what that was about, but when Emma stepped from her car, his thoughts scattered.

TWENTY

Captain Jack's Fine Dining
March 23
7:30 p.m.

Emma started toward him, her black coat billowing around her lithe body and her blonde hair gleaming under the lights.

Angel. His angel.

The message to move propelled him forward. "You're lovely."

"You don't look so bad yourself."

She grinned, and once again, he found her flirting, charmed him. It wasn't polished, but natural.

"This place is amazing."

Killian wrapped his arm around her waist and led her toward the door. "Good food and a romantic atmosphere, or so I'm told."

"Oh?" Emma hummed. "Is that your way of saying you haven't brought one of your floozies here?"

He grinned at her jealousy. "No, Doc. You're the first."

"Good to know, because I don't share."

They walked onto the ship, and she left her wrap in the coatroom.

The comment reminded him of Dylan asking if he was looking for Ms.

Sunday. It also reminded him of seeing her looking cozy with Tyler a time or two.

"Doc," Killian tugged her close enough to whisper, "neither do I."

"Share?" Emma lifted a brow. "With whom?"

"Tyler. You two looked mighty cozy at Molly's house last fall."

"Reade, party of two," the hostess called before he'd gotten the answer he wanted ... no, needed, to hear.

Emma's red dress showcased her firm behind, and with every step, it became a little harder to keep his eyes lifted.

Bloody hell!

"Your server will be with you shortly."

Emma leaned across the table, a mysterious smile playing along her mouth. "Now, Killian."

"Aye?"

"About Tyler."

Did he want to hear this?

"We're friends and ..."

But what type of friends?

"I helped him find a kitten for his daughter, Bethany."

"And?"

Her grin tugged at his heartstrings.

"Just friends. But shouldn't I be asking you about all your floozies?"

Killian brushed a kiss over her fingertips and glanced up underneath his brows. "I'm where I want to be."

Her gaze raised from their locked hands to clash with his, and heat rushed over him.

"You are?"

"I am."

"That's good, Killian," Emma whispered. "So am I."

The spell weaving around them was broken when the server cleared her throat several times.

"Are you ready to order?"

Killian winked, then ducked his head to study the menu. Emma went to his head. How was he to handle that?

As their meal continued, any residual doubts about dating Killian dissipated, and Emma fell more under his spell.

"You're not what I expected," she confessed when their salad plates were replaced with their main course.

"I'm not?"

"I don't think so."

"Isn't that a good thing?"

"Well, yeah." She hesitated for a beat before offering, "What I'm trying to say in my inept way is, I'm sorry."

"You're sorry?" His eyes crinkled. "About what, Doc?"

"For jumping to conclusions about you. It's just ..."

Should she tell him about her father?

The heat from his eyes held her captive. "What is it, Emma? Is it your father?"

"How?" she asked breathlessly.

He lifted that damned brow as if to say, '*Come on.*' "Open book, remember?"

Emma blew out a breath and took a proverbial step forward, which she hadn't expected. "My father is Peter Foster."

"Emma."

His husky voice tugged at something deep inside, and slowly, she glanced up. Killian's tender expression was unexpected. It caused her heart to flip several times and wove the strings between a little tighter.

"He's your father, Doc. That's all that's important."

His comment relaxed her, and before she second-guessed her decision, Emma shared. It wasn't an in-depth psychoanalysis, but it was something that felt right.

"What about your family, Killian?" she asked, hoping he would reciprocate. "I know you have one brother, but what about your parents?"

A look crossed his face, telling her his past held pain—just as hers.

If our past shapes us into the people we are, was it what drew us to each other?

"Never mind." Emma backed away. "It's not a big deal."

Killian reached across the table and took her hand. "It's important to me that you care."

"But your parents are off limits," she murmured, "just like the whole story behind your move to Swan Harbor.

Killian's face flushed, making her wonder if she'd pushed too far. But then a sheepish look crossed his face, and he ducked his head. "Old habits."

"Change is not always easy. We both know that."

"*Touché.* All it takes is meeting the right person."

He squeezed her fingers before letting them go and leaning back in his chair.

Boundaries.

"It's your typical broken home story." Killian's gaze drifted across the room, taking on a faraway look. "When my parents divorced, my mum went back to England, and we haven't heard from her since. But life goes on, right? And finally, Dad, Liam, and I are in a good place."

"Seems we've both made peace with our pasts," Emma murmured. "Is that what drew us to each other?"

"Just a lost girl finding a lost boy?"

"Or is it a lost boy finding a lost girl?" Emma countered.

"Do you believe that? That people change for someone else?"

Several expressions crossed her face while she pondered his question. Was she thinking about more than just their changes?

"I believe people can change *because* of someone else ... not *for.*"

Was that true? Had he changed *because* of Emma? Or had the changes started with Violet's death? Or were the changes from before?

"Have you heard from Elsa lately?" he asked when his thoughts were becoming too deep.

"Elsa? Why?"

Killian shrugged, thinking about his last conversation with Liam. "No reason, really. It's just ..."

"Just what?" She hesitated for a beat before replying, "I called her last week on my way home from Randy's. Again, why? Did Liam say something?"

Killian thought back on his conversation with Liam. His brother was cranky, something new since seeing Elsa.

"It was more what he didn't say," Killian replied.

"The next time I talk to Elsa, I'll ask." Then, a confused look crossed her face, and she once again dropped her gaze.

Killian glanced over his shoulder to find Captain Jack watching their table. As soon as their eyes met, the older man gave a faint bow and disappeared.

"What is it, Emma?"

Emma glanced up, her gaze immediately going over his shoulder.

"It's nothing." Except the tone of her voice told another story.

"If it upset you, it's something. Remember, sharing your burdens helps."

Her face lightened, and she giggled, sending his heart into overdrive.

"I saw Captain Jack," Emma whispered. "He acts like he wants to say something, but never does."

"Probably wants to ask if you've ever treated swans."

"Swans? Sadie said the same thing."

"There's one that shows up around April or May," Killian explained. "Beautiful bird, but he seems so alone."

"He?"

"According to Captain Jack."

The memory of the beautiful white bird swimming around the harbor, close to the ship, made him think of his life before Emma. How, even though company had been available, he'd still been alone.

"Swans mate for life," Emma murmured. "Maybe his died, and he's looking for another. He's pretty far north, though, so it's kind of odd."

"You like your job, don't you?"

"I do. But where did that question come from?"

"You."

"Me?"

"Aye, Doc. You. Tell me a story about Summer and her puppies."

"Summer and her puppies?"

"Any more strawberry incidents?" He lifted a brow in question.

"No," she laughed. "But ..."

While Emma talked, Killian couldn't look away. She was animated and practically glowed. So different from the woman he'd first met at Sally's.

"Are you ready to go?" he asked when she stopped to take a breath.

"I guess." Her smile faltered. "Is everything okay?

Killian signed the credit card slip and pushed it aside. "I need ..."

Emma licked her lips, and he began to doubt they were going to make it outside. He glanced around, thinking of a nook, a private room, a cabin, anywhere they could be alone.

"You need?"

"You, Doc," he whispered. "I need to kiss you, and I don't think you want it happening here unless we can find a quiet room."

Emma jumped up and tossed a sexy smile over her shoulder. "You coming?"

It was all Killian could do to maintain a little decorum and walk slowly. What he really wanted to do was race after her, toss her over his shoulder, and press her against the nearest wall.

Patience, Reade. Patience.

EMMA'S LIPS TINGLED WITH ANTICIPATION WHEN THEY LEFT THE restaurant. The tension between them was an almost palpable thing, bubbling just beneath the surface. It wouldn't be long before it pulled them under.

"Do you have a specific destination in mind?" she asked when Killian didn't immediately tug her into the shadows.

He squeezed her waist, tucking her a little closer to his side. "Let's go to my place. We'll have privacy. Besides, I didn't tell you about the gifts the kittens had waiting for me when I arrived home."

Could she trust him not to push for more than she was ready to offer?

He hadn't done or said anything untoward, and they had spent hours together at her place.

So maybe the real question was, *could she trust herself?*

Her phone buzzed, and sending him an apologetic look, she checked her message.

Damn. Not how she wanted to end the evening.

"Killian, I'm sorry, but this is an emergency." Emma pulled her professional cape out, unlocked her car, and tossed her purse inside. "Dinner was wonderful, thank you." Then, because she couldn't stop herself, she kissed him and climbed into her car. "I'll call you."

Emma realized how abrupt she sounded. Except, what waited ahead had her thoughts splintering. She wrapped her cloak a little closer around her and tightened the strings. It was going to be a long night.

With the Spanish galleon in her rearview mirror, Emma pushed everything away and focused on the task that lay ahead. Rene was losing her pet of almost thirty years. The pain she felt had to be indescribable. Right then, though, Emma's job as a veterinarian was to take care of Romeo. A medical diagnosis that caused a significant amount of pain—something that was being taken into consideration.

Without the ability to walk or run, his quality of life was a factor. *Romeo* was her primary concern. As an animal doctor, euthanization was a part of the field and not one to be taken lightly. She was relatively new to the profession and had only performed the procedure a handful of times. But the voluntary taking of a life hadn't gotten any easier.

Just an injection, and the animal went to sleep—pain-free. Even knowing it was best for her patient didn't stop the sick feeling in the pit of her stomach. Plus, because she was friends with the family, it added another layer to an already complex issue. What would her role be this time?

When she parked in front of the house, the lights around the barn were bright.

"You can do this." She grabbed her medical bag, a change of clothes, and started toward the barn.

Rusty met her before she reached the door. "I'm sorry about this, Emma," he sighed. "Rene checked on Romeo this evening and knew it was time. It's already hard enough, so ..."

"It's okay, Rusty," Emma sympathized. "Killian will understand when he finds out where I went."

He nodded slightly and led her toward the barn. "Roland's already in bed." A somber sigh escaped, but he said nothing else until just before they entered. "We just thought it would be easier, you know?"

"He's six, right?" At Rusty's nod, Emma continued, "Probably a wise decision. This way, you can explain it in your own words. Are you ready?"

"Is anyone ever ready to say goodbye to their pet?"

"No." She forced down the lump in her throat. "I could lie and say it's not a big deal. But it is and will be for quite some time."

"Rene's with him now." Rusty looked away, uncomfortable with his emotions. "I just wish I could make it easier for my family."

"Be there for her. Expect her to second-guess her decision. The pain will dim with time, but ..."

"Just love her," Rusty murmured.

"Your being there is what matters. Right now, though, I should change clothes. Heels and straw aren't a good mix."

Rusty left her in a small office, and when the door shut, Emma took several deep breaths. The need to lean on someone made her wish she'd told Killian where she was going. Even though she'd 'shared her burdens' regarding Captain Jack, it wasn't something that came naturally ... yet.

Maybe afterward, you could go by his apartment.

A few weeks ago, she would have scoffed at the thought. Tonight, though, she could fully admit one of Killian's hugs sounded pretty damn good.

Emma stripped off her date clothes, pulled on scrubs, boots, and her professional mask.

Never let them see you cry.

"Here we go." She squared her shoulders and stepped through the door.

Seventy feet of space separated her from where Romeo lay at the other end of the barn. As she walked, Emma focused only on placing one foot in front of the other. She knew her pace was slow, but with every step, she was that much closer to causing pain to people she called friends.

Emma could hear Rene crooning to the *Equus caballus* as if he were a child. His massive head lay draped over her legs, and she gently stroked the side of his muzzle.

"Rene," Emma whispered. "Are you sure?"

Rene glanced in her direction long enough for Emma to see the pain etched across her face.

"No," she breathed, her tears falling silently onto Romeo's hair. "But he's ready, aren't you, big guy?"

Emma gave Rusty a slight nod, placed her bag close to the horse's head, and pulled out her supplies. When she inserted the needle into the bottle, she met the eyes of her patient. The look in his served to calm her fears, assuring her she'd done everything she could, and he trusted her. *It's time,* they seemed to say. With that last thought, she slowly lifted the plunger, and the syringe began to fill.

The Langley Ranch
March 23

10:30 p.m.

Rusty's text, apologizing for interfering with his date, alleviated many of Killian's questions. Her quick departure had temporarily short-circuited his brain. Once he knew the reason she'd driven off—he'd gone after her.

When he entered the barn, Emma was bent over her medical bag. It wasn't until their eyes met he could see her true feelings.

I'm here.

He lost track of how long he stood watching, fighting the need to go to Emma. Instead, he waited for her to come to him. When she closed her bag and whispered a few words to Rene and Rusty, he held his breath.

Would she, or wouldn't she?

"Killian." Emma walked straight into his arms.

He folded her close, feeling the fine tremors running through her body. "Can you leave?"

"Yes."

"Come on." Killian led her from the barn, and with every step, he could feel her adrenaline letting down until she sagged against him. Once that happened, her knees buckled. He swung her into his arms and carried her straight to his car.

"But ..."

"Shush, Doc," he lightly scolded. "You're in no frame of mind to be driving. I'll get your car back to your place in one piece."

She nodded and closed her eyes, her ability to hold herself together, amazing him.

"I'll have you home shortly," he whispered.

The drive was quiet—so quiet, he kept checking to see if she'd fallen asleep. However, every time he glanced in her direction, her eyes were open, staring off at something only she could see.

"Here we are, love," the word slipped from his mouth, not because he'd forgotten her name, but because that's what she was ... his love.

Veterinarian Clinic

March 23
11:00 p.m.

EMMA FELT LIKE SHE WAS IN QUICKSAND—HER BRAIN AND BODY functioning very slowly, and all she wanted to do was sleep. It took some effort, but finally, she unlatched the seatbelt just as Killian opened her door.

"Thank you."

"Lean on me," he instructed, directing her toward her home. "Do you have your keys?"

She gave him the keys and, once the door opened, went straight to her office, where she stored her medical bag.

"I was ... happy to see you," Emma admitted shyly. "I should have told you where I was going—"

"—But sharing our burdens doesn't come easily, does it?"

"No," she sighed. "Plus, I knew it was going to be hard, but maybe next time."

"Oh, Doc." Killian tugged her into his arms. "We're a pair, aren't we?"

"Are we?" Her gazed with his. "A pair, that is?"

"In my mind, we've been a pair for quite some time."

Emma's knees threatened to give out, just not from a letdown of adrenaline. This time, it was all because of the man holding her. He took her breath away and made her feel so much she couldn't resist him. She carded her fingers through the silkiness of his dark hair and offered her mouth. It didn't take long for her to be completely lost in his kiss.

TWENTY-ONE

Veterinarian Clinic
April 12
9:00 a.m.

WHENEVER HER THOUGHTS WERE ALONE, MEMORIES OF BEING with Killian washed over her. They were on a journey together, but they weren't in a hurry to reach the finish line.

His kisses were tender one moment and steaming hot the next. When he touched her, the heat burning inside grew a little hotter, and her pulse raced a little faster. While they hadn't moved their relationship to the next step, it didn't stop her imagination.

Emma settled on the sofa next to Killian, the movie **Pretty Woman** *playing on the television.*

He draped his arm along the back of the sofa and periodically toyed with strands of her hair. Every time his finger brushed across her skin, the spark inside burned a little brighter.

"Look at him, Doc." Killian nodded toward the TV, where Edward was attempting to drive a stick shift. "His driving skills aren't worth shi—"

Emma crammed popcorn into his mouth. "Be nice."

"Hey, Doc," his pitch dropped, "I'm always nice."

She struggled to maintain some kind of distance between her and the potent attraction she felt for Killian Reade. Her pulse raced, and the fire inside burned a little hotter.

"Edward's one of you."

"One of me?"

"Aye, love." He whispered a butterfly kiss behind her ear, and the fire inside expanded. "He's a planner. Do you think he makes lists, too?"

Emma leaned away just enough to allow her blood to settle. "Don't knock my lists. It's important to know where you're going."

"Have you arrived?" Killian asked in a tone laced with an underlying question she didn't understand.

Their gazes clashed, and the look in his caused her heart to flip. The way his bottom lip glistened tempted her to taste. The way the low light from the television brought out the highlights in his hair and scruff made her want to touch. And the way his eyes were tender one minute, then quickly morphed into passion-filled, told her to throw caution out the window. How was she to fight such a potent combination?

You can't.

Killian must have read something in her gaze, as slowly he leaned toward her until their lips met. He tasted like salt and butter from the popcorn and something indefinably unique to him. Any reason keeping them from moving to the next level floated away. She relaxed back against the sofa, and his mouth worked its magic. Their labored breathing mixed with the sounds of the movie until, suddenly, there was silence.

Emma lifted her head and glanced at the quiet television. Edward's shirt was unbuttoned, exposing his chest. Unconsciously, her gaze went to the V at the base of Killian's neck. Several opened buttons showed a light dusting of chest hair that begged for her touch. Begged for her to bury her nose against his warm skin.

When Vivian's head disappeared from the screen, Emma held her breath, waiting for what came next.

"Come here."

He tugged her close, and their mouths crashed together with a force she hadn't expected. It wasn't sexy or tender, but raw and exciting. Except she couldn't get close enough.

Their kisses grew steamier, and their hands reached for places yet explored.

Killian pressed her a little firmer against the hard ridge behind his zipper, and their hips danced in a rhythm all their own.

She wanted more and dug her fingers into his taut behind. Suddenly, he leaned away and wrapped one hand around hers.

"Give me a minute here, Doc."

"But..."

"Bloody hell, Emma," Killian groaned. "You think I like blue balls?"

Emma leaned back enough for their eyes to meet. "Then why?"

"Emma!"

"What?"

"Where were you just now?" Sadie teased. "The look on your face says it was someplace very nice."

Emma's face flushed. "Nowhere! I was right here. Did you, uhh, did you need something?"

Instead of being put off by Emma's caustic tone, Sadie laughed. "Spoilsport."

"Sadie..."

Sadie giggled, but set a pile of papers on the desk. "Look at the first quarter numbers! You made a profit!"

"What?" Emma glanced through the papers that showed her first quarterly summary for the year. It wasn't much, but ... "This is good news, Sadie. Thank you. Is there anything else?"

"I completed your taxes, too." Another set of papers were set on the desk. "If you sign here and here, I'll take care of it before I leave."

"You answer phones, schedule, make coffee, *and* complete taxes?"

"Sure. My degree's in accounting."

"Wait," Emma frowned. "You're a Certified Public Accountant, and you're working for the pittance I pay you?" At Sadie's sheepish grin, she continued, "What gives?"

"Let's just say," a dreamy smile crossed Sadie's face. "Love rescued me from a life of dreary number crunching. Besides, I prefer fraud investigations, and there's not a big call for those in Swan Harbor. So, here I am."

"And I'm grateful. What am I going to do without you while you're on your honeymoon?"

"I have a suggestion."

"Just as long as it's not one of Killian's floozies ..."

Sheriff's Department
April 12
11:00 a.m.

AFTER ALMOST TWO MONTHS, KILLIAN STILL HADN'T FOUND THAT last elusive piece to the 'dog killer' puzzle. They had clues, but so far, none were enough to narrow their search—just not tire type or car color.

He'd hoped knowing the potential hair color would help. However, there were still too many names on the list. Bloody hell, even Amy and Dylan fit the profile. They had light hair and drove dark cars with the right winter tires.

Killian blew out a breath. "What are we missing?"

"It has to be right in front of our faces," Rusty grunted.

"One would think, but I just don't see it."

"Maybe it's because you're too tired," Rusty quipped. "Why is that? I thought your carousing days were behind you."

"The girls have decided the middle of the night is the best time to play," Killian sighed. "And they aren't happy unless I'm in the middle."

A loud noise had Killian immediately facing the door to see Dylan's wife giving him the evil eye. "Bloody hell, Molly. Did I forget to do something?"

"No," she snapped. "But what did you just say about your girls?"

"My girls?" Killian glanced at Rusty for help. But his blank stare said he was also in the dark. "What about my girls?"

Molly frowned. "I, I thought you were interested in Emma."

"I am."

"Then how can you be involved in," she lowered her voice, "those kinds of games with other women?"

"Those kinds of games?" Killian grinned, finally understanding her anger. "What kind of games did you think I was talking about?"

"You know," she lowered her voice, "sex games."

"Oh! That's what I thought you meant." Killian's smile grew when his boss came into view. "Don't tell me Dylan hasn't asked you to play sex games."

"Why, that's," she sputtered. "That's beside the point."

Dylan slipped his arm around Molly. "Do I want to know what's going on?"

Killian laughed when she said nothing. "Molly's concerned about my nightly activities. She doesn't think Emma would approve of my girls."

"Why wouldn't she approve?" Dylan questioned. "After all, she gave them to you."

Molly's gasp caused all three men to laugh. "I'm sorry, Honey. Killian's girls are his kittens, Trudi and Nina. Right?"

"Aye. Would you like to see their pictures?" Killian offered his phone.

"Oh, don't get him started," Rusty groaned on his way out. "He's like a new father."

"I'm sorry, Killian," Molly gave him a chagrined smile. "I jumped to the wrong conclusion."

"That's how gossip gets started."

"I really am sorry. I just ..."

"Was protecting your friend," he let that hang for a few seconds, "or was there another reason?"

Molly set the books she'd brought on his desk. "Emma's been so happy. I like seeing her that way."

Killian's heart flipped, and what felt like a sappy grin crossed his face. "I like seeing her that way, too."

"I'm glad." Molly rolled her eyes. "Again, I'm really sorry. I'll even let you choose which book to read to the class next time."

"Thank you. And Molly," he waited until she looked at him, "Emma is the *only* one I'm interested in. She has nothing to worry about."

"You're sure about that?"

"Positive."

"We're heading to the Beach Shack for lunch," Dylan offered. "Want anything?"

"No, thanks anyway. Since Gray's parents are back in town, I'm meeting Mary at Sally's.

"Mary and Clint are back in Swan Harbor?" Dylan smiled. "Good. Maybe they can hurry our house along, and we can move home."

"Wilby would love that," Molly exclaimed before she disappeared down the hall.

"Why is it you're meeting with Mary?"

"She was a big help last summer with the runaway teen case," Killian explained. "I thought maybe she could help me figure out the '*why*.'"

"Like a psychological profile," Dylan hummed, "that's a good idea."

"I'm not expecting much on the actual perp," Killian went on. "I'm hoping she can help me understand the perp better."

"Sounds good," Dylan replied. "Keep me posted. I'd better check on my wife. She's probably on the phone, giving Clint a hard time."

Killian slid the papers into the appropriate folders and locked them in his bottom drawer. If he were lucky, when he returned, he'd have an idea of where to go next.

Sally's Diner
April 12
12:30 p.m.

EMMA DROVE BY THE SHERIFF'S DEPARTMENT JUST AS THE GLASS doors were pushed open, and Killian walked out. It was a fight to keep going, but since Maggie was expecting her, she waved and pulled into Sally's parking lot.

Before she'd released her seatbelt, Killian opened her door, tugged her into his arms, and kissed her.

"What was that for?" Emma asked breathlessly.

"Can't a guy just kiss his girl when he wants?"

She kissed him again. "Anytime is fine with me. But I'm running late for a lunch date. Are you heading into Sally's for lunch?"

"I'm meeting Mary, Gray's mom. I'm hoping she can give me a few answers regarding our dog killer."

"The psychiatrist?"

"Aye."

"Still no leads?"

"No specific ones." Killian's blue eyes captured hers. "I promise you, Doc. I'm not giving up."

Emma studied his intense gaze. His brows were lowered, and the set of his jaw told her how much the case affected him. "I know you won't." She hugged him, taking a moment to enjoy his warmth. "Fingers crossed, Mary gives you some ideas."

Killian kissed the top of her head and led her into Sally's. "Thanks, Doc. I'll let you get to your meeting."

"See you later."

Emma squeezed his hand one last time before starting toward a booth near the back.

"Doc," Killian called before she'd gone far. "Do you have any plans after your last appointment?"

"No, why?" She wiggled her eyebrows suggestively. "Need me?"

Killian glanced around, as if making up his mind about something. It wasn't long before he wrapped her in his arms and dipped her into a swoonworthy kiss. "Always, Doc. I'll be at Giennie's waiting for you."

He was already across the room and in conversation with Mary before Emma gathered her wits. *Guess the cat's out of the bag.* She took another few steps and came face to face with a trio of Killian's discarded women.

"Emma," Chloe smirked. "He's quite the kisser, isn't he?"

"What?" Emma exclaimed, more shocked by the venom in the other woman's voice than by the words.

Morgan took a step closer. "She said he's quite the kisser, isn't he?"

Emma's gaze clashed with those of the third woman's. Instead of anger, Belle's showed sadness, embarrassment, and resignation.

"Excuse me." Belle pushed past and ran out the door.

"She doesn't like to share." Chloe shrugged. "But we don't mind, do we, Morgan?"

"Not at all." Morgan licked her lips, and her blue eyes narrowed. "He's man enough to handle all of us."

"At the same time," Chloe whispered. "A few adjustments might be needed to accommodate a fourth, though."

"Is there a problem, ladies?" Killian slid his arm around Emma's waist and tugged her against his chest.

"No, no problem." Morgan ran her long red nails down the sleeve of Killian's leather jacket. "We were just inviting Emma along the next time we get together, weren't we, Chloe?"

"Morgan's right," Chloe smirked. "Just inviting the new animal doctor to join us. Later, Lover."

Emma considered tripping them as they pushed past, but decided it wasn't worth it.

"You know that I," Killian began before Emma placed a finger over his mouth.

"I know, Killian," she assured him. "But while your kiss staked your territory, I wasn't about to strut around and start a fight over you. I'm not a female *Phalaropes*. I'll see you later."

She walked away with her head held high and slid into a booth across from a woman who appeared to be in her mid-sixties. "I'm sorry I'm late. I ran into a few pests."

Maggie barked out a laugh. "I saw that. Was that your young man? He's quite the hunk."

"Don't let him hear you say that. His ego is big enough already."

"Reminds me of my late husband," Maggie mused. "Looks to die for, but a heart of gold and totally devoted."

"How can you know that?"

"When he looked at you," Maggie offered. "It was as if you were the only woman in the room."

Maggie's comment gave her a warm feeling. Emma smiled. "Interesting. Maybe that's a conversation for another time. Tell me a little about yourself."

"I was Sadie's teacher at Swan Harbor High. Did she tell you that?"

"She did," Emma nodded. "Science, right?"

"Biology."

Emma learned Maggie Pierce moved to Swan Harbor over forty years ago as a new bride. Her husband, a Lobsterman, was away often, and she devoted her time to those she taught. While her life was full, and she loved her students, there was a need inside for more.

"More? Such as adoption?"

"You could say that," Maggie chuckled. "Just not what I think you mean."

"Not kids?" Then a light went off, and she remembered Sadie's recitation of Maggie's menagerie: *Equus asinus, Felis catus, Canis lupus familiaris*, and *Capra aegagrus hircus*. "Animals, right?" At Maggie's nod, Emma continued, "Sadie said you have a donkey, cats, dogs, and goats."

"And I just added a *Bos taurus*," Maggie laughed. "I can't turn away anything in need."

"A cow, too? But how do you handle all of those alone?"

"Are you considered a sanctuary of some kind?"

"I wish," Maggie sighed. "But it takes money."

The conversation reminded Emma of her mother's new endeavor. "You know, Maggie. I think we can help each other."

⚜

Sheriff's Department
April 12
6:00 p.m.

Several hours later, Killian was still thinking about Emma's comment when he'd staked his territory by kissing her. Was that what he'd been doing? While they hadn't been overt, in public at least, he'd assumed after their display at Randy's, everyone knew they were together. Had he subconsciously been showing Morgan, Chloe, and Belle he was involved with Emma?

Bloody hell, yes!

He could accept that. What about Emma's comment, though? A *Phalaropes* was a red-necked bird, and the females fought for the male's attention. Was she saying she *wouldn't* fight for him? Or was she saying she trusted him and knew he belonged to her? They'd grown close but hadn't taken the next step. What were they waiting for?

You'll know when you know, his inner voice reminded him. *It's all about timing.*

"What has you so deep in thought?" Rusty asked as he entered the room.

"Just thinking," Killian murmured. "I'm glad you're here, though. I spoke to Mary today, and she had some interesting things to say."

"Oh?" Rusty dropped into his chair and propped his feet on his desk. "Do tell."

"I hoped Mary could give us an idea why this was happening."

"And why it suddenly stopped," Rusty added.

"That too," Killian grumbled, annoyed at his partner's impatience. "One idea we discussed at length was whether the person had targeted dogs, *because* they were seeking attention.

Rusty frowned. "Could she give you any reason as to *how* killing a dog could gain someone positive attention?"

"No. Nor could she tell me why they suddenly stopped."

"Could it be *because* of a specific person?" Rusty suggested.

Killian frowned and unconsciously rubbed his thumb back and forth just below his bottom lip. "So they wanted to hurt one of the people whose dog was hit, and the others were decoys?"

"It makes sense."

"Mary also suggested the person may have stopped *because* they got what they wanted. Of course, it could be the opposite, as well. The person didn't get what they wanted, and they were regrouping."

Rusty grimaced. "Oh, damn."

"Aye. It's cocked up."

"Did she give us any good ideas?" Rusty retorted.

"Mary wondered why dogs were targeted but not cats. It reminded me of the farmhouse."

"The one where you and Emma rescued the kittens?"

Killian nodded and explained several things that seemed off when they'd entered the house.

"It was cold enough to freeze the balls off a brass monkey outside. But once we were inside, it was warm enough for the kittens to survive."

"That's the house with the bags of cat food, right?"

"Another unexplained situation," Killian acknowledged.

"Do we know who owns the house?" Rusty wondered aloud.

Killian shook his head, already thinking about the next step in their quest. "No. I spoke to Gray, whose company wants to purchase the land. Except without a name, they can't find anything in the Registry's Office.

"So, there's no way to track it down?"

"Not without a break." Killian glanced at the clock. "Look, it's late. You should get home to your family.

Rusty wasted no time in grabbing his coat and leaving Killian alone with his thoughts. There was a problem he needed to solve, but it wouldn't happen until the last piece was slipped into place. In the meantime, a *Phalaropes* was waiting for him at Giennie's Gym.

TWENTY-TWO

The Lighthouse Inn
May 4
3:00 p.m.

Emma sat next to Killian, their fingers laced, watching Sadie and Gray pledge their lives to each other. Since college, she'd been to friends' weddings, but then, she was either alone or with Elsa. Attending one with her boyfriend was a new experience, making her struggle with what to think and how to feel.

She surreptitiously glanced at Killian, curious about his thoughts. Was he like her, and when he'd been to a wedding in the past, the words were just sounds without a message? Sitting next to someone she cared for, though, felt different. She wasn't only just hearing, but listening to the words.

... To have and to hold from this day forward ....

What would that be like—to know someone was pledging to be beside you ... always? Would it feel heavy, as if you were carrying a huge responsibility? Or would it be freeing because you would never be alone?

Neither had parents nor grandparents with whom they could discuss marriage. Both sets divorced young, and while her father had remarried, he was still in the honeymoon phase. What did it take to make a marriage last?

... till death do us part.

Was that even possible? To be married to one person until one of you dies? If so, does the love between the two people remain the same? Or does it change?

What about her feelings for Killian? Did she love him? Or was it just infatuation? If she loved him, then how did she know if it was the *till death do us part* kind?

"I now pronounce you man and wife. Gray, you may kiss your bride," Judge Coleman intoned in his deep, booming voice.

Gray, never one to let an opportunity for a little public display go, kissed Sadie. The heat between the two was almost palpable. So much so, Emma expected to see fog on the windows.

"Would you say he's marking his territory, Doc?"

Emma frowned, wondering if she'd heard him correctly. "Marking his territory? You mean like a dog?"

"You told me I was 'marking my territory' when I kissed you at Sally's the other day," Killian murmured.

"Was I wrong?"

When he didn't answer right away, she half-expected him to deny it. Their relationship had taken a turn since their kiss at Sally's ... just not *that* turn.

"No," he whispered. "Should I apologize?"

"Would you if I said yes?"

"Bloody hell, of course!" Killian seated her at the table they'd been assigned. "But I wouldn't mean it."

"Good."

Killian slid his arm along the back of Emma's chair and brushed his thumb down her neck. At her cheeky smile, he nuzzled her temple. "Is that all you're going to say?"

"What do you want me to say?"

"That if the opportunity to 'mark my territory,' as you call it, arises, you don't have a problem with it."

"Okay." Emma nodded across the room to where Chloe, Morgan, Belle, and Catherine were looking for their table. "It might keep your floozies away today."

"I never dated Catherine," Killian felt the need to point out.

"Oh?" Both Emma's brows rose. "Should I ask why not?"

"Dylan."

"Warned you off, did he?"

"Something like that."

"Molly filled me in at Sadie's bridal shower," Emma went on. "But I really hope Sadie seated them on the other side of the room."

"If she didn't, are you prepared to act like a *Phalaropes* and fight them for me?"

"No."

"No?"

"No. I don't need to."

Killian's heart sank a little. "But ..."

"There's this."

Emma cupped his jaw and pressed her lips against his. Her soft touch reconfigured his confusion into electricity and sent his blood running south.

The passion that always flamed between them when they kissed was tempered, but it still spiked his pulse. Emma skimmed his bottom lip with her thumb, and if they had been anywhere else, he wouldn't have allowed it to end.

"Marking me, Doc?"

She slowly opened her eyes to meet his. "Is that a problem?"

Killian's chuckle was dark and dangerous. "You know better than that, Doctor Foster." He kissed her fingers. "I told you once, I always rise to the occasion."

The scrape of a chair had her turning away without answering. Except, every time someone new sat down at their table, he fought the need to grin. Within several minutes, Rene and Rusty, Amy and Shawn, and Ben and his date, Lilly Mason, were seated, leaving two chairs vacant.

"Who are we missing?" Killian nodded at the empty chairs.

Amy picked up the place card. "Harper Taylor."

"Captain Taylor's daughter," Killian added, relieved none of his past dates would be seated at their table.

He'd just begun to relax and enjoy being around his friends with Emma at his side when Harper entered the room.

"Bloody hell," he murmured when Tyler James seated Harper, then sat down next to her.

Killian tightened his hold on Emma's shoulder. When he glanced at her, it was to meet her twinkling eyes.

I know what you're doing, they seemed to say.

Oh yeah, and what are you going to do about it?

Emma stifled a chuckle at Killian's look and decided to *show* him exactly what she planned to do.

She slid her hand onto his thigh. His quads tightened, and their gazes clashed.

His look challenged her. *You wouldn't.*

Watch me.

The material of his tux pants was thinner than those of his usual denim. It allowed her to feel the warmth of his skin.

She squeezed.

Skimmed.

Tapped.

Rubbed and patted.

Emma kept a constant motion. She trailed her fingers up the inside and then down the center. Up the middle, then down the outside. Never stopping for long.

Killian's quick inhale had her glancing sideways at him.

You're killing me.

I know.

Have mercy on a man, Love.

Okay.

Emma had barely lifted her hand when Killian linked their fingers and pressed hers firmly onto his thigh.

"I like your touch. You have my permission to pick up where you left off later."

After being so close to him for so long, her nerve endings were hyperaware. Every touch, look and sound acted as a spark tossed in the center of kindling. The fire was ready to be ignited.

"Your permission, huh?" she forced out. "I'll remember that."

"See that you do."

His hot breath blew across her ear, sending a shiver straight down her spine. It lodged in her core and started a trembling that was a struggle to ignore.

See, Emma, her inner voice seemed to taunt. *Play with fire, and you just might get burned.*

Several hours later, Killian was leaning against the bar, waiting for Emma, and casually surveying the guests.

"Bloody hell, Rusty." He gestured to the crowd. "I never realized there were so many light-headed individuals in Swan Harbor."

"And many variations," Rusty noted as Clint and Mary danced by.

"I hadn't thought about that," Killian grimaced. "Clint's salt and pepper hair could just as easily match the clue as Mary's."

"And did you consider new blondes?" Rusty nodded toward where Audrey and Leroy were dancing. "I heard she wanted to see if blondes have more fun."

"I really didn't need to hear that."

"When you're at a wedding and working, you shouldn't look at everyone as if they're our perp. Go dance with Emma."

"She's busy helping Sadie get ready to leave or something like that."

"So, the only way for you to keep busy is to scan the group for our mystery person?"

"And?" Killian's brows arched. "What else would I do?"

"Dance?"

"I don't see you dancing while Rene's busy," Killian grunted. However, since he was only interested in holding Emma, he turned back to the room to see Mary and Sydney approaching the bar.

"Nice wedding," Killian remarked.

"It is," Mary smiled. "I wasn't sure we'd get everyone home, but we did."

Killian followed her line of sight to where her sons, Gray and Cameron, were deep in conversation with Clint.

"Are Jessie and Cameron staying long?"

Since Killian was subleasing their apartment, he wondered if he'd need to find a new place to live.

"Unfortunately, no. They're leaving for Africa tomorrow. However, I didn't interrupt to talk about my family." She gently touched Sydney's arm. "Since I've been back, we've been working on his memory."

"That's great." Killian hesitated. "Any luck?"

Mary nodded. "A little. But Sydney, why don't you tell them?."

"I keep having these flashes of Buster," Sydney began.

"It's not a good memory, is it?" Killian guessed.

"No," Sydney sighed. "I hear Buster yelp and run to help him, but there's someone bent over his body. And that's it. The image fades before I can really examine it."

"You can't tell who it is?" Rusty asked.

"Not really," Sydney admitted. "I can't tell you if it's a man or woman, or if they spoke, or ..."

"Is there anything else?" Killian pushed. "Anything at all?"

"I think they were wearing a hat or scarf on their head." Sydney exchanged a look with Mary. When his attention returned to Killian, surprise raced across his face.

"You remembered something else, didn't you?" Mary murmured.

"I could see hair." Sydney's eyes sparked. "Light. The person had light-colored hair."

Killian sent Rusty a dangerous smile. *We're getting closer.*

"You've been a big help, Sydney. Thank you."

"We're going to catch this person," Rusty added. "Please let us know if you remember anything else."

"Thank you, Mary," Killian's gaze went back to the doctor. "You've been a big help."

"Let me know if you have any other questions," Mary told them before leaving to be with her family.

"We're close, Rusty," Killian murmured. "Just a few more pieces." Some subtle change in the air pulled his attention across the room to where Emma had just returned. His breath caught, and he couldn't get to her fast enough. "Now, though, I'm going to take your advice and go dance with my lady."

"There's a first time for everything," Rusty muttered. "Enjoy your dance."

Emma's smile was sexy and just a little mysterious as he started toward her. He wanted her touch, and if he had his way, that wish would come true before the night was over.

Bloody hell, he wanted her. His balls tingled, a shiver raced up his spine, and that invisible current connecting them grew stronger.

"Hi."

"Dance?"

He didn't give her a chance to answer, but pulled her into his arms and whisked her away from the others.

"Did you miss me?"

"Always." Killian tucked her a little tighter against his chest. "We'll talk about it later, though. Right now, I just need to hold you."

"Just hold me?"

"Not hardly," he growled. "However, until it's considered appropriate for us to leave, I'll just have to settle."

EMMA RELAXED AGAINST HIS CHEST. "WORKS FOR ME."

The ever-present electrical current between them ignited, creating sparks across every nerve ending. Sparks she wanted to feel and not explore. Her scientific mind, though, had other ideas and set up a simple hypothesis.

If Emma and Killian touch, then an electrical current shall be felt every time.

The spark was there ... and it was hot. So hot, her thought processes were sluggish, and her wayward thoughts started down a path that very well could get them in trouble.

She pressed a kiss to the soft skin of Killian's neck, just above his collar. His quick inhalation said more than words. Their thoughts were aligned.

"How much longer do we need to stay?" Killian whispered.

"Why? I thought this was what you needed."

"But, Doc," he purred, "my needs have grown."

"Oh?" She shivered as her girly parts began to dance.

"Aye."

"You don't like dancing?"

"Oh, dancing is just fine, Doc." Killian tilted his head until their eyes met. "But a few other ideas are becoming more important."

Emma grinned. "Are they only ideas, Killian?"

"That's what I said."

"I'm not sure I'm interested in ideas."

Killian's eyes flared. "No? Then what would interest you?"

"Actionable ideas."

"Oh, I would be up for that."

"Really?" She kissed the underside of his chin. "Care to give me a preview?"

His brow arched, and his eyes darkened. "Gladly." He kissed her, but the kiss wasn't one meant to take deeper—it was one meant to tease. "I'd start with something like that and then see where it goes."

"I think I'd be up for that."

Killian chuckled, and the sound rippled across her skin. Her nipples beaded, and a part of her wanted to drag him off the floor. Then, from the corner of her eye, she noticed Sadie and Gray saying their goodbyes.

"It looks like they're ready to leave."

"Bout bloody time," Killian whispered as they followed everyone outside.

Through the shower of birdseed, the newlyweds ran toward their get-a-way car. Sadie held her bouquet aloft. "Ready?" she cried, her gaze catching Emma's.

Did she want the bouquet?

No!

Yes!

Maybe!

Emma hadn't decided what to do when Sadie tossed the bouquet directly to her. Before she tried to catch it, someone shoved her aside.

"I caught it!" Audrey shouted with a big smile. "Sorry, Emma, but my man needs a bigger push than yours."

"You go, girl," Emma grinned. Inside, though, she struggled to decipher her feelings. *Sadness?* No. *Disappointment?* Maybe. *Confusion?* Definitely.

When she glanced over her shoulder to find Killian watching her, any thoughts but being alone with him faded. She laced their fingers. "Take me home."

The heat in his eyes made promises, causing her knees to shake.

"Let's go, Doc."

Almost by mutual agreement, their conversation on the way home steered far from the intimate. They talked about the wedding, conversations they'd overheard, and Aruba—where Sadie and Gray were going for their honeymoon.

The tension in the car didn't lessen much until Killian said he'd spoken to Sydney. It left Emma to ponder why someone would stand over Buster's body.

Were they trying to help him?

Possible, but why deliberately run over a dog and then decide to help? That made no sense.

Were they making sure he was dead?

Maybe. If he wasn't, that could have explained the tire tracks over the dog's body. But again, why? There wasn't evidence indicating the same thing hadn't happened before.

"Emma," Killian's tense voice raised her awareness of where they were. "Why are there lights on in your clinic?"

"Maybe I forgot to turn them off. I'm sure it's nothing." She was on her way inside before the engine completely died.

"Doc, wait."

Emma waved him off as being overprotective and continued toward the front door. But before she could open it, Killian wrapped a firm arm around her waist and pulled her back against his warm body.

"Hold on. Don't go off half-cocked."

The site of his 38 had her rethinking her actions. "Why?"

That was when she realized the door was ajar. But had someone forgotten to close it completely, or was there an intruder?

"Millicent." Emma's blood ran cold with fear. "I need ..."

"To calm down." Killian shoved her behind him and pushed the door open a little wider. "Come on."

When they stepped inside, the hairs on the back of Emma's neck stood up. She tightened her fingers in the back of his jacket and looked around.

"Killian, someone's here, or Millicent would have met us at the door."

"Go call Dylan."

"No! I'm not leaving you alone."

He gave her a dirty look and led the way toward her office. The sight caused a lump to lodge in her throat and made it hard to breathe.

Someone had destroyed the room. Filing cabinet drawers were empty, and her desk was swept clean. Empty cages were upended, and her go-bag of medical supplies were spread on the floor.

Killian tugged her against his side, but whether it was for comfort or to keep her from doing something stupid, she wasn't sure.

"Do you hear that?"

She nodded, but couldn't discern what she was hearing. The sounds were confusing. There was a rhythmic pattern to them—hums instead of banging and a melody instead of silence.

They moved closer to the door leading to the surgical wing. Emma tightened her hold on Killian's hand, and with every step, her fear climbed a little higher.

He pressed his palm on the door and slowly pushed it open. Suddenly, a cat meowed, causing her nerve endings to stand straight up.

Emma's panicked eyes met Killian's, and without thinking about her safety, she ran inside.

"Millicent!"

TWENTY-THREE

Swan Harbor General Hospital
May 9
5:00 p.m.

Killian stepped into Swan Harbor General Hospital six days later. He'd decided it was time to find the answers instead of running from them. Maybe if he could get his thoughts organized, he could explain them to the woman who held his heart.

He took a deep breath and rapped three times on Doctor Mary Hunter's office door.

Strangely enough, when Mary opened the door, her expression did show surprise.

She stepped aside and invited him in. "I was wondering when I'd see you, Killian."

"You were? Why?"

"I'm assuming you have questions similar to Emma's."

Emma was here? You stupid git, of course, Emma was here.

"And what question is that?" Killian grumbled, reminded yet again of his many shortcomings.

Mary raised a brow as if to say, '*Oh really, you're going there?*' making him instantly regret his outburst.

He brushed his hand through his hair and tried again. "I'm sorry. It's just ..."

"Come sit." Mary indicated the sofa. "Talk to me."

"I know our actions often have consequences," Killian began. "But was it my actions that caused the ... situation?"

Mary sighed sympathetically. "That's what I thought had you worried. But no. It's not your fault."

"Are you sure? I didn't—"

"Killian," Mary replied. "I'm sure. However, before we wade into the weeds too deeply, I must remind you of patient confidentiality laws. Therefore, I can only say so much."

"I understand. I would appreciate any insights you have that might help me make sense of everything."

Mary smiled, which somehow relaxed him.

"Emma pushed past you and ran into the room first." Mary took him back to that night.

"Aye. It frightened me," Killian sighed. "Then I glanced around and realized what I was seeing and hearing wouldn't connect."

"Tell me."

It didn't take much for Killian to drop back into the memory. The fear, confusion, and frustration from that night were there ... waiting.

"Killian?" Emma's confused voice penetrated the fog from what he saw.

He tugged her back enough to whisper. "Emma, get Millicent and go call Dylan."

"But ..."

"Please. I'll be alright."

Once Emma started toward Millicent's cage, Killian took several steps in the direction of the intruder. Who was she? Why was she wearing Emma's typical work uniform? White tennis shoes and pink scrubs, topped by a long white medical coat, and her blonde hair tied into a ponytail. Strangely enough, the intruder's demeanor was calm, almost as if she were at home. How else could he explain her behavior?

Killian hesitated, taking stock of how calm the black cat on the table in front of her appeared, comfortable with whose hands were stroking its fur. At her feet, several more cats wound around her legs as if waiting for their turn. That they trusted her meant something. Right?

"Can I help you?" He took another few steps.

"Oh, hello, the woman greeted him in a voice that sounded familiar—yet different." She picked up the black cat and turned to face him. "Doesn't he look pretty?"

For the first time, she lifted her head, and their gazes clashed.

Killian struggled to make sense of what he was seeing. "Bloody hell! What the ...?"

"Oh, I'm sorry," the woman continued. She put the cat down and brushed at the black fur sticking to the front of her coat. "We've not been formally introduced, but I've heard so much about you. I'm Doctor Emma."

He barked out a laugh. "Doctor Emma?" Killian spit out, and the feeling he'd somehow cocked up rushed through him. "You're not Emma Foster!"

*"Okay." 'Doctor Emma' smiled indulgently. "But isn't that who **you** want me to be?"*

Killian frowned, his thoughts still trying to catch up with what was in front of him. "Why pretend to be Emma?"

*'Doctor Emma's' smile turned coquettish, her body language became flirty and more relaxed. She sashayed closer, her mannerisms not wholly foreign to him. "Oh, silly. I think **you** know why. It wasn't my plan, but we wanted her to be happy."*

She stepped closer and started to touch him. Her perfume turned his stomach, reminding him of the few evenings they'd spent together.

"Don't touch me." Killian grabbed hold of her wrist, his voice icy. "What in the bloody hell are you playing at now?"

"Lacey! My name is Lacey," she said each word carefully. "I'm the one in charge. If you have any questions, you ask me."

The way she crossed her arms, cocked her hip, and smirked reminded him he'd also seen that behavior before.

"What are you doing? Can't you take a hint? I don't want you. There! Is that plain enough?"

'Lacey's' expression crumpled, and once again, the woman's appearance altered. Her head dropped, her shoulders rounded, and her chin trembled. "I

told her it wasn't a good idea," she sniffed, her voice no longer confident and flirty but timid and childlike.

"Stop it, Belle!" Killian demanded. "What are you talking about now?"

"I'm not Belle!" The woman shook her head sadly. "I'm Lori. This was all Lacey's idea, and now it's all ruined, and we'll have to go away."

Killian glanced over his shoulder to see Dylan standing just inside the room. "Emma said there was an intruder. But why's Belle dressed like Emma?"

The woman's chin lifted. "My name is Lori. Lacey is pouting because she knows I'm going to spill everything."

Killian's eyes met Dylan's. "Maybe she's had too much to drink."

"Does Belle do drugs?"

"I'm right here," 'Lori' mumbled. "But no! We do not do drugs."

"Your turn," Killian said to Dylan. "I'm tired of her games."

"You aren't asking the right questions." 'Lori's' voice took on a sing-songy quality.

"No?"

"No," 'Lori continued. "I gotta secret."

Dylan took several steps closer to Belle. "Okay, I'll bite. What's your secret?"

She pursed her lips and placed her finger over them. "Shh, don't tell anyone, but I know who hit poor Wilby."

Before hearing Dylan's dog's name, Killian's attention had wavered. However, the possibility of finding that last piece of his puzzle had him moving closer. "You know who hit Wilby?"

"It was Lacey." Lori seemed to shrink. "It just made me sick. But she thought it would keep the new veterinarian busy so Belle could spend time with you."

The way her blue eyes pleaded with him made him nauseous.

"You're telling me Belle killed those dogs," Killian bit out, "for me?"

"Not Belle," she corrected, "Lacey. Except you still wanted Emma. That's when I convinced Lacey to allow Doctor Emma to join us. We wanted Belle to be happy."

She picked up one of the cats and rocked it slowly. A few seconds later, she began to sing the same song from when he'd arrived.

"Killian, I know what you're thinking, and this wasn't your fault."

"But," Killian cut another glance in the woman's direction. "How do you explain that?"

"This is bigger than we can handle. I'm going to call Mary."

Killian returned to the present, his thoughts just as chaotic as when he'd arrived. "And you know the rest."

"I do. But even knowing it wasn't your fault, you still have questions. Am I right?"

He'd spent the week comparing his actions with Belle versus those with Tia, Chloe, or Morgan. While he'd realized he hadn't treated one woman any differently, he still didn't understand why everything.

"What's D.I.D.?"

"Where did you hear that term?"

"I overheard some nurses talking," Killian admitted.

A look of exasperation crossed Mary's face. "I see. It seems another talk about patient confidentiality is warranted."

She paused for a minute, making Killian think she was trying to decide how to parse out her words.

"D.I.D.," Mary began, "stands for Dissociative Identity Disorder. It's the ultimate cloak, or mask if you will."

"Wait a minute." Killian grabbed onto the cloaking comment, especially since he'd been on a journey to shed his. "The ultimate cloak? So, it's a way of hiding the person beneath?"

"In a way," she acknowledged. "When someone has D.I.D. or multiple personality disorder, their identity has split. It usually happens to protect them from an emotional trauma."

"Was Belle aware she had D.I.D.?"

Mary grinned. "This isn't about Belle. I'm speaking in generalities."

"Understood," Killian nodded. "So, in *general*, does the person know about the others?"

"Alters," she clarified. "The person with the disorder has alters. As far as your question is concerned. Some know, others suspect, and many have no idea. Every case is unique."

While Mary talked, Killian worked to filter through the pieces of information.

"If I understand this correctly, you're saying the disorder occurs to hide the person from something, and the alters are the masks."

"That's one way to look at it. Typically, the alters have their own 'purpose'... some are stronger, others are shy.

The alters Killian met *had* been different. Lacy appeared confident, a planner, and a flirt. He suspected she'd been the one hanging onto his every word at Randy's the last time he'd been there.

Whereas the one who shared the secrets, Lori, was a little shy but calmer, a peacemaker and caretaker. Had he seen her before? Was she the one he'd called Emma? Or was that Belle?

"Why Doctor Emma?" That alter had taken was imitating someone else.

Mary's brown eyes sparkled as if to say, '*People better than you have tried.*' "What does Emma do?"

"Treats animals," Killian murmured, thinking about the hair found under Buster's body. It had matched the blonde wig Belle had been wearing. "So ostensibly, one alter hit the dog."

"And the other tried to fix it," Mary added.

He had his answers, but it was still difficult to wrap his head around. How was it possible for several personas to live inside one person, and no one knew it was going on?

"What is it, Killian?"

"If Belle," he held up his hand to stop Mary from interrupting him, "has D.I.D, and no one knew she needed help, then how can we be sure the people we meet are who they say?"

A slight grin crossed Mary's face before she relaxed and gave a subtle nod.

"That's a fair question. After everything that's gone on around you, it makes sense for you to wonder. But you are a son, brother, friend, investigator, boyfriend ..."

"I'm afraid I've been a total cockwomble when it comes to being a boyfriend," Killian responded wryly.

"Cockwomble?" Mary laughed. "That's a new one."

"It means I'm a moronic idiot," Killian grinned. "It's one of my father's favorite words."

"Cockwomble," Mary snickered. "I'll have to remember that the next time Clint is in the doghouse."

Killian laughed. "I'll apologize the next time I see him."

"Oh, don't worry about him. We've been married a long time."

Killian knew little about longevity in a relationship. He wanted to learn, though, with Emma.

"To continue with my point, here's a simple way to think about it," Mary went on. "Because alters usually serve a specific purpose, they truly are like masks. They come and go when needed. When Killian Reade needs to function as an investigator rather than a friend, you don't become someone different. You put on your professional hat and go to work."

Which was how he remained detached when dealing with an accident.

"Hats," Killian repeated, liking the simplistic way of viewing how people moved through their daily lives. Not always using a 'cloak' to shield, but a mask to handle the task at the moment.

"I'll let you get back to work. Thank you for your time."

"I'm glad I was here," Mary replied. "Call if you have any more questions."

Killian said goodbye and left the hospital feeling lighter than when he'd arrived. So much so that as soon as he reached the parking lot, he pushed the 'Emma' button.

"Hello," her sweet voice came across the line, except it held fatigue—most likely because of him.

"Hi, Doc," Killian murmured huskily. "I'm sorry I've been such a cockwomble."

When Emma laughed, he immediately relaxed.

"If that means you're sorry you've been such a jerk, then yes, you have," she confirmed. "But don't think I'm letting you off the hook that quickly."

"No?" The *Rhopalaceras* in his gut took flight.

"I'm expecting some serious groveling."

The butterflies landed and a warm place grew in the vicinity of his heart.

"I think that can be arranged." Killian took a deep breath and plunged forward. "Mary said you'd stopped by."

Veterinarian Clinic
May 9
6:15 p.m.

EMMA LET GO OF THE BREATH SHE WAS HOLDING, KNOWING THERE was only one way he would have learned that.

"I did. You too?"

"Aye, love," he admitted. "I thought I …" his voice trailed off as if he wasn't sure what else to say.

"You were worried you'd caused Belle's problems," Emma replied. "Did Mary assure you her issue began a long time ago?"

"She did, but how did you know about Belle? About her ... issues?"

"Leroy," Emma sighed. "Audrey works at the hospital, and ..."

"The hospital is a hotbed of gossip."

"I tried not to listen," Emma giggled. "But my boyfriend was being a cockwomble."

"Aye, Doc. That he was." Killian went on almost shyly. "I was wondering. Would you go out with me tomorrow night? If you like, we can talk more."

Her heart took off like a herd of *Equus caballus*, making her breathless. "I'd like that, but just be prepared to grovel."

"Don't worry, Doc. I know what I need to do."

"Bye, Killian."

"Bye, Doc. I miss you."

Before she could respond verbally, the line went dead, so she sent a quick text.

> Emma: I miss you too.

His response caused the butterflies to swarm. After a week apart, with only limited conversation, she'd thought a lot about what he meant to her. About what they meant to each other. He not only gave her the courage to remove her cape, but he filled those empty spaces in her life. Empty spaces she'd not known needed filling.

"You look happy." Maggie startled her, almost causing her to drop her phone. "I'm sorry. Were you thinking of your young man?"

Emma laughed at Maggie's nosiness. "Yes, mother. We're going out tomorrow."

"That's nice." A dreamy look crossed Maggie's face. "I do enjoy a good love story."

"It's been a slow burn one, but ... I think you might be right."

"I know I'm right," Maggie winked. "Just make sure to be safe."

Emma's mouth dropped open, unsure if she heard what she thought. Then she got a good look at the twinkle in Maggie's dark eyes. '*Yes, you did.*'

"We haven't," Emma sputtered before realizing she didn't need to spill her sexual history to her office help.

"Well, okay then," Maggie laughed. "But I am a science teacher, so ..."

"I'll remember that," Emma muttered, "and make sure I'm prepared."

She doesn't have to know you're on the pill.

"It's always important to be prepared," Maggie quipped. "Anything else?"

"Not—" Then she remembered Maggie's question regarding an abused horse. "Is Rene going to help you with Ruari?"

Maggie grinned. "Not only is she going with me to pick up Ruari, but she's giving him her barn. I think she's excited about having a horse around again."

"I thought she might be."

"You're having dinner with Molly tonight, aren't you?"

"I am," Emma grimaced. "She'll have a lot of questions about what happened."

"And you're afraid you don't have all the answers."

"I know I don't."

"Tell her what you can. She won't push."

"Oh, I know," Emma hummed. "Might be a night for ice cream."

"Isn't every night a night for ice cream?" Maggie laughed.

Sheriff's Department
May 9
6:30 p.m.

HEARING DYLAN CALL HIS NAME CUT THROUGH THE FOG surrounding Killian.

"What are you doing here so late?"

"I traded shifts with Eric," Killian explained. "I met with Mary earlier and wasn't sure how long it would take."

He signed the last form, stuck it into the dog killer case file, and handed it to Dylan.

"That's definitely the strangest case I've ever solved. I just wish ..."

Dylan straddled a chair close to the desk and glanced through the file.

"Did Mary explain that Belle's issues weren't your fault?"

"Aye."

"Did you make promises to Belle?"

"We'd only been out a couple of times and never to my apartment until that night." He blew out a breath. "It's all just so bloody mind-bending."

"That, I can agree on. But that's not why I stopped by. Look what came in the mail." Dylan tossed a large envelope on top of the desk.

Killian slid several 8" x 10" glossy pictures from the envelope. "Bloody hell. Where did these come from?"

"Krystal found another file of the night in question. It ended up in a different folder or something."

Killian flipped through the photos, knowing if he hadn't seen it with his own eyes, it wouldn't have made sense. There were three pictures—each with a time-stamp seconds apart. One showed Belle, dressed as Doctor Emma, behind the wheel of a car. A second had her getting out of the car, and in a third, she was kneeling next to Shawn's fallen dog. The facial expressions in each image were completely different.

"Lacey," he pointed to the picture of the person driving. "Lori ... or maybe Doctor Emma, here and here." He indicated the last two. "It confirms what I surmised when speaking to Mary. One hit Buster, and one tried to heal."

"At least we know, right?" Dylan sighed.

Killian stuck the photos in the case file. "Will do. Is there anything else before I head back out on patrol?"

Dylan picked up the children's book lying on Killian's desk. "Let me guess. Nighttime reading for Trudi and Nina?"

"Hardee har har," Killian proclaimed. "Trudi and Nina are into Doctor Seuss."

"*One Fish, Two Fish*?"

"*The Foot Book* is more their style," Killian shot back.

He frowned, realizing how eerie it was that several of the books he'd read to Molly's class aided his journey.

"What is it?" Dylan asked soberly.

"I was just thinking how *Small Knight and George,*" he tapped the book, "paralleled Belle's case."

Dylan frowned. "How so?"

"Neither George nor Belle were exactly what they seemed. It's somewhat disconcerting," Killian continued, "and makes me rethink the people in my life."

"And Emma?"

Killian couldn't hold back his smile. "I don't need to wonder about my feelings for Emma."

"And?"

"I can't tell you before I tell her, now can I?" he winked. "Besides, I have some groveling to do first."

"Good luck with that," Dylan chuckled. "You know women."

TWENTY-FOUR

Sally's Diner
May 9
8:00 p.m.

MOLLY PUSHED HER PLATE ASIDE AND LEANED FORWARD ON THE
table. "Talk to me about Belle."

"You did that on purpose." Emma mimicked Molly's pose. "Start with the
idle chitchat, and then boom, go for the jugular."

"Oh, come on," Molly laughed. "I'm not that bad. Am I?"

"You know what happened."

"Well, yeah," Molly hummed. "You're a doctor, though. Surely you
understand better than I."

"But I don't work with people," Emma pointed out. "My patients are
what you see is what you get. A dog's a dog—a cat's a cat—etcetera, etcetera."

Emma was sure the look Molly gave her made the first graders in her class
nervous.

"Have you ever known anyone with multiple personalities?"

"I'm assuming you're not referring to Lisa, who behaved one way with me
but another way with the cute boy in our class?" Molly arched a brow,

pushing Emma to continue, "How about Shannon, who was my friend to my face and then stole my idea for my senior thesis?"

"You know what I'm asking," Molly murmured. "I'll understand if it's too hard to talk about."

Did she want to talk about it? Yes, and with Sadie away, talking to Molly made sense.

"Alright," Emma gave in. "However, if we talk, I'm going to need chocolate."

"Deal!" Molly grabbed the server, Peyton. "One Double Brownie Fudge Sundae, please. Now talk."

⁂

Sheriff's Department
May 9
8:30 p.m.

KILLIAN PULLED INTO THE DEPARTMENT PARKING LOT, ALREADY making plans for his evening. There'd be a little groveling, a little talking, and, if he was lucky, a whole lot of kissing.

Don't get ahead of yourself.

He wasn't. Just wishful thinking.

Grovel first. Kisses later.

"I know." Killian pulled open the door just as Dylan was leaving.

"Whoa," Dylan exclaimed. "Who's raised your ire?"

"Sorry, Mate," Killian sighed. "Just been a tough week."

"I get that. But if you're already back, it must have not been too bad out there."

It took Killian a minute to realize he was being asked about the patrol. "I'm sorry. I traded a future shift with Brian. Decided there was something I needed to do that couldn't wait."

"And would this involve Emma?"

"Perhaps," Killian grinned. "I've behaved like a right git this week, so ..."

"I've been there," Dylan shared. "Flowers and candy work."

"Ice cream," Killian grinned. "Then maybe a movie."

"You're learning." Dylan motioned across the street. "Emma met Molly at Sally's. You could take her dessert."

"Emma's at Sally's?"

"She is," Dylan laughed. "And if I know my wife, she's pestering Emma about last weekend."

"That's good to know. Thanks."

Killian hadn't gotten far when his phone buzzed.

> Dylan: Use protection.

"Bloody hell!"

Good thing he'd taken care of that when he was in New York. If not, it would have been broadcast around town before he'd even made it back home.

"Talking to yourself again, Reade?" teased Walter Manning, the evening Desk Sergeant.

"You caught me, Manning," Killian laughed. "How's it hangin'?"

"Long and loose and full of juice," rolled off Walter's tongue with nary a consideration of who might hear.

"What?"

Walter chuckled. "Got me a new girl. Been getting me some. How about you?"

"I don't kiss and tell."

"Your missus probably appreciates that," Walter chuckled.

The phone rang, taking Walter's attention, giving Killian a moment to make a quick change and slip out a door.

The lights from Sally's were the beacon that drew him across the street. When his gaze landed on Emma, she was laughing. He wanted nothing more than to rush inside and pull her into his arms. If he did so, what kind of reception would he receive?

Sally's Diner
May 9
8:45 p.m.

Emma licked the chocolate off her spoon and dropped it on her plate. "Why did we eat that again?"

"Because you needed chocolate courage to talk about the Belle situation."

"I'm trying to learn to share my burdens more." Emma shrugged. "It's just not easy."

"Being vulnerable never is." Molly scooped up another bite of ice cream. "Are you done?"

At the last minute, Emma dug her spoon into a gooey lump. A movement outside caused her to hesitate before she shoved it into her mouth.

"If you're not going to eat it, I will," Molly teased.

Almost by rote, Emma shoved the bite into her mouth, her gaze finally returning to her companion.

Molly narrowed her eyes with concern. "Emma? What is it?

"Killian."

Molly grinned. "He's waiting for you."

"But why?"

"Well, duh," Molly clucked. "Go get him."

Should she?

"Go," Molly encouraged.

"Okay. I'll pay on my way out.

"I've got it. Just practice safe ..."

"Driving," Emma interrupted. "I will, Mother."

With not one but two women reminding her to practice safe sex, Emma was tempted to look around. Was there a sign that read, 'Ready for sex?' following her around?

She pushed the door open and lightly touched the back of Killian's neck when she sat down. "Are you waiting for someone?"

"Perhaps. How was your chocolate confection?"

"How did you know I ate chocolate?"

Killian skimmed his thumb along her lower lip and held it aloft. "See, chocolate," he replied before licking it off.

That was all it took for Emma's imagination to take off.

"The chocolate was good. If you had gotten here earlier ..."

When Killian didn't jump in with one of his well-placed innuendos, Emma looked a little closer. He was tense, his expression somber. Was he still worried that he was somehow responsible?

"Killian? What's going on?"

"Nothing, Doc."

Emma lifted a brow and waited. It was several minutes before he kissed her fingertips and closed her hand between his.

"I came for you."

"But?"

"I was trying to decide the best way to approach you."

"How to approach me?" She frowned. "Why would you have to think about that?"

Their eyes met, and the message hidden in his had her locking her legs to keep her butt on the chair.

Oh, mama! I am in so much trouble.

"I'm sorry, Doc." Killian's soft voice touched something deep inside. "I've pushed you more than once to share your burdens, and yet ... I've failed to share mine."

While Emma wasn't sure Sally's was the best place for their conversation, with the genie out of the bottle, it couldn't be put back.

"Oh, Killian. I want to lie and say it didn't hurt. To say I would have behaved differently, but ... I can't." Her voice broke. "What I can say is, I get why you thought what you did."

"That's all you're going to say?"

"Yes."

"No promise not to do it again, or want me to sign in blood?"

Emma smiled. "If you promised, you'd just break it someday."

"Doc." Killian tightened his hold on her hand and leaned in a little closer. "I really am sorry, and I'll try not to let you down."

"And I'll do the same. But ... we're humans, and we aren't perfect."

"Is that your subtle way of saying you only find perfection with *Animalia*?"

She dimpled. "You know me so well."

"I'm working on it, Doc. But there's still much for me to learn. And," he popped the D, and a puff of air landed on her lips. "I'm sure going to love doing it."

The heat from his eyes left no doubt what was on his mind.

"Oh?" Emma leaned even closer, knowing she was playing with fire. "Then what are you waiting for?"

"What am I waiting for, indeed?" Killian whispered just before their lips touched.

It had been six days since he'd kissed her, and she'd expected hard with a touch of impatience. Instead, his lips were soft—taking a moment to get reacquainted.

The heat between their mouths grew hotter, giving a spark to the embers. Flames exploded, reaching higher and higher, threatening to tug them in. It ratcheted the fire, pushing it to grow a little bigger. Pushing it to climb a little higher.

Emma's feelings quickly spun out of control, to where she wanted nothing more than to crawl onto his lap and offer him everything. If she wasn't careful ….

"Wait." Emma leaned back, increasing the distance between her and temptation. "Didn't you have to work tonight?"

"Aye. But I switched with Brian."

"Why?"

"Don't you know, Emma?" Killian's husky voice sent shivers racing across her skin. "I wanted to be with you."

"You traded your shift for me?"

"Aye."

She kissed him again, but this one was shorter—its heat tempered. Her feelings were too raw … her need too great. It would only take one ember for all hell to break loose. Sally's was not the place she had in mind for that to happen.

"Do you have plans for the rest of the … night?" Emma tossed out quickly.

"Groveling."

No matter how hard she tried, she couldn't keep her giddy smile at bay, nor the *Rhopalocera* from fluttering in her belly.

"Good. Get Trudi and Nina and meet me at my place."

While she waited for him to respond, her heart raced, and her hands trembled. Seconds later, the quiet was shattered when Killian jumped up and grabbed her hand. "What are you waiting for? Time's a-wasting."

❧

Emma's Apartment

May 9
9:45 p.m.

SSINCE SHE'D BEEN HOME, THE TINY FLUTTER IN EMMA'S STOMACH swarmed into a kaleidoscope of *Rhopalocera*. Her heart galloped as quickly as a herd of *Equus caballus*. The combination made her as breathless and giddy as a schoolgirl.

And you love it.

She did. No more denials. Killian *was* her friend, but he was *so* much more.

You love him.

"I do!" Emma whirled from one task to the next, wanting—no, needing—time to move faster.

Knew it was going to happen.

The feelings rushing around inside were delicious, and she wanted everything to be perfect. And then she stepped back and observed the scene. When she did so, her insecurities returned, pushing her to tone down the seduction.

It took her several moments. Once she was satisfied, she laid the DVD on the table. "Now, it won't appear like I just want to jump his bones."

But you do.

"Shh," she giggled, hearing his car in the drive.

However, several minutes later, when he hadn't knocked, she peered outside. The view that greeted her had her grabbing a bag of treats and a string before running down the stairs.

Emma approached his car and saw Killian's very fine denim covered behind as he reached into the backseat.

"Can I help?" Emma knocked on the window softly.

Killian's startled eyes met hers. "Don't open the door, Doc. The girls are free."

"Bested you again?"

He started the car to lower the window enough she could hear him without his having to yell. "Can we not talk about it?"

"Who's the boss here, Killian? Will you be like this with human children?"

Their gazes locked, creating a germ of something inside she'd never before experienced.

"I'm sure you'll set me straight if I am." His husky voice promised more than she'd expected. Just not more than she wanted ... a family of her own—with him.

Her emotional response had her blinking rapidly to clear her vision. She held out the bag of treats. "Would you like to try?"

His gaze dropped to her mouth, to the base of her neck, before bouncing right back up. "Just help me get the bloody kittens, Doc. Other matters require my attention."

"Oh?"

Killian growled, and because that turned her on, Emma shook the treat back. "Let's try the easy way first."

Thankfully, within seconds, one furry face peered over the front seat, where Killian could grab her and place her back into her pen.

"That was simple." Killian thumbed over his shoulder where Trudi was watching his every movement. "Houdini is a bit trickier."

Hunger, or jealousy, won out as, after another shake of the treats, Trudi jumped close enough to be caught. Killian stuck her in the pen, allowing Emma to open the door and remove the cage.

"Come on, you big softie. Grab your bag and follow me. I need to tend to your war wounds."

Once inside, Emma set the kittens free and pushed Killian into the bathroom. She laid out several rags and medication before taking his right arm.

His skin was warm, and when she glanced up, their eyes met. There was such heat in his blue depths that her throat clogged with emotion.

"We've been here before, haven't we?"

"Aye, love. We have." Killian's warm breath blowing across her cheek sent shivers racing down her spine. "But at that time, I couldn't do this." He whispered butterfly kisses from her cheekbone to just beneath her ear.

Emma's heart raced, and she couldn't resist returning Killian's kiss. "I agree. This is much better."

Killian tangled his fingers in her hair and angled his head enough to deepen the kiss. Heat spiraled around them, causing Emma's knees to buckle.

She nipped his lower lip, needing a little distance. You're distracting the doctor. Let me finish."

"Oh, alright," he pouted. "Once you're done, though, can I get back to distracting you?"

"I would despair if you didn't," Emma hummed, moving to a scratch on his neck. "When was the last time you clipped Trudi and Nina's nails?" His wide eyes widened in surprise. "Never, huh?"

"I might hurt them."

"How did I know that's what you were going to say?"

KILLIAN BIT BACK HIS COMMENT WHEN EMMA PUT SOMETHING ON his neck that set him on fire. "What the bloody hell are you doing to me?"

"It's liquid Band-Aid. If I put the other kind on your neck, removing it would be a lot worse."

"But it hurts."

"I'll kiss it when I'm done."

Killian gave her a dirty look, but she was wearing her 'doctor's face,' meaning it was a fight he couldn't win. "I won't forget."

Emma grinned. "I won't either. Just sit still. It will be over in a minute."

"Says the woman causing the pain," Killian grunted.

She kissed him and then returned to what she was doing. First, the cold liquid, then a fiery sting, followed by a kiss, were tracked several places along his skin. His patience was wearing thin, but just before it ran out, she was done.

"Is that it?"

"Well ..." Emma placed another kiss on his neck, then one on his lips. "Will that do?"

"And if I say no?"

She dropped another kiss on his mouth before stepping back. "Ready for the movie?" Emma hooked a finger in the V of his shirt and tugged him along behind her. "Where did you leave your bag?"

Her rapid-fire questions and topic switch had him feeling like he was wading through molasses.

"On the table," he replied, feeling much like Danny did in the movie *Grease* when he was introduced to a Sandy he didn't recognize. Gobsmacked.

"Go ahead and put it in my room." Emma pointed toward her inner sanctum. "I'll get the movie set up."

"What are we watching, Doc?"

"An *Officer and a Gentleman*," she tossed a smile in his direction, and her gaze bounced off his.

Killian wrapped an arm around her from behind, pulling her back against his front. "Another girl saves the boy movie?"

Emma stepped away to insert the DVD. "There's boob."

She's nervous. But why?

Aren't you?

Was he? The answer no came easily. He knew how he felt about her.

Tell her.

"Emma." Killian waited until she looked at him and then reached for her. "I love you." Then, not wanting her to feel pressured to return the words, he took his bag into her bedroom.

BEFORE SHE COULD COMPLETELY PROCESS KILLIAN'S WORDS, HE was gone. Once she did, her heart flipped, and a fire started deep inside. Her knees trembled, and she fought to control her breathing.

"He loves me."

"I do."

Emma glanced up to see Killian standing just outside of her room. He started toward her, each step bringing him a little closer.

"Killian?"

"Emma." That sexy brow of his arched, and the look in his eyes had her reaching for the back of a chair. "I do love you."

"That's good," she whispered. "That's very good."

"Yeah?"

"Yeah." She met him halfway and slid her arms around his neck. "'Cause I love you too."

Killian's blue eyes flared seconds before he crushed her against his chest, and their mouths crashed together. Holding back was no longer an option, and as if it was the most natural thing in the world, she opened and let him in.

Her hands tangled in his shirt, and she wanted nothing more than to push him onto the sofa and climb on. Except that would require putting distance between them—something she wasn't ready to do.

Just like their first kiss, when their lips parted, Killian touched his forehead to hers. "Are you still nervous, my love?"

"How did you know I was nervous? I was just …"

"You're an open book and all. Remember?"

Emma rested her head against his chest for an extra second, working to make sense of her thoughts. "I didn't mean …"

"Come here, Doc." He stretched out on the sofa and tugged her down in front of him, spooning her back to his front. "Let's watch your movie. After all, you promised me boob."

With his heat surrounding her, she felt safe while, at the same time, it ratcheted up her awareness of her soft parts pressed against his much harder ones.

Watching the movie would be like two hours of foreplay. Would they make it through the movie with their clothes on? For some reason, she rather doubted it.

TWENTY-FIVE

Emma's Apartment
May 9
10:30 p.m.

It didn't take long for Killian's body to notice how close he was lying to the woman he loved. Even though he knew what he wanted, he had no intention of rushing her. While she hadn't said anything, the tension radiating from her body said he was doing just that. Or, at least, the way his body reacted to hers was moving a little faster than she wanted. How did he change that, though?

He'd recited the Miranda Rights more times than he could count. Yet, even after repeating the same forty-plus words, his dick was still hard, ... and he still wanted.

A whiff of her hair, the touch of her hand, or the wiggle of her ass against his most vulnerable flesh sent ideas coursing through his system.

He'd moved on to reciting state laws when the scene on the screen proved to be the bucket of cold water he needed.

"It was too your fault," the young boy cried, *"you told her you'd be back."*

The boy's feelings were not unlike those he'd felt when his mother left them. Betrayal. Loneliness and a loss of innocence.

"When my mother left, I felt much like that boy." Killian hesitated, as going dark and deep wasn't what he had in mind for the evening. "Loving you has filled those empty spaces, losing her left behind."

Emma squeezed his arm. "Oh, Killian. You do the same for me."

Her response had him holding her a little tighter and burying his face in her fragrant hair. Emma had relaxed slightly, yet it still wasn't enough. He needed an innocuous subject for her to think about.

"That's a lot of power he's got between his legs," Killian noted when the male character in the movie rode his motorcycle across the TV screen.

Bloody hell, Reade! You're trying to move the subject away from sex.

I know! I'm such a dick.

There you go again. Move the conversation away from your crotch.

"Emma."

"Hmm."

Killian tucked Emma a little more underneath him and kissed her briefly. "I want you with every fiber of my being. But you were nervous, and I ..."

"I was nervous," Emma interrupted. "That doesn't mean I didn't want to jump you."

"Is that all you want me for?" he teased. "You want my body to use like the floozie's using that bloke in your movie?"

"You're the expert on floozies," she giggled. "That's not the subject we need to discuss, though, is it?"

"You first," Killian turned the tables on her. "Everything was fine until you finished cleaning my wounds, and after that ... your nerves showed up."

"How did you know?" Emma frowned. "I know you gave me the open book line, but how did you know?"

"Your kiss was different. The way you held yourself was stiff. Did you think once you were finished with your task, it would be *I* doing the jumping?"

"No. I, I think the enormity of the next step hit me, and watching a movie together was something ... normal."

"But?"

"You could have kissed the nervousness out of me," Emma blurted.

Killian relaxed as her answer was what he'd surmised. She wanted him, but the pace had quickened a little too fast, causing a disconnect in her thoughts and feelings.

He gently kissed her forehead. "Emma, when we make love, it will be because, here and here," he tapped her head and just over her heart, "agree. Alright?"

"You're right."

Killian preened, feeling much like the peacock he'd compared them to a while ago. "Told you, Doc. Open book and all." His lips covered hers, his kisses light and teasing. "Anything else I can do for you?"

"Maybe a little more right here." Emma tapped her bottom lip.

THE HEAT IN KILLIAN'S EYES TURNED THEM NAVY BLUE. "GLAD–uhh!"

Emma's eyes flew open just as Millicent launched herself from Killian's shoulder to the back of the sofa. From there, she jumped onto her mistress's legs and the coffee table in quick succession. Her offspring immediately followed her, as Trudi and Nina weren't far behind.

"Bloody hell!" Killian sat up. "The little buggers did that on purpose."

Emma chuckled. "You think they planned that?"

"Aye, Doc. We were kissing. They don't like it when we're kissing."

"You're not really mad," she hesitated a beat, "are you?"

It took him several seconds before he would look at her. "Aye." But the twinkle in his eyes and the twitch of his lips belied his statement.

Emma tried to keep a straight face. However, when all three cats jumped back onto the sofa, she couldn't hold it back. Her laughter completely relaxed her, and just like that, her nervousness evaporated. She knew what she wanted —him. Only him, and this time, the power was hers.

She put the cats on the floor and pulled Killian down on the sofa behind her. The way he wrapped himself around her left no doubt what he wanted. She could feel just how much he wanted her in a way he could never disguise. When she moved and his hips jutted forward, the telltale jerk said more than words.

Could she do something about it? Hell yeah, but did she want to? It was an easy answer—no. Instead, she wanted to savor and relish the way he bombarded her senses.

The longer she lay in Killian's arms, the harder it was to ignore the arousal simmering just beneath the surface. If she moved her head, she could smell his soap. If she leaned back a little, she could smell his shampoo. And every time he moved, his cologne caused her heart to race.

Damn! It's supposed to be me who holds the power, not the other way around.

Emma moved her hips slightly forward—away from the fire, instead of back.

Killian caressed the side of her hip, and a shudder raced up her spine. When she was near him, her head spun one minute, and then the next, she felt disconnected from her body. He threw her off balance just by being him. That was something she'd never expected.

Her breath hitched as Zach and Paula were caught in the throes of passion on the screen. Emma closed her eyes, willing her brain not to betray her. It didn't work, and her traitorous mind placed her and Killian in the same scene. When his hand skimmed along her side, she practically hummed in contentment.

"Th-There's," Emma swallowed. "There's the boob I promised."

Killian's chuckle was low, dark, and heady, causing her heart to race. "That's not the boob I'm interested in."

"No?"

"No."

He cupped her breast and brushed his thumb over a sensitive peak. Suddenly, she didn't care if the movie wasn't over or who had the power. She needed Killian.

Emma rolled over and hooked a leg over his hips. "I need your touch. Kiss me ... please?"

Killian growled, "My pleasure," and then his lips found hers.

He pushed her shirt up, and the moment his work-roughened fingers touched her lower back, pinpricks of pleasure skated across her skin.

Emma wrenched her mouth away, tugged her tank over her head, and tossed it on the floor. When she pressed her chest against his, his moan of pleasure made her smile.

"Liked that, did you?"

"Very much." His fingers whispered across her skin. "Show me more."

Her breath stuttered at what was next, but she couldn't stop kissing him. Couldn't take the time to do anything but what she was doing right then.

Emma kissed his chin, his cheek, and the corner of his mouth. She was where she'd dreamed of being for what felt like forever, and neither kittens nor puppies were getting in her way.

Killian's lips chased hers, moaning when she wouldn't stay in one place.

"I need you here." He held her head still and captured her breath with an open mouth kiss.

Those kisses pushed the whirlwind inside higher, making Emma dizzy. The feel of his fingers curling around her breast, teasing the tip until it was hard and begging for his kiss.

"So good," he murmured, and her heart stuttered. "So good."

A flick of his tongue. A brush of his hand. A whisper of his lips, and Emma couldn't stay still any longer.

Come on ....

She tugged his shirt higher in search of smooth skin. When he removed it and tossed it onto the floor, her breath caught, waiting for that first moment when her chest rested against his lightly furred one.

More! ....

With a few arm contortions, her strap slid down her shoulder and off her arm, freeing her breasts. The touch of her nipples against the soft hairs of his chest was electric.

How had she waited for this?

Killian touched, teased, his hands never still, but it wasn't enough. She wanted—needed more than she could have imagined.

Emma pushed her hands into the back of his jeans and pressed her fingers into the top of his taut behind. His muscles tightened, and his hips surged forward, pressing that hard wedge behind his zipper right where she needed him. A storm was brewing, and it wouldn't take much for it to be set free.

Their lips and tongues tangled, and her hips settled into a rhythm, but still, it wasn't enough. When she heard the theme music, indicating the movie was almost over, she was ready for a different position.

"Killian."

"Emma."

He latched onto her earlobe, causing little shivers to work their way up her spine.

What he was doing felt good. So good, that she had to fight not to give in. "No, Killian." She pushed against his chest. "What are we doing?"

"Bloody hell, Doc!" Killian dropped his head against her shoulder. "I can't ... don't." He shuddered against her as he worked to regain control.

Emma cupped his cheek. "Killian, you have it so wrong. I should have said, why are we here when there's a big bed with clean sheets in the other room?"

"Why indeed?" He gave her a hard kiss and, in one smooth motion, wrapped her in his arms and sat up. "I'm ready."

She couldn't deny she was just as eager as he, but when she sat up, the feeling of being watched had her doing a passable job of covering herself with her bra.

"I've already seen them, Doc." Killian hooked his index finger in the center of her bra and tugged. "You've no need to cover up."

"I know, but," Emma indicated the three cats, "they're watching."

Killian pulled her into his arms. "Oh, Doc. What am I going to do with you?"

"You mean you don't know?"

He palmed her ass and pressed her hips into the cradle of his. "I might have an idea ... or two."

"I should hope so." She nipped his chin. "With your reputation and all, I'd hate to be disappointed."

"You know you're playing with fire, right?"

"Promises, promises."

Killian swung her into his arms and kissed her thoroughly.

"What are you doing?"

"What the song said." He gave her a cheeky smile. "I'm lifting you up where you belong."

"That's corny."

"But you love it."

"I love you."

Mere inches separated them as their gazes locked. His mouth hovered just over hers, and with every step closer, tension grew a little stronger. With every step, the intensity burned just a little brighter. It didn't take long before she could no longer handle the heat.

Killian had been inside Emma's bedroom one time, but unwilling to remove his mouth from hers, he felt his way toward the bed. As soon as the floor covering changed, he pushed the door shut.

"Can't have voyeurs, now can we?" he whispered against her mouth.

The low light from the bathroom helped guide him. Once his shins hit the bed, Killian lowered Emma's legs, allowing her to slide down his body. Soft skin glided over his chest, sending his heart rate skyrocketing. Small hands slid through his hair, circled his flat nipples, and hooked in the top of his jeans. The heat generated by the friction between them had him rethinking slowly.

"Come here." Her nimble fingers toyed with the button on his jeans, popping it before he was prepared.

"Careful, love." He closed his hand around her wrist when she reached for the zipper tab. "Those aren't quite the teeth marks I have in mind."

"I'll kiss it and make it better."

"I'm too close, Doc." Killian pushed her back and meant to follow her down until a movement stopped him. "Millicent, how did you get in here?"

Emma propped herself up on her elbow. "She sleeps in here."

"Not tonight, she doesn't," he retorted. "Bloody hell, Emma." Killian carried the cat to the door. "It's a bloody conspiracy. We are alwa—"

When he turned back around, the vision before him rendered him silent.

"Beautiful."

Emma had tossed her bra and sleep pants onto a nearby chair. She was sitting in the center of her bed, all pink and shiny, and so perfect tears sprang to his eyes.

"You're lovely."

"You make me feel that way."

"I'm glad."

With each step closer, his body hardened a little more. "I'm sorry, Doc. I wanted to take it slowly and get acquainted with every part of you. But I'm too close."

"There's always next time."

"As you wish."

He pushed down his pants and boxer briefs, then took another step closer to the bed. Their eyes clashed as he removed the foil packet from his back pocket and laid it on the bedside table. Killian hesitated, and time stood still while he anticipated what came next. Every wrong turn, wrong step, wrong word had been leading him to this moment where nothing was wrong, and everything was very, very right.

"It's time."

Emma licked her lips, and he had to tighten his fists to keep from jumping her.

"Oh, boy, is it." She stretched out the words, pursing her lips forward, and his knees trembled. Sparkling eyes met his, and his knees almost gave out.

"I need you."

"Then take me," she whispered, and her hot breath mingled with his.

Their mouths collided in an all-out assault of lips, teeth, and tongues. It became impossible to think when all he wanted was to feel. A touch, a lick, a gentle suck.

"I love you."

Killian nipped at her collarbone, skimming his hand down her side. His tongue swirled around a valley, and his lips played homage to a peak. Her moans, pants, and the movement of her body told him what drove her closer to the edge.

The tenuous hold on his control was crumbling, but he couldn't stop. She was too sweet, and he'd been waiting too long. Her heart raced, her body trembled, and with a few well-placed strokes to her most sensitive parts, she fell apart in his arms.

"It's time."

"Hold on, love." Killian reached for protection, but her hand was there first.

"Let me."

Emma ripped open the packet and slid the contents in place with one smooth motion. Then, with a smirk, she pushed him over and climbed on.

"Ready?"

Before he could say anything, her heat surrounded him, and she started to move.

"Oh, Emma," Killian groaned, even though he knew words couldn't explain what he was feeling. For the first time, he understood the difference between making love and sex. One was with the body, and the other ... involved his heart.

She was soft and smooth, and the need to take hold and drive climbed closer. His body trembled, it bucked, and coherent thought flew away as they fell over the crest together.

❧

Emma was sated and relaxed when Killian returned from the bathroom and pulled her into his arms. "That was …"

"I know."

"So, Doc," he began, his lilt exaggerated. "How did you become so proficient in covering my co—mph?" Her hand silenced the rest.

"I don't care for the word used that way. That word refers to a *Gallus gallus domesticus*. You don't have a rooster between your legs, do you?"

"Well," Killian palmed himself, "it is rather splendid." When he turned onto his side, his eyes sparkled with mischief. "Don't you agree?"

"Yes, Killian." She lifted him slightly and squeezed. "It is very impressive."

His smile made her heart flip several times.

"Thank you." Killian kissed her softly. "Now, Doctor Foster," he pulled her hips closer to his, "the proficiency story, please."

His expression touched something inside. It was territorial and curious at the same time.

"It's not what you're thinking."

"How do you know what I'm thinking?"

"Open book." She laughed at his surprise. "Really, it's all quite innocent."

"Oh?"

"Kit," Emma began. "Our sophomore RA decided we should learn about protection. She brought assorted fruits and vegetables for us to practice protecting."

"Fruits and vegetables, huh?"

Emma laughed, the memory of the day still fresh in her mind. "Yes, we had cucumbers, squash, bananas, and carrots."

"You dressed each one?" Killian rolled over and hovered above her.

With his mouth so close and his body pressed against hers, Emma had a hard time keeping her thoughts straight. "Ye—yes. I had the fastest f-f-fing—fingers."

He kissed her, his mouth never settling for long. "Only the fastest fingers, Doc? Were there other competitions as well?"

"Ye-ye-ye ... yes," Emma commanded her tongue to work. "Tori and Aurélie beat me out for the fastest mouth."

His tongue invaded hers. "Yours feels perfect to me."

Emma carded her fingers through his hair and pulled his mouth back down. "So does yours."

The kiss continued, quickly reviving the heat between them. She looped her legs over the back of his and pressed their hips together.

He was close, so close that all she needed to do was adjust just a little.

"Killian, don't tease."

"Who me?"

"Please?"

"Tell me who won?"

It took effort to remember what he'd asked before spitting out, "Aurélie. She said it was because she was French. Now, be quiet and kiss me."

"As you wish."

His mouth touched her, and she decided thinking was highly overrated.

TWENTY-SIX

Sheriff's Department
May 12
8:30 a.m.

Killian left Paula's Pastries, confused by the reception he'd just encountered. He didn't think he'd acted any different. His smile felt the same, and he hadn't been whistling. Yet his sixth sense said the whispers and indulgent smiles were aimed at him.

Why was that?

His trip through the department wasn't much better. Brian snagged a donut on his way out and snickered. Amy giggled, then quickly turned away. Even Sydney, the stoic old newsman, smirked.

He was wearing clean clothes, and his hair wasn't sticking up in several directions. But his reception, both at Paula's and at work, was off.

"Bloody hell, Rusty," Killian grumbled once he made it to his office. "Have I grown an extra head?"

Rusty snatched a donut and then studied him. "No, no extra head, I can see." However, the twinkle in his partner's eyes said something *was* going on.

"Then why am I getting strange looks? They whispered at Paula's. Brian snickered, and even Sydney cracked a smile. You know that doesn't happen very often."

"I'm sure it has something to do with knowing how you spent your weekend," Rusty grinned.

"My weekend?" Killian frowned. "No one, well, except Dylan, knows."

Rusty tapped the side of his neck. "Then how do you explain that?"

Killian's hand automatically went to his neck, where Emma had latched on sometime during the night. But since he was wearing a black T-shirt, it wasn't covered.

She gave you a hickey.

"Bloody hell!" Killian's face flamed. "I should have worn a collared shirt."

"Seems so."

"That's all you're going to say?"

"What do you want me to say?" Rusty laughed. "You've been around the block a time ... or two. I'm sure you knew what you were doing. Just be prepared."

"Be prepared?"

"For the questions."

Killian's brows rose. "What kind of questions and from whom?"

"They'll want to know when you're taking the next step," Rusty reported.

"Marriage?"

"Lover's Cave comes before marriage." Rusty sketched out something on a piece of paper and handed it over.

Killian glanced at the rudimentary map Rusty had drawn. "It's a cave?"

"A small one, yes."

"The prim and proper mayor got down and dirty with you in the sand?"

"Well, there was a blanket, and it didn't smell like horse." Rusty grinned. "But hey, don't knock it until you've tried it."

"What's so magical about this cove? I'm doing quite well on my own."

"I'll give you that," Rusty acknowledged. "But there's a legend to the cave."

"Of course there is. This is Swan Harbor, after all."

"I think you'll appreciate the cave's legend. Especially if you want forever with Emma."

Just a few months ago, he'd hoped for a minute of Emma's time, and yet, after leaving her that morning, forever was what he wanted. It couldn't hurt to listen.

"Okay," Killian sighed, not quite yet willing to admit just how much.

Veterinarian Clinic
May 12
5:30 p.m.

EMMA STARED AT THE EMAIL THAT HAD JUST ARRIVED. A PART OF her had been prepared for it, but the part that wasn't ... was a bit weirded out. What did one say to the father you hadn't seen for years?

You'll figure it out.

Would she?

Share your burdens, remember?

"Emma?" Sadie sashayed into her office, suntanned from her honeymoon in Aruba. "What's wrong?"

"Wrong?" Emma shut down her computer, wondering if out of sight, out of mind would work. "There's nothing wrong."

Sadie tsked several times. "Is it Killian?"

"He's fine." Emma smiled, fighting a grin that felt a little too big.

"I thought so, but that's a talk for later. Something is going on, though. Tell Aunt Sadie what it is."

"It's not that big a deal," Emma huffed. "My father sent me an email, and I'm a little surprised, I guess."

"Okay. Why?"

"Geez," Emma sighed. "First, Killian tells me I'm an open book, and now you're reading my moods. Can't I have private thoughts from anyone?"

"This is Swan Harbor," Sadie laughed. "Things have a way of happening when they're supposed to."

"Serendipitous," Emma murmured, remembering Killian's comment about their do-over meet.

"Something like that." Sadie nibbled on her bottom lip, lost in her memories. "There really is no place like it. But what did your father say that has you rattled?"

"He wants to see me when he comes east," came out in a rush.

Sadie sent her a toothy grin. "See, that wasn't so hard. So why are you worried?

Emma searched for the words to explain what was going on inside. "I grew up Peter Foster's daughter. Big-time movie star and an all-around lousy father. Swan Harbor, though, has been *mine* since I drove across the town line. I don't know if I'm ready to share."

Sadie propped her elbows on the desk. "Emma, you belong to Swan Harbor, and it belongs to you. Nothing can take that."

"I'll think about it." Emma glanced at the time. "Aren't you here late?"

"Oh, don't play that card with me." Sadie playfully wagged her finger. "I'm not trying to interfere—just help."

"I know, and I appreciate it," Emma sighed. However, there was still a disconnect between the feelings of the child and the understanding of the adult. "Is that why you came in here? To meddle?"

"Ha!" Sadie laughed. "That was just a bonus. I wanted to tell you Sydney called, and he's adopting Summer's puppy."

"I thought he might." Emma grinned. "I think it will be good for him."

"He and Buster were inseparable for a lot of years."

"And now, he'll always have a little piece of the dog he loved," Emma replied, happy something positive had come out of the ordeal.

Sadie sighed, still a little put out that she missed all the excitement. "He named the puppy George."

"George?" Emma laughed. "As in *Small Knight and George*?"

"That's where it's from." Sadie's eyes sparkled. "Seems Mr. Hot, Hunky, and Gorgeous impressed Madison when he read to the class."

The nicknames Sadie had bestowed on Killian all those months ago definitely fit. "He is easy on the eyes," Emma dimpled. "And his accent ..."

Sadie leaned a little closer. "And now—?"

Here we go.

"—I've solved the problems regarding your dad's visit," Sadie continued. "And told you about George. Now, we have time for you to tell me about your weekend."

"Are you sure?" Emma glanced at the clock. "It's pretty—" She was saved when their phones buzzed simultaneously.

"Don't think I'll forget," Sadie mouthed as she left the room, her phone glued to her ear.

Emma swiped her thumb over her screen.

> Killian: Good evening, Doc. Meet me for dinner tonight?

Anytime she didn't have to worry about cooking was a plus, as far as she was concerned.

> Emma: Name the place and the time, and I'll be there.

> Killian: Lover's Cave in an hour. Follow the lights.

> Emma: Lover's Cave?

> Killian: A map is on its way. Hurry!

When the map arrived, Emma frowned. Based on what he'd sent, Lover's Cave was somewhere close to the lighthouse, down by the water. But what was it, and why were they having dinner there?

She went to ask Sadie and found her staring out the window, wearing a dreamy expression. "Waiting for Gray?"

"How did you know?" Sadie gave her a sheepish smile. "Am I that obvious?"

"Just a little," Emma teased. "But I was hoping you were still here. Can you tell me how to get to Lover's Cave?"

"Oh, ho ho," Sadie smirked. "You know the legend about Lover's Cave, don't you?"

"No .... But I'm assuming you do."

Sadie looped their arms and steered them to more comfortable chairs.

"Legend has it that if a couple makes love in Lover's Cave, they will be betrothed before the year's end."

"Betrothed?" Emma repeated. "That sounds so old-fashioned."

"It's an ancient legend," Sadie shrugged. "I think it goes back to the beginning of Swan Harbor. But it worked with me, Molly, Jessie, and our friend, Cassie. Isn't that what you want?"

"Where is it?" Emma asked, pointedly ignoring the question.

Sadie glanced at the map and indicated a spot at the base of a cliff. "It's quite a romantic location. Large boulders guard it, and once you get around those, the mouth of the cavern is heart-shaped. I'm sure it used to be much larger. Inside, you can build a fire, and there are ledges on the walls for candles. It's like being in a romantic bubble."

Her words stayed with Emma as she changed into leggings and boots before leaving. She didn't care what the legend said about making love outside —there was no way. Doctor Emma Foster was too practical to allow that type of romance to sweep her away.

Lover's Cave
May 12
6:30 p.m.

It took Killian hours to set everything up. Now that he was done and knew Emma was on the way, his nerves kicked in. While Rusty explained the legend, he wanted to scoff—and then, he'd arrived. There was a feeling about the area that was different. In a way, it felt alive, and if he closed his eyes, vision after vision raced through his head.

By the light from the lighthouse, a pirate ship glided toward the cove. He could hear music and laughter. Could feel the love and heartache. The walls held memories, many of which would never be known.

The sputter of Elli's engine had him leaving the thoughts of the past behind and going in search of Emma. When he rounded the boulders, she was walking toward him. She was a vision, and she was his.

"Good evening, Doc. Did you have any difficulty finding your way?"

"No, your map was perfect. And this is very impressive." Emma waved her hand toward the path where he'd placed a hundred luminary bags. "Thank you."

She leaned against him and offered him her mouth, which he happily accepted. She tasted hot and sweet. "You taste like chocolate," he murmured just before helping himself to another kiss.

"Hungry?"

Killian tucked her against his side and started back toward the cave.

She gasped when they reached the cave's mouth, her expression one of awe. "You did this ... all for me?"

"It was noth—"

Emma placed her finger over his mouth, stealing his words, and gestured around them. "Killian, *this* isn't nothing. It's something that took work and ... more than anyone has ever done for me."

A tear slid down her cheek, but before he could wipe it away, she continued into the cave. He'd set luminary bags in the grooves of the rock walls and spread several blankets on the ground. Next to them, a picnic basket waited. The scene was set for seduction, and she wasn't running. It was another sign of just how far they had come.

"Killian, it's perfect. But you've not brought any of your floozies here, have you?" she teased.

He wrapped an arm around her waist and pulled her close. "What do you think? Do you really think the Killian Reade you met in Sally's last fall would have frequented a place like this? Especially a place with such a legend."

"So, you know about that?" Emma murmured. "I wondered."

"Rusty filled me in." But since he didn't want to make her feel pressured, Killian turned on soft music and swung her around.

"Dance with me?"

Emma stepped into his arms, and time ceased to matter. He'd chosen every song in the playlist, and each one reminded him of a time he'd spent with her. Some were from the New Year's Eve party, others from Randy's or the movies they'd watched. The music wrapped them in a sensuous bubble. One where everything outside their bubble no longer mattered. Their focus was only on each other.

He stole kisses, most of which were freely offered. It wasn't until her stomach growled he loosened his hold. "Hungry?"

"Sorry." Emma let go of a light laugh. "I guess I am."

"Let's feed you." Killian guided her toward the blankets and began searching through the food basket.

"Sally's?"

"You don't think I cooked?"

She lifted a brow, pushing him to add, "You were right. It's from Sally's. She likes me."

Emma giggled. "Everyone likes you."

The basket held cold chicken, fresh croissants, fruit, and a bottle of chilled lemonade.

"I'm very likable. Don't you agree?"

Her eyes sparkled from the many candles. "Well, you do have several redeeming qualities."

"Only several?" He paused. "Care to elucidate?"

A red grape disappeared into her mouth, and the way her cheeks hollowed and expanded as she sucked the juice had the saliva in his mouth drying.

The little minx is trying to get a rise out of me.

"No, I don't think so." Emma grinned. "Your head's big enough already."

And one of them is getting bigger by the second.

"Tell me about work," he tossed out, determined to move the conversation into a more neutral territory.

Emma ate another grape, and then took a drink. Her expression said, *That is sour.*

"Need some sugar?" Killian cupped the back of her head and planted a firm kiss on her mouth. "Think that's enough?"

"Oh, you!" Emma licked her lips. "*That's* one of your likable traits."

"My kisses?"

"Well, those too." She smiled, one so sweet that if he hadn't already been in love with her, he would have fallen right then. "You're also corny."

"But you love it."

"Guilty." Emma dumped the entire packet of sugar into her glass. "As for my day ..."

Killian watched several expressions cross her face. When she started talking, it was about making home visits and vaccinating horses at the Martin Farm. The uneventful, even relatively mundane, procedures made him think she was working her way around to something. Until she was ready, he'd listen, as that was one of his favorite pastimes.

When he finished eating, he packed away the leftovers and pushed the basket aside. As he'd hoped, Emma scooted closer and draped her long legs over his.

"Sydney adopted Summer's puppy. He's bringing George for his shots next week."

"George?" Killian chuckled. "Not exactly a typical *Canis lupus familiaris* name, is it?"

"You're getting quite good at that." Emma playfully shuddered, but her eyes spoke of awareness. "When the syllables roll off your tongue, my whole body tingles."

"I'll remember that the next time I'm planning to seduce you."

"I'm sure you will."

Their eyes locked, and the current that was always between them pulsed. It pulsed, growing stronger, threatening to pull them together.

"You asked where the name came from," Emma continued. "Another female fell under your spell. Her name is Madison, I believe."

"Ahh, Madison, of the auburn curls and bright blue eyes," Killian snickered. "I think she's six going on twenty-six."

"You're very observant ... for a man."

"I am very observant," he agreed. "For instance, I observed a certain magazine hidden in one of your desk drawers."

"My desk?"

"Aye, Doc." He trailed his finger up the inside of her leg to settle on her thigh. "And in case you were wondering—I marked the pages I liked best."

"It's research," she sputtered.

"I'd be happy to help you with your research," Killian quipped, "Anytime and Anywhere."

"I'm sure you would."

"Now, though." Killian wrapped his hand around her ponytail to hold her still. He leaned toward her, closer ... and closer. "*Felis catus, Canis lupus familiaris, Rhopalocera, Coccinellidae,*" he recited, dropping kisses on her lips, cheeks, and eyes.

Emma carded her fingers through his hair, attempting to take the upper hand. He pushed back for a handful of seconds until he gave in. After all, they wanted the same thing.

Killian opened, welcoming her in. Their lips and tongues dueled, their movements rapid, pushing the other toward an ending they both wanted. He let her lead for only so long before taking control of the kiss. It became slow—languid, one twining around the other in a leisurely fashion. Emma moaned, and the sound went straight to his dick. His body was primed and ready, and if he didn't watch out ....

"Doc," he whispered, his mother never straying far. "What else happened today?"

"Wha—?" Emma leaned back, breaking the contact between their lips. "Open book?"

"Aye, Doc."

"It's nothing ... much. I invited my dad to come to Swan Harbor when he flies east. Now," she cupped his head and tugged him back down, "kiss me."

"Gladly," his lips teased hers, "but we'll discuss your father's visit later if you want."

"Much later," Emma moaned, holding his head still and pressing her lips against his.

The fire burning inside was unlike anything he'd ever experienced. One second, the flames were a roaring inferno, and the next, a gentle flame.

"I need you."

Emma groaned, and with a few adjustments, she wrapped her legs around him and aligned their parts. Her softness pushed against that hard wedge behind his zipper. He slid his hands into the back of her leggings and cupped her arse. Every time she moved, he thrust forward, and the tingling in his balls grew a little stronger.

His one functioning brain cell cried, '*Frottage is one thing, but what about skin?*'

Killian slid his hand under her back and found soft, smooth skin.

"Let's go. I want you now." Emma scooted backward and started to stand up.

"Then have me." Killian tossed his jacket in one corner of the blanket and reached for the hem of his shirt.

"Killian, wait. We're in public."

"Trust me, Doc," he whispered. "Tonight, right here, it's only me and you."

"Promise?"

"I promise."

Killian slid his hands up her side and swept his thumbs across her tight peaks.

Everything she wanted to do to him and everything she wanted him to do to her was telegraphed in her eyes.

Trust me.

I'm here for you.

He saw the moment she gave in to the storm brewing between them.

"Race you."

The two words were the sweetest he'd ever heard.

"I love you, Doc."

"And I love you." She tugged off one boot. "Hurry."

Killian whipped his shirt over his head and tossed it in one direction. His pants were thrown in another.

They met in the middle of the pallet, and when her hard nipples mingled with the hair on his chest, the heat nearly set his skin on fire.

"Heaven."

"We're getting there." Killian followed her down onto the warm blankets. "Hold on tight. It won't be long now."

TWENTY-SEVEN

Veterinarian Clinic
May 21
5:30 p.m.

When Rusty pulled up in front of the vet clinic, Killian was relieved to see Emma standing at the door.

"Who's this?"

"I don't know," he admitted. "We discovered Belle's family owned the old farmhouse, and when Rusty and I arrived, we found her.

A concerned look crossed Emma's face, and then she indicated where he should take the patient.

"What do you want me to do?" Killian asked as soon as he'd gently placed the dog on the table.

"Can you hold her still for me?"

For the next few minutes, Emma gave him instructions, and he followed. It gave him time to watch her while she worked—something he'd not had much of a chance to do. Her movements were fluent and confident while she examined the stray dog, making him realize just how in awe he was of her abilities.

"What's going on, Doc?" he asked when the dog's breathing continued to grow more erratic.

Emma grinned. "She's having puppies. Unless there's a problem, all we need to do is make her comfortable."

Killian carried the dog into the back room and placed her in one of the larger pens.

Instead of settling, though, the dog immediately began nosing around in the blankets. "What's she doing?"

"Creating a nest."

Emma laid several more rags close to the new mother and then took a step back. Her tender expression as she cared for the mother dog had him reaching for her.

"Come here, Doc."

Emma placed her hand against his chest, holding him back. "You smell like dog."

"I can remedy that." He removed his jacket and unbuttoned his shirt. "Would you care to help?"

"Stop. Go take a shower."

"Join me?"

"Alone." Emma pushed him toward the door. "I'll stay with the new mama."

Killian stole a kiss and ran up the stairs, where he wasted no time jumping in and out of the shower. When he returned, he settled next to Emma on an old sofa not far from the *Canis lupus familiaris.*

It wasn't long before the mother dog's breathing grew louder, her body straining to expel the pups.

"I feel like we should be doing something."

"Like what?" Emma snickered. "Hold her paw and feed her ice chips?"

"Ha ha." He turned back to the cage just in time to see the first puppy slip from its mother's body. When the dog immediately began attending to her newborn, tears sprang to his eyes. "Words fail me, Doc."

Emma rubbed her cheek against his shoulder. "I understand. Even though I've seen hundreds of births, it still takes my breath away."

The sound of her voice had Killian surreptitiously peering down at her. Her expression was one of pure joy. "You love your job, don't you?"

"I do—very much. It doesn't feel like a job."

He'd known for some time he wanted to spend the rest of his days with her. Seeing her like this, though, had him thinking of his life before. Thinking of how cold it had felt.

"Do you remember when you asked what brought me to Swan Harbor?"

"How could I forget?" Emma murmured. "You ignored the question the first time, and the second ..."

"I said a life was inadvertently lost because of me."

She draped her legs over his lap, and her expression was contemplative. "Are you finally ready to share those burdens, Killian?"

Was he?

"I never wanted my darkness to touch you."

"Killian, I love you. That will never change."

He knew that, but even after all the soul-searching, it was still a difficult topic to discuss.

"While I was with the NYPD, I worked undercover. You knew that, right?"

"Only because Elsa told me," Emma smirked, making him feel like a cockwomble for not telling her himself.

"Sorry. It's just ..."

"Hey." She placed her finger over his lips. "You don't have to ..."

Killian dropped his head against her shoulder and, for several minutes, just breathed, inhaling her scent until, once again, he was calm.

"The last case I was involved with ..."

He'd been tasked to infiltrate a gang run by Santora Callandra—a known drug and arms dealer. From there, he tried to explain how the case had affected him differently—even from the beginning. How the things he'd seen and done had made him feel dirty, an uncomfortable situation at best. But as he continued to share, the cold milling around the edges of his mind drew closer, threatening to overwhelm him.

Somehow, Emma understood what was happening and took his hand and effectively drove the cold away. As the tale grew closer to the end, she again anticipated what he needed and wrapped her arms around him.

The longer he spoke, the farther away he seemed, and several times, he had to stop and gather his words before continuing.

"I remember everything about that time as if it were yesterday. I received an anonymous tip hinting at internal strife within the organization. However, after spending hours checking in with several informants and coming up empty, I drove home. When I climbed out of my car, that sixth sense I'd developed while undercover grew hyper-aware and shouted for my attention. Unfortunately, I ignored the warning and didn't call for backup."

His chest grew tighter, and his heart raced as he moved toward the worst part of the story.

"I took the stairs two at a time to the third floor and peered around the corner. The hallway was empty, and as I sprinted toward my apartment, I had my gun out and ready. And then ...."

His brain registered Violet running toward him, shouting, "Ian, you'll never guess ...." at the same time, it processed Santora's right-hand man stepping around a corner with an AR-15 in his hands.

"No!" Killian screamed, diving for the little girl just as the spray of bullets flew, hitting her small body and driving her into his arms. As soon as they hit the ground, he brought his gun up and around, but before he could fire, he heard pop-pop-pop and then silence.

Emma's quick inhalation brought him back to the present.

"She was gone," he murmured. "While I was numb, I continued to do my job until backup arrived. As soon as I was able, I called my lieutenant, resigned, and a week later, I moved here. After that, I just existed until a flash of yellow caught my attention."

"Elli," Emma breathed.

"Aye, love." Killian kissed her. "You made me feel again." He punctuated each word with a firm kiss,

Emma cupped his face, and the look in her green eyes mesmerized him.

"Oh, Killian, sometimes you take my breath away."

"Only sometimes?" Killian teased, never allowing their lips to lose contact for long.

"You know what I mean."

"Aye, love. Forgive my poorly placed humor."

"One of those 'hat' things?" Emma murmured, likening his comment back to Mary's explanation of having many personas.

"Something like that."

His lips were soft, and she could feel the need to shut out the world for a while, seeping closer. Just as soon as she knew if he was safe.

"Was Santora caught?"

"Aye." Killian nodded, but a flash of something behind his eyes caused her breath to catch. "I heard a rumor his lawyers were filing a motion to have the charges dropped. If that happens ..."

"But you're here," she tightened her arms, "and safe ... right?"

"I'm safe, Emma." He tugged her back against his chest and tucked his chin on her shoulder. "Santora knew me as Ian Jones. And thanks to my captain in New York, Ian Jones died in a fiery crash not long after Violet's death."

Dozens of questions floated in and out of her head, but with Killian wrapped around her, holding her tightly and a new life in front of her, she let it go.

Hours later, Emma had showered and was nursing her second cup of coffee while Killian dressed for the day. They'd been dating for months, and she'd seen him with his gun. Except, even when he'd led her into her own house, worried there was an intruder, she hadn't given much thought to the life-or-death reality. Until he'd shared his story. Watching him slip into his shoulder holster as easily as he would his shirt caused the enormity of the 'what ifs' to grow inside.

If it hadn't been for that little girl ....

What kind of person are you to be happy someone else had died?

Tears sprang to her eyes, as she didn't know how to answer that question. Be happy it wasn't him and the life of another was lost. Wish it were different, and he ....

"Hey, hey," Killian tugged her into his arms, "you can't think like that."

Emma relaxed, her nose automatically burying into the soft skin at the base of his neck. "Open book?"

"Aye." He kissed the tip of her nose and leaned his forehead against hers. "Emma," the huskiness in his voice had her opening her eyes to see a variety of emotions swimming in his. "I've, I've thought the same things you're thinking now, but it doesn't change what happened."

When Killian kissed her, the fine tremor in his lips shook her more than she was willing to acknowledge. She could taste the hazelnut flavor of his coffee and smell the mintiness of his toothpaste. But those were external and not what made him special. Nor were they important to them as a couple. What mattered was the way he made her heart trip, her knees weak, and her pulse race.

"I'm sorry. Just seeing you slip on your gun somehow made it real. Logically, I know you're right. Emotionally, well ..."

"I know, love." Killian tightened his hold. "I'm here."

"I'll be okay."

He stepped back, and his blue eyes delved into hers, making her fight to maintain control. The more she loved, the harder it became.

"Walk me down?" he asked, allowing her to relax when he didn't push.

"Definitely."

"I'll call you later," Killian murmured against her mouth.

Emma's breath caught, and she wasn't sure what came over her. She knew he needed to leave, but the spark fanned upstairs suddenly ignited.

His lips consumed hers, and with a groan, he backed her against the wall. Was it the roughness of his jacket pressing against her unbound chest or the cool air blowing under her robe and across her bare nether regions that sent her want spiraling? She didn't know or care. His story of life and death was too real. She needed to know he was alive. Needed him to make her feel alive.

One of Killian's hands settled against the bare skin of her lower back. His fingers kneaded her tense muscles. His pinky slid up and down between her ass cheeks, spreading the tingles farther and farther—until no part of her skin wasn't involved.

He parted her robe with his other hand, baring her breast for his exploration. Pinching, sliding, cupping, his fingers molded, stroked, and circled the tip until her nipple stood firm, waiting for what came next.

In the back of her mind, Emma's lone functioning brain cell shouted, *'Lawsey, it's a good thing Leroy hadn't worked overnight.'* But Killian sucked her earlobe into the hot cavern of his mouth, weakening her resolve and her knees.

Knowing Sadie was going to be late released her last hesitation. A tug of Killian's shirt allowed her hands to find skin. His back was warm, the muscles smooth and supple beneath her fingers. He released her earlobe to nibble across her cheekbone, his hot breath sending shivers down her spine. A kiss on one corner of her mouth. Another on her chin before his tongue joined to lave down one side of her throat, stopping periodically to feast on her skin.

Emma moaned, and his name sounded like a prayer as he slid lower.

"Look at me." Killian nipped the side of her breast.

She forced her eyes open, meeting his, dark with need. *Watch me,* they seemed to say. Involuntarily, her chest pushed forward, seeking and encouraging his descent. When Killian latched on, Emma's thoughts shut down, and all she could do was feel.

A flick of his tongue. A stroke of his finger. His lips and hands were all over and everywhere, and with every touch, her desire grew. The feelings quickly became too intense, too big, and she needed more. She pushed him back far enough to rip open the button on his jeans.

"Careful love."

Emma heard the rasp of his zipper, and with a few creative moves, he gave her exactly what she needed—him. She ignored the creaking of the building as it settled around them. Ignored the roughness of the wall behind her. Her entire focus was on him and where they were touching—that place where they were connected.

"I love you," he emphasized with every thrust forward.

There was no holding back, and before she was ready for it to end, Killian hit the perfect spot, and stars exploded in front of her eyes.

"That's it, love," Killian shouted, meeting her in that hazy aftermath.

Emma wrapped herself around him, holding on as shudders continued to work their way through her system. "That was ..."

"A bloody lovely way to start the day."

"I agree, but," she relaxed her hold and allowed her feet to once again touch the ground, "it—" The doorbell cut her off.

"Who the bloody hell is that?" Killian tucked himself back into his jeans.

Emma quickly worked to retie her robe with shaking hands. "Killian, I can't ..."

"Calm down, Doc." He kissed her cheek. "Go. I'll get the door."

On shaky legs, Emma rushed to the small powder room. She leaned against the closed door, her breathing still rapid, her body still tingling from their coupling. What had come over her?

Well, duh, Killian.

"Not quite over me." She giggled, but there was no disguising the woman in the mirror had been well and thoroughly loved. The bee-stung lips and whisker burns on her neck and chest gave it away.

"And I still wear his smell." Emma ran a brush through her hair before opening the door, ready to find out who rang the bell.

Once she left the powder room's safety, she could hear the distinct vibrations of two voices. Killian's and ....

Why was her mother in her house?

"I'm sorry to just show up like this," Ava was saying. "I left several messages on Emma's phone to let her know I'd be stopping by."

Left messages on her phone? Her phone!

Emma mentally slapped her forehead. While waiting for the new mom to have her puppies, her phone had died. It was still charging in her office.

Okay, you can do this. She tugged the belt on her robe a little tighter before making her presence known.

"There you are, love." Killian stepped forward and took her hand.

"Mom, I'm sorry ..." Her fingers tightened around Killian's. "We, uh, were up all night with a new mother."

A corner of Ava's mouth curved. "I'm sorry to drop by like this. But I'm meeting with Maggie in a few minutes and have something for you. Is this a bad time?"

Ava's twinkling eyes moved to Killian before returning to Emma's. "Your beau was just telling me he's on his way to work."

"He was?" Emma's startled gaze went to Killian's. "You're leaving?"

"Aye, love." Killian kissed her cheek. "But I'll introduce your mother to Daisy and her brood while you shower. How's that?"

Which will give you time to get it together.

"Perfect, thanks." Emma kissed him again, and, with a few words to Ava, ran up the stairs.

Joanne's Gems
May 22
10:00 a.m.

KILLIAN PARKED IN FRONT OF JOANNE'S GEMS, A SMALL, FAMILY-owned jewelry store not far from Randy's. He'd known he wanted to marry Emma for a while, and now that he'd shared his story with her, he felt he had the right to ask. But the variety to choose from confused him more than helped.

Are you sure this is what you want?

Bloody hell, yes!

Then you'll know.

"Can I help you?"

Killian turned toward the husky voice and uttered words he'd never expected to say, "I, I want to buy a ring."

"Oh, that's wonderful. Come on in. By the way, I'm Joanne, and you are?"

"Killian, Killian Reade."

"And your intended?"

"Emma." Killian grinned at her use of the old-fashioned word. "Emma Foster."

"Oh, Doctor Foster," Joanne smiled. "She's such a lovely girl. My Dolly adores her. The last time I was there, I took home Tiger. He's a little spitfire."

"You adopted Tiger?" Killian chuckled. "I have two of his siblings."

"What are their names?"

"Trudi and Nina," he supplied. "They're my first pets."

"Well, that's quite a big step. And now marriage. It seems you did something right."

Had he?

Aye, you big git! You changed!

"Maybe I did," Killian exclaimed, trying to picture one of the rings beneath the glass on Emma's finger.

Joanne was patient, and while she explained about diamonds and cuts and sizes, he asked questions. Once he'd relaxed, Killian found it easier than he'd imagined, and the process was painless to everything but his wallet.

On his way out, he came face-to-face with Sadie.

"Bloody hell," Killian groused. "Can't a man do anything in this town without running into someone he knows?"

"Let's see," Sadie chuckled and pretended to think about it. "No. Try growing up here. Everyone knows you."

"You can't tell Emma you saw me," Killian decided to be proactive.

"Oh?" Sadie's grin grew. "You were shopping for Emma?"

"Who else would I be shopping for?" he retorted. "Of course, it's for Emma."

"And are you going to ask her to marry you?"

He thought about saying, '*Why else would I be in here?*' However, at the last minute decided what she didn't know couldn't be spilled.

"Guess you're going to have to wait and see." Killian winked and pushed past her. "Catch you later."

When he reached the office, he stored the ring in his locker. He'd know when it was time.

Veterinarian Clinic
May 22
10:30 a.m.

After another shower, Emma found her mother sitting on the sofa, holding a cup of hot chocolate and talking to Millicent.

"Hope you don't mind." Ava held up her cup.

"You're fine." Emma sat on the other end of the sofa, feeling a bit awkward. "So, you're meeting with Maggie this morning?"

Ava grinned. "In an hour or so." Then, she changed the topic. "It looks like you took my advice about Killian."

"Your advice?"

"That if you have something good, you should hold on tightly," Ava reminded her. "Looks like you were holding on tightly."

"Mother!"

"Sorry," Ava giggled. "I feel like I missed those awkward moments when you were growing up."

"So, you're making up for them now?"

"It's nice to see you happy." Ava smiled impishly. "But Swan Harbor has been good for you."

"It's become home."

"I'm glad. But teasing you isn't the reason I stopped by. I have something for you." Ava dug through her purse for a minute before pulling out a small envelope.

"What is it?"

"Open it."

The envelope rattled, and when Emma upended it, a tarnished bracelet dropped into her hand. "It's an old charm bracelet?"

"It is." Ava showed her a photo. "I wanted to have it cleaned first, but ..."

Emma glanced at the picture, and her eyes grew wide. "She looks like me, but she's older and has dark hair."

"That's your Grandma Rose," Ava replied. "She was my mother's mother, and she's holding me."

"What are you, about two in this picture?" Emma glanced at the entire picture, but her uncanny resemblance to the woman kept pulling her attention back. That's when she saw what the woman wore on her arm. "It's the bracelet."

"It is."

"That picture and this bracelet arrived in the mail a few days ago. The only other thing in the package was a piece of paper that said, *'For Ava,'* written in dainty handwriting."

Emma frowned. "A package? Who was it from?"

Ava shrugged. "I don't know. It came from an attorney's office. I've been trying to get in touch with them. Do you want me to send the bracelet to be cleaned?"

"No, that's alright." Emma stretched out the bracelet to look at the charms. She could see a heart, the number two, a key, something that was round, and what she thought was a duck. "I'll take it to Joanne's the next time I'm in town. Thanks for this. Grandfather never talked much about grandmother and her side of the family."

"I know," Ava sighed. "He thought it would be too sad, but I always wanted to know more. Maybe this will be my kick in the pants to start looking. Now, though, I should go. I'm sorry my timing was so bad."

Emma bit her tongue to keep from responding and walked her mother down the stairs. After all, she had a *Canis lupus familiaris* family to check on.

TWENTY-EIGHT

Sheriff's Department
June 1
9:00 a.m.

KILLIAN PROPPED HIS 'ENGAGEMENT' EVIDENCE BOARD ON AN easel and stood back to observe. A part of him realized he'd been a bit zealous, but he wanted it to be an event they'd never forget. With only a few hours until the big moment, double- and triple-checking his lists kept his nervousness at bay.

"Are you still obsessing over every little detail?" Rusty teased.

"Aye. I just …"

Rusty waved at the board. "Come on, Romeo. For the past few weeks, you've planned every detail as if you were solving a crime. This is a proposal. It's supposed to be from the heart."

"And that's not what I'm giving her?" His voice rose as just a tinge of panic crept in. "I'm trying to remind her of our journey. I just don't want her to have any doubts. Do you really think I went too far?"

"Well," Rusty raised a brow and pointed at the numerous lists, "music, movies, books …"

Which reminded Killian of another part of his plan. "Is Rene going to …?"

"Everything is taken care of. Thatcher and Maggie are covering the clinic, Sadie is taking Emma to the Foxy Lady, and afterward, Rene will be at Sally's reading to Roland."

"Good." Killian scanned the board one last time. "I keep thinking I'm forgetting something, though."

Rusty laughed. "Well, if you are, check in with your geriatric spies. I'm sure they'll set you straight."

"Hey," Killian chuckled. "The geriatric network is amazing, and during this time of year, they blend in easily. I'm sure Emma has no clue."

"Right," Rusty joked. "Because Rupert, Glynnis, and Lois are so subtle."

"Do you think she's noticed?"

"I'm sure you're fine," Rusty assured him. "Don't worry so much."

"Easy for you to say," Killian muttered.

"Relax, Killian," Rusty patted his shoulder on his way out. "Everything will be okay."

"Can you guarantee that?" Killian grumbled as the other man disappeared.

Foxy Lady
June 1
10:00 a.m.

Emma parked Elli in front of the Foxy Lady, and before her fingers even touched the ignition key, she heard it. Just like had happened over the past few weeks, she could hear music from the movie *Grease*. She was tempted to stay in the car to see how long the song would play. But with Sadie giving her the evil eye, she took a chance and opened the door. The music stopped, just like every other time.

"Any chance you heard that?" Emma asked as soon as she'd stepped from the car.

"Heard what?" Sadie frowned. "Janet scolding me for being late?"

"The music. I've been hearing it a lot lately."

Sadie linked their arms and started toward the salon. "Sounds like you're overdue for a massage."

Emma could admit she'd been a little distracted, but to begin to hear things ....

"Maybe." Except something about the concession felt off.

Once inside, Emma followed Sasha toward the back of the salon. When she passed the waiting area, she was distracted where, on one of the televisions, the same song she'd heard in her car was playing.

"Sasha," Emma thumbed back toward the television screen, "*Grease*? That's not typical."

"It was requested."

"Requested?" Emma began, only to realize she'd been left behind.

"Here's your robe." Sasha handed, but unlike other times, the esthetician's shuttered look didn't welcome conversation.

Emma quickly changed, and while she waited for Sasha to return, she kept thinking about the music in her car and the movie playing at the spa. Was she imagining coincidences that weren't there?

"Anything new?" Emma tried to engage Sasha in conversation when she'd returned.

Except Sasha only gave a one-word response and continued spreading wax.

Is it me? Emma wanted to ask. But the whisper of what could have been her name had her tuning into the words of others.

... Emma ...

Was that Sadie's voice?

... doesn't ...

... know ...

He ...

I ...

... charge ...

And Janet's?

Are they talking about me or just talking?

"There, that wasn't so bad, was it?" Sasha chirped.

The overly false voice threw Emma off. "What?"

"You should get dressed for your massage," Sasha asserted. "We wouldn't want to anger Janet."

"Heaven forbid we anger Janet," Emma grumbled.

When Sasha didn't move for several seconds, Emma's brows shot up. "Well?"

Sasha gave her a sheepish smile. "I'm sorry." She ducked her head, and when she glanced back up, her expression was neutral. "When you're ready, you can wait for Janet next door. I'll see you toni— … later."

After she'd left, Emma didn't waste any time taking her things to the next room. She was greeted by the light scent of jasmine, the soft sound of waves, and an already prepared massage table. Once she placed her belongings on the counter, she climbed onto the table, lay on her stomach, and waited.

The cool room and relaxing environment lulled her into a state of peacefulness. If she concentrated, she could hear the murmur of a voice and the soft sounds of footsteps, but the longer she lay still, the harder that became. And then … silence.

Emma lifted her head just in time to see the small monitor on the wall come to life. A scene from another movie she'd watched recently, this one showing Zach lifting Paula from *An Officer and a Gentleman*. Then, just as quickly as it had appeared, the screen went blank.

"Sorry, I'm late." Janet rushed in before Emma could make sense of anything.

"S'alright," Emma slurred.

She could hear Janet bustling around, feel the cool breeze when the blanket was folded back, and smell the massage oil. Then, firm fingers dug into her trapezius muscles on either side of her neck.

"You have knots," Janet grumbled.

Emma grunted when Janet used her elbow to press on the knot as she worked to convince the muscle fibers to relax.

"There," Janet let up on the pressure. "That wasn't so bad, was it?"

Not for you, Emma thought, but it came out as a groan when Janet's elbow found its way into another knot.

"Relax, Emma. You're undoing all my hard work."

"I'm trying."

She focused on the sound of the waves coming through the speakers. Several minutes later, she relaxed, feeling much like she had no bones.

Janet's touch lightened, and then Emma heard the first buzz of voices through the wall.

… good …

… tonight …

I know …

No ... surprise ....

It sounded like Sadie's laughter, and then there was nothing. Once again, she felt like the little girl on the outside who wanted to fit in.

"You're done," Janet declared briskly. "Helen will be waiting for you once you're dressed." She scurried out the door just as silently as she arrived.

Emma slipped into her leggings and reached for her sweater. Just as she pulled it over her head, the monitor burst to life again. This time, a scene from *Dirty Dancing* was playing. It showed Baby running into Johnny's arms.

"That's it." Emma yanked on her shoes and went looking for answers.

Except with Helen waiting for her, she didn't get far. "It's about time. I was ready to come get ye."

"Wait! What about?"

Helen just shrugged and hurried her along to be shampooed. But with the room's meditative music and low lights, discussion was impossible.

The warm water and strong fingers combing through her hair helped clear her mind. After the shampoo was rinsed away, her head was wrapped in a hot, moist towel, and another was placed over her eyes.

While she lay still, Helen massaged lotion into her arms. It was long before others arrived, and Emma once again heard whispers.

Yes ...

... her ...

He's ...

... train ...

Almost as if she were hearing something she shouldn't, Helen quickly rinsed her hair and guided her to another room. Yet, the remaining time she was in the Foxy Lady, she kept feeling like she was interrupting conversations.

Paranoid much, Emma?

Shut up! What are you talking about? Unlike other times when in similar situations, Emma wasn't tempted to pull out her cloak and hide. It didn't stop her from wanting to rush home, though, to *her* place.

"Lunch?" Sadie suggested as soon as they stepped outside.

"Oh," Emma sighed. "I thought I'd just ..."

"Stop." Sadie linked their arms. "Doesn't a grilled cheese and a milkshake sound good?"

"You're thinking Sally's." Emma allowed her friend to pull her along. "We probably can't even get a table."

Sadie ignored the potential problem. "I bet we can. Come on."

While they walked, Sadie filled her in on the gossip she'd heard in the Foxy Lady. Emma half-listened while the other half attended to the elderly gentleman she'd seen more than once lately.

"We're being followed."

Sadie glanced over her shoulder. "That's just Rupert. He probably came into town with his wife, Lois, and her sister, Glynnis. Didn't you see them at the spa?"

Emma's answer was lost when they walked by an electronics store, and the scene of Edward arriving in the limo in *Pretty Woman* appeared on a monitor. Like dominoes, before that scene had been completed, the next monitor showed Danny and Sandy from *Grease* flying into the sunset. Then, a third had Lee Stetson proposing to Amanda King.

"Sadie, wait." Emma frowned at the blank screens. "Did you see that?"

"See what?" Sadie redirected them back toward Sally's. "The new computer you're planning to buy me for the clinic?"

"Don't be cheeky," grumbled Emma.

"You're just hangry." Sadie tugged open the diner's door. "Let's eat."

They slid into a booth close to where Rene and Roland were sitting, their heads close together, reading a book.

"And they laughed and giggled, and then he proposed," Rene read.

It was the book Killian had given her on Valentine's Day.

And the music you've been hearing?

Were from movies they'd watched. The pieces were there, floating around in her head. If she could just ....

"Hi, Emma." Roland peered over the back of the booth. "Are you and Killian going to laugh and giggle and then get married?"

"Married?" Emma glanced from Sadie and then to Rene for clarification. "Killian and I aren't engaged to be married."

"Oh?" A slight pucker developed between his big brown eyes. "I thought ..." he began, only to have Rene's hand cover his mouth.

Rene slid from the booth. "Let's go home, Roland, and let Sadie and Emma eat in peace."

"But Mama," Roland dimpled, "I was gonna ask ..." Once more, Rene's hand once more covered his mouth.

"Sorry," Rene apologized. "He's excited because Maggie is coming to work with Ruari, right?"

Emma watched as a silent message was exchanged between mother and son.

"Right!" he exclaimed. "See you tonight."

"Tonight?" Emma repeated, noting identical 'deer-in-headlights' looks on Rene's and Sadie's faces.

"He means later," Rene exclaimed quickly. "We'll see you later." With a wave, she rushed him out the door.

Sadie started jabbering so quickly that it made Emma dizzy. However, those pieces she'd gathered started forming a picture.

"Something is going on." Emma gave Sadie a pointed look. "Isn't there?"

"Going on?" Sadie squeaked. "What could be going on?"

"You tell me." Emma leaned on the table. "For the last couple of weeks, I've been ..." Suddenly, the pieces clicked. "Killian's involved, isn't he?"

"My lips are sealed," Sadie winced. "And please, don't ask any more questions."

"But ..."

"Trust me, Emma," Sadie replied softly. "Trust him."

It took several minutes before her hands stopped shaking enough to release the leather seat she'd grabbed onto.

"I can do that. But," Emma glanced around, making sure they were still alone. "If this is 'supposed' to happen tonight, he's not mentioned going out."

"Oh, poop!" Sadie grabbed her phone and quickly sent a message.

Emma giggled, suddenly feeling much lighter than she had in weeks.

Sheriff's Department
June 1
2:00 p.m.

"Bloody hell!" Killian read Sadie's text.

> Sadie: Are you sure you 'asked' Emma out tonight?

He had, hadn't he? They'd talked about an assortment of topics, but .... Had he cocked up again?

Killian: I'll be by to pick you up at 7:00.

Emma: Pick me up? For what? I was planning on a quiet night to read a few journal articles.

"Bloody hell!" Killian grimaced, thinking he'd been right. He *had* forgotten something.

Killian: Forgive me, Doc. I should have asked sooner. Will you go out with me tonight? I've planned a special evening for us.

Emma: How special?

Killian: Very.

Emma: Does it involve clothing?

Killian: I thought we'd go dancing. Afterward, though, clothing will be optional.

Emma: ;-) I'll see you at 7:00.

From there, Killian moved on to his network.

Foxy Lady Women: ✓
Rupert: ✓
Sanders Electronics: ✓

The fact he'd resorted to Emma's list-making hadn't escaped his notice. However, if the night turned out as he planned, he didn't mind.

It wasn't long before he received the message Emma was on her way home, and he could check one more thing off his list.

Sadie: ✔

With that taken care of, Killian headed to his apartment to change. Once there, the *Rhopalocera* played havoc with his stomach, especially after reading Rene's text.

> Rene: I'm sorry, Killian. Roland almost spoiled the surprise, but I think I covered.

With his heart racing like a herd of *Equus caballus*, he checked on his list one more time.

Rene: ✔*, but barely.*
Suit: ✔ *It was hanging on the door.*
Ring:

Killian grabbed his jacket and stuck his hand in the pocket where he'd placed it earlier. "Sod it," he grumbled when the ring wasn't there. Finally, he mentally retraced his steps.

"Bloody hell!" He'd left it in his locker.

⁂

Veterinarian Clinic
June 1
6:30 p.m.

Since returning to the clinic, Emma tried to focus on work. However, her thoughts kept returning to Killian's plan.

Somehow, he'd involved the entire town of Swan Harbor. No longer was she the little girl standing on the outside looking in. She was the one in the middle. The town's motto of being a haven for lost hearts had come true for Emma Foster. In more ways than one, her heart had found what it wanted.

With a few minutes before she needed to get ready, Emma unpinned her list and spread it on the desk. She'd been fifteen when she'd written her first goal.

Goals equal success

Graduate from High School. ✔
Graduate with her Bachelor's. ✔
Get into Veterinarian School. ✔
Graduate from Veterinarian School and pass her licensure exams. ✔
Get a job. ✔
Make Business a success. ✔, as according to Sadie, they were consistently operating in the black.
Hire a staff. ✔, as she had Sadie and Leroy, and even Maggie, who offered to help when needed.
Make new friends. ✔, and since the entire town seemed to be in on her surprise, she was apparently earning more each day.
Partner? While the idea of a partner had merits, she'd decided to put it off until later. She had, however, been happy when Doctor Thatcher offered his services part-time.
Find a man. ✔ She hadn't been looking and had tried to ignore the pull she'd felt from the beginning. But as Molly liked to say, the heart wanted what the heart wanted, and her heart had won out.
Fall in love. ✔. She couldn't pinpoint the exact moment she'd known she loved him. It might have started that night in New York, then continued when he'd turned around with Trudi in his hands. Plus, there was the evening he'd helped her clean the strawberry mess or when he'd told her he was adopting two kittens. Some days, she felt as if she'd been in love with him forever, and other days ... it felt brand new.

But falling in love had been the last goal written on her list, as she'd never allowed herself to think beyond. Until today ....

If he asked her to spend her life with him, they would be a family. Was she ready?

When her heart felt like a flower blossoming in spring, and she couldn't completely take a deep breath, she had her answer.

Fall in Love. ✔
Get Engaged.
Marriage.
Family.

With an almost giddy sense of anticipation, Emma pinned the list back on the board.

"Emma?"

She barely had time to pretend she was involved in something before Killian strolled into her office.

"You're not ready, Doc. Is there a problem?"

"No, no problem." Emma rushed by him and started toward the stairs. "I'm on my way. I'll hurry."

KILLIAN WATCHED THE SWAY OF EMMA'S HIPS AS SHE RAN UP THE steps ahead of him. He'd been nervous when he stopped at the department to get her ring. But when he'd caught her pinning her list on the board, his nervousness faded. Nothing felt more right than having Emma as his wife.

"What do you think, Millicent?" He brushed his hand down the cat's back and showed her the ring. "Think your mistress will like it?"

The cat pawed at the object before giving it a dainty sniff and butting her head against his arm. He took the strength of her purr as an affirmative response.

"I can't wait to give it to Emma."

"Killian?"

Killian stuck the ring deep into his pocket and greeted her. "What is it, Doc?"

"Nothing. I thought I heard you talking to someone."

"Just Millicent. She wanted to know when you'd be home."

"Oh, she did." Emma grinned. "What did you tell her?"

"That she wasn't your mother." Killian spun her around and brought her close for a kiss. "You look lovely, Doc."

"Thank you. I wasn't sure what to wear." She shrugged as if to say, '*This is what you get.*'

"I think you'll like it."

Killian kissed her again, and as they started to the car, he mentally checked off one more item on his list.

Pick up, Emma. ✔

✿

ONCE THEY WERE ON THEIR WAY AND KILLIAN WAS HOLDING HER hand, Emma was calm ... ready. Having a man fight for you until you could no longer ignore your feelings for him was every little girl's dream. Except, it hadn't been a dream Emma Foster had given much thought—until Killian.

When they left her property, and he turned in the opposite direction she'd expected, a tiny doubt crept in.

"No hints as to where we're going?"

He kissed her left hand. "Trust me."

"I do."

While they drove, his thumb was in constant motion, brushing rhythmically over her knuckles. It kickstarted the current that was always between them. She could feel it growing faster and burning brighter than usual. Almost as if it, too, knew something different was in the air.

"Here we are."

Sally's?

Killian rushed from the car and moved quickly to open her door.

Sally's?

He held out his hand, and a dozen questions flew through her head.

Trust me, his expression said.

Emma gave him her hand, and the fine tremor beneath her fingers said more than words.

The moment was big.

Killian led her onto the sidewalk and took both her hands. "Emma, it was less than a year ago when I stepped onto Main Street, and a flash of yellow crossed my path."

"Elli."

"Aye, love. Elli. You restarted my heart that day and made me *feel*—something I hadn't done for a very long time. It wasn't long before I fell in love."

"Just like I fell in love with you, Killian Reade."

"That's very good to hear."

Killian lowered to one knee, and when their eyes met, he was holding a diamond solitaire.

"Will you marry me?"

She'd expected the question, but actually hearing him say the words brought forth tears. Unable to get the words out, Emma nodded, not wanting to blubber like a fool in the middle of town.

"Is that a yes?"

"Yes," Emma cried. "Yes, I'll marry you."

Her knees gave out, but Killian was there to catch her. "I've got you, Doc. May I?"

"Please."

It was a struggle to hold her hand still for him to slide the platinum band onto her finger.

"Perfect," he whispered against her lips.

Emma sank into the kiss, happier than she could ever remember being. Her heart raced, and the butterflies in her stomach swarmed.

"Now what?" She held up her hand to admire the diamond. "Is it time for the 'clothing optional' part of the evening?"

Killian chuckled and turned her to face Sally's. "Hardly, my love. There are a few people inside who want to celebrate with us."

"Oh, Killian," Emma sighed when she saw who was standing in the window. "Not only did you invite the entire town, but you also invited my mom and Elsa."

"Ready to go inside?"

When she'd arrived at Molly's all those months ago, she'd been afraid to walk into a room full of strangers. That time was behind her, though, as for once, she was anxious to be the one in the middle of everything.

"Race you."

And with that, another check was added.

Engaged. ✓

EPILOGUE

Sally's Diner
June 1
9:00 p.m.

Elsa took a glass of champagne and found a corner in the back of Sally's Diner. Since she'd learned about Killian's plans, something inside of her had changed. It wasn't until she watched him propose to her best friend, Emma, that she understood her feelings. She was jealous.

Her gaze drifted to Liam, Killian's brother, and the man she'd been 'seeing' for months. Their attraction was instantaneous, and she'd thought they were going somewhere. The reality, though, was something very different. He treated her like his friend. Not the woman he couldn't get out of his head. Not the woman he wanted to spend his life with, and certainly not the woman he loved. Except—she didn't believe he *couldn't* love her. It was more that he wouldn't *allow* himself to love her. How was a girl to fight that?

She wanted a man to look at her the way Killian looked at Emma. The spark between them was there at the New Year's Eve party. Even then, it spoke of forever.

What about her, though? Was Liam her forever, or was there someone else out there waiting for her?

Her attention trailed from Liam to Tyler James. At one time, he'd starred in her dreams, and she'd thought he was her future. Until he went back home and ....

"Do you know him?" Ava, Emma's mother, joined her in the back of the room.

"Who?"

Ava arched a brow. "The hottie you've been staring at for the last few minutes."

"His name is Tyler James," Elsa replied. "The first time we met, we were sixteen."

"The first time?"

"Caught that, did you?" Elsa sighed, wishing she'd watched her words. "Emma and I saw him in concert a few years ago. The connection was still there, and I thought, maybe, but," she shrugged, hoping Ava would let it go.

"He didn't call?"

"No, and according to Emma, he has a daughter, so he wasn't pining for me. Plus, since I've been doing my residency at Queen's Court, my time has been limited."

Ava stared for several seconds as if to say, '*Okay, we'll play it your way,*' and moved the conversation back to Emma and Killian.

"They look happy, don't they?"

"They do."

"But?"

Crap!

"But nothing," Elsa replied. "I was just thinking about how Emma tried to run from her feelings, and now look at her."

Ava gently bumped her shoulder. "Maybe you'll be next. Here comes your young man now. We'll talk later."

"There you are, love." Liam turned his sexy smile in her direction. "I've been looking for you."

Was that when you were dancing with several of the lovely females? Or could it have been when you were speaking to the sheriff?

"I'm sorry." She smiled, one that felt very unnatural, but knew Liam wouldn't notice. "I've been right here."

His navy eyes bore into hers, and for a second, Elsa could have sworn he wanted to say something. Then, as always, his feelings were masked with a neutral expression.

"Would you care to dance?"

Elsa held his gaze, waiting ... for what, though she wasn't sure.

"You want to dance?"

"I do," his voice dropped an octave, "with you."

"I'd like that."

Liam tucked her against his chest, and like every other time when they touched, tingles raced across her skin. Was he aware of the spark between them? Or was she imagining the slight catch in his breathing?

"Did you talk to Killian?" she finally asked when she was in danger of letting down her guard.

"Not yet."

"I thought it was important."

"It is." He lowered his hand slightly and pressed her closer, holding her like she was special, and he couldn't get close enough. "I'll get to it. Just not now. I'm where I want to be."

Elsa laid her head against Liam's chest to hide her expression. He confused her by saying the right things *sometimes*—by doing the right things *sometimes*. But after seeing how happy Emma and Killian were, it had her asking—was sometimes enough? Unfortunately, she was no longer sure.

The music ended, and Elsa took a step backward. "Thank you for the dance."

"Elsa, wait I ..."

"Come with me." Emma laughingly linked their arms. "We haven't had a chance to get caught up."

Elsa glanced at Liam, but again, his expression was closed, telling her the moment had passed.

"Killian needs to talk to Liam anyway," Emma continued, leading her to the back hallway, where it was a little quieter.

Elsa grabbed Emma's hand as soon as they were seated. "Let me see that rock."

Emma held out her hand. "He didn't do too badly, did he?"

"Not bad at all." Elsa relaxed against the wall. "I'm glad I was here to share the moment."

There, that sounded normal, didn't it?

"I'm glad you were here, too." Emma's smile turned serious. "We need to talk about you."

"Me," Elsa exclaimed. "Why me? This is your big day, and no—"

"Stop," Emma cut her off. "What's going on between you and Liam?"

"I—"

"Don't do that, El," Emma muttered. "Talk to me."

Oh, the irony. It's always been the other way around.

"Wait, a minute." Elsa frowned. "Will the real Emma Foster please stand up? Is this Killian's doing or Swan Harbor's?"

Emma blushed. "A bit of both, I think. Killian started with, 'I've been told sharing your burdens helps,' and I found myself doing just that."

"Which is so not you."

"No," Emma agreed. "It's not, and sometimes I still forget, or Killian has to pull it from me. When I do, though, things look different."

Elsa could relate, as there were times when she'd talk to Liam about a patient or something that annoyed her at the hospital. He had a way of helping her better understand what was going on. Frustratingly, he rarely reciprocated, preferring to keep work issues at work. On the one hand, she understood the why behind his behavior, but it also hurt. She'd grown up in a home where her parents talked to each other about everything.

"And then there's the town," Emma continued. "From the moment I arrived, it's felt like home."

"I'm happy for you and Killian." Elsa blinked the tears away. "You've found your happy ending."

"And now we need to work on yours."

"Well," Elsa sighed dramatically. "I need to pass my boards and—"

"You'll be fine." Emma wagged her finger playfully. "You of the photographic memory will be just fine. I'm talking about you and Liam, and you know it. Wouldn't it be perfect if you and he …?"

While Emma was talking, there were several times Elsa wanted to laugh. Not because she didn't like the future being described, but more because it was almost too perfect.

"Oh, Emma," Elsa murmured. "You, of all people, should understand the future we want isn't always the one we're meant to have."

"I know," Emma sighed. "But until you open yourself up to the possibilities, you'll never know."

"Seems my talk in January did some good," Elsa chuckled. "That still doesn't change the fact that I need to finish my residency and find a job. Then we can talk about what's next."

"Find a job?" Emma frowned. "Didn't Queen's Court offer you one?"

"They did, but I've gotten several other offers. I just want to make sure I take the right one, you know?"

"The right one, what?"

Elsa glanced up into Liam's concerned eyes.

"The right one, what, Elsa?"

"Job," Emma answered before Elsa decided what to say.

"Job?" Liam glanced from one woman to the other. "But you have a job at Queen's Court."

"I do." Elsa stood so Liam wasn't hovering over her. "And I've explained this, but apparently, you either didn't listen or don't remember."

"What are you talking about?"

"Liam," she dropped into her no-nonsense physician's vocal pattern. "I took my Family Practice boards last month. In a few weeks, I'll finish my pediatric residency at Queen's. Yes, they offered me a job. But so did a hospital in DC, one in Florida, and one in Tennessee. Then, in October, I'll take my pediatrics boards. So, yes. I need to choose what's right for me. Now, if you'll excuse me. I'm going to take a little walk. We'll talk later, Emma."

"But it's dark," Liam muttered as she walked past.

"Relax, it's Swan Harbor," Killian responded.

Elsa rushed through the partygoers and outside.

Crap!

What had gotten into her? She never lost her cool.

Her feelings propelled her down the sidewalk without paying attention to where she was going. It wasn't until the paved area gave way that she knew where she was—the pier.

On one end stood Captain Jack's Fine Dining, which was built inside a seventeenth-century Spanish galleon. The other end of the pier was anchored by Siren's Song, a music club she knew belonged to Tyler.

Elsa leaned against the railing and tilted her chin up to the breeze. She replayed her behavior and had to admit it wasn't her finest moment. With that admission came the realization she needed to apologize—if not to Liam, at least to Emma and Killian.

When she started toward Sally's, the road veered in multiple directions, making her hesitate. Then, seemingly out of nowhere, she was greeted by a black and white dog.

"Bandit, get back here!" a man yelled.

"Well, hello." Elsa scratched the dog's head. "Did you run away too?"

"He didn't wait." Bandit's owner held up a leash, but his attention was on her instead of his dog. "You're lost."

The simple statement threw her. "Lost? No ... yes ..."

In more ways than one.

"I'm Captain Jack. Come, child. I know just what you need."

"What I need? How do you know what I need?"

"Oh, not me, per se." He clipped the leash onto the dog and began walking. "This is Swan Harbor, where the heart always knows."

*Curl up with a copy of **Brothers, Hope & Hearts**
and rally behind Liam and Elsa. He's lovable but stubborn.*

QUICK AUTHOR'S NOTE:

I'm one of those writers who flies by the seat of my pants. For the most part, Kittens followed the same pattern. However, as the *'Hope'* story (Books 2 – 6) started floating around in my head, I dropped a few hints about what's ahead. As you continue reading, see if you can spot them. I will say where Emma & Killian's story goes through here is pretty cool.

I've created a playlist for the *'Hope'* books. On my website, www.sophiebartow.com, you can find each 'couples' song. You can also listen to the entire series on either YouTube or Spotify.

Swan Harbor's Hope Playlist.

Moving right along ...

If you enjoyed reading *Kittens, Puppies & Love,* and would like another scene up for my newsletter. My newsletters are sent on the 5th, 15th, and 25th of each month and include a lot of tidbits. Book sales, giveaways, teasers, new releases, and early releases. I've even been known to toss in one or two of my favorite recipes or a picture of my cat or dog.

In Emma and Killian's extra scene – Bunnies, Bunnies, Bunnies, Hayden pulls Killian into a situation, and instead of asking for help, well ... Timeline-wise, it fits between chapters 26 & 27.)

Just click here - **<u>Bunnies, Bunnies, Bunnies</u>** to get the secret link.

Thanks for hanging with me this long.

Until next time,

Sophie

P.S.

In Book 3, *Brother, Hope & Hearts*, Elsa leaves Liam and NYC behind to start work in Swan Harbor. When danger brings Liam to town, and he finds out someone from Elsa's past lives there – well, let's just say Liam Jones is quite stubborn when it comes to finding out why he's like he is. However, his transformation was a lot of fun to write—especially when you learn what label he gives himself.

Read on for a preview of
Brothers, Hope & Hearts

SOPHIE BARTOW

Brothers, Hope & Hearts

HOPE & HEARTS 3

EPILOGUE

Sally's Diner
June 1
9:00 p.m.

Elsa took a glass of champagne and found a corner in the back of Sally's Diner. Since she'd learned about Killian's plans, something inside of her had changed. It wasn't until she watched him propose to her best friend, Emma, that she understood her feelings. She was jealous.

Her gaze drifted to Liam, Killian's brother, and the man she'd been 'seeing' for months. Their attraction was instantaneous, and she'd thought they were going somewhere. The reality, though, was something very different. He treated her like his friend. Not the woman he couldn't get out of his head. Not the woman he wanted to spend his life with, and certainly not the woman he loved. Except—she didn't believe he *couldn't* love her. It was more that he wouldn't *allow* himself to love her. How was a girl to fight that?

She wanted a man to look at her the way Killian looked at Emma. The spark between them was there at the New Year's Eve party. Even then, it spoke of forever.

What about her, though? Was Liam her forever, or was there someone else out there waiting for her?

Her attention trailed from Liam to Tyler James. At one time, he'd starred in her dreams, and she'd thought he was her future. Until he went back home and ....

"Do you know him?" Ava, Emma's mother, joined her in the back of the room.

"Who?"

Ava arched a brow. "The hottie you've been staring at for the last few minutes."

"His name is Tyler James," Elsa replied. "The first time we met, we were sixteen."

"The first time?"

"Caught that, did you?" Elsa sighed, wishing she'd watched her words. "Emma and I saw him in concert a few years ago. The connection was still there, and I thought, maybe, but," she shrugged, hoping Ava would let it go.

"He didn't call?"

"No, and according to Emma, he has a daughter, so he wasn't pining for me. Plus, since I've been doing my residency at Queen's Court, my time has been limited."

Ava stared for several seconds as if to say, '*Okay, we'll play it your way,*' and moved the conversation back to Emma and Killian.

"They look happy, don't they?"

"They do."

"But?"

Crap!

"But nothing," Elsa replied. "I was just thinking about how Emma tried to run from her feelings, and now look at her."

Ava gently bumped her shoulder. "Maybe you'll be next. Here comes your young man now. We'll talk later."

"There you are, love." Liam turned his sexy smile in her direction. "I've been looking for you."

Was that when you were dancing with several of the lovely females? Or could it have been when you were speaking to the sheriff?

"I'm sorry." She smiled, one that felt very unnatural, but knew Liam wouldn't notice. "I've been right here."

His navy eyes bore into hers, and for a second, Elsa could have sworn he wanted to say something. Then, as always, his feelings were masked with a neutral expression.

"Would you care to dance?"

Elsa held his gaze, waiting ... for what, though she wasn't sure.

"You want to dance?"

"I do," his voice dropped an octave, "with you."

"I'd like that."

Liam tucked her against his chest, and like every other time when they touched, tingles raced across her skin. Was he aware of the spark between them? Or was she imagining the slight catch in his breathing?

"Did you talk to Killian?" she finally asked when she was in danger of letting down her guard.

"Not yet."

"I thought it was important."

"It is." He lowered his hand slightly and pressed her closer, holding her like she was special, and he couldn't get close enough. "I'll get to it. Just not now. I'm where I want to be."

Elsa laid her head against Liam's chest to hide her expression. He confused her by saying the right things *sometimes*—by doing the right things *sometimes*. But after seeing how happy Emma and Killian were, it had her asking—was sometimes enough? Unfortunately, she was no longer sure.

The music ended, and Elsa took a step backward. "Thank you for the dance."

"Elsa, wait I ..."

"Come with me." Emma laughingly linked their arms. "We haven't had a chance to get caught up."

Elsa glanced at Liam, but again, his expression was closed, telling her the moment had passed.

"Killian needs to talk to Liam anyway," Emma continued, leading her to the back hallway, where it was a little quieter.

Elsa grabbed Emma's hand as soon as they were seated. "Let me see that rock."

Emma held out her hand. "He didn't do too badly, did he?"

"Not bad at all." Elsa relaxed against the wall. "I'm glad I was here to share the moment."

There, that sounded normal, didn't it?

"I'm glad you were here, too." Emma's smile turned serious. "We need to talk about you."

"Me," Elsa exclaimed. "Why me? This is your big day, and no—"

"Stop," Emma cut her off. "What's going on between you and Liam?"

"I—"

"Don't do that, El," Emma muttered. "Talk to me."

Oh, the irony. It's always been the other way around.

"Wait, a minute." Elsa frowned. "Will the real Emma Foster please stand up? Is this Killian's doing or Swan Harbor's?"

Emma blushed. "A bit of both, I think. Killian started with, 'I've been told sharing your burdens helps,' and I found myself doing just that."

"Which is so not you."

"No," Emma agreed. "It's not, and sometimes I still forget, or Killian has to pull it from me. When I do, though, things look different."

Elsa could relate, as there were times when she'd talk to Liam about a patient or something that annoyed her at the hospital. He had a way of helping her better understand what was going on. Frustratingly, he rarely reciprocated, preferring to keep work issues at work. On the one hand, she understood the why behind his behavior, but it also hurt. She'd grown up in a home where her parents talked to each other about everything.

"And then there's the town," Emma continued. "From the moment I arrived, it's felt like home."

"I'm happy for you and Killian." Elsa blinked the tears away. "You've found your happy ending."

"And now we need to work on yours."

"Well," Elsa sighed dramatically. "I need to pass my boards and—"

"You'll be fine." Emma wagged her finger playfully. "You of the photographic memory will be just fine. I'm talking about you and Liam, and you know it. Wouldn't it be perfect if you and he ...?"

While Emma was talking, there were several times Elsa wanted to laugh. Not because she didn't like the future being described, but more because it was almost too perfect.

"Oh, Emma," Elsa murmured. "You, of all people, should understand the future we want isn't always the one we're meant to have."

"I know," Emma sighed. "But until you open yourself up to the possibilities, you'll never know."

"Seems my talk in January did some good," Elsa chuckled. "That still doesn't change the fact that I need to finish my residency and find a job. Then we can talk about what's next."

"Find a job?" Emma frowned. "Didn't Queen's Court offer you one?"

"They did, but I've gotten several other offers. I just want to make sure I take the right one, you know?"

"The right one, what?"

Elsa glanced up into Liam's concerned eyes.

"The right one, what, Elsa?"

"Job," Emma answered before Elsa decided what to say.

"Job?" Liam glanced from one woman to the other. "But you have a job at Queen's Court."

"I do." Elsa stood so Liam wasn't hovering over her. "And I've explained this, but apparently, you either didn't listen or don't remember."

"What are you talking about?"

"Liam," she dropped into her no-nonsense physician's vocal pattern. "I took my Family Practice boards last month. In a few weeks, I'll finish my pediatric residency at Queen's. Yes, they offered me a job. But so did a hospital in DC, one in Florida, and one in Tennessee. Then, in October, I'll take my pediatrics boards. So, yes. I need to choose what's right for me. Now, if you'll excuse me. I'm going to take a little walk. We'll talk later, Emma."

"But it's dark," Liam muttered as she walked past.

"Relax, it's Swan Harbor," Killian responded.

Elsa rushed through the partygoers and outside.

Crap!

What had gotten into her? She never lost her cool.

Her feelings propelled her down the sidewalk without paying attention to where she was going. It wasn't until the paved area gave way that she knew where she was—the pier.

On one end stood Captain Jack's Fine Dining, which was built inside a seventeenth-century Spanish galleon. The other end of the pier was anchored by Siren's Song, a music club she knew belonged to Tyler.

Elsa leaned against the railing and tilted her chin up to the breeze. She replayed her behavior and had to admit it wasn't her finest moment. With that admission came the realization she needed to apologize—if not to Liam, at least to Emma and Killian.

When she started toward Sally's, the road veered in multiple directions, making her hesitate. Then, seemingly out of nowhere, she was greeted by a black and white dog.

"Bandit, get back here!" a man yelled.

"Well, hello." Elsa scratched the dog's head. "Did you run away too?"

"He didn't wait." Bandit's owner held up a leash, but his attention was on her instead of his dog. "You're lost."

The simple statement threw her. "Lost? No ... yes ..."

In more ways than one.

"I'm Captain Jack. Come, child. I know just what you need."

"What I need? How do you know what I need?"

"Oh, not me, per se." He clipped the leash onto the dog and began walking. "This is Swan Harbor, where the heart always knows."

Curl up with a copy of **Brothers, Hope & Hearts** *and rally behind Liam and Elsa. He's stubborn but lovable.*
https://books2read.com/brothershopehearts/

Sign up for my newsletter and download a Killian and Emma scene.
Bunnies, Bunnies, Bunnies
https://www.subscribepage.com/swan-harbor_bonus_scenes

Purchase a copy of
Brothers, Hope & Hearts
https://sophiebartow.com/book/brothers-hope-hearts/

BROTHERS, HOPE & HEARTS
SWAN HARBOR'S HOPE BOOK TWO

Forever begins with a little hope...

When Elsa Winters realizes the man she loves won't allow himself to love her back, she flees New York City to start a new life in Swan Harbor. The comfort of being there with Emma, her best friend, and dealing with her new pediatric practice, help distract her. Except, Elsa can't forget the man whose eyes spoke to her.

Paramedic Liam Reade knew Elsa was dangerous to everything he'd come to believe. But words from his past have him thinking he doesn't deserve a happy ending and he lets her walk out of his life. However, fate had other plans.

An enemy from his brother's past threatens, and Liam rushes to Swan Harbor to warn Killian. The town's hope soothes his battered heart, pushing him to rethink his idea of the future. As the danger surrounding them grows, can Elsa, Liam, Killian, Emma, and their friends work together to save Swan Harbor before everything blows up around them?

When hope is all you have, is it enough?

Purchase your copy, read an excerpt or watch the trailer.
Brothers, Hope & Hearts
https://sophiebartow.com/book/brothers-hope-hearts/

BIBLIOGRAPHY

Gow, N. (2010). *Ten Big Toes and the Prince's Nose*. Illustrated by Stephen Constanza

Dewdney, A. (2005). *Llama Llama Red Pajama*

Armitage, R. (2007). *Small Knight and George*

ABOUT THE AUTHOR

Sophie crafts small-town mystery romances that weave intricate plots with richly developed characters. Her female leads are intelligent, resourceful, and resilient, while her male characters, often stubborn, exude sexiness, wit, and a protective nature. She delights in building slow-burn romances, savoring the tension and delaying that first kiss for as long as possible. No matter the trope, every story she writes has a happy ending.

After a fulfilling 30-plus-year career as a speech-language pathologist, working with adult post-stroke and Parkinson's patients, she is enjoying her new journey. With their four children spread out, Sophie and her husband live in South Florida. They share their home with a spoiled dog named Bandit and an equally pampered cat named Irma.

You can find her on her website: **https://sophiebartow.com/** *Sophiexo*

facebook.com/SophieBartowAuthor

x.com/SophieBartow

instagram.com/sophiebartow

goodreads.com/sophiebartow

bookbub.com/profile/sophie-bartow

pinterest.com/SophieBartow